Preying On Generosity

By
Kimberly LaFontaine

PREYING ON GENEROSITY
© 2007 BY KIMBERLY LAFONTAINE

ISBN 10: 1-933113-79-0
ISBN 13: 978-1-933113-79-1

First Printing: 2007

This Trade Paperback Is Published By
Intaglio Publications
Walker, LA USA
WWW.INTAGLIOPUB.COM

CREDITS
EXECUTIVE EDITOR: TARA YOUNG
COVER DESIGN BY VAL HAYKEN (photography@valeriehayken.com)

DEDICATION

In loving memory of Sam J. Lea (1977-2005), the most tender, dedicated, wonderful man I've ever known. We all miss you dearly.

When I search the sky on a crisp moonlit night, a tight feeling in my chest tells me you finally found your happiness. So be it.

ACKNOWLEDGMENTS

This book is also dedicated to Bug, whom I adore and appreciate very much. Your faith in me is what kept me going through the storm. You are a beautiful, wonderful, amazing woman. Thank you for all the hours you spent reading this manuscript and providing invaluable feedback. And thank you for asking the tough questions that made this book so much stronger.

Nae, I promise one of these days I'll break most of my bad grammar habits so you won't have to make my written pages scream with red ink. Thanks for the long hours correcting and for that crazy, ridiculous night of Krispy Kreme doughnuts and Starbucks coffee that got the book done.

Tara, my Intaglio sister and editor, thank you for all your support—professionally and personally. And thanks for putting up with all the late-night calls and bazillion text messages. You're awesome.

And Sarah, my dear friend, the best listener I've met in a long time, you've made my life so much richer for being in it. Someday, we'll find that magical happiness we're searching for.

For my friends Shaun and Kara, who love to tease me about my lesbian fiction addiction, and for their baby boy, Hayden, to whom I will someday have to explain what I write. I have no idea how I'll pull that one off.

And all my other friends who put up with my babbling about the written word: Mark and Ria, who are so far away but faithfully follow my work; Diana, Sayre, and Danielle, who will tell anybody willing to listen that I'm an author; my brother and sister, who both brag about my books but are too embarrassed to read them; and my parents who are so proud and never ashamed.

Chapter One

The caller states her neighbor's dog is barking loudly and does this all the time. She wants officers to check on the dog and make it stop, so she can put her children to bed." Crackle, crackle, scan. "...medical emergency at 7276 Airport Freeway—trouble breathing." Crackle, crackle, scan. "...signal twelve. Repeat, signal twelve: white male; appears to be in his early thirties; found face-down in the kitchen of his apartment. Officer requesting homicide unit and back-up for crowd control."

"Shit!" Angie Mitchell snapped out of her lazy reverie and grabbed the nearest notepad on her desk with one hand, knocking over a soda can in her desperate search to find a pen with the other. Cursing under her breath, she sat very still for several seconds—notepad and pen ready—waiting for the police scanner to pick up that last channel again. It had been the north patrol unit, she was sure of it.

And she wasn't wrong. After less than a minute, the police scanner picked up the chatter again, and dispatch repeated the address for responding officers. She quickly jotted the information down in barely legible writing, shouldered her purse, clipped the remote police scanner to her belt, and limped down the long aisle of empty reporter cubicles toward her boss's desk, leaning heavily on her recently acquired crutches.

"Tom!" She startled him, and he jumped midbite, spilling bits of a deli sandwich down his crisp blue shirt. Scowling, he dabbed at a mustard stain with a napkin.

"Sorry about that," Angie muttered, trying not to laugh. "There's been a homicide—big crowd at the scene—and I need to head out."

"Shit!" he said with feeling, checking his watch. 10:11 p.m. "You better hurry. We've only got about an hour."

"I know, I know. I'm on it." She hurried down the hall muttering and cursing all the way.

A crime reporter's night is sometimes like that—nothing going on for hours until it's almost too late to gather enough information to get a story in the paper before it goes to press. And Angie wasn't used to the night shift. She was only covering that shift as a personal favor and had been fighting the urge to crawl under her desk and take a nap all night. No, she was the *Fort Worth Tribune's* morning crime reporter. She was used to coming in early, making dozens of calls to the five gazillion little towns surrounding Fort Worth and asking dispatch operators if there had been any major crimes overnight. With all the morning news stories covered when she came in at three p.m., she'd been left to babysit the scanner and hope that nothing happened too close to deadline.

But the feeling of utter dread and stress drained as quickly as it had surfaced, morphing into barely suppressed excitement. Try as she might to feel annoyed or frustrated or stressed out, she couldn't squash the adrenaline rush. She simply couldn't help it. Angie, if nothing else, was a hard news junkie at heart. And seldom is there harder news than a homicide. Unless it's a double homicide. Or triple.

She made it down the rickety elevator to the ground floor, hobbling along with her crutches at a risky pace. The *Tribune's* parking lot was half-empty at this time of night, with many gone for the day. Angie stopped beside her brand-new Mitsubishi Eclipse and carefully balanced on her good leg while she stowed the crutches in the backseat.

Only two months before, she could have run down the stairs and hopped into her car. Her average response time was usually about as good as your average cop's—two minutes flat from receiving info to being in her car and on the road. But an investigative lead on a story gone badly had nearly killed her. She'd been lucky to escape with a scar from a bullet and a broken leg. And her bosses had expected her leave of absence to last longer than a month, but Angie's restlessness had kicked in, and she'd demanded to be put back on the schedule.

She'd furiously argued her way through her boss's apprehensions, saying there was absolutely no reason she couldn't make a few phone calls and sit at her computer, both of them knowing perfectly well that she wouldn't stay in the office. Not if something big happened. But Tom had caved—more because he needed the stories than because he thought she was ready.

Using her tattered Mapsco, she found the location quickly and zoomed off toward northeast Fort Worth, one hand holding the steering wheel, the other a cigarette. Taking a turn off Beach Street, she found the crime scene immediately. There was no way to miss it—flashing blue lights everywhere, a dozen cop cars, and yellow crime scene tape marking off half of an apartment building. Dozens of people were milling about, smoking cigarettes, staring, some somber-faced, others gawking excitedly.

An officer stepped in front of her car and indicated she should roll down the window. After she flashed her press pass, he waved her over to a spot where she could park. Angie complied and checked her watch. 10:27 p.m. No doubt the TV crews would show up within the next few minutes and accost the officer in charge. She had about five minutes to find whoever that was and get some info before the media circus began.

While she was fumbling with her notepad and crutches, someone tapped her on the shoulder. "Miss Mitchell, I thought you might show up."

She spun around, wondering who the hell was demanding her attention at such a crucial time. She had to crane her neck upward to meet the eyes of the speaker, a man with a boyish face and shockingly vibrant red hair.

"Johnny Key, Fort Worth's newest homicide detective. First day on the job. I believe we have an appointment for coffee tomorrow morning." He held out his hand and smiled. Angie blinked at him and grasped his hand, not entirely surprised by the strong grip. "Lance pointed you out, and I thought I'd come on over before I'm whisked away." He jerked his thumb over his shoulder, pointing out the police department's public information officer, Lance Tucker.

"Shouldn't you be in that apartment over there?" She smiled back at him, indicating the unit that was being guarded by several

11

officers. "Not that I mind you coming over. I do need some info from you."

His responding laugh was warm and bright, and Angie couldn't help but like the man.

"Tell you what—give me ten minutes and I'll be back over. You're first in line, no matter how many TV guys show up," and before she could say anything, he wandered over to the apartment in question and disappeared.

Struggling with her crutches, Angie made her way to the crowd and began interviewing the more mournful-looking people she could find. Rejected by several, she finally found someone willing to answer a few questions. Within minutes, however, the TV crews showed up, and what turned out to be a group of grieving friends quickly dispersed. But not before Angie managed to obtain a phone number and some usable quotes. Detective Key tapped her on the shoulder again and waved away other approaching reporters with a smile and a laugh—"One at a time, guys, no pack journalism tonight, okay? Go to Lance for that."

"So are you ready for this?" he asked once the others were out of earshot.

"Yeah, shoot," she said, pen and pad at the ready.

"Male, white, thirty-two years old. He was reported missing earlier this evening by his parents, who also called his friends. Three of them stopped by to check on him, one of them had a key. They opened the door and found him face-down on the kitchen floor, apparently beaten to death. No, we don't really suspect the friends because it appears he has been dead for a couple of days, though we don't know how long, and we can't rule out anybody, either. The medical examiner hasn't come to inspect the body yet."

He paused while Angie scribbled furiously, trying to keep up. She noticed he'd stopped speaking and she asked, "Any signs of forced entry?"

"The friends had a key," he repeated patiently.

"They did, but did the killer? I mean, couldn't he or she have forced entry, stolen his keys, then locked up? Was the door locked?"

He gave her a contemplative look and smiled. "They told me you were good. But we all knew that from your own publicity."

Angie blushed and cursed under her breath. No quick retort

came to mind, especially since he was right. At least about the publicity part, which ties back in with the investigative lead gone badly and all that. She cleared her voice and demanded, "Well?" not looking at the detective.

"Yes, there were signs of forced entry—scratches on the lock. We haven't yet been able to locate the man's wallet or a key ring."

"ID?"

"Come on, Mitchell. You know better than that. The medical examiner hasn't come yet. We haven't even informed next of kin. And before you ask—I saw you talking to his friends—no, I won't confirm any names they may have given you."

"Okay..." She chewed her pen for a second, thinking. "Hey, what about the state of the apartment? Was it wrecked? You know, any signs of a struggle?"

"Why, yes there were," he replied with a touch of sarcasm and a bemused smile. "Broken glass on the floor. Upturned furniture."

"Blood on the body?"

"You want some gore for your story?"

She gave him a sheepish grin. "No, I want details. If there's no gore, there's no gore. If there is, there is. Out with it."

He suppressed a laugh, apparently not wanting to offend any onlookers.

"Off the record?"

"I don't do that."

"Damn, you're tough. The others at the station warned me about you. The chief gave me a whole lecture on dealing with Miss Angie Mitchell, just so you know." He paused and lowered his voice. "Seriously, Angie. Can I call you Angie?" She nodded. "Okay. Seriously, I came to Fort Worth from Dallas because I wanted to get away from serious shit like this. The body's pretty messed up. I'll tell you he was found half-naked—still had his briefs on, the rest is missing. He was bound in what appears to be silk scarves. Gagged with the same. There's more, but I can't give it to you yet. Obviously, we're still investigating. But my gut tells me this was no crime of opportunity or passion. No, this was something much, much worse. But I don't want to see that last bit in the paper tomorrow. Not until I can confirm what my gut's telling me. Got it?"

"Yes, sir."

"Call me Jay. And I have to get back inside. See you tomorrow?"

"Starbucks at nine o'clock. And thanks, Jay."

He nodded and slipped back through the crowd before the TV reporters could get to him. They glowered at Angie as though she was a traitor, and she tried desperately to hide the smirk that wanted to break across her face.

She hadn't exactly been popular with them lately. For the previous month, she'd been denying interviews, making snide comments when a camera guy or girl started following her around at a crime scene. She'd allowed only one interview, and that was because it was an Associated Press reporter. And Angie liked The Associated Press. She'd told the reporter the whole story about how she stumbled across a strange homeless man down at Sundance Square one day, how he told her about another man who was beating and killing people out on the homeless strip—a seedy area under Interstate 30 where homeless people spend the night. Well, where they used to spend the night before she started writing her stories about the strange deaths, the disappearing people, the man named John Carpenter who'd found a following. Most of the homeless didn't go there anymore, the memories were just too painful. And the city had approved more funding for homeless shelters anyway.

Angie had gotten more threats with each follow-up she wrote. Her car was trashed. And finally, after many articles, she met with a city council aide who blew the cops' theory about Carpenter out of the water. Whereas investigators thought Carpenter just wanted to start a gang to terrorize people, he'd actually been hired by Councilman Ted Henry, a bigoted racist who wanted "his streets" cleared of bums. After meeting with the aide, she was kidnapped by Carpenter's thugs, beaten by Carpenter, then shot by Henry while she was trying to escape. She'd only barely survived.

The following weeks were chaos. Every news station and publication in the area—and some from out of state—had wanted to interview her. But Angie thought it was pointless and didn't want to give the story. She'd hoped giving that one interview with the AP would solve that problem. Other news agencies could just reprint the story, after all. It was kind of hypocritical for a journalist, she knew, but it was her life. And being in the news was

14

interfering with her job. It was bad enough that they kept running stories and interviewing the police and city council about the incident. Now she couldn't go anywhere without somebody recognizing her and showering her with praise or launching into a lecture.

So now the other reporters weren't exactly happy with her, and Detective Key's little game of favorites wasn't going to help. But she allowed it just this once and reveled in their annoyance.

Angie sighed and checked her watch, turning her back to them. 10:56 p.m. She leaned against a nearby wall and dug her cell phone out of her pocket and punched in an all-too-familiar number, catching a glimpse of the *Tribune's* night shift photographer snapping pictures across the street.

"Okay, Tom, are you ready? It's a front-pager, you'll see. Here it goes: A thirty-two-year-old Fort Worth man was found beaten to death in his apartment late Friday, where he had apparently..."

Angie drummed her fingers on the steering wheel, waiting for her apartment complex's access gate to open. The rickety old thing made an awful screeching sound and reluctantly swung open while she repeatedly punched her code in the keypad. Her patience was beyond wearing thin. It was after midnight—she should have been home more than an hour earlier—and she'd been held up more than once along the twisty route home. First she'd had to stay on her boss's orders to make sure no further updates from investigators were forthcoming. He'd finally released her at 11:30 p.m., and she'd happily hopped in her car, eager to get home, only to take a wrong turn and end up on a windy little road without a turn-around possibility for five miles.

It didn't matter that she knew most of the streets in Fort Worth. The sprawling city outskirts still held a few pockets she'd never had to visit, and those narrow, dimly lit roads with deep ditches on either side didn't allow for quick little mistakes.

When she finally managed to find the correct street out after a frustrated consultation of her trusty Mapsco, she was stopped at an accident site on Interstate 30. She'd been stuck for twenty minutes, furiously debating whether her car could handle a little offroading—maybe drive through the shallow ditch to the access road to get around the lanes blocked by emergency crews. But after watching a Ford Escort get stuck, she resigned herself to waiting.

Angie peeled through the gate and swung her car hard to the left, coming to a screeching halt in her allotted covered parking space. She crammed her notepad roughly into her purse and cursed furiously, realizing she'd accidentally taken the *Tribune's* police scanner home with her. A big no-no. But there was no way in hell she'd turn right around and drive all the way back downtown. They could just wait until the morning. It wasn't like anybody worked overnight and would need it anyway.

Still fiddling with her purse, she was startled by a knock on her driver's side window. Her scowl disappeared the second she turned to see who it was. The previous forty-five minutes of frustration drained away into nothingness as a soft warmth slowly began to build in her stomach and finally reached her eyes.

"Lauren." She sighed happily and unlocked the door.

Soft lips she'd been craving all day met her own, and she lost herself for a few minutes, reveling in the tenderness and sweet smell of lavender that was so distinctly Lauren. Strong arms wrapped protectively around her shoulders and pulled her closer, the woman's hands kneading her back soothingly, while long raven hair tickled her cheeks. When they finally parted, a small whimper of protest escaped her lips and her lover chuckled knowingly.

"I was wondering if we should send out a search party," Lauren murmured in a husky voice, her breath tickling Angie's ear and making her shiver involuntarily. "We got bored and went for a walk and were just about to head inside."

Angie cleared her throat with difficulty. "Homicide. Sorry I'm so late."

"Yeah, we figured it was something like that."

"We?"

"Jimmy's here. Don't tell me you forgot about our plans tonight."

Angie shook her head, stalling. She had forgotten, but she would never admit it. Her mind racing, she finally came across the thread of conversation from nearly a week before. "Right. Club 1970. Tonight," she finally said, trying to hide the sheepish grin that wouldn't quite stay off her lips.

Lauren sighed and nodded, standing up. She helped Angie gather her things and walked her over to their waiting friend, who'd busied himself smoking a cigarette and staring at the half-sickle moon during their intimate embrace. When Jimmy realized Angie had gotten out of her car, he turned and smirked at her, holding out a hand, clearly indicating she should hand over her things, so he could carry them inside.

Angie stared at him blankly for several seconds. The two of them, Lauren and Jimmy, had been playing mother hen since she'd gotten out of the hospital. They did everything from cook her meals to sometimes—much to her protest—carry her around. She took guilty pleasure in allowing Lauren to bathe her, though she was far from needing that sort of help. But that was something altogether different than letting them think she was incapable of carrying her own purse. She had a broken leg, after all, not two broken arms.

A strong streak of pride reared itself, and she sighed exaggeratedly, hoping to convey her disapproval.

"Oh, don't give me that crap," Jimmy said and laughed. "Aren't you tired? I heard something about you being at a crime scene. I bet you ignored your doctor's orders and stood around there for at least an hour. Just give me your freaking purse."

She couldn't help but smirk in return because he had her pegged. Again. He always did, whether she liked it or not. Jimmy, for all his sarcastic frankness, was terribly perceptive, something that had actually helped her more than once.

She tried staring him down—met his sky blue eyes full on—but knew it was a lost battle. If there was one thing they had in common, it was their sheer stubbornness. And she was too damned tired to play the game of wills that night. After several seconds passed, she dropped her eyes and handed over her purse and sweater without further protest.

"That's better," he said smoothly, his smile all white teeth and victory. He turned to Lauren. "Why don't you get your stuff, so we can head out?" He took a closer look at Angie, stepping around her and inspecting her back appraisingly, and added, "Unless you want to change first."

"And exactly what are you implying?" Angie demanded, her

eyes narrowing.

"Your shirt is stuck to your back, honey. Unless you're going for that 'I'm sweaty and sexy' look, I'd suggest you change." Out of habit, he took a quick step back to avoid the usual retort—a playful but hard slap. Immediately, though, an evil grin replaced the silly smirk as he apparently realized Angie couldn't exactly hobble forward fast enough to catch him. "I knew there was something good about that cast."

"Lauren?" Angie turned to her lover, who'd been watching the exchange with a grin that slid off her face a split second after their eyes met.

"No problem." Lauren nodded and caught a retreating Jimmy with five long strides. He yelped when she slapped his backside a bit harder than intended.

Angie leaned against the stairway railing with folded arms and listened to the following argument with typical amusement. A yawn threatened to surface, but she squelched it quickly, wishing she hadn't had such a late night. She wanted to hang out with them at the bar, had been looking forward to it all week. It had only slipped her mind because she'd been so focused on her story and had allowed its details to take over everything else.

There was little else she enjoyed more these days than spending time with Lauren and Jimmy, regardless of what the evening's entertainment was. Over the last few months, she'd gotten to know both much better; they'd worked their way into her hectic life, claiming large chunks of her heart and thoughts— something that for years she'd reserved only for family. And her best friend. It was more than a gigantic leap forward for the workaholic reporter who'd once been emotionally distant.

The biggest change, of course, was Lauren. The way the woman had sauntered straight past her defenses was still slightly unnerving. The fact that she was a woman was becoming less of an issue, though Angie had fought against the attraction like crazy until she'd reached a breaking point—a time and place in which she could have run away forever but chose not to.

Watching the rather loud exchange between her lover and their friend—they were acting like misbehaved children, running around the parking lot, shouting, and giggling—Angie couldn't imagine what her life would be like if she had shut Lauren out, if she'd put the "it's just a phase" stamp on the issue. The thought alone was enough to make her feel uneasy, as if she desperately needed another kiss to confirm the last six weeks had been real.

And then there was Jimmy, the brutally honest, goofy guy who ignored her attempts to shut him out emotionally and demanded friendship. He used to be her source for everything techno geek-related while she still wrote computer articles. He owned his own computer tech business and knew a ton of experts.

As far as she knew, he went around the Metroplex to people's homes and fixed things. Sometimes he set up networks for small businesses. He seemed to have an awful lot of free time, though, and Angie was both grateful—he'd been around a lot during her recuperation—and envious. If she had as much time as he... There were so many things she'd do. Write a book. Cuddle with Lauren. Travel. Jimmy did none of those things. For all Angie could tell, he goofed around a lot, went to his favorite bar to hit on guys, went to the gym, and surfed the Internet.

Having him as a friend was both refreshing and frustrating. Refreshing because he wouldn't buy into any of her bullshit and instead called her on it, frustrating because he was restless, reckless, and had the wildest ideas that usually meant trouble, the most recent of which was disappearing in Mexico for three days and blowing off his tech gigs. He'd called her up, giggling. "I called in sick. It was a weird conversation. I decided to put myself on suspension."

Whatever. She loved him anyway, and that was all that mattered. At least she had a social life now, unlike before when her highlight was building simulated cities on her home computer and doing laundry.

Jimmy and Lauren came running up to her, half breathless, apparently remembering that they were supposed to be well on their way to the bar. Angie reluctantly let them help her into Jimmy's new Pontiac Firebird. He'd had to replace his old one two months prior, after landing it in a ditch during a summer thunderstorm.

She inhaled the scent of new car and smirked, strongly suspecting that he sprayed the sports car every day with a freshener to retain the scent. Digging around the backseat, her suspicion was confirmed when she found a bottle of the stuff.

With a devious smile, she slipped it between the seat cushions, mentally giggling at the thought of him searching frantically for the damned thing. Serves him right for teasing her about her shirt.

Club 1970 was Jimmy's favorite hotspot. Cringing at the smell of stale beer, Angie's eyes watering under the assault of a cigar smoke cloud hanging in the air, she had to force a smile on her face. It was the type of place she'd never visit on her own, but since it was her friend's favorite place to have a few drinks, she'd just have to tolerate the dingy establishment. It was also the only gay bar in Arlington, a Fort Worth suburb sorely lacking in gay venues. They didn't have time to head out to Dallas since it was already so late. Angie sighed and let her eyes adjust to the dim lighting.

Jimmy's walk took on a slight strut and his voice dropped an octave as he ordered their drinks from a redheaded bartender he'd been interested in for weeks. Angie and Lauren pointed not-so-discreetly and giggled, watching as their blond friend lighted up a cigar importantly, blowing puffs of smoke in a way he clearly must have thought was sexy. He was in full flirt mode, just like always.

The redhead handed over three bottles of beer and scurried off to the other end of the counter without a word, eyes barely leaving the counter. Jimmy sighed, his shoulders sagging slightly.

"Someday, my friend." Lauren cuffed him lightly in the shoulder and took her beer when he made it to their table. "Aren't you seeing somebody already anyway?"

"Yeah, what's up with that?" Angie smirked and took her beer as their friend slid into the chair they'd reserved for him.

He sighed and puffed on his cigar, took a long sip of beer, and sighed again.

"Justin's out of the picture," he finally answered, the words not entirely laced with his usual indifference regarding his previous partners.

Neither Angie nor Lauren had actually met this Justin, but their friend had babbled on about him on more than one occasion. Angie had actually been on the verge of pressing for a double-date, so they could meet the guy. Damn, she thought, slightly deflated. So much for that idea. Jimmy was so weird about relationships. If you could call them that. Every time she asked

20

about Justin, she got a different answer as to how things were going. One day, he'd say it was no big deal. The next day, he'd say he and Justin were really going somewhere.

"What?" Lauren snapped, immediately catching his barely hidden tone of resignation.

"Now don't get all protective on me," he snapped back, the words enunciated so sharply it was clear he wouldn't tolerate any arguments. "My own fault. You know how I am. And it doesn't matter anyway. We only saw each other five times. Who cares, right?"

Lauren opened her mouth to say something, looked as though she thought better of it, and took a swig of beer instead. She peeled off tiny pieces of the water-logged label and began setting the scraps on the table. Jimmy picked at a nail and said nothing.

Angie's eyes darted from one to the other, not following what wasn't being said. There had to be some history there she hadn't discovered yet. She wanted desperately to ask what it was but knew it wouldn't be a good idea, would likely send the evening into a downward spiral, especially considering how the two of them were acting. She swallowed her questions and instead scooted her chair a little closer to Jimmy and touched his arm reassuringly. "Hey, if you need us, we're here, okay? Sorry it didn't work out." She paused for a second and waited for a response, but he continued to say nothing. "Okay… How about you tell us about that bartender?"

He ceased fiddling with his nails and looked up at her. His eyes darted to Lauren and fixed on her face until she nodded silently. Jimmy laughed abruptly—a bit more high-pitched and forced than his typical bright chuckles—and started babbling about Matt the bartender, fluffing his hair nervously and checking over his shoulder frequently to make sure the man in question was nowhere near.

Angie bit back a startled yelp when Lauren's hand clenched convulsively over her own, the knuckles white with tension. Angie knew Lauren loved fiercely, deeply and wondered if there was more to her apparent anger than a simple thick protective streak. She resolved to get to the matter the second they got home, regardless of how late it was or how long the conversation took.

But the second Jimmy dropped them off and they stepped into

21

her apartment, Angie was in Lauren's arms and roughly dragged to the bedroom, where her lover put all thoughts of talking out of her mind.

Chapter Two

S tarbucks was unusually crowded for a Saturday morning, but Angie had no trouble locating Detective Key—his flaming red hair painted a brilliant contrast against the gray walls in the far corner. He spotted her quickly and beamed, standing up to offer her a seat when she approached.

"Hey there. I wasn't sure you'd make it after last night and all. What time did you finally make it home for some sleep?" she asked, returning his strong handshake.

"Sleep? Me? Never." He laughed and took his seat. "We were up there for hours after you left. Cleared the scene about seven o'clock. I figured it was a moot point to sleep after that." He paused, thinking. "Why don't we get the update out of the way before discussing more interesting matters? Oh, and I took the liberty of ordering a caramel latté for you, hope you don't mind. It seems the staff is quite familiar with you."

Angie grinned. "I come here almost every day. What did you do, tell them you were expecting me and dig for gossip?"

"A good cop always does his homework," he said and shoved her cup a little closer. Angie took a sip and closed her eyes in utter contentment. No matter how many of those sickeningly sweet coffees she ordered, the reaction was always the same. She hardly went a day without one and wasn't ashamed to admit it. Yes, the staff knew her. They probably made rent on her tips alone. Well, maybe not, but she did blow a good chunk of her paycheck at the coffee shop every month.

She dug out her notepad and pen and looked inquiringly into Detective Key's appraising eyes. She thought she saw an intense curiosity there, but it slid away so quickly she wasn't entirely sure

23

she hadn't just imagined it. Not that it really mattered.

"Okay." He took a deep breath and let it out slowly. "Here we go: The guy's name is Ben Whittaker. He's a Fort Worth native and worked down at the GMC plant in Arlington. We ID'd him through his friends and a couple of pay stubs we found. We spoke with his supervisor, who told us he'd failed to show up for work the past two days. The medical examiner placed his death around late Wednesday or early Thursday." He paused to let Angie catch up before continuing. "His family lives in Richardson. He wasn't married, doesn't have any kids. In fact, he was gay, and we think that might have something to do with this crime."

Angie's head snapped up from her note-taking. "Hate crime?"

"Maybe. There are some indications that it might be, though we're still investigating. And no, I can't tell you what those indications are." He gave her determined look a pointed frown and shook his head. "No, Angie. It's a guilty knowledge issue— something only we and the killer know, and that's the way it needs to stay. When I interrogate people, I ask tricky questions, and they usually let something important slip. If the details show up in the news, they know what not to talk about. And you've already said you don't do off the record, so that's it. Got it?"

Grumbling, she nodded. Sure, she'd let it go. For now. Maybe he'd let up later.

"Anyway, this guy is messed up. And yeah, you can write that I said he's 'messed up.' There were some things in that apartment that no person should ever have to see. And I refuse to elaborate on that."

"He's messed up? So you think a guy did this?"

"Yeah."

"What did the killer do that a woman couldn't?" she demanded indignantly.

He snorted and shook his head. "Whittaker was a gym nut— you know, pretty muscular, bulky arms and chest—had a membership at the YMCA downtown. We found him bound, gagged, and beaten all to hell, but that wasn't the cause of death. What I didn't tell you last night, and I'll explain why some other time, is that his throat was slit. Straight across, quick and efficient. No hesitation marks. Our guy, unless he was already unconscious, would have fought back—bound, gagged, and everything. You'll have to forgive me for thinking that a woman would have a hell of a time holding our vic tight enough to make such a clean cut if he was struggling. I mean, his chest was, like, this big around," and he spread his arms wide so Angie could see his point. "You know how hard it would be for someone to do that? It would be hard enough for a tough guy, let alone a woman, unless she was built like a refrigerator.

"So yes, we're pretty sure the killer is male. As to how old or what he looked like—not a clue. We haven't found any witnesses, and as far as we can tell, the guy wasn't dating anybody."

"Why do you think he was gay?"

"The rainbow posters in his apartment and stickers on his car were a big clue. His friends confirmed it. His family was also aware of his sexual orientation."

"So why do you think it was a hate crime?"

He snorted and shook his head. "Angie, Angie, Angie. You think you can get me that easily? Like I said, there are indications, and no, I won't go into what they are."

She jotted down several more notes, flipping over the sixth page in her notepad. He was being a lot more forthcoming than she'd expected, much more so than any of the detectives she'd ever dealt with. Even if he wasn't going to give her the details she wanted so badly. She opened her mouth to say something about it, then decided she'd be pushing her luck by commenting on the fact that he was giving away more than the other Fort Worth detectives did.

But she needn't have been so careful because the next thing he said was, "That should be enough for a good, strong follow-up. Do me a favor, include my cell number in that story in a fact box or something so people who may know something about what happened can give me a call, okay? I help you, you help me, and we have a beautiful working relationship."

"I'm not done, you know," she snorted, realizing she'd just become his public relations monkey. It wasn't as bad as it sounded—he was right—but she felt the urge to drag more bits of information from him just to prove she was a tough reporter.

"Really?" He drew the word out and leaned forward with interest. "Fine. Fire away."

How come, Angie grumbled internally, is it always so hard to come up with a decent question when somebody challenges you, especially when their eyes pin you in place? She thought of several questions but discarded them, realizing they'd already been answered. Finally, one popped into mind.

"Who was the last person to see him alive?" She caught his smirk and added, "other than the killer?"

"As of right now, and that might change, it was a close friend who works out at the gym with him. According to his friend, they hit the weights and jogged a couple of laps Wednesday evening about six o'clock. The friend said Whittaker left about seven and said he had some business to take care of. Unless somebody saw him after seven o'clock, that's all we have. And I'm really hoping somebody did see him after that. If so, they really need to give me a call."

He stopped abruptly and took a sip of his coffee. Detective Key set the cup back on the table and rubbed his eyes, stifling a yawn. "I guess I did leave a piece out that you needed, huh?" he asked and forced a smile. "Put away your notepad, please. I think that's enough."

Angie remembered that he said he hadn't slept and frowned, doing as he asked. She had enough for her story and some info on people she needed to track down for interviews. She expected that he was ready to discuss what he'd called "more interesting matters" earlier, but before she could start any pleasant chit-chat, he started drumming his fingers on the table and scowled.

"You know, this homicide really bugs me," he stated flatly and sucked a breath of air between clenched teeth. His hand was balled into a fist, and it looked like he had to resist slamming it on the table. "I take this shit personally. It's different when somebody gets shot in a drive-by or gets dumped in a lake," he continued, seething. "But fucked-up shit like this is a disgrace! His friends have been crying to me all night about how good of a guy he was. I mean, some crazy asshole tied this guy up and beat him for days! *Days*, Angie. And then he slaughtered him like an animal. Our killer is a freaking maniac. A sexual predator. And he's good at it. I promise you, this will happen again. It will happen on my turf, and this guy won't stop until we put him away!"

And for the first time during her three-year career, Angie stared at a source in open shock. Sure, she'd been blindsided before, had been surprised. But what she felt at that moment, gawking at the disheveled detective—his hair standing on end, his coffee-brown suit wrinkled from more than one day's usage—was a desperate desire to run out of the room. Not because she couldn't take it, but because it was so shockingly unprofessional from such an authority figure that she couldn't think of a single damned way to respond. Other than by staring.

She ordered her butt to stay planted firmly on her chair, and the only sound she made was a stifled gasp that sounded more like she was clearing her throat.

He was so livid that he was trembling. What made his outburst worse, he surely should have known, was that he did it in front of a reporter. In front of her. Not that she would be writing a story about it—people just freak out sometimes, and so long as it doesn't harm anybody, there's no sense in writing up an exposé. Leave that for the tabloids. But one thing was immediately apparent: Perhaps he hadn't left Dallas because he wanted to get away from such terrible crimes, as he'd said. Maybe he'd left because he'd been booted out. Clearly, he didn't have the whole "staying detached" bit down very well.

Seconds passed. He continued to shake with anger; Angie continued to stare. She still couldn't think of anything to say. Of course, she felt the same way he did. She wasn't so callous that violent crimes didn't shock her or piss her off. But she dropped that sort of talk and attitude at the door, so to speak. It just wouldn't do for anyone to think she attached herself to the people she wrote about, whether they're dead or alive. So she couldn't exactly verbally agree with Detective Key.

Still searching for an appropriate response, a thought crossed her mind and slammed home. It was more of a question, really. She suddenly wanted to know who had been killed that he'd loved and had made him become a cop. Because it was unlikely that he'd be this passionate simply because he cared about his fellow man. There are exceptions, sure, but they are pretty rare and hard to find. No, he had all the signs of a man who has been terribly wronged.

Finally, he looked her directly in the eye. This time, she could see the mask that slid into place as he smiled and his dark eyes lightened considerably.

"Don't mind me," he said softly. "Yeah, it's not normal, but it makes me a better detective because I loathe the people who killed my victims. I obsess. And because I do that, I don't give up. Ever. Best you know that about me now, so I don't surprise the hell out of you again later." He paused and took a sip of coffee before meeting her eyes again. "Let's talk about something else. You, for example. Let's talk about your passion and how it gets you in trouble. Detective Ramirez said something the other day about you not being altogether forthcoming about your own little run-ins with lowlife scumbags..."

The first follow-up article was easy to complete—write up what she'd gotten from the detective, send it over, have her editor post it online—45 minutes from start to finish. Then she'd wandered over to the YMCA, conveniently located across the downtown office on Taylor Street, and had tracked down the friend who'd last seen Whittaker alive. Her excitement at finding Roger Sanders so easily quickly faded, though, when he demanded an off-the-record interview. Some people are so scared to see their names in the paper... But this guy had a point. He was worried about a backlash from the killer, and Angie could hardly blame him. And she supposed she could complete an article without his narration of Wednesday evening's events, but it wouldn't be nearly as strong.

With much patience, she discussed the importance of writing a full account—emphasis on the full—and how only he, as the last person who'd seen his friend alive, could possibly help shed some light on what had happened. Angie generally loved being a crime reporter, what with all the action and high-profile pieces she could write. But talking to mourning friends, especially when they didn't want to talk, was definitely on her top ten list of least favorite things about her job. It took well over an hour to get five paragraphs worth of on-the-record information from the still-hysterical friend. He'd only stopped by the gym to let the staff know what had happened to Whittaker.

And then it took another twenty minutes and three cigarettes to convince herself that she wasn't a horrible person for harassing Mr. Sanders during such a terrible time in his life.

On the last cigarette, standing on the street corner outside the

Tribune's office, she decided it was a good thing that others' pain still affected her like this. And maybe it wasn't such a bad thing that Detective Key had similar issues. Maybe, and she hoped this wasn't true, she'd get over it quicker someday. She was only twenty-five years old, after all, and had been on the crime beat for less than six months. But she'd be damned if she became one of those reporters who went to a homicide in the morning and could be found laughing about the gory details at a bar later that evening.

The sun glared high overhead when Angie finally left the office in a mad dash to make it to class on time. She'd cut it awfully close that afternoon—talking to the landlord, the family, the neighbors, and crafting her story carefully until well past two o'clock—before heading out. She'd forgotten about her weekly appointment. Again. And she'd already been reprimanded for her tardiness more than once.

Angie graduated from the University of Texas at Arlington years before. On her graduation, she'd said her good riddance to the place quite happily. She'd always maintained that school was an unpleasant but necessary thing. Her cumulative GPA reflected that attitude.

But during the first week of her recuperation at home after being shot, being cooped up and restless, she'd had the wild idea that she should go back to school, at least to try it out, and take a class to further her career. It was just one weekend course, an undergraduate class on an introduction to forensic criminology. Sure that she'd learn lots of definitions and cop knowledge, she'd forced Lauren to drive her down to the university, so she could fill out her application and sign up.

Three weeks in, she wasn't exactly regretting her decision but was wondering exactly how much practical, instantly usable information she was going to learn over the next twelve weeks. Not to mention that she already had an unpleasant reputation among her peers due to an embarrassing incident Professor Laney had caused on the first day.

"Now that we've all introduced ourselves, I'd like to elaborate on Miss Mitchell's all-too-humble introduction!" Angie groaned internally, remembering. "How many people know who she is other than—what did you say?—'a degreed student who wants to learn more about forensic investigations'?"

Of thirty students, three raised their hands, and Angie had begun to stare at her desk in dreaded anticipation. Professor Laney called on one of the responding students who eagerly said, "She's that reporter from the *Tribune* who was shot by that city council guy. I saw it on the news. She'd been writing about them and got kidnapped! It must have been terrible."

And Angie distinctly remembered muttering something like, "Good for you, you stupid, know-it-all little…"

"Very good!" the professor had praised. "So we have an investigative reporter in our midst! Better watch what you say." And then she'd laughed at her own joke as if it had been the funniest damned thing in the world. That wasn't the worst of it, though. During the two following classes, the professor had called on her at nearly every other question about crime scene etiquette or similar matters, something Angie thought was incredibly annoying.

That week surely was going to be worse. There was no doubt in her mind that Professor Laney had read the morning paper, knew she'd been to a crime scene the night before, and would drag as many details out of her as she could.

"Yeah, well, this time I'm going to tell her to read tomorrow's paper," she grumbled, hitting the gas a bit harder to shave off a couple of minutes. Professor Laney, even if she liked Angie, wasn't too keen on late-comers. And she'd made that perfectly clear in front of the whole class the prior Saturday.

With a flood of relief, Angie slid into her desk with two minutes to spare, her cast resting on a pulled-up chair. Since she'd forgotten about the class, she didn't have her books or notebook. Sighing, she pulled her nearly scribbled-full notepad out of her purse and flipped to an empty page, and waited. Sure enough, the professor strode in with a particularly eager gleam in her eyes, holding a newspaper, immediately calling attention to Angie's most recent article. This time, though, she read entire paragraphs out loud.

"…a dozen police cruisers blocked off parts of the parking lot, as additional officers had been forced to respond for crowd control. Apartment residents and friends of the victim pressed in on the crime scene tape until officers threatened to issue citations."

She paused importantly. "Now officers couldn't actually issue citations unless people step over the caution tape or tear it down, right, Angie?"

Angie sighed again and simply nodded.

"Right. Let's continue. '…investigators said they found signs of forced entry—scratches around the door's lock—but have not yet determined whether the killer forced his way inside or tried to alter the crime scene. Key' (that's the detective, class) 'said furniture had been upturned inside the apartment, and investigators found broken shards of glass on the floor, indicating signs of a struggle.'"

Professor Laney took off her reading glasses and chewed on one end during a lengthy pause, allowing the class to mull over what she'd read. Angie stared into space, trying her absolute best not to appear thoroughly annoyed.

"So what do you think? Yes, you over there—haven't got your name memorized yet, sorry."

"Is it possible the killer staged the whole thing? I mean, maybe they had a rendezvous, and the guy offed the other guy and then he, like, threw some shit around to make it look like a break-in."

The professor grunted and considered her student's theory, though Angie saw her lips grow thin in a bit of an incredulous frown. It was satisfying in a terribly inconsiderate sort of way. But her satisfaction didn't last long.

"Angie?"

She suppressed a groan, again wondering why exactly she'd decided to enroll in this class. "I don't think so." She could hear the mumble of protest from the back row and continued, undeterred, "What you didn't read was that the police released only the fact that he'd appeared to have been beaten to death and that he was bound and gagged with silk scarves. But they released information this morning that the cause of death was in fact a slit throat."

She paused, briefly considering her next words.

Deciding what she wanted to say was nothing that wouldn't be in the paper the next day, she added, "I don't think the killer would have gone to the trouble of altering the crime scene if he were just going to leave a body laying around that shows all the signs of premeditation. We don't know this yet, but I'd be willing to bet the killer brought those scarves with him and perhaps the murder weapon. And so why leave the body and all that evidence if he's going to make it look like a break-in? That would be pretty stupid. And I don't think this guy is stupid. He probably knows that people don't tie up other people and beat them half to death, then slit their throats if they just want to steal some shit."

"My thoughts exactly!" the professor shouted happily and placed the newspaper on her desk.

The class debated the crime for the following half hour, until the students finally ditched the subject and moved on to discussing sections of their textbooks. The lecture wasn't half bad for once. For the first time, Angie learned bits and pieces of information she could actually use at some point. If only her professor wouldn't insist on dissecting her work every weekend, it might make for a valuable course. Chewing her lip nervously, she decided she'd shoot her prof an e-mail that evening to share her thoughts on the matter and hopefully put a stop to it.

When class ended two hours later, she quickly gathered up her things and hobbled out the door, not wanting to be caught for another private discussion with Professor Laney. She made it out just in time, too, with the help of another student who distracted the professor with several questions about the lecture. She thought she caught sight of a disappointed frown and didn't care.

Halfway home, Angie cursed furiously, realizing she'd nearly forgotten about her dinner date with Lauren. She was so scatter-brained lately that her lover had actually commented on it more than once. They'd joked that it was because Angie had fallen on her head while trying to escape that councilman, but she knew Lauren's joking was laced with not-so-hidden concern. Angie pulled an illegal U-turn at the next stoplight and headed back down Cooper Street, determined not to be late and let on that she'd let herself go off the mark again.

Lauren had saved them a booth at La Isla, a fast-becoming favorite Mexican eatery. Angie got a lingering look that was more appraising than friendly but let herself be helped into her seat. Wondering what was wrong, she opened her mouth to ask but was cut off with a knowing smile.

"Forgot, didn't you?"

"Er…"

"It's almost six-thirty and it only takes five minutes to get here. You're late."

"Um, couldn't I have needed to talk to my professor?" she tried lamely but knew the excuse wouldn't fly.

"You'd have said something immediately," Lauren said, the ever-more-familiar note of concern softening her voice. Angie thought she didn't look disappointed, more like she'd expected this to happen. "Seriously, you've got to ask your doctor about this. It's not normal, okay? It's just not and I'm tired of arguing about it. Last night—we can let that one slide because you'd been busy with work. But today, and the dozen times it has happened over the last week... I'm just worried."

Angie sighed. It was a familiar argument and she was tired of it, too. The first two weeks in the hospital, she'd blamed it on the drugs. The second two weeks out, she'd blamed it on getting the drugs out of her system. But the last two weeks—well, she didn't exactly have an excuse anymore. Damn.

Angie fiddled with her napkin, rolling and unrolling it, then stared out the window at passing cars. She hated this, hated having to be taken care of and being forced to reveal a vulnerable side of herself she could hardly bear to show.

She was strong. She was independent. She'd been accused more than once of being bull-headed and not asking for help when necessary. But her body was broken. It simply didn't fit with the image she had of herself and it pissed her off.

Finally, she met her lover's eyes and simply nodded. It was good enough for Lauren, who gave her an encouraging smile and dropped the issue. For now. Angie knew she'd be questioned on Monday about a specific appointment time, and there'd be hell to pay if she couldn't give that information. She pulled out her notepad and jotted down a note, put a star next to it, and showed it to Lauren.

"Starred and everything. Good enough?" She didn't dare admit that she'd been avoiding seeing her doctor, not wanting to hear any bad news about her head. Surely, she argued internally, it was just an aftereffect or something. It had better be anyway.

"Yeah," Lauren said, clearly relieved. She picked up her menu and set it back down after about five seconds. "I don't know why I bother looking. We both know what I'll get."

"Pollo con mole. No doubt about it."

They eased into a soft laughter and started chatting about the coming week. After placing their order, Lauren's hand inched across the table and grasped Angie's fiddling fingers. She had to fight the urge to withdraw her hand, gritting her teeth to avoid looking over her shoulder to check if anyone had noticed. If Lauren followed her thought process, she didn't show it. After a minute passed and Angie didn't hear any mumbled conversation—imagined or otherwise—she relaxed.

She was still getting used to this whole dating a woman thing. Lauren was her first. And after they'd met, she'd fought like crazy to invent all sorts of reasons why her body reacted to the woman, other than that it was attraction. The tingling sensation she felt every time she touched Lauren—that happened still—was just intrigue, fascination. Right. The way her heart raced when she heard that rich voice speak was just infatuation. Uh-huh. The way her voice caught when Lauren said her name was coincidence. Sure.

It had been, simply put, a losing battle.

The dust in her world was still settling after the upheaval Lauren had caused. At least Angie didn't feel as if things were spinning out of control anymore. And even if they were, she thought fiercely, Lauren was worth it. The warmth and safety she'd brought into her life was invaluable.

As she stared across the table into her lover's eyes, she couldn't believe that only two months before they'd just been friends. How many weeks she'd wasted worrying... But the build-up had carried them through Angie's tragedy and had allowed for a solid foundation that held them afloat during her recuperation. Now it seemed they were finally granted some time to get to know each other better, to simply love and live.

Angie suddenly wasn't interested in their meal at all and set aside her fork, reaching across the table with effort—her cast proving difficult to maneuver—and touched her lover's face. With courage she hadn't yet been able to muster in a public, non-gay establishment, she pulled from a well of that newfound warmth and security and said without a whisper, "Let's have the waiter box up our stuff and get out of here. I want you. Right now. And I don't think I can stand another minute without being in your arms."

It was more than a gigantic leap. And she knew it.

Her words took barely a second to register on Lauren's face, and when they did, the woman's eyes grew wide and she dropped her fork and knife at the same time and scooted out of the booth to track down their waiter. When she returned, she slopped their food in their respective boxes and handed them to Angie, lifted the smaller woman up—crutches and all—and practically jogged them out to her car, a lopsided grin plastered across her face.

Preying On Generosity

Chapter Three

A ngie squinted against the bright light bouncing off her bathroom mirror and fumbled with the faucet, filling a nearby cup with cold water. She reached into the medicine cabinet for the near-empty bottle of Vicodin, balancing precariously on her good leg. She popped a couple of pills and gulped the cool liquid, sighing, hoping the medicine would kick in soon and wipe away the searing pain that seemed to throb all the way from her toes to her hip.

She leaned against the counter, taking deep breaths, willing the pain to seep away. Minutes passed slowly. Finally, she looked up at herself in the mirror, preparing to brave the trip back to the bedroom where Lauren was softly snoring.

Angie caught sight of her disheveled appearance—tufts of her short blond hair sticking out in every direction—and snorted bemusedly, shaking her head even as the corners of her lips curled in a tiny smile.

She made a silly face at her reflection but suddenly stopped to take a closer look, leaning forward with her hands resting on the sink. The dark circles under her grass-green eyes that had made her look so hollow and stressed over the past few years had all but disappeared in the last month. She supposed it was because of the extra rest she'd gotten while she'd been on leave from work. But she preferred to think it was the warmth and safety she'd felt with Lauren that had erased the constant tension.

Then Angie's eyes fell on the angry red, silver dollar-sized scar that painted a sharp contrast against her pale skin half a hand's width below her left breast. Her look lingered there as a familiar icy feeling flooded her chest, forcing her breath out in

painful bursts as her heart rate sped up. A few inches higher...
Well, she wouldn't be standing in the bathroom—or anywhere else
for that matter. She forced her eyes to close and counted to ten,
viciously shutting out the image and memories attached to it. She
felt slightly faint and swayed before catching herself, shaking her
head as though it would help clear her mind. Angie cursed under
her breath—sick with helplessness and a touch of self-loathing for
allowing her emotions to get out of hand. Again.

It had been a clean through-and-through—straight through the
back, out through the front. With time, she knew, the matching
scars would pale and she wouldn't feel like passing out when she
saw them anymore. But the thought didn't make her feel any better
or less horrified.

And she didn't want to feel like this, not at that moment, not
when she'd just spent half the night making love to the most
amazing woman she'd ever met. She took hold of that thought,
wrapped it around her like a security blanket. She forced snippets
of conversation to surface—Lauren talking about her family,
Lauren recounting countless stories of when she'd been overseas
with the Peace Corps in Africa and Micronesia.

She could hear the stories. She could almost see the way her
lover's eyes lighted up every time she spoke about her studies at
the university. God, how the woman loved to learn... But Angie's
nightmare kept interrupting, refusing to be denied.

It was like swimming in a lake wearing armor. It was like
trying to breathe in a sandstorm. Angie slapped her face and shook
her head. She was stronger than this.

Her eyes still shut, Angie struggled against the tide of fear,
summoning the overwhelming feelings of satisfaction and love
that had consumed her until she'd fallen asleep, that had spread
through her dreams until she'd awoken and come into the
bathroom. Slowly, images of their lovemaking flashed through her
mind, flushing color back into her cheeks and along her neck—
sweat-dampened skin, ravenous lips and teeth, Lauren's dark,
beautiful eyes, and knowledgeable hands.

Through the haze of unpleasantness, a smile finally surfaced.
Angie clung to the images like a lifeline. She lifted her hand to her
face, touching her flushing cheeks, and could smell Lauren's sex
on her fingers. Her eyes fluttered shut as she inhaled the musky

scent and let it overwhelm her.

A wave of desire crashed through her so hard, she couldn't stifle a desperate moan. Her eyes snapped open with fierce determination, and she recklessly made her way back into the bedroom, not caring that she jarred her throbbing leg, ignoring the lightning-hot pain that ripped through her. She slid into bed, between the sheets, spooning her naked body around the taller woman, her eyes half-lidded as she took in the smell of lavender and sex—the back of Lauren's neck slightly salty on Angie's exploring lips.

She ran her hand along her lover's side from shoulder to hip, dipping suggestively, casually along the lean-muscled body, seeing if Lauren would awaken and show interest. The soft snoring stopped abruptly, interrupted by a startled gasp.

Encouraged, Angie grasped a full, heavy breast and pinched a nipple already erect with more force than patience—just the way Lauren liked it. Her initial tentativeness had died away over the previous month, when they'd explored each other's bodies at length, charting the differences and preferences.

Angie ran her teeth along Lauren's neck, dipping her tongue into the hollow behind the woman's ear, delighting in the tremble that shook her lover's body when she wrapped her lips around the soft earlobe and bit down, rolling the flesh between her tongue and teeth.

Her insides tightened with frantic urgency when Lauren moaned under her touch. Angie slid her hand away from the beautiful breasts, down along her lover's taut abdomen, past the wiry dark curls, fingers slipping through slick folds to find her lover's center with practiced ease. She swirled three fingers, coating them on all sides, returning again and again to tease the swollen nub, while Lauren trembled and bucked, crying out in sweet desperation.

"Angie," she moaned hoarsely. "Please...please...please..."

Angie's breath was becoming as erratic, her resolve to draw out Lauren's pleasure crumbling with each gasp for air. She bit a struggling shoulder hard and plunged her fingers through the aching entrance. Lauren cried out in satisfaction, her hips bucking to match the rapidly increasing rhythm.

She slowed and held her fingers still for several seconds,

savoring the feeling of entering her lover, of being inside her, surrounded by trembling muscles, and having Lauren at her mercy. Lauren cried out and struggled, gasping, unable to demand what she wanted.

Angie inched her face closer to Lauren's ear, pressing in, and murmured, "I can hardly stand not touching you like this, not being inside of you, not feeling you quivering around my fingers or hearing you moaning my name. I love you..." And she thrust her fingers inside hard, then again and again—Lauren's moans a continuous melody in her ears—until she could feel the rhythmic tightening that meant her lover was close.

Lauren's legs jostled the bed and kicked at the covers, bumping Angie's rough cast—a long groan of frustration escaping her lips. Angie knew she was trying to control her mutinous legs, was concerned even on the verge of ecstasy of causing her any harm.

"Let it go," Angie demanded, her fingers punctuating the commanding words with sharp plunges. And Lauren finally let go, crying out, her body shuddering as a thin sheen of sweat broke out across her back where their bodies pressed together. Angie murmured soft nothings in her lover's ear, her heart racing with unquenched need but a deep satisfaction filling her regardless.

Seconds passed in silence, broken only by Lauren's calming breaths. Angie tried to will herself to lie still, but her body began to tremble and she ground her teeth.

She couldn't do it. A muffled whimper escaped her lips while she tried to suppress it by nuzzling her face against Lauren's back.

She was suddenly pinned to the mattress—the taller woman not bothering to waste time on foreplay—those long fingers sliding straight to Angie's core in one swift move. She let out a startled cry, her eyes wide with surprise and pupils shot through with desire. Those long fingers seemed to touch the very center of her body, felt as though they'd crawl up through her insides and burrow under her heart, squeezing—a tantalizingly slow rhythm that made a voice in Angie's head begin to scream, unable to surface, the echoes prickling along her skin like mutinous armies of marching ants. More, she needed more.

She tried to buck with her hips, pushing up with both legs, and pain ripped along a cord from toe to groin, the fingers seemingly driving it in deeper, tears sliding hotly down her cheeks. The movements stopped, and Angie's eyes snapped open, catching a bleary look of dismay on Lauren's moonlit face.

"No!" she shouted and grabbed the retreating hand, throwing an arm around her lover's neck and pulling her forward with such strength that Lauren collapsed on top of her, the woman's trapped hands pressing roughly against her swollen clit.

"Don't stop," Angie pleaded, her voice thick and scratchy, her vision unfocused. Eyes black in the dim light searched her own as seconds passed. Lauren's tongue slipped out and hesitantly traced the path of tears, seemingly torn between her concern and Angie's need.

Angie cupped Lauren's face and crushed their lips together in a forceful kiss, her tongue demanding entry, moaning against the soft lips and reluctantly welcoming mouth with surprising ferocity. Her lover whimpered and she released her at once.

Lauren stared down at her with wide eyes and licked her lips, clearing her throat. A series of unreadable emotions crossed her face, her lips forming a protest that never come out, halfhearted or not.

Finally, Lauren gave a gentle thrust, then another, the palm of her hand grinding Angie's center. Her arm was still firmly locked around her lover's upper body, keeping them close as the rhythm picked up speed. Angie's eyes found those dark, beautiful orbs and she lost herself, overpowered by the emotions reflected there. Tiny explosions erupted from deep within where those fingers impacted with each driven plunge, a blazing fire scorching her skin inside and out as she screamed and went limp—the desperation quelled at last.

She collapsed, her arm sliding off her lover's shoulder and hitting the bed with a thump. Her heart pounded in her ears so that she could hardly hear anything else, the beat thrumming along her sensitive folds and down her broken leg painfully.

"Are...are you okay?" Lauren whispered, softly kissing her neck, the words laced with fear.

"Yeah," Angie half-lied. Truth was, she felt both beautifully sated and horribly jarred. But the pain was receding quickly, and she suspected the Vicodin had finally kicked in. "Yeah, I'll be fine. Don't worry." She cleared her voice and closed her eyes.

"You did what I wanted you to do. More, in fact." And she felt a tingle run along her spine and released a shaky breath. She let out a half-laugh and sighed.

"Your leg..." Lauren began but was shushed with a finger on her lips.

"No, I said don't worry. My brain was focused on things other than remembering that I can't push up with my broken leg, okay? It's not like this hasn't happened before."

Silence. Lauren's eyes dropped for a few seconds as she turned her head and studied the cast, before returning to patiently waiting green eyes. Her right hand reached to touch and trace the bullet scar, softly trembling. Angie could see her lover's jaw muscles clenching and unclenching, her breath forcefully even.

Angie grasped the lingering hand and drew it away from the scar, pulling her lover close, the dark hair tickling her neck as the woman snuggled closer and the trembling calmed.

She clenched her eyes shut, fighting the sickening feeling that came with thinking about the whole mess, tried to force out the visions that would give her nightmares. Her eyes burned with unshed tears, but she'd be damned if she'd ruin the night for them. She drifted off into an uneasy sleep, listening to Lauren's deep breaths.

On Monday afternoon, Angie stepped out of the physical therapist's room, fighting the urge to scream and break something. She felt like she'd spent the entire hour squelching myriad stinging words, along with tears of frustration and pain, as her therapist pushed on her foot—toes toward the shin, just an inch or two of movement—and forced her to do still-agonizing, upper-body stretches. Everything felt stiff and abused. And when Lauren met her in the waiting room, she said nothing, limping on her crutches instead toward the door, a deep scowl cutting across her face. Her lover followed silently, carrying Angie's purse. When they made it out to the parking lot and into Lauren's car, her dam of resolve broke and she let off a string of profanities that made Lauren cringe and grit her teeth.

And to think that she had to leave work early every other day for this shit.

Angie sat in the passenger seat, fuming. Lauren didn't dare

say anything. Angie had taught her that no reason or encouragement after these sessions would have any effect. Under other circumstances, Angie might have thought it funny how Lauren tiptoed around her, a forcibly polite smile on her face. But it wasn't funny. She was in pain. And she appreciated the silence and the simple help her lover offered—a ride to and from the hospital.

It would take an hour or so for her to cool down, after she'd gotten home and had a piece of comfort cheesecake bought for that very reason. Until then, all bets were off.

An hour passed. Then two. Finally, after Lauren started to fidget and mutter—the woman tended to think out loud and didn't realize she did so—Angie finally opened her mouth and said, "I have to do something about this. I mean, the therapist said I wasn't making very good progress. I can't go limping around forever, Lauren. I just can't. The worst part about this whole thing is that I can't go running anymore to blow off steam. I need that. But she said I may never run again."

Lauren got off the easy chair and slid into a spot next to Angie on the couch, wrapping her arm around Angie's shoulders, twitching muscles on her forehead clearly showing that she was trying to keep the worry out of her voice the best she could.

"It's only been a few weeks. We'll practice at home. They gave you exercises, right?" Angie nodded. "So we'll do the exercises. Plenty of people beat the odds. So don't give up."

Angie sighed and stared at the empty plate where a fat slice of cheesecake had sat before she'd wolfed it down in huge, furious bites. She was getting weaker, she could feel it. She'd been so fit for so long and now, well, she felt like shit half the time and it pissed her off. But she couldn't continue to just sit there and fume. Lauren didn't deserve it and a familiar stab of guilt bore straight through her chest.

"Sure," she said and forced a smile. She snuggled closer to her lover, her mind racing for a topic that would steer them away from the unpleasant conversation.

A smirk erupted across her lips. "So you're going to be old soon."

Lauren snorted and shook her head. "Twenty-nine is not old, you know."

"Sure it is—one year away from thirty, one year away from being over the hill."

"Over the hill!? At thirty? You're so full of shit sometimes..."

But she never got to finish the sentence because Angie's nearest hand shot to a well-known spot between Lauren's ribs that was dangerously ticklish, hitting her mark with calculated accuracy.

Lauren screamed and giggled, gasping for breath while threatening a counterattack when the phone rang. Reluctantly, Angie allowed her prey to get up and get the damned ringing thing. Lauren handed the cell phone over with a smirk and whispered, "Saved by the bell." Ha-ha.

"Hello?" Angie grumbled.

"Hey, ditch your lady friend and meet me at the coffee shop," an urgent voice whispered loudly, laced with scarcely contained laughter. "In twenty minutes."

"Hi, Jimmy. You'd better be kidding..."

"Just do it, okay?" He spoke in a normal voice. Lauren tried to snatch the phone away, but Angie swatted at her hands and shook her head.

"Fine. Twenty minutes. I'm assuming you mean the one across the street from your apartment."

"That's the one." He hung up before she could respond.

Angie sighed and pushed herself off the couch, reaching for her crutches nearby.

"I don't know what he wants, but it had better be good," she grumbled at no one in particular. "I love seeing him, but I really don't feel like driving right now."

"I could give you a lift, then go take care of some things," Lauren suggested and got up to grab her keys.

"Sounds great," Angie said with more than a little relief. Driving had become a bit of an effort with the knee-high cast—her seat needed to be pushed back a little more than was comfortable, forcing her to stretch for the pedals with her right foot—but she managed because she had to for work. You can't have a crime reporter who can't drive to crime scenes. But it had helped that she'd broken down and purchased the Mitsubishi Eclipse with an automatic transmission instead of a manual gear-shift the way she usually preferred. But she couldn't very well use the clutch with a broken leg. Imagine hitting stop-and-go traffic... No, the automatic was just fine. It was the extra trips that weren't work-related that got on her nerves and made her leg ache in dreaded resignation of the extra jostling from potholes and speed bumps. At least when someone else drove, she could position her leg for better control.

Exactly twenty minutes later, Lauren dropped her off at the Starbucks on Beach Street, where Jimmy rushed out to help her and shooed Lauren away. She pretended to pout but finally gave up when she couldn't get a word out of Jimmy about the impromptu rendezvous. With a quick kiss goodbye, Lauren hopped back into her car and sped away.

"This had better be good, Mr. Has-No-Understanding-Of-Other's-Needs," Angie grumbled as she hobbled off toward the coffee shop entrance. Jimmy raced ahead in typical fashion and held the door open for her.

"It is good, you'll see," he said with a quick bow, ushering her inside, where he insisted on pulling out a chair for her and bought her favorite coffee.

Angie stared across the table while he made pleasant chit-chat. She began to seriously frown while he went on about his computer tech business. She scowled by the time he started babbling about the weather and finally cleared her throat, pinning him hard with her eyes, her fingers drumming an irritated rhythm on the table.

"Er, right. The reason I called you out here." He finally noticed and smirked. "Patience is a virtue, you know." He avoided an across-the-table smack and leaned back in his chair, making damned sure that he was out of reach. "Sorry, been cooped up all day. No computer gigs this week. My clients are behaving for once—not pulling viruses off the Internet or installing shit programs they don't need that clash with other software..." Angie raised her eyebrow threateningly. "Right, I'll cut to the chase."

"It's about damned time," she mumbled, wishing they'd at least picked a table outside so she could wile away her boredom by smoking cigarettes. As the thought crossed her mind—that she was bored—she suddenly realized how unusual it was for her friend to beat around the bush. Wasn't he usually the frank one?

"Come on, let's go find a table outside so we can smoke," she said, her tone much less aggravated than before. "And you can tell me why you're pussy-footing around whatever it is you want to discuss."

She caught a sheepish grin before Jimmy turned away and collected her purse.

They sat at the far end of the building at a rickety table rather the worse for wear. Jimmy lighted two of his own cigarettes of frilly vanilla flavor and handed her one—a gesture that reminded her distinctly of the first time they'd ever had a personal conversation.

"Basically, I've done something drastic and after much deliberation, decided I need to consult someone about it," he began, took a drag of his cigarette, and exhaled dramatically. Angie sucked back a bemused laugh. "It's about Lauren's birthday."

Ah. Her curiosity flared, and she wondered what he could possibly have done that his longtime friend might disapprove of. Of course, this was Jimmy she was thinking about. And Jimmy was full of ideas ranging from bizarre to impossible.

"You didn't hire a stripper, did you?"

"Nothing like that, no." He chuckled, his eyes crinkling with mischief. Perhaps she shouldn't give him any ideas. "No, it's something a bit less likely to get me in trouble with both of you. Don't worry. You see…" He paused, steeling himself. "I kind of booked a show for her, thought she might want to let loose for her birthday."

"You what?" Angie nearly shouted, dropping her cigarette. Her friend lunged for it, nearly knocking the table over, and handed the half-smoked thing back to her.

"That bad?" he mumbled, frowning.

"Well…" She thought hard and fast. Would Lauren freak out? It wasn't like she didn't enjoy performing with her band, Fearless. And she had nothing to worry about, really. The woman was a fantastic singer, very Melissa Etheridge-esque. But she did have some control issues, especially when it came to performances. To Angie's knowledge, she usually spent a week or two rehearsing nearly every night. On the other hand, that was only secondhand knowledge, and she'd never witnessed the before-the-show antics. "I don't know. Tell me the band knows about the gig."

"Of course they know. Do you seriously think I'd pretend to be the band's manager, print fake business cards for such,

46

schedule a gig, and not tell anybody about it? What if they weren't in town or something?" He gave her an incredulous look, to which she responded with a shoulder shrug and a nervous half-laugh.

"They know. They think it's cool. They have some minor worries about her freaking out. Damn it, I thought this would be a good thing. She hasn't had a gig since you went to the hospital, and the band's getting restless. It'll be good for her, don't you think?"

Angie gave a reluctant nod. Lauren had to get past the whole mess as much as she did. And performing just might do the trick.

"When is it?"

"Friday night at ten p.m. at the Art Bar in Deep Ellum," he said with flare.

"Shit! That's a big deal, Jimmy. She's gonna freak."

"It's just a small bar..." he began, his voice lowering to a whisper.

"In Deep Ellum on a Friday night! And don't give me that 'it's just a small bar' crap. I know that place. On Fridays, it's freaking packed. Bands perform on the roof. Everybody can hear them. How the fuck did you get her band in that place?"

"I did some work for the management for free, brought them some video footage from her last concert," he muttered, his voice strained. "It'll be really good for the band. Maybe we should tell her. I was going to ask that you lure her down there, but I guess that won't work."

"No, it won't. And you should know better than that. Y'all have been friends way longer than I've known her, damn it." She sighed and lighted another cigarette. He had meant well and that's all that should matter. Of course, if Lauren refused, the Art Bar was highly unlikely to ever book Fearless again, and it was a big break. "I'll talk to her tonight. I'll make her agree to it. They still have a few days to rehearse—maybe she won't freak out."

They smoked in silence for a few minutes. Jimmy was muttering something about "unreasonable" and "if only she'd recognize her own talent." Angie agreed, but didn't say anything. She knew it was an old argument between the two of them—Jimmy insisting she should ditch her studies and go for the singing career, Lauren dismissing that choice with fierce determination, saying the rock star life just wasn't her calling.

"Hey, when did you book it anyway?" Angie broke the silence, sincerely curious.

"Four weeks ago."

"Don't you dare tell her that," she warned, coughing on smoke inhaled too quickly. "I'm not going to give her a time frame. If she knew she could have been obsessing about vocals for the past month, she'd flip."

"Deal."

The talk didn't go well at all. Jimmy had driven her home, and the second Angie got inside, she joined her lover on the couch and told her everything. Lauren had jumped up and cursed for five solid minutes. Then she'd ripped her cell phone out of her purse, furiously punched in her lead guitarist's number, and yelled into the phone for another ten minutes. By the time she'd hung up—voice hoarse and dark—she'd already picked up her things and was headed out the door with a brusque, "Gotta go rehearse. Don't wait up."

To Angie's relief, Lauren hadn't turned down the gig, but only because she'd shouted about what a great break it was over Lauren's string of furious ranting.

She sat on the couch and sighed into the silence, rubbing her throbbing upper leg absentmindedly. Well, hell. The mess would make for an interesting week.

At eleven o'clock, she wondered if Lauren would come back at all that night.

"Jimmy and his ideas," Angie grumbled to herself, hobbling into the kitchen to fix herself a sandwich. "Stupid, stupid, stupid," she continued as she slopped a heaping pile of raspberry jam on the white toast. "He doesn't have to put up with her while she freaks out all week," she muttered while slapping on a generous amount of peanut butter. She continued to mumble around mouthfuls while she made her way to the porch.

She flopped down on a plastic lawn chair and sighed, munching silently. She stared at the horizon, watched the twinkling plane lights heading toward DFW International Airport. The air was stale and muggy; the humidity clung to her skin and hair like a sticky blanket. A car alarm went off nearby and a neighbor's dog started barking. Angie thought about lighting a cigarette when she finished her sandwich, but the air was so stiflingly hot that the thought made her feel almost nauseated.

Her cell phone rang. She dug the buzzing thing from her pocket and flipped it open.

"Yeah?" she said, reaching for her pack of cigarettes out of habit but setting it aside.

"Wazzup?" a vaguely familiar voice nearly shouted in a way reminiscent of that silly "Scary Movie" flick. Angie checked the caller ID and didn't recognize the number.

"Er...not much," she said after several seconds passed. "How're you doing?"

The responding bright laughter reminded her of that awful crime scene. It couldn't be... "Detective Key?" she asked, slightly incredulous.

"Yup, and call my Jay," he chuckled into the following silence. "I was just calling because we've collected some new evidence you may be interested in. Who'd you think it was?"

"I...well, I just didn't expect you to be so..." She hesitated, searching for a descriptor.

"Goofy?" he suggested.

"Yeah." She paused. "What's the new info?"

"Several people came forward after reading your article and gave us some leads." He paused. "Looks like our killer might have been out to find a poor sucker with a good heart."

The following days were a blur of business such as Angie hadn't known for months. She'd rushed to the office early Tuesday to type up the info she'd received the night before—a bizarre follow-up piece based on witness accounts from patrons of a Fort Worth gay bar. They'd called the Crime Stoppers hot line and told police that they'd seen Whittaker at the Funhouse, a hole-in-the-wall bar off Lancaster Avenue, about eight o'clock the previous Wednesday. Apparently, he'd come alone and had been chatting with the bartender for a while before he was approached by a redheaded man he didn't seem to know.

"Now some of the guys said that redhead wasn't hitting on him or anything," Detective Key had told her. "They said he was polite and kept his distance, sat a couple of barstools down. It doesn't seem like our vic was looking to pick up some guy, and the redhead wasn't looking to hook up, either. That's what they say it looked like." He'd paused then and let out a long sigh.

"Angie, we have three guys telling us they heard the redhead say something like, 'So can you help me?' And then our vic nodded, paid his tab, and they left together. The guys think his first name was Chris but couldn't be sure. He paid his bill with cash, so there's no record. The guys told us that they were eavesdropping but not too closely. And they said the guy who asked for help was talking to Whittaker for about an hour or so. They left around nine thirty p.m., which gets us a hell of a lot closer to the time of death window."

Of course, investigators couldn't be one hundred percent certain that he was the last person to see Whittaker alive or that this Chris guy was the killer. But the detective was right about their meeting being conspicuously close to the "late Wednesday or early Thursday" time of death. Or maybe the redhead took some money in the parking lot or had his car jumped and left, leaving Whittaker to go somewhere else. Who the hell knew?

Angie was extremely careful in the crafting of her article, writing very diplomatically that "the man is being sought for questioning."

As soon as she'd completed the piece, just in time for lunch, a factory caught fire and exploded in the industrial district of Fort Worth. Black smoke had billowed from the building full of chemicals, and even though it was miles away, the emerging smoke had blown straight into downtown. She'd rushed to the scene, joined half an hour later by six other *Tribune* reporters who fanned out to collect information and witness accounts from nearby business managers, hysterical workers, police, firefighters, and city leaders. She'd been stuck late into the night.

The next day, a Wednesday she'd hoped would be nice and quiet, turned out to be a day filled with a crazy carjacker and wild police chase and the arrest of a major crack dealer in the seedy Stop Six neighborhood.

Thursday wasn't much better, and Friday followed hot on its heels with a terrible six-car pileup on Loop 820 and an underground gambling business bust in Parker County.

She'd spent her nights recuperating—miserably alone—after hard days of standing around crime and accident scenes for hours.

But there was no way in hell she'd have told her boss how much it hurt or that she couldn't do it. No, she would as soon have jumped in front of the Trinity Railway Express.

As per Angie's predictions, Lauren wasn't around much to help her relax. But she couldn't really blame her. The woman was rehearsing like mad at night and attending classes at the university for her graduate program by day. Lauren could barely keep her eyes open when they did manage to find an hour here or there, and Angie contented herself with early-evening naps and cuddling. She told herself that the hectic week was almost over, and Lauren's anxiety should pass after her gig was over.

Angie stepped into her quiet apartment at seven o'clock and frowned. She was late and had expected to be admonished by her surely nervous lover. She checked the bedroom, and finding it empty, pulled out her cell phone to see what was going on. She called Lauren and got her voicemail. Then she called Jimmy.

"I'm so glad it's you!" he shouted and she held the phone a couple of inches farther away from her ringing ear. "We'll be over in about twenty minutes. You have to talk some sense into her." He hung up before she could respond, and she groaned.

Angie ran a quick bath and gingerly got in the tub, her cast hanging over the edge as she scrubbed herself clean and washed her short hair with record speed. There was no time for her usual ritual of sprinkling bath salts in the steaming hot water and playing some nice classical music if she'd have to spend time "talking sense into" Lauren—whatever that meant.

She heard them unlocking the door just as she'd put a few finishing touches on her makeup. One last check of her appearance—rather punk with her hair styled in a wet spiky look, wearing a low-cut, tight black shirt, matching black skirt, and a knee-high boot, her cast covered with an oversized black sock—and decided it'd do. Not bad for twenty minutes, anyway. She put on some silver hoop earrings and added a thick, chainlike choker necklace, a present from her lover.

Angie hopped into the living room and sat next to Lauren, whose face had taken on a grayish pale tinge and whose hands were shaking. Jimmy had taken the liberty of raiding the fridge and handed them each a bottle of Shiner.

Angie slid onto the couch cushion next to Lauren and pulled

her in for a long, demanding kiss—her hands tangling in the windblown, jet black hair. The dark eyes grew wide and Lauren struggled at first, but Angie persisted, softening the kiss, her tongue dancing on her lover's lips. If she could get her to respond, Angie thought, pressing her upper body in close, maybe she could break through this fit of anxiety.

Lauren's eyes fluttered shut, and after several seconds, her lips finally parted. Angie dove in for a searing kiss and didn't let up until she felt the reverberating moan in her mouth. They both gasped for air when she broke contact, moving to nuzzle Lauren's neck.

"Happy birthday," Angie whispered into an all-too-tempting ear, pleased to see the slight tremor that ran through Lauren's body. "If you're this freaked out, don't go. I don't care what anybody thinks." She paused, nibbling on the nearby earlobe. "But I was looking forward to seeing you on stage again." She closed her eyes, remembering the last time she'd seen Lauren demonstrate her vocal abilities. "Hey, do you remember that night at Division One?"

Lauren nodded silently, her hands beginning to fidget again. Angie trapped them with her own and squeezed.

"You were so sexy in those leather pants. In fact," she lowered her voice so their friend couldn't hear, "right before I came up there, I was fantasizing about you in those leather pants. I imagined your teeth on my neck, your hands running up my back, your..."

The balcony door clicked shut as Jimmy stepped outside. Angie continued to whisper in Lauren's ear, saw the color flush back into the woman's cheeks, and didn't stop until she felt strong hands run up her bare thighs and slip below her skirt.

And by then it was too late to protest the skillful hands and tongue dipping into her cleavage. Her body wouldn't have allowed it. Angie halfheartedly struggled, torn between the spreading warmth between her legs where Lauren's hand had disappeared and the knowledge that Jimmy was on the balcony waiting. But the internal debate ended when Lauren's fingers slipped beneath her panties and teeth closed over a still-covered, taut nipple. She gasped, her head thrown back in complete surrender, hands digging into her lover's scalp, pushing her closer.

Lauren slid off the couch and spread Angie's legs wide, trailing hot kisses up her inner thighs, strong fingers massaging her hips as they slowly moved in anticipation. Dark hair disappeared under Angie's skirt, and she sucked in a sharp breath of air when she felt her panties pulled aside and a hot tongue ran the length of her folds.

Half an hour later, Angie opened the balcony door, a lopsided grin plastered on her face. She flopped down in the lawn chair and lighted a cigarette. Jimmy took one look at her and burst out laughing. She shook her head and took a drag, exhaling slowly.

"She'll do it," she said with a smirk. He immediately fell silent. "She's getting ready right now. Give her half an hour or so. I told her to take her time."

"Damn..." he said and snorted. "If I'd have known that's all it took to calm her the fuck down, I'd have dragged her butt over here sooner."

"That's not all it took," Angie said, mischief sparkling from her grass-green eyes.

His smile crumbled and a frown slowly spread, his eyes narrowing suspiciously.

"What do you mean?"

"You pretended to be manager, now you get to be manager. Guess who gets to announce Fearless on stage and entertain the crowd while they take a break?"

His eyes grew wide, and he jumped out of his chair.

"No, no, no," he squeaked. "I don't do well on stage. You can't be serious."

"You do it or she stays here and we take our fun to the bedroom," she deadpanned.

Jimmy started pacing, stopped to light a cigarette, and resumed pacing. He muttered something about "damned freaking girls" and "make a fool of myself" and "have no choice." Finally, he stopped, by which time Angie had finished her cigarette and started to get out of her chair. They stared at each other for a full minute.

Then, "Fine. But we're talking about what the hell I'm supposed to say all the way there."

"Fine." She repressed a giggle at his stern expression. "She was going to do it either way, but since you so readily agreed, you're stuck."

And this time, it was Angie who got smacked on the shoulder. She yelped, surprised, and raised a hand to return the favor when the devilish gleam returned to his eyes.

"Don't touch me with that, I have a pretty good idea where it's been." And with an agility she'd never have expected of him, he slipped by and shut the door, locking her out before she could even blink. She frowned at the door for several seconds and tried the doorknob again. She still couldn't get inside. She sat back down in the chair and laughter slowly bubbled up from her stomach and burst through her lips, her shoulders shaking as she closed her eyes and drew in lungfuls of rich, summer-scented air with each shoulder-racking laugh.

Chapter Four

"Er...Hi! I'm um...here to...uh, introduce the band Fearless." Long pause. "Yeah, they're pretty cool."

Jimmy gripped the microphone with knuckles white from tension, and his voice rose a quarter octave with each word. He dropped the mike and it screeched, making the crowd hold their hands over their ears and shout their disapproval. The boos would come soon if he didn't pull himself together, and Angie was regretting her decision to force him into this.

If he'd known that she and Lauren had had to furiously argue with the manager to allow this, he'd have killed them both. Oops. Too late now.

She waved frantically, trying to get his attention while he stared at the audience with a deer-caught-in-headlights look. Standing near the stage, she could see sweat pearl on his forehead and his hand shake. Shit.

Finally, she caught his eye and he mouthed something nasty. A couple of teenagers behind her started snickering, and when she shook her head disapprovingly, they laughed obnoxiously loud. The murmuring crowd quieted, craning their necks, trying to see what was going on.

Angie lost her patience. "Come on, Jimmy."

"Yeah, get on with it, Jimmy!" several people shouted from the back row.

And suddenly, he started laughing.

"Damned reporters, feisty things, aren't they?" he asked, his hands trembling less.

Angie closed her eyes. Not again.

"I'll have you know," he continued, "that this one up front

here is particularly feisty. Has to be, if she can put up with her girlfriend, Lauren Lucelli, Fearless's own fearless lead singer. Bit of a troublemaker if you ask me." He paused for a second, the corners of his mouth twitching mischievously in a way that clearly was supposed to say "serves you right" to Angie.

He opened his mouth to continue but was cut off by a shouted, "Hold on, did you say the little blonde up front is dating this Lauren chick? We have lesbians in the house?"

The teenagers behind Angie started snickering again and clapped her on the back in what they must have thought was a guy-to-guy-like way. There were a few catcalls, and Jimmy chuckled into the mike.

"Indeed," he said, a slight tremble in his voice giving away that he was trying to contain his laughter.

"Is the singer hot?" a male voice shouted.

"Angie?" Jimmy asked, taking a few quick strides to where she stood, and shoved the mike in her face. She'd gone pale by now, not entirely sure that being outed in front of a tightly packed straight bar rooftop was a good idea. She shook her head. Jimmy persisted, encouraged by the jeering crowd.

She mouthed, "I'm going to kill you," before mumbling an agreement into the mike.

"Hey, we can't hear you!"

"Damn it, I said she is fucking hot!" Angie huffed, much, much louder than she'd intended. Applause erupted through the muggy night air, and she thought she heard muffled laughter from backstage. She may have imagined it. Regardless, her face turned scarlet and she had a damned strong urge to bolt.

"Jimmy, get her on stage! Quit fooling around!"

Great. She was crammed on a rooftop full of frat boys and horny straight guys who wanted to check out her girlfriend. Angie pulled a cigarette out and lighted it, exhaling angrily as an ugly green head she didn't know existed reared itself.

"Okay then! Give it up for Fearless!"

Jimmy left the stage, a bounce in his steps, and made his way over to Angie, where he immediately cuffed her in the shoulder. The band members trekked out bravely and snatched up their respective instruments to catcalling and stomping feet. The floor seemed to shake as the band skipped a few first words, going straight to the music with a heavy number Angie didn't recognize.

Lauren stood center stage, feet shoulder-width, clad in those tight, black leather pants that Angie thought increased her lover's sexiness factor considerably. Lauren's long hair was down loose and wild, her eyes lined heavily with smoky-dark makeup. Her fist clutched the microphone, and when the drummer abruptly stopped, Lauren let out a howl that sent shivers down Angie's spine. The audience, too, stopped jeering—shocked. Lauren threw her head back for the full ten seconds of unleashed rage. When her breath ran out, her eyes snapped on the crowd, blazing fiercely, and she shouted: "Got your attention? Good. Because this is pretty fucking important."

Angie knew the people in the street had probably stopped dead in their tracks. The band was performing on the rooftop, after all, and there was no way in hell they would have missed Lauren's amplified screaming. She pictured them staring up at the two-story building and couldn't help but glance sideways at the rest of the audience, catching many pairs of wide eyes and open mouths, extremely puzzled expressions.

The crowd pushed in on the stage, forcing Angie against the barrier, while Jimmy shoved at people behind them pointing out her cast with vicious words.

The beat picked up where it had left off, though slower, more dramatic, forcing Angie's attention back to the stage. The lead guitarist ripped a strangled series of power chords while Lauren closed her eyes and dropped her head as though steeling herself, her body beginning to sway with the melody.

"Two shadows meet in the night, darkness suffocating/ They share a secret, a lie, a cutting grief—deathly hot/ Dawn will tear them apart, rip their hearts/ Rip their hearts, blind their eyes, if they're caught/ And it won't matter how they met, how they loved/ That they dream, that they hurt, that they bleed/ And it won't matter that they die every night/ With the crushing sun, the scorching heat/ Those words of fire that make them believe."

Angie's heart nearly stopped. Lauren's voice had gone ragged, emotion-roughed, angry. She dropped her cigarette and didn't notice. She'd only seen the woman perform a couple of times, and yes, Lauren was always intense. But the raging fire in her eyes was unexpected and made her breath hitch.

She stared into those dark eyes across the stage that fixed the audience with a look so icy-hot they went completely silent.

"The night is short, already gray sky breaks/ See their tears, hear their cries, feel them tremble/ One last touch, crushing lips, daylight takes/ Takes the night, the comfort, fuels the fight/ They stand together, two women melding/ And comes the blasting sun, the razor light/ Comes the day with fiery words, righteous delight/ And they fight! Can't hold back, can't run/ Can't shield their eyes or walk away or die with the night."

The music stopped. Angie's whole body had gone rigid, her fists balled, shaking. She was quivering, seething. How dare they, she thought. How dare…

"How dare you deny/ Another woman's right to love/ How dare you deny/ A force of nature that's not a choice/ How dare you believe/ It's not sacred/ It's not precious/ It's not pure/ As pure as any woman's love/ How dare you take away my life/ How dare you turn your eyes/ And pick the self-righteous sentence/ That of destruction and fear and hate.

"Open your fucking eyes/ Look into their eyes/ listen to their cries."

Complete and utter silence—only the sounds of passing cars and the dampened techno beat next door.

The electric guitar suddenly ripped through the silence—the melancholy melody mind-numbing and eerily mournful at first, until the pace suddenly changed and the drums kicked back in— depressing minor chords switching to hopeful majors. The solo was quick, though, and ended with Lauren's voice, a quieter anger seeping in, almost a whisper.

"How dare you whisper/ How dare you stand by/ Let us cry/ Let our love die/ Open your eyes/ Fight the lies/ Don't just stand there/ Averting your eyes.

"We won't go back into the shadows again/ Our quiet anger has boiled too long/ See through the blinding hate/ See through the lies/ Look into your souls/ And don't deny."

For several seconds, it seemed as though the crowd didn't realize the song was over. The music had stopped abruptly. Lauren's legs trembled slightly, and she raked a hand through her hair nervously.

Then two sets of hands started clapping, then three, then four.

Within seconds, the roof was filled with wild applause. A dozen people shoved through the crowd toward the exit and were followed with angry shouts of outrage. Lauren's scowl faded slowly, her eyes focusing, apparently stunned. She took a rattling breath and whispered a few words to the lead guitarist before turning back to the audience.

"I'm damned surprised you liked that," she said, fixing the crowd again with her dark eyes. "Knowing how y'all vote around here."

The crowd booed and began verbally abusing the people who had left the rooftop. They shouted. Screamed. Vied for her attention with calls of, "We'll see about that!"

Slowly, Lauren's lips turned upward and she gazed at Angie, her eyebrow raised. Angie's lips twitched and she nodded her approval.

"Right. So you like political songs. 'Cause we can play some nice fluffy shit. Unless you want to hear more politics?"

Cheering approval and stomping feet. Lauren turned to the guitarist and nodded, and a melody Angie recognized about women's rights followed. Then another new song about the war in Iraq, followed by a number about a woman named Cindy Sheehan, a mother who'd lost her son in the war and was staging a protest at the Western White House—the president's ranch near Crawford—demanding to meet with him so he could explain why her son had died.

Lauren had been busy. Angie was pretty sure she hadn't written since they'd started dating, the recent fiasco having eaten much of their time. No wonder she'd been so exhausted the past week. And nervous—the seeming lack of ease from the first time she'd seen Lauren perform was practically nonexistent. Of course, that last little concert had been in a small Arlington bar, and most of the patrons had apparently known her or the band.

It was completely different to play in Deep Ellum. But the band had won the crowd over with that first risky heavy number. After a set of ten songs, Fearless announced they'd be taking a twenty-minute break, and Angie made her way to the back of the rooftop at the bar, where Jimmy had secured five barstools by threatening a group of frat boys that Fearless would leave if they didn't get a drink. They vacated their spots, but not before ordering the bartender to add a pitcher to their tab that they left on the counter for the band.

The lead guitarist slipped onto a stool next to Jimmy and said something that Angie couldn't quite hear, jerking her thumb over her shoulder. Angie followed their gaze and caught a glimpse of raven hair, her lover surrounded by a group of animated people. Jimmy jumped up and headed toward the commotion.

"We're not doing too bad, eh?" the guitarist asked.

"Hey, Dawn," Angie responded, tearing her eyes away from the scene where Jimmy had grabbed Lauren's arm and was shoving people aside with a forced smile. "I had no idea you girls had been so busy. Lot of new songs. Great stuff, by the way. I think it's going really well."

"You know, when your girl heard what Jimmy did, she was a mess. She showed up all crazy-like and went into this long freak-out about how we needed new material and shit."

Dawn laughed and poured herself a drink. "So we went to the nearest gas station and bought a couple of newspapers, then went to the bar and decided which topics to tackle."

Another woman slid in beside Dawn and snatched the pitcher of beer, immediately filling a mug for herself.

"You telling her about Monday?" she said.

"Yeah," Dawn said and snorted. "Anyway, we spent the rest of the night writing lyrics. That first song was a Lucelli original. I wrote the Sheehan number. Tristan here got stuck with the Iraq deal."

"I wouldn't say stuck with it—wasn't that hard," Tristan said.

Angie sighed with relief when Lauren finally plopped down next to her, a bemused smile on her face. She accepted a mug of beer that Tristan handed her and took a long sip, sighing contentedly.

Angie gazed into her lover's dark eyes for a long moment, her hand resting on a leather-clad knee.

"You did good," she said simply. She wanted to say more, and Lauren looked like she'd have liked to respond, but a gangling thirty-something guy with mousy brown hair squeezed through the crowd and stuck out his hand with a brusque, "Ryan Orr, *Dallas Alternative*, music reporter." An arrogant smile cut across his face as he introduced himself to the rest of the band. Lauren gave him an inquisitive stare, shared by Angie and the others.

"So," he began with an air of nonchalance, his hands confidently in his pockets, rocking on his heels. "I see you won the crowd over. Good job. Tough group, usually—known to boo a lot at newbies. When I got your press release, I almost tossed it in the trash. I don't usually do pieces on complete unknowns. But I was bored and thought I'd come see what you're all about. Got a bit more than I expected. I'll admit that. You've got some Melissa Etheridge in you, don't you think? Maybe a little Fiona tossed in. Some Curtis, some Aerosmith-esque guitar work. Heavy lyrics. I get so sick of all the whiney, pretentious, existential crisis shit you can expect for the most part these days. Nah, you're old school. Good with the bitterness. Which is coming back, so that's definitely not a bad thing." He took a deep breath after rattling all that off and opened his mouth to say more, but Lauren cut him off.

"Excuse me, but what press release?"

"This one, got it right here," he said, his arrogant look fading a touch, replaced by a smirk. He pulled a crumbled piece of paper from his pocket and handed it over.

"But we didn't..." Lauren began and trailed off, reaching behind her and snagging a Jimmy arm, forcing him to face her. "You didn't."

"Um, I kind of did," he stammered, his eyes widening at her threatening scowl.

"No matter," Ryan cut through the tension. "I'm here, I'm writing about this. No way around it now. Could I have a business card? I knew that thing was written by an amateur when I scanned the page for contact info and didn't find any. Quite a mess if you ask me."

Lauren's eyes snapped on the music reporter and pinned him effectively. His smile faded, but only a touch. Angie suspected that she might be annoyed with Jimmy, but no way she was going to let this stranger criticize his work. "I don't have a business card," she growled.

"Um," Jimmy nearly squeaked. "You do now. And you have a Web site. And some CDs, and I had the management put cards on every surface in this place, and..." He stopped at her blank stare. Sighing, he fished through the black leather "man bag" that Angie and Lauren had teased him for carrying earlier in the night. He pulled out a CD and card, handing them over to the waiting music reporter. "Happy birthday, Lauren," he said quietly.

For a couple of seconds, she looked outraged. But Angie could see the wheels churning rapidly behind those dark eyes and the scowl slowly dissolved. And then Lauren began to laugh, her shoulders shaking.

"Yeah, okay," she finally managed. "So you have our card and our CD that I'm assuming was recorded during our practice sessions?" Jimmy nodded at her raised eyebrow. "So am I to take it you think we're quite lucky for your presence, Mister—what did you say your name was?"

Angie had to swallow a laugh at the man's startled expression. Yeah, he surely did think Fearless was lucky for his interest. And she sincerely doubted he was used to being treated this way by relatively unknown bands. But he was in for a big surprise. Though Lauren may have all the talent in the world, she'd expressed time and again that she didn't want the rock star life. And the laugh that Angie bit back was echoed with abandon from Fearless's guitarist and drummer. Lauren smirked and took a sip of beer while the man recovered.

"I guess you don't give a shit about publicity. Is that it?" he said, the smile gone.

"Nope. This isn't a career for any of us, more of a hobby and sometimes a fundraiser. So you can drop the tone that so clearly says you think we should kiss your feet and beg for some press, okay? Play nice and we might—stress on the might—grant you an interview."

Mr. Orr opened his mouth and closed it, clearly at a loss for words. Well, Angie thought, he had gone about the whole thing the wrong way. And good for Lauren for shutting him down. Angie could read the internal debate as various expressions flitted across his face. Finally, he settled on a much more politely interested smile and shook his head.

"You have a point and I'll think about it," he said, his tone much less aggressive. "Just don't run off after the show, okay? Can I find you here afterward?"

"Probably," Lauren said and smiled, satisfied. He nodded and left the bar area.

She turned on Jimmy, who was grinning sheepishly.

"You really did it this time," she started but couldn't keep the amusement out of her voice. "And you know what? You didn't do half bad. Got us the gig, built a Web site, got us business cards, maybe a little press...even CDs. Thank you. It's been a wonderful birthday. But I swear, if you pull another stunt like this without fair warning, I'll have to kill you. This week has been freaking insane."

He crushed her in a relieved hug and ruffled her hair, releasing her reluctantly and with piercing loud laughs only after she complained of having breathing difficulties and began to tickle him in self-defense. Angie watched the two, shaking her head.

And when Jimmy got back on stage to announce Fearless coming back, he wasn't nearly as nervous the second time around, a giddiness marking his sarcastic comments and bouncing steps. The band followed up the first act with a second set of fast songs that kept the crowd lively. The numbers weren't nearly as heavy —save one on a woman's right to choose—and they ended with a sexy cover of AC/DC's "You Shook Me All Night Long," a song that left Angie's mouth dry and eyes heavy-lidded, visions of what she'd do to the singer once they stepped foot in her apartment flooding her mind.

The rooftop had grown so tightly packed that the management wasn't letting any more patrons up the stairs. And when the band finished, ready to leave near midnight, the crowd called after them for several minutes, demanding an encore.

It was one o'clock by the time the band had packed away their instruments and secluded themselves with their friends and Mr. Orr at the all-night grungy coffee bar, Insomnia, up the street. The music writer had been much less arrogant when he'd approached them the second time around, and Lauren had permitted an interview after the band took a vote and agreed it might do them some good. The friends bought a round of Rocket Shakes— banana-chocolate espresso milkshakes—and sat for an hour, taking the music writer's rapid-fire questions in turn.

Before they'd left the Art Bar, the establishment's owner had shown up, much to the management's discomfort, which seemed unsure whether his unannounced appearance was a good thing. It seemed he'd been called by a few regulars who wanted to let him know how freaking packed the bar was. He stopped by and kept saying, "Good turnout, good turnout," and practically ordered the band to book a repeat performance the following month, a greedy smile plastered on his face as he took in the crowd and busy bartenders.

He'd also handed a check to Jimmy for a thousand dollars—rather cheap by Deep Ellum standards, but much more than what the band usually got. Lauren had snatched it away and stuffed it in her pocket, vowing to wire the money to her fellow Peace Corps buddies who were still in Micronesia, where she herself had been stationed for a year prior to meeting Angie. That's what the band usually raised money for—though it sometimes went to fellows in Africa or South America, depending on where the band felt the greatest need was.

Jimmy had been crushed with hugs by the band members after this last surprise that he'd kept so successfully secret. He promised to negotiate a higher rate for their next Art Bar performance. Fearless took a vote and made him their official manager, promising him a hell of a lot of work for no pay at all. The man had blushed, surprised, and had worn a pleased smile the rest of the night, spouting off ideas all the way back to Fort Worth.

It was nearly three o'clock when Jimmy finally dropped the pair off at Angie's apartment. She hobbled inside, her good leg and armpits throbbing from the effort of standing on her crutches for hours, but a nervous smile crossed her lips as she fumbled with the keys, eager to get inside and give Lauren her birthday present.

But she never made it past the living room. She was scooped up into her lover's arms and placed carefully on the couch—Lauren's rough and eager kisses demolishing the image of a red envelope well-hidden in the file cabinet. By the time the roving hands made their way under Angie's skirt, she forgot about the present entirely. And even her ringing cell phone couldn't destroy their passionate celebration.

Angie awoke with a start. Her skin was coated with a thin sheen of cold sweat, hair plastered to her forehead. The details of her nightmare slipped away before her eyes could focus, but it didn't matter. She knew what she'd been dreaming about—that hate-filled voice in her face, breath stinking of cigar smoke and cognac, a 9 mm revolver pointed between her eyes. She forced her gasping breath to slow and desperately focused on the pleasant smell of her lover nearby.

The realization that she was lying in bed slowly forced its way through the haze of confusion and fear. Her mouth was dry and sticky. Her hands clammy. She sat up with effort, her whole body stiff.

Carefully, she crawled out of bed, extracting herself from the arm that was clamped around her waist. Lauren made a whimpering sound of protest in her sleep but didn't wake.

Angie grabbed her crutches and made her way into the kitchen, desperate for a glass of water. The liquid slid down her parched throat in cool relief as she drained the glass in long gulps. She leaned against the counter for several minutes, lost in thought.

The aftereffects of the nightmare faded, leaving an empty feeling behind. She hugged herself, shivering slightly in her nakedness as the air conditioner blasted coolly along her sticky skin, raising unpleasant goose bumps and forcing her nipples to contract painfully.

She shuddered, running a hand through her disheveled hair. She felt wide awake, despite the fact that the clock on the wall read five a.m. She'd been asleep for barely an hour. She tried to force a feeling of exhaustion to take hold but couldn't do it.

Her cell phone lay on the coffee table where she'd dumped her purse unceremoniously, its contents spilled across the surface. A red light was flashing in the dark and she stared at it curiously. Who the hell had called so late?

She limped over to the table and picked up the phone, flipping it open and hitting the speed dial for her voicemail.

"One new message, received at 3:04 a.m., from an unknown number." Pause. "Angie, this is Jay. Thought I'd help you out since your article gave us some leads. We've just been called to the scene of another signal twelve. M.O. sounds the same. I guess that unlike some people, you actually get to sleep at night. So just give me a call when you get this. Address is 7900 Arlington Court, apartment 107. Village Grove complex. See you."

She cursed under her breath and shot a look at the wall clock. Less than two hours—there was a chance investigators would still be at the scene. Damn it, damn it, damn it. She struggled with her purse, sending objects flying as she dove for her notepad and a pen. She replayed the message and jotted down the address.

Then she abruptly stopped.

"It's freaking five o'clock in the morning," she muttered, setting the phone and notepad down. She should go back to bed. She should forget about the whole thing until her alarm blared at eight, ordering her out of bed for her morning shift. She should snuggle up to her beautiful lover, inhale that sexy lavender scent, and fall back to sleep.

She sighed. It wasn't as if the crime scene was going anywhere. It wasn't like she couldn't just call the detective back in a few hours, get the story later, right? Right.

But that adrenaline burst that came with big news had already shot straight through her system. And if she thought she'd been wide awake before, she was even more awake after hearing that damned message. Her shoulders shook with silent laughter as she resigned herself to the fact that she wasn't going to let it go, that she would instead get dressed as quietly as possible and leave Lauren a note, after which she'd hobble out to her car and drive to 7900 Arlington Court, apartment 107.

Daylight broke as she pulled into the complex and found the cop cruisers and the familiar homicide unit van and spotted a man dressed in black slacks and a black polo shirt—his flaming red hair sticking up in the back—speaking with a group of uniformed officers within the confines of crime scene tape sectioning off a staircase. Yellow streaks of light cut across the horizon and cast a somber atmosphere. She stashed her purse under the driver's seat and grabbed her notepad, stuffing her car keys in her pocket, a pen tucked behind her ear.

Angie's hair was still a mess, having refused to flatten in her brief attempt to tame it with water and a comb. Eyeliner was smudged most unattractively. She probably looked like she'd fallen out of bed and grabbed the first wrinkled pieces of clothes she could find—the green skirt she'd picked not quite going with the pink blouse she'd chosen from her closet in the dark. But what the hell did it matter? She'd successfully made it to a crime scene before six a.m.—definitely a first for her, and by the looks on the cops' faces as she limped over on her crutches, a first for them to see a reporter at such an hour. Detective Key caught sight of her, shook his head with a smirk, and waved her on over.

Chapter Five

I can't believe you made it," Detective Key said, gripping her outreached hand tightly. "And just in time, too. We got the search warrant about an hour ago and just finished our preliminary. The medical examiner is on his way."

He gave Angie a once-over, his eyes fixed on her crutches and rigid posture. "Why don't we go sit on the bench over there, and I'll give you the rundown?"

"Sounds good," she said with more than a little relief. She was damned lucky she'd skipped her nightly Vicodin dose, or she wouldn't have been able to drive to the scene. But without the painkiller, she was starting to feel miserable. Only one more week, she recited mentally over and over again as they made their way to a bench near the apartment complex's office. Only one more week and the cast that went inches above her knee would be downgraded to one that went halfway up her shin. So she'd been told, anyway. And she prayed it would make a difference.

"Better?" the detective asked with a note of concern in his voice.

"I'm fine," Angie lied. "So what's the deal with this one?" She pointed at the apartment guarded by uniformed officers. "Your message said it sounded similar to the last murder."

He fixed her with cop eyes that clearly said he didn't believe she was "fine" but let the issue go after several seconds of silence. He pulled off his purple latex gloves and stuffed them in his pocket, retrieving a notepad. His eyes scanned it for a few seconds.

"Yeah, it's very similar," he finally said, looking back up at her. Angie had her notepad out and pen ready. "Here are the similarities: Our vic is male, in his early thirties—thirty-three to be exact—his throat was slit clean, he was gagged and bound with silk scarves, and looks like he was beaten. He also wasn't found right away. We're guessing he'd been dead for about two days or so, though we haven't confirmed that yet. The ME will tell us in a little while. He was also gay, apparently single—we're still checking on that—and lived alone. His apartment is wrecked just like the last one."

He paused and ran a hand through his hair, closing his eyes briefly, his brows furrowed and angry. He took a deep breath as Angie stopped writing and watched the expressions flit across his face. His eyes opened and she dropped her look back to her notepad.

"The differences are troubling," he said slowly, drawing the words out. "Our vic's car is missing, unlike the other case. The indications are that this is another hate crime, and I still can't elaborate." He leaned closer and lowered his voice to a near whisper, though no one was standing nearby. "But the indications in this apartment are much worse than in the last—more violent and aggressive. It seems the killer wants urgently to get his point across."

"You think the cases are linked? I mean, definitely linked—not just maybe?" Angie whispered back, her tone alarmed.

"Yes," he said and stood up and began to pace. Three strides right, three strides left—scowling. He looked over his shoulder at the other officers and forced himself to stop, resuming his seat next to Angie. His left foot tapped agitatedly on the concrete.

"I wish I could tell you it was a copycat murder, Angie, but there's no way. You know that guilty knowledge thing I told you about? The reason why we can't just give you all the gory details? Well, there are certain things a copycat couldn't possibly have known. I was very careful with the press, and our guys don't blab about shit like that. They know better. And there are signs in that apartment that make it look almost exactly like the other one." He sighed and took a sharp breath, releasing it between grinding teeth. "It is my belief that we have a serial killer on the loose. Sure, we only have two bodies—for now. But it took a while to find this one. And the last one. Who the fuck knows how many more there are?"

Angie almost dropped her pen.

"Jay," she began, questions racing through her mind, but she tucked them away for the time being. She put a hand on his shoulder. He'd told her this would happen. And he'd been right. His shoulders sagged, and she wasn't quite sure why she knew that he felt responsible, but she knew it with certainty. "What are we going to tell people?"

She'd never used that question before. The answer had always been simple: Tell her readers every single detail she could pry from the cops, use the facts, and weave the tale as tragically or as coldly as the facts dictated. But as she combed her brain, she couldn't remember the last time a bona fide serial killer had been on the loose in Fort Worth, aside from Henry's thug, John Carpenter, who'd had help with the killings, a different situation altogether.

They sat in silence for several seconds. Then Detective Key cleared his voice. "This is what I want you to print. I know it's up to you and your editor, but if you can fit it in, write this: There is a serial killer on the loose. He's targeting single gay men in the Fort Worth area. According to our investigation, the killer seems to be meeting his victims in bars. At least that may have been the case in Whittaker's murder. Gay men should be extremely careful who they take home with them."

"Okay, I'll do my best," she said and took special care in jotting down what he'd said to the tee. No paraphrasing. She'd try to get it in as a direct quote. And just maybe, it might help some guy out.

They talked about the details for another half hour. Angie was just about to get up and make her way back to her car, where her laptop lay waiting under the front passenger seat, but a woman in a red Chevy pickup pulled up. She got out and ran toward the cops, her face ghostly white.

"Oh, my God, no!" she yelled, ripping straight through the crime scene tape.

A uniformed cop caught her around the waist and she struggled. Two more cops took her arms, trying to calm the woman as she began to wail, shaking her head. Angie flinched at the scene, knowing exactly what had just happened. It was only a matter of whether the woman was family or a friend. Angie remained rooted to the spot, unable to tear her eyes away. Detective Key told her to sit tight and took quick strides toward the screaming woman, who slapped at officers wildly.

He laid an arm around the woman's shoulders, whispering words into her ears, and ordered the uniformed officers to let go. He gently steered her away when she sagged against his side. Her knees buckled, but he held her up. They went around a corner and disappeared.

Angie stood up weakly, balancing on her crutches. She limped back to her car and unlocked her passenger door, dragging out her laptop. She sat in the seat and booted it up, forcing the image of the distraught woman from her mind as she spent the next half hour composing her article.

When she was done, she checked for nearby wireless Internet signals and pirated an unsecured one from what she assumed was either the front office or a nearby apartment. After she e-mailed the story to her boss, she checked her watch. 7:03 a.m. If she wanted to beat television, she'd just have to brave his wrath. If she didn't, there was no point in her having come out to the scene so damned early. She counted to ten, steeling herself, and punched in Tom's home number.

"Who is it?" a sleepy voice asked, alarmed.

"Tom, it's Angie. Did I wake you?"

"Hell yes, you woke me up. It's the freaking weekend. The world doesn't exist before eight a.m. on the weekends, damn it. This had better be good."

"We have a serial killer in Fort Worth. I typed a story and sent it to you already. It needs to get online ASAP."

Silence. Then she heard rustling that she assumed meant her boss was getting out of bed. "Say that again," he demanded, his voice much more alert. Angie repeated herself and waited. She heard more rustling and the distinct sound of a computer booting up. Her good foot tapped impatiently as she waited for him to open his e-mail and say something. Just as she was about to break the silence, he let loose a long string of profanities.

"Sonofabitch," he finally finished. "I'll call Jake, get his ass out of bed so he can put this shit up." She was promptly put on hold. The sun was starting to beat down stiflingly, and she felt a trickle of sweat run down her back. After a few minutes, Tom was back on the line.

"Okay, it'll be online in a few minutes. What the hell are you doing out there this early, anyway?"

"Got a call from Detective Key at three a.m. Didn't check it till five and came straight here. I was having trouble sleeping."

"Is there a crowd like last time?"

"No. A woman just showed up, though. But that's it."

"Okay, I'll wait an hour or two before sending a photographer. Give me a call when you have another update."

"Will do," and she hung up, now desperate to get out of the sweltering car. She wandered back to the bench and waited. An hour passed. People started to gather at the crime scene tape—neighbors whom she interviewed. Another half hour passed as she typed up the new info and sent it to her boss to include in the online story.

It was the only way they could beat television, really. And the *Tribune* of late had put a strong emphasis on pushing for more and faster online updates.

The detective still hadn't returned, and the photographer Tom had promised showed up, quickly snapping pictures.

It was nearly eleven o'clock before the first television crew pulled into the parking lot. They approached Angie, hoping she'd share some information. But she remained tight-lipped and referred them to her online story. Grumbling, they wandered off and set up camp three feet from the crime scene tape. She called Lauren and told her where she'd slipped off to in case her note had gone unnoticed, promising they could meet downtown at Starbucks at four o'clock and that she'd call if anything happened that would force her to cancel.

To hell with the Saturday class and Professor Laney. The crime was a hundred times more interesting and she had three absences she could use. That Saturday would just have to be the first. And if the professor had a problem with that, she'd just have to bribe her with a detailed account for the following class. She shot off a quick e-mail to said professor with that promise—just in case—and hoped playing hooky wouldn't get her in trouble.

Her phone rang. She didn't recognize the number but picked up anyway.

"Angie, it's Jay. Listen, you need to meet me downtown as

soon as possible. Call me when you get there and I'll come get you," and he hung up. What the hell? Sighing, she tucked her laptop under the passenger seat and hopped in her car. The television crew watched her with narrowed eyes, likely wondering why she was leaving so early. She shot them a dirty look and pulled out of the complex, hitting the gas hard.

She made it to the police station in ten minutes flat and called Detective Key. He met her in the lobby and led her down white, sterile hallways and back behind a heavily secured door. She started to ask what this was all about, but when she rounded a corner and stepped into a conference room, she suddenly knew. The woman from the crime scene sat in a chair, eyes red and puffy from hours of crying.

"Miss Lockett, this is Angie Mitchell."

Angie walked around the conference table and held out her hand. The woman accepted with trembling fingers but dropped her hand quickly, eyes darting around the room. Angie took the seat next to the woman while Detective Key stood by the door silently.

"You're the reporter who got shot, aren't you?" the woman muttered, her eyes still fixed on the table.

Angie shot a look at the detective, completely at a loss. Then she cleared her throat and said, "Yes. That's me, unfortunately."

Miss Lockett nodded and said nothing else for several seconds. Instinctively, Angie knew she'd have to let her speak first. She waited, her hands resting on the table politely. She took a closer look at the woman, noticing how young she looked— probably not much older than Angie herself. A tear trickled down Miss Lockett's face and splattered on the table. She brushed it away angrily and finally spoke, voice shaking.

"Do you care about your stories as much as they said on the news?"

Angie blinked at the unexpected question and swallowed hard. She considered it and chewed her lower lip. "I'm not supposed to, but yeah. I guess I do."

Blue eyes fixed on her and searched her face for several more seconds.

"And do you care about this crazy motherfucker who killed my brother?"

Angie nodded silently.

"Mr. Key said you'll treat this right. And I want to say something to that crazy sonofabitch who killed Chance."

Again, Angie simply nodded and put her notepad on the table, plucking a pen from behind her ear. She looked up expectantly.

"You better quote me on this shit, too," Miss Lockett said forcefully.

"I can't promise..." Angie tried in her most patient tone but was cut off.

"You promise, damn it!" Her voice rose threateningly, but Angie didn't flinch against the sharp words.

"I promise I'll tell my boss how important it is. I swear I'll type it in my story. But I don't control the paper. You have to understand that."

The woman's hands started shaking uncontrollably and she shook her head, fighting.

"Fine," she finally agreed, forcing her voice to lower. "If you give it your best shot."

Angie agreed and took Miss Lockett's full name and age, then some other random information, easing her way into more complexities, hoping it would give the woman some time to calm down a little more. People will say some pretty nasty stuff when they're upset—especially when they're grieving—and she wanted to give her a chance to compose herself before stuff like that came out.

Sandra Lockett, it turned out, was probably the last person to hear from her brother while he was still alive, aside from the killer. She told Angie that he'd called to cancel a movie date with her four evenings before, telling her he had to help some guy out and would be over late that night. They'd fought about it. He never came over. When she didn't hear from him, she got pissed off. She waited a couple of days and tried calling him but only got his voicemail. She went by his apartment but got no answer when she hammered on his door. The next day, she filed a missing person report. The cops waited twenty-four hours, then conducted a welfare check at the apartment at 2:30 a.m. Saturday.

They ran plates on the cars in the lot, but none of them matched his. Finally, they decided to bust down the locked door.

"Enough," Miss Lockett finally shut the conversation down. "Here's what I really want you to write. My brother was a decent, loving man and how dare anybody cut him up. The cops are going to get you, I know it. I'm going to pray every night that they do. I'll help them any way I can. And by God, you'll pay for this, you sick, twisted..." and she let loose a long string of profanities before her voice cracked and she broke down in tears.

"Thank you," Angie said softly, giving the woman's shoulder a gentle squeeze before standing up. She pulled out a card and placed it on the table. "Here's my business card. My cell phone number's on the back. Call me if you think of anything else." She paused. "And I'm very sorry about your loss."

Miss Lockett didn't respond, and Angie stepped around her quietly and left the room. Detective Key followed her outside and walked her to the lobby.

"I don't normally do this sort of thing," he said earnestly, grabbing her arm and forcing her to stop. "So don't ever expect it again. She asked for you specifically, repeatedly, and I finally just gave in because she refused to answer any more questions until I called you up." He paused. "Beats me what she thinks this will accomplish, but thanks for coming so quickly. Maybe now I can get some more information out of her. Call me in a couple of hours and I'll give you the guy's name and some updates." And just like that, he dismissed her and brusquely strode off.

Angie stared after him, not knowing whether he was pissed at her or not. Then she stared down at her notepad—pages of scribbled comments in blue ink—an unbelieving look in her eyes.

She shook her head and left the police station, still baffled. Still unnerved—the look of pure hatred on Miss Lockett's face blocking out all other thoughts, still swimming before her eyes as she pulled into the apartment complex on Arlington Street.

The skin on Angie's arms and face was painfully tight and had turned a deep shade of pink hours earlier. It was almost time to leave the scene. She'd updated the story six times already, and Miss Lockett's comments had made it online without protest from her boss—would make it in the next day's paper, too—though they'd chopped off the last words that were simply unprintable.

"Almost there," she muttered, eagerly accepting a bottle of Gatorade that the *Tribune's* photographer handed her. She rubbed the cool container across her face and neck. And just when she thought she couldn't take it anymore, a familiar car pulled in the parking lot and she fought the urge to shout excitedly. Sandy-haired Mark Thompson strode up, a fresh notepad in hand.

"Thank God," she said, and started to give the *Tribune's* night police reporter the rundown, but he cut her off, pulling a couple of printed-out articles from his pocket.

"Unless there's something you know that's not in your stories, don't bother. You need to get the hell out of the sun, Angie. I knew you were stubborn, but damn. That's gonna hurt tomorrow," he said and shook his head. "Go on, I can handle it."

He gave her a dismissive wave and she nodded, hobbled over to her car, and slid into the scorching thing, immediately cranking up the air conditioner and rolling down her windows. Hissing, she took the steering wheel, touching it only with the tips of her fingers. It may have been mid-September, but it felt more like August—a digital sign she passed on the highway reading 106 degrees Fahrenheit. She found a parking space on Third Street near Starbucks—practically a miracle for a Saturday afternoon in Sundance Square—and actually made it to the coffee shop on time to meet Lauren, who was waiting patiently.

Angie almost cried with relief when the air conditioner hit her full blast as she stepped through the door. Lauren waved her over and stood up in alarm when she saw the deep pink, flushed skin.

"Damn it, Angie," she muttered and rushed off toward the counter, returning seconds later with a large cup of ice water. "Drink this—slowly. I think I have something for that burn in the car." She jogged out of the shop and down the street, returning minutes later with a bottle of car-heated aloe vera gel that was a bit more liquid than it should have been. Despite Angie's protests, Lauren started spreading the stuff on her face and arms and along the base of her neck, her throat, and the part of her chest that the low-cut blouse didn't cover. She was still in the process of doing so when they were interrupted.

"Isn't that sweet," a familiar voice said and chuckled, the speaker sliding into the booth. Angie looked up, startled, and swatted Lauren's fingertips away from her, smiling sheepishly at her boss.

"Got bored at the office?" she asked, trying not to smirk at his hideous Hawaiian shirt and khaki shorts. He looked like Santa taking a vacation at the beach. Just take away the beard and add a touch of geek and he certainly looked the part. "Going casual today?"

"Like you should talk—nice pink shirt, by the way—goes well with your sunburn, doesn't go so well with the green skirt." He paused. "Good updates. Good story. Looks like you've got your work cut out for you next week. I have a feeling this won't go away anytime soon. And I was thinking…" He paused again, his eyes darting to Lauren. He looked like he was debating whether to continue, but then said, "We should do our own investigation. What do you say?"

Angie's heart rate picked up. She couldn't help it. Every time someone mentioned investigative reporting, that happened. Her eyes, too, darted to Lauren, whose polite look of interest had suddenly turned a touch darker, her lips thinning into a narrow line.

"Er…I think it'll be interesting," Angie said.

"This isn't going to be like last time, is it?" Lauren demanded.

"Oh, no," Tom said, his eyes a tad wider than before. "No, no, no. It had better not be. I don't think any of us want to go through that again. No, I'll assign a couple of reporters to help you out, Angie, go to places with you if for nothing other than to provide support. And you won't be going to any seedy parts of the city. At least not alone."

Her first thought was to protest, to say she could do the damned story alone. It was different, right? Right. So she tried to convince herself. But her throbbing leg was a painful reminder and not easily ignored. Very slowly, she nodded her agreement.

"Okay," Tom said with a smile, clearly relieved. Angie was pretty sure he wouldn't have been so hesitant without Lauren sitting across the table, the woman's brows furrowed in disapproval. Angie's second thought was to be annoyed, but she squashed the feeling as soon as it popped up. The concern was real and justified. So she'd be working in a team. Journalism shouldn't be about getting front-page glory by oneself anyway.

"So we'll have a meeting Monday morning, discuss ideas." He slid back out of the booth and said his goodbyes before picking up an iced green tea and heading back to the office.

The two women sat in silence for several minutes, Angie

playing with her napkin, Lauren staring out the window. The aloe vera started to work and sent pleasant tingles along Angie's skin. She sighed. It wasn't as if her lover didn't have reason to dislike the idea of her doing more investigative reporting work. Look where it got her last time. But damn it, it was her job and she loved it.

"I don't want you pulling any stunts," Lauren whispered, taking Angie's hand and squeezing it gently. "I don't want to be overbearing or anything, but I have a bad feeling about this. And I tend to trust my gut."

"I'll be careful, I promise. This is not like last time. Sure, there's another whacko running around, but I'm sure Tom will come up with some ideas that won't require me to go into any dangerous areas. We'll probably just do background reports on the victims' lives and their last days, maybe some in-depth pieces about gay bars, that sort of thing. It's not like we're going to take over the detectives' jobs or anything. Don't worry. It'll be okay."

"You're probably right," Lauren sighed. "I shouldn't worry. Didn't you once say it would drive me crazy?"

"Yeah, I think I did say that once or twice." Angie chuckled and shook her head.

After they left Starbucks, they spent the rest of the afternoon lazing around the apartment, their cuddling only interrupted by Angie's insistence in watching every news broadcast to see what the television crews had gathered, just to make sure she hadn't missed anything. It just wouldn't do for her to be shown up by TV after the huge head start and exclusive interview she'd gotten.

They checked out the Web site Jimmy had built for the band and listened to the CD he'd produced on his home computer from the band's practice recording. And despite Lauren's list of criticisms of each and every song—"If I'd known we were going to hand this out, that we were recording, I'd have insisted we do" such-and-such!—it wasn't half bad in Angie's opinion. She burned herself a copy and stuck it in her car happily.

She'd popped a Vicodin the second they made it back to her place, which made her feel a hundred times better and slightly goofy. She prank-called Jimmy several times from her home phone, a number he didn't recognize, and didn't figure out it was her until the seventh call, when Lauren couldn't contain herself anymore and burst out laughing. Angie got a colorful lecture, which made her laugh even harder, until Jimmy threatened to come over and teach her a lesson. She hadn't believed he would do it and called his supposed bluff, which resulted in her getting doused with a water gun when Lauren let the red-faced man into the apartment half an hour later.

He wasn't really that mad. Angie suspected he just wanted an excuse to come over. And she didn't mind that a bit. With Jimmy, it was always good times.

The fresh crime scene had erased the mental picture of a red envelope stashed away for Lauren until it suddenly popped into Angie's head late in the evening after Jimmy left. She'd jumped out of her lover's cuddling arms and hobbled over to the filing cabinet. But once she opened the bottom drawer, her fingers had trembled with nervousness. She couldn't come up with a good enough excuse as to why she'd sprung up like that when Lauren wrapped her arms around her waist and looked over her shoulder curiously.

Angie had held her breath, wordlessly handing over the envelope on which she'd sloppily scribbled, "Happy Birthday." The two women had looked at each other for a long few seconds— Lauren giving her an encouraging smile, Angie mentally berating herself for buying what the other woman would surely feel was completely inappropriate.

Then Lauren's eyes had dropped to the envelope that Angie finally handed over. She tore it open quickly. Her long fingers slid inside and retrieved a couple of airline tickets—roundtrip, Dallas to New York City, set for mid-December.

Lauren's lips parted to say something, shut, opened again, and she finally managed a simple, "Wow." Angie hadn't noticed the flitting expressions but heard the single word. She was studying her tightly clasped fingers. She muttered something, shook her head, and cleared her throat, trying again.

"I, um...I thought it would be nice to get away," she whispered. "Just the two of us, you know, just for a weekend. I hope that's okay."

The next thing she knew, she was pinned against the wall, lips curling around an earlobe, a hungry voice whispering hoarsely, "It's a wonderful idea. A few days with you in a hotel far away sounds like a lot of fun…"

And her lover proceeded to show her all the devilishly devious things she intended to do in a hotel far from home. The demonstration left them both gasping for air—breathless in a heap on the floor hours later.

Preying On Generosity

Chapter Six

Angie grunted and squirmed, her fists clenched, her body language practically screaming, "That's enough, let me go, damn it." But she didn't say a word. She bit back another scream and whimpered instead. Her eyes squeezed tightly shut, she summoned the last of her strength and pushed as hard as she could.

"Good," Lauren murmured. "Just a little more and we can stop."

Right. That's what she said the last three times, Angie grumbled internally past the lighting-hot pain that shot from her toes to her knee as she tried to push against Lauren's hand with the tips of her toes. If the woman said "just a little more" one more time, she was going to scream for real.

Her leg felt as if it were on fire. If she pushed for another second, her skin would surely melt away. She didn't have bones in her ankle—no, knives were there instead. And they were itching to surface, slicing her muscles along the way. The encased limb was an offending monster. It should be chopped off. And burned for spite.

Angie shook her head and pushed harder, ignoring the single tear that squeezed past her eyelid and slid along her nose, wetting her upper lip. She could do this. She could ignore the spots dancing behind her closed eyelids. She had to.

Lauren was counting seconds—"five, four, three…"

Finally, when she thought she'd pass out, "…one. You can stop now."

Angie released the breath she was holding and gasped painfully, letting her head fall back against the couch cushion, her whole body sagging. The exercises, or "torture sessions" as she was beginning to call them, were damned hard. The physical therapist said she should do them at least once a day. She wanted to kill that therapist.

Her eyes were still closed as she forced her breathing to calm and tried to banish the sadistic plans to torture the person who came up with the exercises. She heard retreating footsteps and running water. A warm hand touched her bare shoulder and she finally dared to open her eyes. What she saw was the most wonderful sight in the world: a Vicodin in Lauren's hand and a glass of water.

She snatched the offered pill without hesitation, even though it was mid-afternoon. It wasn't as if she had to drive anywhere or do anything. She'd tried hard to limit her intake of heavy painkillers—taking them only at bedtime so she could make it through the night without waking every time she jostled the cast in her sleep. But after the torture session, hell, nobody should blame her for popping a pill.

Angie sighed and let her eyes slide shut again. Lauren settled on the couch and pulled her close, lightly running fingers through her short blond hair.

Her leg was a throbbing, burning, wretched thing. But it was no longer covered in a blanket of acid. And maybe there were bones in there after all, healing slowly. Maybe she shouldn't chop it off quite yet.

"Better?"

"Mmm," Angie responded without conviction.

They sat in silence for several minutes until Angie broke it with, "Tell me a story."

"A story?" Lauren paused. "You're the storyteller."

"Blah-blah-blah. You have lots of stories. Tell me..." she thought about it for a few seconds before continuing, "...about you and Jimmy." A thought occurred to her. "About why you reacted the way you did when he said he wasn't dating Justin anymore. What was that about?"

Her question was met with a grunt. The fingers that had been trailing lazily through her hair and along her scalp suddenly stopped and fell away. Angie was beginning to think she wouldn't get an answer when she heard Lauren take a deep breath and let it out slowly.

"About Jimmy and I." Lauren hesitated and took another deep breath. "Listen, Angie, there's a lot of stuff we haven't talked about, and I... Well, there are some things I don't know if you'll want to hear."

Angie opened her eyes and let the room come back in focus. She turned her head slowly to see the nervous look on her lover's face. Lauren was gnawing her lower lip, fidgeting at an errant thread on her worn jeans, her eyes focused there.

Angie was torn. She didn't know whether pushing for an explanation was the right or appropriate thing to do. There were still pockets of insecurities in her that sprung up when their dynamics changed. Even if only temporarily. Lauren was supposed to be the woman oozing with self-confidence. The woman at ease with herself. At least most of the time. Angie was supposed to be the one who questioned herself and was nervous half the time. And she wasn't sure what the hell to do when things changed.

But she was also the one with the won't-be-denied curiosity. And it shot through her with such ferocity that she couldn't help but race for the words that would get her lover to open up. She thought through possibilities, discarded several, before opening her mouth and saying, "You can trust me. You should know that."

Lauren looked up from her fidgeting fingers and searched Angie's face. She leaned forward and touched their lips together, brushing lightly—just a simple touch for comfort—before the troubled look softened. She nodded and began to speak.

"We've known each other for eight—no, nine—years." She paused and ran a hand through her hair. "I was bartending in a dive in Dallas. He was a regular. After a while, we just hit it off..."

She was twenty-one and stupid, she told Angie with a smirk. He was a twenty-four-year-old hell-raiser. "A hell-raiser?" Angie interrupted with a laugh. Lauren gave her a no-nonsense look with a raised eyebrow, and she shut up.

"Anyway, he'd wait for me until I got off work—usually around midnight—and we'd hit the streets. We'd go to all the bars and blow our paychecks. He was working for some computer company. I can't remember which one, not that it matters, though I

"Anyway." Lauren cut through her thoughts and laughed nervously. "What else do you want to know, Miss Reporter? Should I tell you about my boring childhood, my goofy parents, the day I nearly kicked my brother's ass for enlisting, or how I came to be in a band? What'll it be?"

Angie gave her a long once-over but decided she'd let the tough stuff go. For now. She felt a little drained herself—both from the torture session and hearing the depressing story. She was also worried about Jimmy and understood better why Lauren was so protective toward him. The story painted a whole new picture of the person she'd known as a silly, sarcastic goofball.

When she thought of Jimmy, she always saw his smirking lips and twinkling eyes. She could hear his high-pitched, ringing laughter, his booming voice in a crowd. He was the red-faced man who stormed into her apartment with a water gun and doused her head to toe. He was the one who had teased her about her attraction to Lauren, had made her laugh through her confusion with his suggestive eyebrow wiggling and innuendos. He was definitely not a man who would allow his world to be reduced to punches and emotional ruins. But, it turns out, he was. And she hated that—didn't hate him or Lauren for telling her—just hated that it had happened at all. It wasn't right. And the thought added to the well of quiet anger for so many injustices in this world.

She didn't bother asking if they'd called the cops on this Adrian asshole. She didn't want to know if he'd been part of their drug circle. She could read those truths between the lines, even if she didn't want to.

What she really wanted was to show up on Jimmy's doorstep and give him a hug. But how could she do that when he didn't know she knew? She didn't know what she'd do the next time she saw him. She didn't want her eyes to fill with sympathy. She said as much to Lauren.

"His story is my story. He knew it would come up eventually. If you want him to know, just tell him we had a talk about my junior year in college. He won't be mad. Just don't feel sorry for him—he hates that—and don't ever mention the name Adrian."

Angie nodded. That's what she'd do when the time was right.

Something had changed in Lauren during that conversation

88

about the past. Angie could almost feel it as if it were something tangible. And yet she couldn't put her finger on it. She watched the other woman carefully, trying to figure out what it was. Maybe it was a new trust and respect. Maybe not. Maybe it was the Vicodin. But she didn't think so.

Then she saw it. Lauren's shoulders seemed straighter, her chin held higher. Her hips swayed when she walked. She seemed more sensuous. And definitely more light of foot. And it suddenly dawned on her that Lauren had worried about telling her. It wasn't just the hospital fiasco that had strained her. Or the recuperation. Or her exhaustion during the past week. Lauren was almost giddy, as though she'd been carrying around a ton of bricks and found a reason to set them down. The woman wasn't ashamed of herself; Angie was pretty sure of that. And there was no reason to be. People screw up. Good people—strong people—fix their screw-ups. Lauren had pulled a one-eighty.

But, Angie thought, if she'd had to tell Lauren a story like that, she'd probably have been nervous as hell, too. They hadn't been together that long yet. There was still a certain degree of uncertainty—not that either of them thought the other would leave, surely—but placing such trust in another is hard enough. Let alone after only a couple of months. And if it went well, she'd be just as happy. And damned relieved.

And that's what it was—pure and utter relief. No doubt about it.

She sighed and rubbed her forehead, deciding it was time to think about something else and get the images of Jimmy on that living room floor out of her head. She started thinking about her upcoming assignment. She couldn't focus on it for long. She was too drained. Her eyes drifted shut and she began to doze.

A sharp knock on the door scared her so badly she jumped, her racing pulse making her a little lightheaded.

"I'll get it," Lauren called from the bedroom and came jogging around the corner. She unlocked the door and snorted. "Oh, it's you," she said, and Angie heard the sarcasm in her voice. She turned and peeked at the door to spot Jimmy standing there.

"It's nice to see you, too," he said flatly and strode into the apartment.

"Oh, I'm sorry," Lauren said, fluffed her hair with much

exaggeration, clearing her throat. She raised her voice a couple of octaves and said, "I've missed you so very, very much. I don't think I could have gone another second without seeing your face! Come to me, darling. Thank God you're here."

Jimmy raised an eyebrow, set down a bag he'd carried in, and took two quick steps toward her. He dropped to his knees and grabbed her around the legs, throwing her over his shoulder. He managed to stand—with a rather loud grunt—and began walking toward the living room with hesitant steps and a huffed, "I always knew I'd sweep you off your feet someday."

"If you drop me," Lauren growled, trying not to giggle, "I'm going to kill you."

Angie felt it was a valid concern. That he was able to pick up the tall woman at all, in her mind, was a damned impressive feat. But she couldn't hold back the giggles and chose to ignore the indignant frown she got from Lauren.

Jimmy's knees began to buckle and he grunted, trying to shift the woman's weight. Angie's eyes widened. Before she could say, "you'd better put her down," he leaned a bit too far to the right and ran into the wall. The two fell to the ground with a crash and lay in a heap on the floor, laughing.

Lauren got up first, still laughing, and tried to make threats on his life but couldn't catch enough breath between laughs to complete the sentence. After several tries, she finally gave up and doubled over. Angie got off the couch, grabbed her crutches, and took a few steps toward the balcony door.

"Jimmy, get off your ass and come outside with me."

He got his feet under him and said a quick, "Sorry, honey," to Lauren before skirting out of her reach in case she decided to give him a playful smack for his efforts. She shrugged and continued laughing, shaking her head.

It was hot out on the balcony, even though the sun had already set. Angie sat down and propped her leg up on another chair while Jimmy stood and leaned against the railing.

"So," she said after she lighted a cigarette and took a drag. "Is there any particular reason for this visit or were you just bored?" She said it with a grin. It didn't really matter why he'd come by. He just did that sometimes—show up unannounced, just because. She was curious, wanting to know what was in the bag he'd brought. It went back to the whole won't-be-denied characteristic.

"Both," he said and returned her grin. "Haven't gotten many gigs lately. Haven't really been trying, though. I'm kind of sick of it right now anyway. It'll pass." He paused long enough to light his own cigarette. "And I brought you girls some chocolate cake."

"Oh, I love you," she said and did a little happy clap before she could stop herself. Next to caramel lattés and cheesecake, chocolate cake was her favorite treat.

They chatted for a few minutes and finished their cigarettes. Angie couldn't help but think about the conversation she'd had with Lauren about him while he stood there looking all relaxed and happy. And she thought she'd wait until the time was right to tell him she knew, but she realized the time would never really be right for something like that. What was she supposed to do—wait until he was depressed? She'd never seen him even remotely upset, save for the time he visited her in the hospital.

He reached for the doorknob and she quickly said, "Hold on," stopping him. He turned curious eyes on her and his smile slowly faded. Angie took out another cigarette and lighted it. He fumbled in his pocket for his pack and lighter and did the same.

She took a deep breath. Lauren had said to just come out with it. She exhaled her smoke and wished it weren't so damned hot outside.

"Are you going to keep me in suspense all night, or are you going to spit out whatever it is that's on your mind?" he demanded with a flick of his cigarette.

"Lauren and I," she hesitated, swallowed hard, and continued, "had a conversation earlier. It was about her junior year in college."

The tightening of his lips was the only sign of surprise he showed. He took a drag off his cigarette and exhaled, turning away from her, resting his arms on the railing.

"About time," he said. "She's been worried about that."

"Are you…Are you okay with it?"

"It had to come up sooner or later." He paused for so long Angie thought it would be his only comment. But he wasn't finished. He flicked his cigarette nervously, sending ash flying off the balcony. "It was a long time ago. And I don't want your pity, okay?"

She nodded. Realizing he couldn't see her, she said, "I don't think sympathy is what you need, Jimmy."

He turned around then and stared at her for a full thirty seconds. "And what exactly do I need, Dr. Angie?" The words were harsh and clipped, perfectly enunciated, stripped of all the sarcasm and wit she was so used to. Her eyes widened and she put out her cigarette in the ashtray, trying to stand.

She stretched out her hand to touch his shoulder, but he pulled out of reach.

"I didn't mean," she tried, fumbled for words, and tried again. "Let me rephrase that. I don't think you need pity because pity would probably annoy the hell out of me if the situation was reversed. I didn't mean anything by it. Hell, like I can give you any advice."

His angry look faded. But only a little. Damn this was hard, she thought, harder than she thought it would be. "Look, I just want you to know I'm here for you if you want to talk. Ever. And if you don't, that's fine. It's your choice. I promise."

He took a long drag off his cigarette and nodded. "Then let's not talk about this again. I've seen a shrink. I'm a little fucked up. But only in the relationship department. Just don't try and hook me up with somebody to get me in a relationship I'm not ready to deal with. That's what everybody tries to do and it really sucks. Promise."

"I promise," she said with feeling and took a step forward. This time, he didn't shy away and accepted her hug.

He tossed his cigarette over the balcony, his shoulders sagging just a little.

"Let's go back inside," he muttered. "I need a drink."

Angie forced herself not to point out that his needing a drink was definitely a sign that he was numbing his pain. She wasn't sure that was a wise course of action, but she'd promised not to force him to deal with his issues. And she wasn't so sure that promise was a good idea but hadn't known what else to do. Hell, she suddenly understood Lauren's frustration with full force.

Another worry. Another issue. It wasn't really hers, but he was her friend. She couldn't help but worry about his well-being. It was another of her character traits, or flaws, whichever way you look at it.

She felt a headache begin to build behind her temples and stifled a groan.

Preying On Generosity

Chapter Seven

A ngie's alarm blared at seven thirty a.m., ripping a startled yelp from her lips in midbreath. She coughed, rolled over, and slammed the flat of her hand down on the buzzing thing. Lauren grumbled a halfhearted protest and wrapped an arm tightly around her midriff.

"Not yet," she mumbled, still half asleep.

Angie didn't want to leave the warm nest—her lover's body pressed against her back—but gently removed the tightening arm around her waist anyway. She had an important meeting that morning, after all. She yawned and rubbed her eyes furiously, trying to rid herself of the sleepy blurriness, struggling with the dampened morning light that fell through the window and hit her square in the face.

Blinking rapidly, she stumbled into the kitchen, poured herself a cup of steaming black coffee, again thanking the creators of time-set coffee machines, and took a scalding sip, her eyes closed. The liquid slid down her throat and hit an empty stomach that gurgled in fierce protest. Sighing, she took another sip before opening her eyes again and allowing them to adjust properly.

Her pantry yielded a couple of energy bars and she munched them in silence, thinking. She mentally scanned through the information she'd gathered at the last crime scene—visions of both victims fleetingly appearing, accompanied by myriad voices from interviews and newscast announcers. Her mind settled on two words: serial killer. A tight knot wrapped around her lungs and squeezed painfully. She could still see the look of fear on Lauren's face when her boss had suggested the *Tribune* do its "own investigation."

And then she heard it—that sound she'd been unable to drown out over the last seven weeks, that piercing scream that had once cut through a muggy summer's eve—Lauren. It startled her so badly that she dropped the energy bar and slopped scalding coffee over the mug's edge, her fingers red and throbbing where the liquid had touched her skin. She shook her head, cursed under her breath for a full minute, and leaned against the counter. "Not real," she mumbled over and over again, counting seconds between breaths, willing her racing pulse to calm.

Lauren had been there when she was shot and had seen the whole bloody mess. That scream that echoed through her troubled mind was the last thing Angie had heard before giving in to the darkness that had swallowed her for days. The wretched sound had caught her off-guard countless times before—in her dreams, in her waking hours—and it seemed impossible to drown out. Sensory memory, they say, is the strongest association, especially in connection with traumatic experiences. She knew the experts were right. And she hated them for it, even if that was ridiculous.

Minutes passed between four-second breaths, eyes fixed on the safety of her empty kitchen, knuckles white with tension as she gripped the counter hard. A tear of frustration rolled down her cheek and splattered on the floor, then another.

"No." Her harsh whisper didn't carry far but seemed to ring in her ears. "No, damn it." Her eyes snapped open. She leaned over the kitchen sink and jerked on the faucet's knob, cool water rushing into her hands. She splashed her face, sending droplets flying across the counter.

She told herself this investigation would be different. She told herself the killer would not hunt her down. She told herself she'd have people at her back, just as her editor had promised. She told herself Lauren's piercing, grief-stricken scream would go away eventually. And while she rationalized away her fears, she didn't really believe that last bit. But her legs ceased trembling and the tears of anger and helplessness dried up.

"Time to see a shrink," she muttered and finished her cooling coffee in quick gulps, discarding the fallen energy bar and ignoring the sick feeling in her stomach. "Can't let this get to me," she continued mumbling on her way to the bathroom, where she ran a hot bath and sank in with a sigh. "He can't get me," Angie muttered while slapping a generous amount of shampoo in her hair, thinking more of Henry than the unknown killer on the loose. And by the time she was done getting ready for work, the fear had morphed into determination, color had returned to her face, and she'd actually been able to smile at her sleepy-eyed lover when she kissed Lauren goodbye.

She locked her apartment door and headed down the stairs precariously. Wind ruffled her blond hair and she looked up at the sky, surprised by the lack of stifling heat, even if it was still early. Thick, murky-violet clouds roiled across the sky and she took a deep breath, smelling the rain that would hit soon. For a full minute, she stopped, leaned into the wind, and closed her eyes, letting the cool air rush over her and whip her skirt about. A sigh escaped her lips. She needed it to rain, to wash away the film of red clay grime that covered everything in sight. She needed the prickling water to touch her face and pound out the demons she wrestled within. There was a purity in rain, a cleansing, healing quality.

But the minute passed and it didn't rain. Not yet. She knew it would come and steeled herself as she slid into the driver's seat of her Mitsubishi Eclipse and put the car in reverse.

The conference room was loaded with a suffocating tension. It poured off Angie in waves of silent fury. She refused to meet her editor's eyes as she set aside her pen and waited for the other reporters to leave for lunch. Their chatter became muffled halfway down the hall. She heard rustling and finally looked up to see anger reflected on Tom's face.

She didn't say anything—wanting him to break the silence first so she could respond with a few choice words. But he didn't speak, choosing instead to stare her down. She took a deep breath and released it slowly, dropping her eyes, deciding it was time to get the hell out of that room. The rhythmic clicking of her crutches snapped along her path back to her desk in the newsroom.

She booted up her computer, still seething, while the damned ancient contraption sputtered to life and reluctantly launched the *Tribune's* ten-year-old operating system. It promptly froze up when she tried to access her e-mail and she groaned in frustration, drumming her fingers on the desk while it rebooted. She knew, at any moment, she was likely to scream.

It wasn't that she'd been assigned a team to conduct the investigation—she'd already decided that wasn't a bad idea. It wasn't even that her boss had yanked her off daily crime stories—she'd expected that. She needed to focus her attention on the serial killer after all. Even the fact that she'd been given a flex schedule—three day shifts, two night shifts—hadn't made her blink.

No, it was the team itself she had a problem with. She'd been expecting sandy-haired Mark to be her right-hand man. Throw in another good, experienced reporter or two and she'd be set. She'd thought such an investigation merited skilled people. But her boss had other ideas. She snorted at his choices: an intern and a yearlong fellow. What the hell was he thinking?

As soon as she'd seen the two when she stepped into the conference room, watched them chatting with Tom, the fellow practically bursting with excitement and gratitude, a black cloud had settled over her head. The reassurance that she'd have good people at her back slid off her shoulders and hit the floor with a thud that rang in her ears, even if the others couldn't sense it. Her hands had begun to tremble as she sat down and refused the proffered muffins and coffee. She'd given Tom a pointed frown which he ignored, save for a subtle shake of his balding head.

"Guess it's just the three of us then?" she had asked, taking out her notepad.

The other two reporters' conversation halted abruptly, and they turned to face her with matching inquisitive eyes. Their looks said plainly, "Aren't we good enough?" It had not been the smartest thing Angie could have said or asked. Just thinking about it made her groan in annoyance. She should have said something more direct, more immediate, such as, "So, Tom, looks like a weak batch if you ask me. Not to be rude, but I'd like somebody who knows what the hell they're doing if we want to do this right. Maybe someone with a bit less naïvety."

Instead, she'd brooded for the rest of their meeting. Sure, she gave her ideas. She'd suggested they profile the neighborhoods where the victims had lived, visit their places of employment, find out what their favorite bars were, track down every associate of theirs they could find. They'd do a timeline piece on both victims, track their activities in detail of their last few days. The team would dig up every piece of evidence and color that they could find about the actual crimes—give Detective Key a more thorough interrogation. They'd attend the upcoming funeral for Chance Lockett. Basically, they'd do everything they could.

Mandy, the intern, had expressed her desire not to attend the funeral. Gavin, the fellow, had outright refused to attend a meeting with Angie and Detective Key, trying very smoothly to slip out of such an obligation with, "But, Angie, he's your source and I wouldn't want to step on anybody's toes."

"Stupid, fresh-faced, can't-deal-with-it rookies..." Angie muttered under her breath, her drumming fingers growing louder.

Tom had said it was a good learning experience. He'd rambled on about responsibility and opportunity to the eager nods of Mandy and Gavin and to Angie's deepening frown. She'd tried to squelch the annoyance, tried to shrug off the uneasiness. But it stuck to her like cling wrap.

There was no way in hell she'd tell Lauren about the lousy meeting. No way would she dare admit to her worried lover that her backup was so inexperienced. Maybe that was stupid and maybe she was blowing the whole thing out of proportion, but her last fiasco, if nothing else, taught her much-needed caution. Despite the red flags and sirens blaring in her ears, she would chase down leads for the investigation anyway. It was her job. And she took her job very seriously. So seriously that she shot off a fiery e-mail of protest to her editor.

No major news broke that day, affording Angie plenty of time for Internet research on the two victims. She found bits and pieces of usable information—martial arts competition results on Whittaker and more recent listings in local charity organizations mentioning Lockett's work contributions. It gave her a dojo to visit and a tutoring center to check out. Her two aides had stopped by the apartment complexes where the men had lived, though they didn't return afterward.

She checked her e-mail again at four o'clock. As per usual, she'd received tons of criticism—"Who cares if somebody killed a man living his life in sin!"—a couple of tips she'd follow, and the tiniest bit of praise. The very last e-mail she opened, however, made her eyebrows shoot up in bafflement.

"There are a lot of details you should be writing about, Miss Mitchell. You're missing the point. Maybe you should ask the police about spray paint. But don't worry. I'm sure you'll get it right next time."

"What the hell?" she muttered, wondering if the person was off his or her rocker. She reread the message three times, shaking her head. It stemmed from a Yahoo! account, and when she checked the listed profile of said sender, it not-so-surprisingly came back with a generic, half-filled-out listing. The listed city did read Fort Worth, but that didn't mean much.

But it was just weird enough... She shook her head at her thought process. It couldn't be. With a bit of a laugh, she forwarded it to Detective Key and shut down her computer.

She was about to leave when Tom came stomping up to her desk, a crumpled piece of paper in his hand.

"What the hell is this?" he demanded, shoving the printout in her face. Her e-mail glared back at her and she had to bite back a sarcastic response. Tom saw the look and frowned. "In my office. Now," he barked and strode off at a pace he had to know she couldn't keep up with. Angie continued to shove various items in her purse at a forcibly relaxed pace—let him wait for her, damn it—and slowly picked up her crutches, hobbling toward his office door, behind which he'd already disappeared.

She stepped over the threshold and closed the door, quietly took a seat, and faced her boss with a politely inquisitive look. "Yes?"

"So you think I don't know what the hell I'm doing..." Tom began, his voice dripping with anger. "You think I don't understand the importance of this story, that I don't give a shit since I assigned Mandy and Gavin to your team." He paused.

"Pretty much," she said, her tone rising a touch.

"Your last investigation was a disaster for the most part," he snapped, and she shrank back into her chair. "You're good, but not this good." He shook the crumpled paper at her before flopping down in his chair. "Damn it, Angie, you can be the most infuriating, most annoying, most stubborn...." He trailed off and snorted, rising out of his chair again. "Those two are damned fine feature writers. They'll get those good little pieces for your bigger stories. Haven't you read their work?"

Angie nodded slowly and cleared her throat with difficulty. "I have, Tom. You're right about the features. It's good stuff. But you heard how they both shy away from dirty work. You heard how freaking naïve they are. You've got to see that if anything happened…" She stopped abruptly and dropped her eyes.

Silence. Tom's phone rang, and he picked up the receiver and slammed it down. Angie looked up at him, a question on her lips that she wouldn't let loose. She watched his angry eyes soften as the seconds ticked by.

"You're scared," he finally deadpanned, realization dawning. He looked so shocked, so utterly bewildered that Angie couldn't hold in the laughter that bubbled up from her stomach. As quickly as it had started, though, it died away and the two stared at each other. Finally, Tom said, "I'll be damned. I thought you were the craziest, most reckless reporter on my staff."

"Guess I learned my lesson the hard way," she whispered.

"Guess you did. We don't have to do this if it bothers you this much. We can…"

"No," she cut him off, her voice rising. "I can do my job." She paused, stalling, but couldn't figure out a way to explain herself without being honest. "There are just…aftereffects, okay? It might take…some time is all. I had an episode this morning and convinced myself everything would be okay because I'd have help. I thought you'd pick Mark and somebody else. I didn't realize when you asked me if I'd do this that you'd give me a couple of rookies. What if…well, I'll get over it."

His eyes searched her face, and he let the silence linger for a few seconds.

"Angie, as a friend, I'll tell you I think you need to see somebody about those 'aftereffects.' As your boss, I'll tell you this makes me real uncomfortable and worried. Tell me now if you can't do it. This is your out."

She fiddled with her hands and forced them to still.

"I can do it," she said, proud of how level her voice sounded. "Please don't take me off the assignment. I'll keep my temper in check. I'll see somebody about the nightmares. And I'll try my best to be nice and trust Mandy and Gavin," she paused, then added with the barest of a smirk, "so long as they don't turn in shit for notes or pull stupid stunts like yours truly."

The corners of his mouth turned upward and he nodded, slowly, deliberately. He crumpled up the paper in his hand and tossed it in the trash.

"Let's pretend that never existed," he said, and he moved his mouse, eyes focusing on the computer screen in front of him. Angie heard the telltale chime that announced a file had been deleted and sighed with relief.

"Now tell me what you've found so far," Tom demanded, leaning back into his plush leather office chair, propping his feet up on the old mahogany desk where a single patch of space was left among the mountains of files and loose papers.

Angie flopped down in her desk chair and leaned back, happy that her home computer was more cooperative than the one at work. She loaded up her favorite game and started building imaginary cities, grumbling when messages of citizens' complaints popped up. She denied their requests with vicious satisfaction. She was about to hit bankrupt and decided to punish the complaining lot with four tornados and a flood. For good measure, she unleashed an alien ship that promptly blasted downtown all to hell. Still muttering about "stupid environmentalists" and "picky commuters," she pushed away from the desk and headed toward the front door, where someone was banging with gusto. A smile spread across her face but fell when she was halfway between her bedroom and the front door. It couldn't be Lauren, she had a key. And Jimmy was supposed to be out with Lauren.

A glance at the clock revealed it was nearly eight p.m. She'd killed three hours on the game, but it was still too soon for her lover to come over. Curious, she opened the door. A brown-suited, sweating UPS deliveryman stood there, holding out a clipboard. Her eyes drifted to a thick, padded envelope under his arm and she frowned.

"Sign here please," the man said, growing a touch impatient. Angie took the clipboard, signed, and took the package. The deliveryman turned on his heel and strode back to his idling truck. Angie shut the door and locked it.

The package wasn't heavy at all. In fact, it felt like nothing was inside. She hobbled over to the couch and sat down, placed it on the coffee table, and stared at it for several seconds. The return address was scribbled in bad handwriting and she couldn't make it out. Tentatively, she picked the package up and tore at the flap.

She slid her fingers inside and felt a silky-smooth texture. Her breath caught. She pulled out a lilac silk scarf with obvious brown splatter stains.

Angie screamed.

"Take my goddamned listing out of your index," Angie growled, the phone squashed between her ear and shoulder as her hands pounded a URL address on her keyboard furiously. "And take it out now! Not tomorrow. Not next week. Got it?"

She hung up and tossed the phone across the room while pulling up her *Tribune* e-mail account and searching for that bizarre message. She printed it out, stuffed it in her jeans skirt pocket, and limped across the apartment, into the living room, where the contents of the package lay on the floor where she'd dropped them—one blood-stained lilac silk scarf, three newspaper articles with scribbled indecipherable messages in the margins. She stopped in her tracks. Should she call the police?

Better yet, should she call Detective Key?

A car door slammed outside. She heard muffled voices and footsteps on the stairway toward her front door. The voices were familiar, one male and one female. A second of indecision caused her to hesitate. Then, as if watching someone else act, her hands snatched the contents, stuffed them back in the padded envelope, and slid the package under a couch cushion.

A key slid in the lock and turned. Angie spotted an errant piece of newspaper clipping and kicked it under the couch. A second later, her heart still pounding dangerously fast, the door flew open.

Jimmy was giggling and nearly dropped a brown paper bag on the floor. Lauren strolled in after him and closed the door, looking at her lover in surprise.

"Going somewhere?" she asked, pointing at the set of keys in Angie's hand.

"Yeah" came the lie quickly. "The detective called, I have to go."

"Another body?" Lauren whispered, her forehead wrinkling.

"No. Just an update. I have to get some information," Angie said haltingly. It was sort of the truth. "What's in the bag?"

"Liquor," Jimmy answered, the giggling gone. "Damn. We were hoping you'd be up for a couple of hours of debauchery. Guess it'll have to wait."

"I'll take a rain check," Angie mumbled.

The two looked at her for several long seconds. She watched the matching frowns appear and realized they were waiting for her to leave. But she couldn't leave without the envelope. Her mind raced.

"Er...my computer's kind of fucked up. Could you take a look at it?" she blurted, forcing her voice to remain level.

"What's wrong?" Jimmy asked, his eyebrow raised.

"It...uh...keeps popping up with this message that says my registry is corrupted or something like that. Go check it out, okay?" At least that was true.

He snorted and shook his head, as though the problem was not really worth his attention or expertise, but wandered off toward the bedroom anyway.

Lauren walked over and wrapped her arms around Angie, nuzzling her neck for only a second or two before placing a quick kiss on her pale lips and pulling away.

"Don't stay out too long, you don't look well," she murmured. "You look shaken. I don't care if it's late when you get back. We can talk."

The comforting arms dropped away and Lauren turned to join Jimmy in the bedroom. She glanced over her shoulder only once before turning away. Angie snatched the envelope out from under the cushion and disappeared through the front door as quickly as she could. With one hand on the railing, the other holding her crutches and cell phone, she hopped down the stairs on her good leg, the package tucked under her chin. When she reached the bottom, she punched in Detective Key's number and prayed that he would pick up.

Three rings—"Damn it, damn it, damn it!"—then four, then five. Finally, on the sixth ring, "Miss me already? I wondered why you weren't pestering me today for an update. Guess I shouldn't have gotten my hopes up."

"He found me," she hissed, fumbling with the car door and her crutches.

"Who found you?" the detective's voice instantly changed, all hints of amusement dropped in a second.

Angie tossed the crutches in the back, slid into the driver's seat, and slammed the door shut. She closed her eyes. The car seemed unusually stuffy despite the daylong reprieve from the late summer's heat—moisture coated the parking lot, drops glittering on her windshield. Sweat trickled down her back and clung to her forehead. She felt like she was suffocating. Even saying the words out loud would give her less air.

"*He*, damn it. The killer. That's who," she shouted. "He fucking mailed me a package. Lilac silk scarf with blood on it. Newspaper clippings. Comments in the margins."

A long pause followed on the other side, only the sound of the signal crackling.

"Lilac? As in, light purple?"

"Yes."

"Get down to the station. Now," he growled and hung up.

She tossed aside the phone, turned the ignition, and put her car in reverse. She glanced up at her bedroom window, which faced the parking lot, and thought she caught sight of dark eyes peering down at her. Angie dropped her gaze to the pavement and left.

Preying On Generosity

Chapter Eight

Angie couldn't hear a thing for the freight train roaring in her ears—rhythmic pounding of a shell-shocked heart that drowned out the blaring horns trailing her Mitsubishi Eclipse as she swung her car hard to the right, cutting across three lanes, barely making the downtown exit. Rain drops splattered on her windshield at odd intervals. She didn't notice. All she could think about was the envelope sitting in the passenger seat, its contents, and its implications.

It was her nightmare come to life. Even without the smell of cognac, the stale cigar smoke, the gun trained on the spot between her eyes. It was still her nightmare. Her lips moved, muttering soundlessly. She wanted to curse, but no words made it past her constricted throat. She wanted to cry—demand, "Why me?"—but it wouldn't come out.

She nearly struck a car at Sixth and Calhoun streets. The vehicle pulled up beside her, someone rolled down the window, and shouted obscenities, a balled fist shaking half a foot from her window. Angie stared fixedly ahead.

Finally, she pulled up to the curb on Belknap Street and parked her car. For a solid minute, she didn't move, hands still on the steering wheel. The package seemed to glow in the light of dusk, the white glaring against the dark car seat.

"I will not fall apart," her voice sliced through the stifling silence—words clipped and harsh. She repeated it. Twice. Then slowly, she reached over and grasped the package, checked for coming traffic over her shoulder, and opened the door.

The humid evening air clung to her chilled skin. She hadn't even realized her air conditioning had been on full blast all the way to the police station. She ran a nervous hand through her hair before opening the back door and pulling out her crutches. She tucked the package under her chin and made her way to the entrance of the police station.

White florescent light streamed through the doorway and fell across the stairs she was navigating with difficulty. A shadow cut through the carpet of light.

"Let me take that," its speaker said, and she heard the urgency in his voice. He'd been waiting for her.

"Okay." She raised her chin and Detective Key caught the envelope before it hit the ground. His hands were covered in latex gloves. She heard crinkling plastic, the sound of the envelope sliding into a bag, and the distinct, rubbery snap of gloves being torn off. She didn't look up, scared of what expression she'd find distorting the detective's boyish face.

The click of a lighter followed, then a long sigh. She smelled tobacco smoke in the heavy air. "Let's go for a walk," he said, stopped, then added, "Just a short one."

"But the package…"

"A few more minutes in the open won't hurt it. I'm sure it's been jostled around plenty—what with it being sent through the mail. We're going to be inside for a long time, Angie. Let's take a few minutes out here first."

Her eyes trailed the ground as they walked. His lighter clicked again and she stopped to take the offered cigarette. Finally, she met his eyes.

Angie had no idea what she'd expected—anger maybe, or frustration. But she thought she caught a gleam in his eye, a spark of excitement. It was gone as quickly as it had surfaced, replaced by a grave look of concern. Maybe he had been excited about this particular new clue. Maybe it was just a trick of the light. Maybe she was in shock and was imagining things. She took a drag of her cigarette and let the smoke out slowly.

"Why would he send me something like this?" she asked, her bitter tone disguised by the noise of a passing truck.

"We'll find out soon enough," he replied simply and gestured for them to head back. His mannerisms toward her had abruptly changed. He was treating her like he'd treated that woman, Sandra Lockett—like a victim and not a reporter—softer, gentler, his bantering and his hardened, bitter sides completely buried. The thought that it should piss her off crossed Angie's mind, but no angry feelings followed. Instead, her shoulders sagged and she trailed after Detective Key.

He led her down the winding crisp hallways that smelled of a thorough and recent cleaning. The police station was quiet at night. No people stood in line at the records department. No one waited in the lobby. But as soon as they cleared the security door, sounds of working officers picked up.

"Sit here," he instructed, and pulled a chair out for her in a cubicle. She sat and leaned her crutches against the wall. "Can I get you some coffee?" She nodded.

He was gone for an extraordinarily long time. It seemed like hours. Angie had fidgeted at first, seemingly fascinated by her knitting fingers and the nondescript blue carpet. Then she'd stared at the wall clock for half an hour. It was getting late, nearly ten o'clock. Finally, as her racing heart began to calm and her senses thawed from the iciness that had clutched her earlier, she allowed her eyes to wander.

A faded picture was tacked to the wall, sporting a much-younger Detective Key—bare-chested and with boxing gloves. A yellowed newspaper clipping announced he'd beaten his opponent. She stared at it, intrigued. The typeset of the clipping looked like it was a couple of decades old. Had she misjudged his age when she thought he was in his thirties? She must have.

A stuffed cactus wearing a sombrero sat on a shelf overhead, one that would dance and sing "La Cucaracha" if its stomach was poked, she knew, but didn't dare try it out with so many serious faces in other cubicles. The sight of it erased her frown, though didn't exactly spawn a smile. Her mother had one just like it in the kitchen in Fayetteville, North Carolina.

Her eyes drifted to linger on the desk's surface, which had so many piled stacks of paper it would rival her editor's. A police photo spread immediately caught her attention. Checking over her shoulder, she picked it up with the tips of her fingers and scanned the six faces—all redheads. It made her wonder if one of the men was responsible for sending the package.

The last bit of frost in her stomach melted. She stared harder at the faces. Her breath quickened. Her heart rate picked up. She gasped.

"Hey, hey, hey," Detective Key chided, snatching the paper away from her. "Didn't know I left that out," he muttered, stuffing it quickly in a drawer before placing a cup of steaming coffee in front of Angie.

She closed her eyes and took a deep breath. "I know one of those guys."

Silence. The detective very slowly sat in his office chair. "What?"

"Bottom left corner. Wide mouth, arching brows, goofy haircut," she replied, voice growing stronger. "He works at Club 1970 in Arlington. His first name is Matt and he's a bartender."

"So he is," Detective Key drawled, pulling out his notepad, jotting down a quick note, then setting the thing aside to pin her with his eyes.

"Is he a suspect? Does that photo spread relate to the case?"

"It relates to *a* case," he tiptoed, not quite answering the question. "Back to you."

Angie grumbled and grabbed her coffee, taking a long sip before meeting his eyes again. "You were gone an awfully long time," she muttered. "Made me wonder if you'd gotten lost or something."

"Had to stop by the lab. I had a conversation with our guys about the notes. Nothing concrete, mind you, just a general idea of what he was trying to say. The handwriting's atrocious."

He paused, picked up his notepad, and flipped back several pages. He scanned the scribbled sentences with his eyes and nodded. Then he produced a manila folder Angie hadn't noticed, from which he withdrew several photocopies.

"It seems our team is well-versed in chicken scratch writing." He smirked, an expression quite obviously aimed at getting her to relax. Not that it helped much. "Not too surprisingly, the return address was a fake. There is no 7226 Calloway Court in Fort Worth."

He'd also taken a closer look at the e-mail she'd forwarded him earlier. He told her he had already subpoenaed the account's records to see if the sender had sent anything else—he, like Angie, believed it came from the killer—but wasn't too hopeful. Anybody could create an account, send one message, and never use the account again.

Sighing, he leaned forward and held out one of the photocopies for her to see. "But these are interesting. Look at this blob next to your name above the article. It says, 'quick learner, good listener.' And this little bit here next to my name says, 'pompous ass.' Guess he doesn't like me much. And check out this piece here, next to the paragraph that indicates the homicide was a hate crime. It says," he flipped to another page in his little notepad and read, "'Indicates? Perhaps more aggressive measures are warranted given the careful construction of this sentence.'" He stopped and looked at Angie.

"This over here is more troubling…" He cleared his throat and pointed to a scribbled paragraph next to a sentence in the article that spoke of Whittaker's sexual orientation. Detective Key had to clear his throat again, and he tugged with one finger at his shirt collar to undo the top button. "If man also lie with mankind, as he lieth with a woman, both of them have committed an abomination; they shall surely be put to death; their blood shall be upon them."

"From the Bible?" Angie asked, leaning forward in her seat.

"Leviticus 20:13. I pulled it up on the Internet. But the passage isn't concluded in typical fashion with the author in parentheses. No, the parentheses here contain the words: 'I am that blood.'"

Their eyes met and lingered for seconds. Angie put out her fingers to trace the words in disbelief but yanked them back when they touched the page. She felt terrified and elated at the same time, outraged but coolly disconnected as though the page existed only in her nightmares, the different emotions all warring for her attention. Her hand trembled slightly. She balled it into a fist to stop the shaking. So the killer thought she was a quick learner, a good listener. That didn't sound so bad.

But he was still a twisted psychopath. The thought of a private encounter made her insides cramp painfully.

"I am that blood," she mumbled, her mind racing.

"We're checking the packaging for prints. The clippings, too. Perhaps we'll find something on the scarf." He waited a beat. "But I doubt it. I'd be willing to bet a year's salary that all the prints will come back as yours or somebody who works in the postal industry. Any DNA we gather will belong to one of the victims."

Angie sagged back in her chair, deflated.

111

"But," he forestalled her depression, "we do have samples of his handwriting—second-best thing to a good fingerprint, unless you have DNA. And it looks too personal, too interested and invested to have been written on his behalf by a second party. No, my gut's telling me the killer wrote this himself."

Angie took another long sip of coffee and let her eyes drift shut against the myriad thoughts and pictures racing through her mind so she could at least make an attempt at sorting them out. She didn't notice that her fingernails were cutting moon-shaped slices in the palm of her clenched right hand.

"Do you think I'm in any danger?"

Detective Key leaned forward and took her right hand, prying the fingers apart.

"I honestly don't know. On the surface, the killer seems to think of you as somebody he can teach, someone who is spreading whatever message he wants to share, though I'm not one hundred percent sure this is all fire and brimstone shit—it's too easy." He rubbed the back of his neck with his free hand, glanced down, and realized he was still holding Angie's hand with his other, and let go. "On a deeper level, he's a cold-blooded killer. He's got to know you'd take this to the police. He's obviously not a moron murderer. Maybe he did this to point us in another direction. Maybe he really did do it because he has an interest in you. It got your attention. And I think that was the point."

"But why my attention?"

"You're the one writing about his handiwork."

"Has he sent packages to other reporters, like to the Dallas paper?"

"Not that I know of, which makes me think he's a Fort Worth local."

He dropped his eyes to the floor and tried to hide a yawn.

Angie drained the coffee mug. "So what should I do?"

"You certainly can't print any of this—not one word—in the paper," he deadpanned. Angie groaned and slammed the mug down on the desk. That's not what she wanted to hear. It also wasn't an answer to her question. Her lips parted to deliver a sarcastic response, but she was cut off.

"It'll compromise the investigation..." His eyes suddenly grew sharper. "On the other hand, if you ignore our killer's 'helpful' criticisms, he might get pissed off and try something truly stupid." He paused a beat. "Damn it."

Angie chewed her lip. She hadn't thought of that. She'd assumed she couldn't possibly write about the package, that she'd have to omit a detail in her investigation. But isn't that what she did last time she was involved in dangerous dealings? Hadn't she conveniently left out the fact that she'd been attacked on the homeless strip—chalked up to stupidity in having gone down there to begin with? Her lips began to sting under the nervous gnawing.

"Er…I think you've just become our very own personal link to the killer himself," the detective ventured, his voice unsure. "If you ignore it, he may come after you, he may not. If you work with it, he may send you more stuff, and we may get more clues that'll help us catch him."

Angie gaped openly at the man. She shook her head violently. If Lauren knew… If her boss knew…

"What should I tell my boss?" she demanded, trying not to sound too frustrated, failing miserably in her efforts. She decided to leave Lauren out of it for now, thinking he might understand the problem with her editor quicker. "I mean, it's not just the danger. It's…it's unethical. I can't be part of the news. It's a conflict of interest."

There, she thought, beat that.

"You didn't seem too concerned with that the last time around," Detective Key retorted, his voice dropping to a whisper. "Isn't it a conflict of interest to write articles on the arrests of men who attacked you? Bet it gave you a bit of a thrill, an unethical satisfaction."

Her eyes widened, not because she was shocked, but because he was right. She suddenly wondered how much he'd dug up on her personal business. He'd said at Starbucks that a cop always does his homework. She had a dark feeling that he'd done more than simple homework.

They glowered at each other for a full minute. Detective Key folded his arms across his chest; Angie mirrored him.

"Look," he began slowly, his eyes narrow and fierce. "You know I can't force you to do this. But the right thing to do in this case, in my opinion, is to let the killer continue to think he sent you a golden nugget and show your appreciation by writing some sort of follow-up."

"Your opinion is a cop's opinion, which will always be that it's more important to get a dangerous man off the street," Angie growled. But even saying it, she knew he had a point. "Besides, how can I write a follow-up without new information? My boss is not going to go for this whole thing, either. Not to mention I would be putting myself in a hell of a lot of danger."

He leaned forward, resting his elbows on his knees.

"Here's what we're going to do about all that…"

It was after one o'clock in the morning when Angie finally made it back to her apartment. She slipped the key in the lock and opened the door as quietly as she could. She slowly eased it open and hissed when the hinges squeaked. She stepped through, leaned her crutches against the wall, and closed it quickly, hoping it wouldn't make the same sound again. With a sigh of relief, she turned the lock.

A tap-tap-tapping just behind her made her jump. With tremendous effort, she forced her tense facial muscles into an acceptable calm, flipped on the light, and turned.

"Hi, Lauren," she whispered, the color draining from her face at the disappointed look that stripped the beauty from her lover's eyes.

Lauren wasn't wearing a T-shirt and boxers—her favorite sleepy clothes—a very bad sign. Instead, she stood, shoulders rigid, her long legs still clad in jeans, her feet encased by her favorite black cowboy boots. She held a scrap of paper between index finger and thumb. "What's this?"

"A newspaper clipping?" Angie received a deepening frown in return.

"Why does it say, 'The most important details have been omitted, but the writer will hopefully do better next time'? Is this what I think it is?"

"You can read that?" she asked, in spite of herself.

"Of course I can," Lauren said flatly. "Or have you forgotten that I taught grown men and women to read and write, that I've deciphered far worse writing than this?" She paused and raked a hand exasperatedly through her hair. "Did you lie to me?"

Angie's heart almost stopped. She stared at the newspaper

clipping that she'd completely forgotten, the one she'd kicked under the couch. Her legs started trembling. She felt like remaining in a standing position was the hardest thing in the world. But it wasn't. What she would do next was.

"Yes," she answered. It was the barest of a whisper.

Lauren opened her clenched fingers and the scrap of paper fluttered to the ground where it lay propped half upright against a discarded pair of shoes. She opened her mouth, closed it, and cleared her throat. "I…" her voice cracked, "…can't deal with this." She took two quick steps toward Angie and raised an eyebrow threateningly. Angie opened her mouth to speak, to explain, but barely a second after she took two steps away from the door, Lauren turned the lock, flung the door open, and jogged down the stairs.

A car door slammed shut. An engine roared to life. Tires screamed as acrid smoke billowed into the air and a car peeled out of the parking lot.

Silence.

Slowly, Angie closed her mouth, shut the door with trembling hands, and turned the lock.

Dark circles lined Angie's red, swollen eyes. The silence in the apartment threatened to suffocate her. She was forced out onto the balcony, where she smoked cigarette after cigarette. She hadn't been able to sleep at all. And for the first time in her career, she picked up the phone and told her boss she was too sick to work.

More important things were going on, damn it.

Screw the *Tribune* and Detective Key with his whacko plans.

Lauren wasn't answering Angie's calls. Neither was Jimmy. He'd left her a voicemail while she was still speaking with Detective Key and hadn't been able to answer. He said he didn't want to get in the middle of a fight. Let Lauren cool off and give her a couple of days, the message said. Everything would be okay. She would get over it.

The sky was thick with promised rain. At that moment, more than ever, Angie needed the clouds to burst, to splatter her face with rain so it could dribble down her neck and back. Lightning flashed, thunder following close behind, and still it didn't rain. The sight brought a flood of memories crashing to the forefront of her mind—Legacy River Park, her lover's first kiss tingling on her lips, their first heated embrace.

Dark gray clouds rolled overhead. She forced her eyes shut against the tears, but it was no use. They slid out and trickled down her cheeks mercilessly.

She lighted another cigarette, drew in the painful breath, and let out a sob. How could she have let this happen? Her fingers crunched around the paper dart, knocking the glowing tip to the floor. She threw the butt over the balcony edge and wiped the tears roughly from her eyes. Angie decided there was no way she'd sit around like this for the next couple of days. She didn't think she could bear it. No, she'd have to track down her lover, force her to listen to an explanation, regardless of how weak her justifications were. Maybe then, Angie thought, she'd at least feel a little less helpless. At least she would have tried to patch up the mess.

She hobbled into the living room, shouldered her purse, and headed out the door, a grim but determined look in her eyes.

It was nearly three o'clock before she caught sight of Lauren. Angie had searched half of the university campus by foot and crutches. Her armpits would surely blister after that exercise. Both her legs were throbbing. She'd already canceled her physical therapy appointment. Finally, when she'd nearly declared defeat, she spotted Lauren trudging along between the University Center and Woolf Hall.

"Lauren!" she shouted, ignoring the dozens of students who turned around to see what was going on. She tried to move faster, thrust her crutches out, and hissed with each impact they made.

Her lover stopped and peered in her direction. Angie felt encouraged, though the other hadn't taken a single step toward her. She tried to quicken her pace even more. Her crutch slipped out of her armpit and she lost her balance, landing her cast leg squarely on the concrete with full force.

Pain ripped up her side and danced before her eyes in white and black spots. She didn't even scream she was so surprised, the breath ripped from her lips. She thought she heard someone shouting, felt an arm around her waist as she let go of her crutches and they fell away.

A familiar hand touched her face and Angie almost smiled, even though she heard something about "hospital" and "damned

116

crazy woman." The hand cupped her face and held her still as her stomach lurched in discomfort. Those dark eyes she loved so much stared back at her, wide and shocked. The whole thing was ridiculous.

Lauren's arms slipped under her and hefted her up. Finally, the pain cut through the haze her body had created to protect her, and Angie let loose a string of profanities that made those standing nearby grit their teeth and shake their heads in bewilderment.

She heard a responding, slightly hysterical laugh and knew she'd be taken care of.

Preying On Generosity

Chapter Nine

T he night's darkness was complete by the time Lauren pulled into the apartment complex off Fielder Street, parked her car, and helped Angie out. The knee-high cast was gone, replaced by the promised shorter one, which stopped three inches below her knee. It was still heavy but allowed Angie more much-needed freedom of movement. She leaned heavily on her new single cane, taking slow and careful steps. A giddy grin cut across her face, induced by the heavy dose of painkillers she'd been given at the hospital four hours earlier.

It had been a long afternoon and evening. After two hours waiting in the emergency room at Harris Methodist Hospital downtown spent in brooding silence, Angie had received a sound tongue lashing by Lauren and her doctor when he finally got to her. The latter had decided to remove the offensive cast a few days early so he could better conduct a series of X-rays to make sure she hadn't rebroken anything. When the verdict came back that she'd been lucky as hell, he'd decided to replace the old cast with the shorter one, had taken her crutches, and given her a cane.

Despite the frustration at having had to endure half the day in the ER, Angie's mood finally lifted when that decision came down. Thank God, she thought, her temper completely dissipated as the good nurse washed her wretched itching leg and smeared a fat amount of lotion across the flaky skin before a new cast was formed around her sensitive limb. And good riddance to the damned crutches.

Lauren had left the room momentarily to use the restroom, and Angie had used the opportunity to ask the doctor about her head. The mention of the many memory lapses had caused a brief look

119

of concern to flit across the old doctor's features and he'd ordered a CT scan, much to her annoyance. But Lauren hadn't protested the extra hour it cost them in the hospital. In fact, she seemed a bit relieved that Angie had brought it up. Especially since Angie had "forgotten" to make that promised appointment and had used every diversion tactic she could think of to avoid a discussion about it.

The doctor had said he'd call with the results in the morning so they could leave. Her lover had muttered something like "it's about damned time" but made no further comment on the matter.

Once the two made it inside, Lauren quickly moved a pile of books and papers and dumped them on the floor so Angie could sit on the couch. Then she made herself busy in the kitchen, whipping up a quick meal. She'd been silent most of the day. Her smile that had graced her lips after the doctor proclaimed that Angie's leg was not broken anew had slid off her face after those first relieved moments. As Lauren brewed a pot of tea, Angie could hear muttered grumblings in the kitchen, pots being banged around, and dishes treated none-too-nicely.

Angie sighed. The painkillers were beginning to wear off and her leg felt hot, her toes swollen bright red. She'd have to pop another set of pills soon, but didn't dare do it until they had the discussion she knew was coming. After dinner, she was certain, they'd trade a few choice words. She hoped that would be the end of it. But her stomach filled with dread, cramping uncomfortably.

She busied herself by looking around the apartment, trying to see if anything had changed. The two didn't spend much time there—they usually met and slept at her apartment a couple of miles east. It wasn't a set rule but had somehow become routine. Angie suddenly wondered if it bothered Lauren.

The most noticeable feature of her lover's apartment was the lack of a television. Where one should have been propped against the wall, a flimsy bookshelf stood, every inch packed with novels, philosophy works—Nietzsche, Lao Tzu, Machiavelli, Rand—and textbooks. Framed photographs lined the white walls, mostly pictures taken in the countries she had visited during her Peace Corps time in Africa and Micronesia, interspersed by what appeared to be exotic tin weapons. A corkboard hung on the far wall, colorful scraps of paper pinned to every available space, save the top right corner, where a picture of Angie hung prominently. She returned her own grinning smile.

Her eyes fell on the coffee table and she smirked. Like every surface in the apartment, it was littered with text books and papers, newspapers, and forgotten coffee mugs. Angie leaned forward and stacked a few items before setting the pile under the table so they'd have room to eat. She grunted in the effort to lean forward and not jar her leg.

A glance at the tiny dining area confirmed that there would be no eating there. The table seemed to be serving as a substitute desk—a laptop perched at the edge, surrounded by CD cases, more papers, and more coffee mugs.

It occurred to Angie that Lauren wasn't nearly this messy at her apartment—always picking up after herself. She wondered then if it was just politeness. Not that it mattered. Lauren was entirely too busy, after all, with her graduate courses in teaching English as a second language and with her band. If she'd had a job on top of that... It was a damned good thing the university picked up the tab as part of her Peace Corps benefits. The grant she'd received on top of that ensured that she had plenty of living-expenses money. Otherwise, Angie thought, they'd never see each other.

She couldn't hold the mess against her lover. Honest.

Her eyes scanned the living room and spotted a beat-up acoustic guitar propped in the corner, a couple of open notebooks spread around its base. The urge to pick up one of those books and flip through the tattered pages was overwhelming. But she resisted the temptation. This was not the time to be nosy. Lauren surely wouldn't appreciate it, not given the current tension between them.

How had Lauren discovered the damned clipping? And how had she guessed so quickly what it was? More importantly, Angie demanded of herself, why the hell hadn't she just told the truth?

It wasn't an issue of trust. Angie trusted Lauren completely. It suddenly dawned on her that she'd only wanted to protect her, to keep the worries at bay, to keep her in the dark. Her shoulders sagged and her head flopped back against the couch. Lauren didn't need protecting, she could take care of herself. Her worries were justified. Her outrage understandable.

The scent of sizzling onions and bell peppers filled Angie's nostrils, cutting through her thoughts. Blues music filtered in from the kitchen, and she realized Lauren had turned on a radio, likely to distract herself. Angie's stomach growled in anticipation, but she closed her eyes and let the melancholy bassoon and saxophone calm her mind.

"Hey," Lauren whispered in her ear, seemingly seconds later. "Time to get something in your stomach. Sorry it took so long. The pills must be wreaking havoc in there."

Angie sat up and rubbed her eyes, realizing she'd drifted off.

"Thanks," she mumbled, trying to will away the grogginess fogging her senses. She took the offered fork and gave a brief smile before shoveling a mouthful of stir fry, relishing the subtle spices the other was so good at choosing.

She risked a glance sideways where Lauren sat and ate in silence. The dark eyes were focused on the task at hand. Angie sighed and took another bite. It was a good dinner. But she would have enjoyed it much more if the dread of what would be said when they finished weren't looming over her head. She cursed herself mentally, added a healthy slap for good measure, and scraped the remaining morsels off her plate and into her mouth. She took a sip of water from the glass Lauren had set on the coffee table, swished it around her mouth before swallowing, and leaned back. Lauren set her fork down that same moment and drained the glass of water in quick gulps that pierced the silence.

Angie dared reach toward Lauren, trying to snag a hand and keep it within hers. But the fingers she grazed retreated hastily. Her throat began to burn and she couldn't choke out a single word.

Lauren stood up and carried the plates into the kitchen, where she unceremoniously dumped them in the sink with a little crash. She took a couple of steps back into the living room and stopped three feet shy of the couch, her arms crossed, her shoulders rigid.

"We need to talk," she announced, and Angie couldn't do anything but nod. Lauren sighed and forcibly relaxed her posture before continuing, though she didn't come closer to the couch, either. "I..." she started, an unreadable expression crossing her face and she stopped, took another deep breath, and tried again. "It's your life, okay? I know that. You're a grown woman. If you want to take risks, that's your business. But after what happened the last time... I feel justified in worrying." She waited a beat, holding up her hand to silence Angie, who'd opened her mouth to interrupt. "What happened with the newspaper clipping is not your fault. You didn't ask for it. But don't you dare lie to me again." The last sentence was spat out quickly, words harsh and clipped. "I mean it. If there's one thing that pisses me off above all others, it's lying." She punctuated the statement by raising her chin defiantly. "I want to know if you're in deep shit, damn it. I want to know what the hell is going on. Don't fucking shut me out again. And don't lie to me."

Angie's eyes widened and she nodded so rapidly it hurt her neck. She cleared her throat, trying to get rid of the burning that held back the words she needed to say. She finally managed an "I'm sorry."

"You'd better be," Lauren whispered, dropping her eyes.

"I didn't know what to do…"

"You should have told me."

"I tried to explain, but you left…"

"After you lied to me."

Silence. Angie fought back the defensiveness that threatened to raise her voice. She studied her twisting hands. "I was scared," she finally admitted to both herself and Lauren.

Feet shuffled across the cream-colored carpet and weight made the worn couch sag in the middle. Angie felt a strong leg press against her thigh and her twisting hands were stopped when Lauren's fingers touched hers.

"I'm sure you were, honey," came the whisper, barely audible. "Please tell me about it—everything, I mean."

Angie didn't want to elaborate, thought she should keep this line of thought to herself. She should keep her mouth shut. But she couldn't. Not now.

"I was scared out of my mind, okay? Scared because some psycho killer sent me some fucked-up shit. And I didn't want… I didn't want you to know because you'd have made me promise to steer clear of the investigation. And I don't think I can do that." Angie turned her hands and grasped her lover's fingers before they could escape. She squeezed tentatively, trembling in the silence that followed. She wasn't explaining it right.

"Look," she turned and faced the woman she loved. "This is really important. To me. To the families that are hurting. Even to the killer, apparently. What I did was wrong, I know, and it won't happen again. I'll tell you anything you want to know." She waited a beat, catching her breath as the words were spilling out unchecked. "You've been hurting since last time. I can see it in your eyes. You mumble in your sleep sometimes. It was terrible—for both of us. But you've got to understand that we have to move on. I was...trying to protect you. Stupid, I know."

Lauren's breath hitched and came out in a sigh. She tugged at her hand, trying to free it from Angie's tight grip, but she wouldn't give. A low growl began in Lauren's throat and she tugged hard, finally freeing her limb. She made to stand up, but Angie leaned in and caught her around the waist, burying her face in the other woman's lap. The legs stiffened.

"Trying to protect..." Lauren muttered. "That much was obvious. But damn it, I don't need to be protected," she said with an annoyed groan. "You're being damned naïve and someone has to point that out. Let me tell you, it's like watching a train wreck in slow motion, it's..." She groaned in frustration, put her hands on Angie's shoulders, and tried to put more distance between them so she could better voice her thoughts. "Look at me," she demanded, her voice raising an octave in frustration.

Angie loosened her grip and finally sat up, tears threatening to drown her vision.

"I know," she whispered. "But I can't just let it go. You don't understand. The killer has taken an interest, and we can't stop now." She risked looking up into the taller woman's face, shrinking back at the shocked and angry look she found there.

"What are you talking about?" Lauren demanded, a storm cloud brewing in her fierce eyes. "What do you mean by *interest*?"

Angie took a deep breath and ran nervous fingers through her sticky hair. This was not going to be easy, but she choked out an explanation, told her about the comments and Detective Key's plan.

Lauren stared at her, mouth open. Her shoulders began to tremble. "Let me get this straight. You're telling me that crazy-ass detective wants you to respond to that e-mail with questions, then wants you to pursue this lunatic investigation of yours, and demands you keep producing articles about the killer?" She plopped back down on the couch with a thud, her knees suddenly too weak to stand. "Not to forget that you're to hang around those crime scenes—a freaking target basically on your forehead—as bait?"

"Not bait, no," Angie shot back. "Remember, he's not after me."

"Oh, right. I forgot. He thinks he can 'teach you something' and share his fucked-up Sodom and Gomorrah shit with the world!" Her voice rose. "I swear to whatever deity you wish—if I see any more damned newspaper clippings or packages, I'll burn them!"

Angie would have jumped up and shouted back, went to do just that, but her cast proved too difficult an obstacle. She banged it against the coffee table and whimpered in protest. Lauren moved to stop her, but she swatted the hands away angrily, slumped back against the couch, and focused all her attention instead on not letting helpless tears surface. Her bottom lip quivered.

A rough thumb wiped an errant tear from her face. Burning, dark eyes loomed less than an inch from her nose and Angie clenched her eyes shut, put her balled fists against her lover's chest. Not now, she thought, not like this. Lips crushed against her own, caught her trembling lip between insistent teeth, a tongue demanding entrance—not asking.

Angie groaned and struggled, her eyes wide. Lauren grabbed her fists and pulled them away—her strength overpowering—and long fingers snaked along the back of her neck, crushing their faces together roughly. She whimpered, her protest growing weaker.

Angie's mind couldn't wrap around the sudden change, the rough embrace. Her mouth parted involuntarily and let the hot tongue slip inside and swirl deep in her mouth. Her body knew what to do and shut down the angry feelings, decimated logic, set fire to the confusion, and transformed it into a desperate need— fueled by the sleepless night and emotional beating she'd given herself. She moaned into Lauren's mouth and let her eyes slide shut, allowed the hands to slip away from her neck, and rip the buttons from her blouse, sending them flying onto the floor and coffee table, down the cracks between the couch's cushions.

The blasting air conditioning didn't have time to chill her exposed chest as hands quickly covered the area and pinched her nipples almost too hard, more than a touch painfully. Angie squirmed against the onslaught that felt more like a conquest than a shared expression of love. But wetness began to pool between her legs and she cried out with relief and protest simultaneously when one strong hand deserted her breast and disappeared under her skirt, grasped her damp panties, and ripped them along the length of her upper thighs.

Teeth grazed her neck, nipping eagerly, leaving marks—claiming her, the thought echoed through the foggy haze. Two long fingers slid into her mouth and she ran her tongue along the length of them, trapped them with her teeth, suckled them greedily. A dangerous growling sound filled the air, and with a shock, she realized it was coming from her own throat. Spots of red light flashed behind her closed eyelids, and she wrenched them open, a gasp of surprise escaping her lips at the predatory look on Lauren's face, the woman's lips curving dangerously, eyes sharp and clear.

"Let go," Lauren hissed, tugging at her trapped fingers.

Angie released the digits, catching a brief glimpse of deep teeth marks that momentarily sobered her. But before she could utter a word, those fingers jabbed deep inside her in one smooth thrust and she cried out. She heard a low, husky laugh in response, punctuated by the hard thrusting hand. She couldn't focus. The room was spinning ever faster with the increased rhythm of the rough caresses deep inside. A hand gripped her jaw and the fingers stopped abruptly.

"You have to trust me," Lauren demanded, her lips suddenly inches away.

"I will," Angie gasped, her hips rocking, trying to resume the ministrations on her own, crying out in anger and desperation when the hand disappeared.

Lauren held the fingers to her kiss-bruised lips and ran her tongue along the length of both digits in agonizingly slow movements, Angie's eyes were glued to the sight, her breathing caught in her chest.

Lauren stopped and dove in for a searing kiss, a touch gentler than before, and Angie grasped her beloved's face, holding her in place for the precious reconnection. She could taste herself inside that mouth and groaned, her hips resuming their rocking motion.

Fingers curled around her hands and pried them away.

"And," Lauren continued, gasping for breath, "you won't protect me anymore," she growled, her hands digging into her inner thighs.

"Not anymore," Angie promised feverishly, wetness coating her cheeks as she realized she was crying. "I need you, don't run away from me. I'm sorry."

Lauren's fingers stopped digging in and turned into a tender caress. She leaned forward and traced the path of tears with her tongue, murmuring indistinguishable words of comfort. "You mean so much to me," she whispered hoarsely, and trailed a burning path down Angie's chest, past the hitched-up skirt, and covered Angie's sex with her panting hot breath and lips, shoving her tongue into the salty-sweet opening as far as it would go.

Explosions of colored light erupted behind Angie's unseeing eyes, and she cried out her lover's name, unable to still her quivering hips, ignoring the pain that shot through her leg as she jostled it and struck the coffee table. Lauren wrapped a protective arm around the cast and held it still, not letting up on her lightning-hot lovemaking.

Angie's hands clenched and unclenched, grasping at thin air. Her mouth was completely dry, her tongue stuck to the bottom of her mouth. She moaned, thrashed, and moaned again.

She felt a pressure below the assaulting mouth, a finger teasing low at her second opening, and her eyes snapped open in surprise. Her dry lips moved to form a question that was silenced when the finger retreated momentarily, touched her slick folds, coated itself, then returned to burrow deep inside—aggravatingly slow—remained still for two or three seconds, then slid out and in again. Angie's moaning ceased immediately.

"I'm going to let go of your leg," Lauren whispered, undeterred. "I need my other hand. Try not to move it." She received a tentative affirmative nod in response.

Lauren dipped three fingers into her mouth as they stared at each other. She had not let up the rhythm with her other hand and Angie quivered in anticipation, whimpering, gasping for air that rushed out as quickly as she could suck it in. The moment seemed infinitely suspended as she stared at the fingers that glistened in the lamp light, matched by a spark of light hitting a thin sheen of sweat and sex on Lauren's cheeks and lips. Angie wanted to lean forward and kiss those swollen lips, lick herself off that beautiful face. The moment shattered abruptly when her lover lowered her hand and slid the digits deep inside—filling her so exquisitely that she felt like she'd explode.

With both hands now, Lauren pumped and turned her head to the side, so she could let her tongue dance along Angie's swollen clit. The rhythm quickened in increments, the dance speeding up. Angie was filling up, felt like her lover was crawling inside, wrapping herself around her, splitting her up the middle to make room for more. Logs were being added to the fire—one by one— each catching fire immediately, burning, burning, scorching her insides until they were molten in the blaze.

She screamed with each tantalizing thrust, writhed on the rough fabric of the old couch, teeth biting down on her lower lip— she could taste copper in her mouth. She couldn't remember why she'd ever been angry, why she'd ever been scared. The world disappeared, and it was only she and Lauren on a lonely plane of heat and fire. She was at the edge of an abyss and thrust her hips harder and harder so she might fall, delighting in the spots that danced before her eyes. And finally, she crashed over the edge, voice raw and heavy, fingers aching from being so tightly clenched, her hips and thighs quivering while she melted back into the folds of the couch.

"Angie?" an urgent voice drew her back from oblivion and she opened her eyes, squinting against the living room light. A soft smile curved her lips and she swallowed.

"Damn," she sighed, the word slurred. She tried her muscles, flexing her abdomen, and found she was completely exhausted. Everything ached deliciously. She rolled her head to the side and bumped her forehead into her lover's nose. A giggle escaped her lips.

"I thought…" Lauren began, then giggled in response, "never mind," and nipped at her ear playfully, ducking her head coyly away. Angie smelled herself and energy returned to her limbs as though she'd taken a good shot of caffeine straight into her blood stream. She flexed her hand and it didn't feel so heavy anymore.

She found Lauren's eyes and growled. "We're not done yet," she announced to the shocked face and assailed her prey with a series of searing kisses.

Moonlight filtered through two sets of blinds in the corner apartment bedroom, laying a gentle pattern of soft white lines that distorted into twists and curves across the crumpled bed sheets. Angie lay on the covered mattress—Lauren's long body spooned at her back—grass-green eyes open, heart beating slowly. It was well past three o'clock in the morning and she couldn't sleep, despite the painkillers in her system.

Long hours had passed in halting conversation after they'd satisfied their needs, words whispered at times, shouted at others, or muttered in reluctant understanding. They'd sorted it out this time, but Angie couldn't help but wonder how bad the next episode would be when she got another package or e-mail or—she shuddered—some other form of contact. For now, they'd agreed to be honest, no matter how unpleasant, but that's where their agreement ended.

Angie thought of the plan and forced back a disbelieving snort.

"You'll have backup," Detective Key had promised. "Just in case. The feds are breathing down my neck. This'll give them something to do. They can tail you, keep an eye on you in case our killer does decide to pay a visit. I don't think he will, but just in case." It had been the only part of the plan that Lauren had taken as a good idea. The rest, as far as Lauren was concerned, was all a bunch of crazy bullshit.

Angie wondered if the feds were already tailing her, wondered if they waited outside for her to leave. She almost snickered. Hope they brought some coffee, she thought and sighed. And no telescopes to peek into Lauren's living room. She didn't want to think about some federal agent getting an eye-full. The thought alone drew red blotches along her cheeks and neck.

She wondered if they'd contacted her boss yet. Unlikely, considering he hadn't called with a storm of heated words. Angie began to dread the coming morning, desperately wishing the whole mess would just go away. But it was not to be.

At exactly eight o'clock, her cell phone rang.

"Angie speaking," she said in a low voice, toweling her hair dry. She'd known who it was the second the phone rang.

"I don't know what you're playing at, but you had better get in my office the second you walk through the door." The line went dead and Angie closed her eyes. So the detective had paid a visit to her boss after all. She dropped the phone back in her purse and rifled through Lauren's closet, hoping to find a suitable blouse.

She could have forced the woman out of bed an hour earlier to drive her back to her own apartment so she could get ready and change, but she hadn't had the heart to do it. Lauren had a class in a couple of hours and would be doing research for the rest of the day. It was almost time for the first round of papers to be turned in, and Angie could tell by the amount of books littering the living room that Lauren expected it to be tough. The woman needed her sleep. So she'd waited until after her morning bath to wake her lover.

Angie found a pale blue blouse that didn't hang off her shoulders like a nightshirt, though it was a tad too big, and slipped it on. She frowned, remembering her own blouse still on the living room floor in tatters. The frown was more of a puzzled expression, heavy with newfound knowledge and skills. They'd been rough. More so than usual. And to her slight embarrassment, she'd liked it immensely. Even if she wasn't too happy about the circumstances under which they'd practically assaulted each other.

A tingle ran down her back and forced a shudder from stiffening shoulders.

Shaking her head to rid the thoughts, she glanced at her clock and gasped. Damn it, she thought, cursing herself for dawdling, and took quick steps into the bedroom.

"Lauren, honey, wake up," she urged, shaking the woman's shoulders. "We need to go get my car so I can get to work."

The other woman grumbled and resisted, half-asleep, and sat up straight with a start when the words registered. "Damn," she swore, rubbing her eyes. "Forgot about that. Give me a minute." She fumbled around the room, snatching a random pair of jeans and T-shirt and strapped on a pair of sandals. "Okay, let's go," she said with a ferocious yawn.

When they reached the university campus, Angie maneuvered quickly with her cane to her car, barely letting Lauren stop her before she got in for a tight but quick embrace.

"Be careful." The words tickled her ear, and Angie took it for the tenderness that it was. She nodded, turned, and kissed the woman soundly, and got in her car.

In the rearview mirror, Angie watched her lover stare after her with a worried frown. The sight didn't make her feel any better, and she decided to focus on the road.

She didn't even make it out of the parking lot when her cell phone shattered her contemplative silence. She rummaged for it in her purse and flipped it open, by now recognizing Detective Key's number.

"Yeah, what's going on?" she demanded without a polite prelude.

"We've got a signal twelve at 8860 Aubrey Lane, Hilltop Vista Apartments complex. I'm pulling in right now. You'd better get here soon. Looks like this one is a bit higher on the profile list."

"What?" she slammed on the brakes right before she hit the main road and dug out her notepad. He repeated the address and she jotted it down. "What profile list?" she demanded, not understanding what the hell he was talking about.

"William Saunders lives at that address. He's the mayor's son."

Preying On Generosity

Chapter Ten

Angie pulled in to the parking lot at 8:58 a.m. Already, the media circus had begun—eight news vans with satellite antennas extended, twenty or so cameramen and women, television and print reporters mobbing the police officer in charge. A crowd of residents heading out to work had gathered, shocked by this early invasion of media and police. Everyone, it seemed, had known the second-story, two-bedroom apartment was occupied by the mayor's son.

She let loose a string of muttered cursing, barely below her breath, but she needn't have worried about being overheard. The excited babbling of the crowd, journalists, and police officers was enough to drown out most everything. She looked up at the sky and spotted three news choppers. This story, she knew, would be the lead on all media outlets. That is, if the medical examiner identified the body as indeed being William Saunders. There was little doubt that it wouldn't be so. But the reporter in Angie demanded she keep her presumptions at bay and not succumb to the sensationalistic excitement until Detective Key confirmed the signal twelve's identity. Even so, a death in the man's apartment was a big deal, and Angie dug out her cell phone and punched in her boss's number.

"Tom," she nearly shouted, still sitting in her parked car, the door open. "I won't be coming in for a few hours. The police have discovered another body. The detective called. It's at the mayor's son's apartment. There are a hell of a lot of reporters here already, a few choppers, a giant crowd." She rattled off the few details she knew quickly. "We need to get something online. A couple of paragraphs at least." She squinted across the parking lot, trying to decipher the apartment number on the door sectioned off by crime scene tape, and gasped. She could just make out two letters of a pink, spray-painted word on the front door—FA—but the view was obscured by an officer. "Hold on," she grunted and got out of the car, taking quick steps toward the crime scene tape, her cell phone held limply in her hand.

The officer scowled at her as she leaned closer, taking steps left and right to get a better view, but he kept changing positions to block the message. Angie groaned in frustration and opened her mouth to shout an order to get the hell out of the way, when the man was suddenly distracted by his police scanner. He frowned, turned, and went into the apartment.

Angie wasn't the only person to let out a startled yelp. The letter she'd been trying to spy was a capital G, and another word above it read, "Die."

"Um, Tom?" she whispered into the phone. "There's a word painted on that door that we can't print in the paper."

"What word?" She told him. "Sonofa... Tell me what it looks like." She described the message. Her other hand was aching to run nervously through her hair, but she couldn't let go of the cane or the phone. She heard the sound of a keyboard being pounded rapidly. "What apartment?" Her eyes found the numerals and she answered the question. She suddenly knew what the "more aggressive measures" referred to and had a good idea of what "indications" Detective Key had frequently alluded to. Tom continued to mutter profanities even as he typed up a few paragraphs to slap online.

"It's the Hilltop Vista Apartments complex," she answered another question and added, "Key said this is where William Saunders lives and there's a body inside. You should probably have someone do a search to confirm that Saunders lives there. I don't think Key would have called if he didn't think this was related to the other murders."

"Fine. I'm sending Gavin and Mandy as soon as they get here. Go get some good stuff. And we're still having our meeting when you get in." The line went dead and Angie sighed.

"You're welcome for the heads-up," she muttered and went back to her car for her notepad and pen. She shoved her purse under her front seat and stuffed the cell phone in the front pocket of her denim skirt.

After weeks of maneuvering on crutches, the new cast and cane provided much-needed comfort. She could walk quicker and less clumsily, make her way through the crowd without having to groan in frustration every five minutes for extra steps taken to avoid bumping people. It was, simply put, perfect timing for such a scene.

Television reporters were rattling off the few bits of information they had. The stations were going all out—interrupting regular programming to announce police had discovered a third victim of a crazed serial killer. She stopped to listen and could barely contain a snort of annoyance at the charged adjectives and sensational action verbs they used—"...the apartment management found the slain victim in a pool of blood with his throat slashed" How did they know that? She needed to find said management. "Detectives believe this homicide is related to two other grisly murders that happened in recent weeks...the serial killer is believed to prey on single gay men, ending their lives in a most terrifying way."

Even as Angie rounded up a few neighbors to interview, her eyes kept sliding toward the door with its painted message. The detective had said he doubted the "fire and brimstone shit." Could he have been mistaken? Could it really be that easy and sadistic?

And each time she started scribbling in her notepad, taking quotes from this neighbor or that, four or five cameras would instantly appear over her shoulder to catch whatever pieces she was extracting. Her sources would clam up, their accounts becoming increasingly stocky. A few choice words didn't make the preying television crews shy away, either. This, she knew, was a true circus. And nothing could be done to stop it.

The police also had not come out for interviews, much to everyone's frustration. But Mandy and Gavin had finally shown up—eyes wide and eager—and she'd delegated the task of describing color and interviewing neighbors with more than a little relief. She needed to find Detective Key. She had to. It was her job. And while Mandy went into the crowd and Gavin marched off toward the apartment complex's front office, Angie pulled out her cell phone and typed a quick text message, not wanting the other reporters to overhear any conversations.

She got a reply within a minute. "Get in car. Wait for call in two minutes. Will give prelim info only. More later."

Angie followed the instructions without complaint and sat in her car, waiting. She'd composed only a single paragraph in her notebook before her ringing phone cut through the silence. "You ready?" came the increasingly familiar question.

"Thirty-two-year-old male, throat severed to the bone, found in the living room, bound and gagged with silk scarves. Prelim estimation puts time of death two days prior. Bruising across most of the upper torso, appearing to have come from several beatings. ME says the vic is indeed William Saunders—his father's on the way. The vic was gay, apparently single. The door wasn't forced but bears scratch marks around the keyhole." He took a deep breath and Angie struggled to keep up. Her writing was atrocious, sloppy words abbreviated wherever possible, scrawled across two pages. Detective Key cleared his throat and shouted a direction to someone in the apartment. "Sorry about that. We've got too many damned people in here." He paused. "The vic's car is still in the lot. You saw the message on the door?" Angie nodded. "Quid pro quo, Angie. You gave me info, I'll give you stuff nobody else will have." He waited a beat before elaborating. "That message on the door was on the walls in the other two apartments. Usually there's more, but I'm guessing the killer didn't want to spend so much time marring the outside of the apartment in plain view. There are no such messages inside this apartment."

"What else does he usually write?"

"Can't tell you that," he said quickly, though she thought his voice sounded different—deflated and tired. "It's bad, bad stuff. You couldn't print it even if I told you. Lots of four-letter words."

"Any other evidence?"

"Yeah, but we're still working on this shit. I'll just say this one is much worse than the last, and I thought that one was bad... More aggressive measures indeed. I've got to go." And he hung up without another word.

Angie punched in Tom's desk number and relayed what she'd learned in rapid-fire, nearly breathless sentences.

"And TV doesn't have this?" he asked, sounding slightly suspicious. "I don't want to know why he gave you this and didn't give it to them. Probably has something to do with that thing he told me about yesterday. Damn it, Angie..." He grunted a few incoherent words. "I want...You stay there another hour, then get your ass back to the office."

Angie hung up and hit the steering wheel with her balled fist. She didn't want this any more than her boss did. It wasn't her fault, damn it. The thought of just quitting and walking away crossed her mind. She hit the steering wheel again and slumped back into her seat, shaking her head, closing her eyes to try and force a calm that wouldn't come.

She'd been so excited when Tom had rescued her from city council hell and given her a fresh start in crime reporting. It had been the happiest moment of her career. Now after the Carpenter fiasco and the latest developments on her current assignment, she couldn't help but think she should have chosen the education beat. No teachers and school board members would be sending her fucked-up packages. No school kids would cause her this much trouble. She'd been given the choice of picking crime or education, and the hard news junkie had pounced on the opportunity to cover bigger stories.

And now...she was in over her head. Continuing was unthinkable. And yet—Angie stared at the message on the door, thought about the victims, their families, and friends.

"Damn it all to hell," she muttered, struggling against the warring emotions of fear and social responsibility, of anger and determination. She got out of the car, walked around the building, and lighted a cigarette. The tendrils of smoke lingered in the stifling heat and the still, humid air. She took another drag, let it out slowly, and closed her eyes. She forced herself to remember the details of what happened the last time she'd followed a story that was too dangerous. The flood of images was jarring and drew an unpleasant shiver down her spine. Cold sweat broke out across her back and made her hands clammy.

A commotion of shouting voices broke through her melancholy reverie. She tossed the half-smoked cigarette on the ground, stomped it out, and headed back toward the crime scene. A large man she immediately recognized was at the yellow tape, shouting at the top of his lungs. Mayor Saunders was suffering a fit of hysterics, apparently not giving a damn that the cameras were recording his outburst. He was flinging words around in desperation, kept saying, "FBI," and made vows to find the murderer himself and kill him with his bare hands.

He was not the mayor at that moment—not the level-headed man Angie had interviewed hundreds of times before. He was a grief-stricken father who was lashing out with the only weapons he had—influence and rage.

Angie stared at him as he shook his fist at police officers, threatened the camera crews, screamed at the crowd to go mind their own damned business. His normally pristine suit was splattered with coffee stains—a sure sign that he'd gone into shock when investigators had called, had spilled his beverage, and not given a shit about it. He spotted Angie and stomped over to her, his eyes blazing fiercely, though tears shimmered at the surface.

"You," he pointed a shaking finger and grabbed her by the shoulders. "Tell me what the hell is going on, or I'll...I'll..." His voice broke and Angie tried not to squirm as his fingers dug in painfully. Camera crews jogged over, surrounding them. They, too, wanted to know what she knew.

She shook her head and whispered, "Not here, mayor, not like this." She tried to indicate with her eyes that they were surrounded by many cameras. His eyes followed hers and he gasped, momentarily sobering. He nodded silently before barking, "Get out of the way," while he shoved people aside and tugged Angie by the arm toward his Mercedes.

Angie got in despite a nagging voice in her head that told her she didn't have to do this. Sure, he was a source that had been most accommodating in the past, but what he was demanding was a police officer's job. And then another voice piped in and said she might be able to get some comments from him. Angie almost hated herself for that second voice.

Once the doors were securely locked and they were obscured from view behind dark-tinted windows in the backseat, he turned red eyes on her and demanded with furrowed brows that she tell him everything she knew.

"I'm sorry," she croaked, her voice straining, before she gave in under his fierce eyes and related the details she'd been given. He stared at her blankly for several seconds, trying to digest the information that his brain didn't want to let in, before letting out an agonized sob that racked his shoulders. His head fell into his hands and he cried for several minutes, the choking sounds interrupted only by wheezing gasps for air. Angie placed a trembling hand on the older man's shoulder and the sounds grew louder.

"Forgive me," he mumbled finally, voice hoarse and thick. "I shouldn't have…"

"It's okay," she whispered, her hand retreating and resting in her lap.

His muddy-brown eyes found hers, and he wiped his face roughly with the palm of his hand. He dropped his piercing gaze and touched the front of his shirt. "Spilled coffee all over myself when they called." Angie didn't need to ask who "they" were.

"My wife is a mess," he continued, his voice a touch steadier, though it wasn't the gruff strength he usually projected. She nodded, not knowing how to respond. She wanted desperately to get out of the car that had grown increasingly stuffy.

"I'm sorry," he said again, resting his head against the window. They sat in silence for several minutes. "Damned television crews will have a field day with that display, huh?"

"Maybe," she said, trying to sound uncertain, though she knew he was right. Her hands twisted nervously in her lap, and the second she realized it, she willed them to still.

"Aren't you going to ask me how I feel? Try to get a quote or something?"

The words were harsh and clipped, stronger even than the last sentence he'd uttered. Angie thought about the question, stared at his trembling fingers, and slowly shook her head. He gawked at her for a full thirty seconds before nodding. "Thank you," he said and reached across to open her door. The popping sound it made almost startled her. She pushed the door open farther and put her legs on the ground. He got out on the other side, shouted at a hovering cameraman to "get the hell out of the way," and slipped in the front seat. Angie barely had time to step aside and close the door before the engine roared to life. He hit the accelerator, peeling out of the parking space and away from the complex. The camera guy glared at Angie, made a snide comment, and stalked off toward the yellow tape.

She stared after the disappearing car, watched it take a corner rather sharply, and disappear down the street. She looked at the blank page of her notepad, slightly unbelieving, but nodded to herself approvingly. It had been the right thing to do, she thought, but decided not to mention the incident to her boss.

The office was unusually loud—televisions turned up to full volume as everyone stopped what they were doing to watch when the news interrupted regular programming to give updates. Angie was standing in front of her boss's office, about to enter the lion's den and brave whatever he was going to unleash, but a scene unfolding on television made her stop. There was the mayor, shouting at officers, threatening the crowd. She sighed and turned away. She didn't doubt that scene would be included in many follow-up reports.

When she'd come back to the office as instructed, her boss had brusquely ordered her to continue working on the story until exactly five o'clock. The decision had baffled her, considering his earlier demand to get her butt back so they could talk. She'd obeyed, a bit suspicious, and had cranked out a lengthy story about the incident. A news researcher had dug up tons of information on William Saunders at Tom's request.

She typed the story, then rewrote it, and had it posted online. Key called, gave her more information, and she rewrote it again. Mandy and Gavin came in, their shirts sweat-drenched from the long hours in the sun, and she worked in their notes. After six versions, she was loath to write it again and was almost happy when five o'clock rolled around. But the momentary feeling of relief quickly fled with each step toward Tom's office.

She turned the door knob and stepped in, her head held forcibly high, her shoulders rigid. Maybe he'd fire her. It was a possibility that had run through her head all day. Or maybe he'd take her off the crime beat. She didn't know what to expect and was shocked to find him seated in his chair, feet propped on the desk, a redheaded visitor sitting opposite. Detective Key rose to greet her with a firm handshake that nearly crushed her fingers.

"Sit, Angie," her boss said, his expression unreadable. A chair beside the detective's had been added. She placed her cane against the wall and sat with apprehension.

"So," her boss drawled, the carefully neutral look still intact. "I understand you've become a piece of the puzzle." He paused, his eyes shifting between Angie and the detective. "Jay claims you're not in any real danger." He snorted, a flash of incredulity flitting across his face before he tucked it back behind the mask. "If I understand this correctly, he wants you to continue with the investigative reporting and take into consideration any 'constructive feedback' the killer sends you." His feet slid off the desk abruptly and landed on the floor with a thud. He leaned forward in his chair, his fingers laced beneath his chin. "Is that about right?"

Detective Key nodded and glanced at Angie. She swallowed a lump in her throat. "That's what I gather."

"You realize this is about the most fool-hearted thing you could possibly do?" Tom snapped and dropped the mask, letting them both see his anger full force. Detective Key didn't so much as flinch and Angie followed his example, letting a grim smile curl her lips.

"Not to mention it's unethical—you've become part of the news! Again!" he continued undeterred, his voice rising. "I swear, Angie, you are the most infuriating, stubborn..." He stopped. "Didn't I just go through that the other day?" She nodded and dropped her gaze to her lap, where her treacherous fingers were twisting nervously again. It was a habit she was determined to break.

"If I may," Detective Key interrupted and cleared his voice. "There were no threats in that package. None. As I understand it, the last time Angie got in trouble, the affair was preceded by numerous threats on her life." He pinned Tom with his eyes until the other nodded, acknowledging the fact. "I've shown you photocopies of the messages. There's nothing to indicate he'd try an attack of any kind."

"But she's part of the fucking story!" Tom nearly yelled, shook his head, and took a deep breath to force back the rest of what he'd wanted to say.

"Yes, she is," the detective growled. "And I need it to stay that way in case the killer decides to send her any more messages because I need to get under his skin. And this is a good way to start." He stood up and began pacing the tiny office. "Besides, if you thought you'd discovered someone who appreciated your craft and just needed a few pointers on how to better write about it, only for that person to walk away the first time you offered some constructive help, wouldn't that piss you off? Wouldn't it disappoint the hell out of you?" He stopped his pacing and let the questions linger in the air unanswered, giving them more weight.

"I don't want him getting pissed off," he said flatly and took his seat.

A tinge of fear muddled Angie's thoughts as she thought of the psychopath becoming angry with her. But only a second or two passed before the fear flip-flopped into anger.

"I'm not going to let some psycho dictate how I write my stories," she spat.

"See?" Tom pointed at her and let out a barking laugh. "She's going to do whatever the hell she wants and get herself in trouble again."

They fell silent. Tom's foot began tapping on the floor, his fingers drumming on the desk. His eyes pinned first Detective Key, then Angie. He sighed, letting the breath out slowly through gritted teeth.

"I could fire you," he said, and Angie had a sense of déjà vu. It was the very same threat he'd made during her last investigation when she'd refused to drop it. She felt incredibly tired all of the sudden and wanted nothing more than to go home to Lauren and lie in her arms.

"Then do it," she said wearily, getting to her feet. "I didn't want this, you know. I didn't ask for it. I didn't ask for it last time, either." She let the exhaustion show in her eyes, allowed her shoulders to sag slightly, dropping the defiance. "I just want to do my job, Tom. And this plan of his is crazy. But I can't help but think of those victims and wish there was something I could do to make the killings stop. And if he really thinks this will help, my conscience won't let me get away with doing nothing." She sighed and grabbed her cane.

"Wait," her boss said and sighed exasperatedly. She turned and faced him, the cane holding her tired legs up.

Tom got up and rounded the desk. "This goes no farther than this room," he demanded. "You won't tell anyone." He grabbed the detective's arm to punctuate his point. "We will consider—consider only—what this crazy-ass person has sent. We will not be bullied by you or him or anybody else. I will hold you personally responsible for Angie's safety. If a single hair on her body is harmed, I'll have this company sue your ass. You will be broke forever. Got it?"

Detective Key shrugged out of Tom's grasp and took a step back, a scowl curling his lips dangerously. But slowly, he nodded. "She'll have protection. The killer may not send her anything else. But if he does, we'll examine every square inch with a microscope. Her efforts will be worth it, I swear."

"What kind of protection?" Tom demanded, his shoulders rigid, hands clenched.

"The FBI is involved—seems they've decided we're not working fast enough," he growled. "She'll have a tail at all times."

Tom glared at the man for several seconds and finally dropped his eyes, nodding. He waved them away dismissively, but before Angie could get her hand on the door, he said, "Angie, if this blows up in my face like last time, if it ends badly, I'll have to terminate your employment. And, Jay, at the first sign of any real danger, I'm yanking her off this assignment. Period. I want copies of anything the guy might send, and I'll be the one to determine how dangerous it is, not you."

A cold spot grew in Angie's stomach, but she squared her shoulders and nodded her understanding before opening the door and stepping back into the busy newsroom. The detective put a hand on her shoulder and said, "Thank you. I need to get back to the scene," before showing himself out.

Angie went back to her desk with heavy-weighted feet and plopped down in her chair. She was about to shut down her computer and get the hell out of there when she saw the blinking red light on her office phone that indicated she had a message. Her heart leapt and she closed her eyes while punching in her code to retrieve it.

"Angie, this is Earl Saunders." Her eyes snapped open and she fumbled for her notepad. A relieved sigh escaped her lips. It was just the mayor. "I was calling to give you some comments but guess you're busy..."

She jotted the message down and called the man on his cell. He answered on the third ring and proceeded to talk about the murder in a steady voice that belied his emotional outrage. She doubted that he'd called anybody else. Doing the right thing, she realized, does bring rewards on occasion. Even if they are few and far between.

"Girl, you look like you're vying for a part in a movie about the undead."

"Shut up and get me a drink." Angie tried to snarl, but a giggle escaped instead. She flopped down on Jimmy's couch unceremoniously and rested her cast on his coffee table while he puttered around in the kitchen.

When she'd left the office, she hadn't felt like heading home quite yet. Lauren would likely be knee-deep in books and papers, typing away on a twenty-page essay she was supposed to hand in the following afternoon. And showing up on Jimmy's doorstep unannounced had struck her as the perfect solution. She needed a good laugh, at any rate.

"So how was work?" he ventured, handing her a cool glass filled with some kind of alcoholic pink concoction. She studied the drink and raised an eyebrow, wondering if it was another one of his experiments. He'd been playing bartender for the past couple of months and some of his drinks were decidedly…interesting.

"It's safe, I swear," he said in mock offense, though his brown eyes sparkled mischievously. "Go on, try it."

She raised the glass to her lips and wrinkled her nose in anticipation. A tropical blend of flavors exploded on her tongue and slid down her throat warmly, soothingly, and her closed eyes opened in surprised appreciation.

"It's a good one, then?" he asked, literally bouncing in his heels as he scanned her expression with utmost concentration.

"Yeah, this one is safe. What's it called?"

"Don't know yet. I'm thinking something very girly, like sunshine or delight or something."

"Or something." She giggled at his annoyed expression and took another sip. She thought she tasted kiwi but couldn't be sure.

"Tell me about your day. I want to know why my little reporter looks like she was attacked by rabid dogs—or maybe it's a fashion statement."

"First undead and now rabid dogs? I don't look like…"

He shushed her with his finger and disappeared for a few seconds down the hallway, coming back with a handheld mirror.

She took it with a scowl and held it up to see what the hell he was talking about. The second she caught sight of herself, she realized he wasn't too far off the mark.

Her cheeks and forehead were sticky with dried, cold sweat, the patches under her eyes darkening again. Her hair was flat in some places and sticking straight up in others—a sure sign of her hands running through it nervously for hours. She looked tired or sickly or both. She sighed and handed it back.

Jimmy sat on the couch and put a hand on her shoulder. He was waiting for an explanation while she chewed her lower lip.

"I'm tired and stressed out," she finally said and sighed. "Work's been crazy."

"So I hear," he drawled, and lighted two cigarettes, handing her one.

Angie took a drag and let the smoke out slowly. "Lauren?" He nodded, looked like he was about to say something, then shut his mouth. "I know, I know," Angie interjected quickly before he could change his mind. "I've learned my lesson. But so has she. We were both out of line and we realize that. As for me, I've come to the decision that I'm not dropping this investigation, nor am I going to discourage any further contact from the killer, as per the detective's wishes."

Silence. Jimmy took a long drag and exhaled sharply. His lower lip twitched twice, three times, so that the corner drew down slightly as though he was fighting a frown. Then a grin split his face abruptly.

"So, Angie Mitchell—investigative reporter extraordinaire—is going to expose the dastardly deeds of this madman, solve the mystery with her cunning intellect, and save the day for queer thirty-year-olds everywhere!" His voice was high and melodramatic, like a queen radio announcer. He slapped his hand on his knee so that she jumped and continued with, "She will use her connection with the madman to lure him into a trap. Having learned from past mistakes, she will survive unscathed in her endeavor." He jumped out of his seat and ignoring her scowl, gestured wildly with his hands while saying, "And damned the man who dares say that none of these deeds is her job or duty, for Angie Mitchell is a woman of superior foolhardiness."

He bowed and made to resume his seat but was slapped

halfway down. He let out a rather loud squeal, surprising himself, and clapped a hand over his mouth, trying to stay earnest and not succumb to a fit of laughter. But Angie started laughing, and he couldn't keep the giggles at bay. Each egged on by the other, they were soon laughing hysterically until Angie had tears in her eyes.

"I am not foolhardy," she spluttered, still laughing.

"Hell yes, you are," he shot back, the giggles subsiding slowly.

She crossed her arms in defiance, but the image she was trying to project was ruined by her laughter-shaken shoulders. The frown also refused to stay in place, the corners of her lips twitching rebelliously.

"You've obviously rationalized the whole thing in your head somehow, but when you strip away the justifications, you've got to realize you're putting yourself in a bit of danger," he said after seconds of back-and-forth glowering attempts. He raised a hand to cut off her objection. "I'm just saying it as it is, Angie." He waited a beat. "But that doesn't mean I'm going to lecture you or tell you to stop. I'm just not going to let you get away with thinking this is some normal, noble thing you're doing. So cut the crap. No more 'social responsibility' blah-blah-blah bullshit. Got it?"

She stared at him for several seconds and finally nodded, dropping her eyes guiltily, and took another sip of his unnamed concoction.

"Okay," he drew the word out importantly. "Now how about we talk about more interesting things? Not that your stubborn insistence to get yourself in trouble is not interesting enough, but we can't go on and on about that forever. Besides, I believe we are way overdue on a shopping trip you'd promised months ago." At her blank look, he wiggled his eyebrows suggestively. "Shopping trip. Toys. In Dallas. Come on!"

Realization dawned and her eyes widened, red blotches creeping up her neck and painting her cheeks.

"Now that's better—a little red to get rid of that undead look." Jimmy laughed and successfully escaped her swiping hand, dodging what surely would have been a nice, hard cuff in the shoulder. He chuckled all the way to the car and down the street.

Chapter Eleven

T he next two hours were decidedly...interesting.
Angie had been expecting a trip to a nice, relatively
safe store like Condom Sense. But no—Jimmy had
taken her to a much darker, more exotic place called After
Midnight, several blocks away from gay Dallas's Cedar Springs
area. She never would have found it on her own, and even if she'd
somehow managed to stumble across the store's location, she
would have dismissed it as an abandoned warehouse.

The nondescript building sat squarely, unobtrusively between
two other warehouses, with a tiny sign on a door that looked like
an employees-only entrance reading, "After Midnight—yes, we're
open," in red, hand-painted letters on a black background. Only
one other lonely car sat in the parking lot. She'd looked at Jimmy,
a blond eyebrow raised skeptically, but he'd only smirked.

He pushed a button on a callbox and waited patiently for a
response.

"Who's there?" a female voice called out.

Jimmy replied, "Your lover from three years past."

Angie shot him a look of bewilderment, but the question she
wanted to ask was interrupted by a buzzing sound. Jimmy opened
the door and ushered her inside, a quickly interjected, "password,"
stilling her curiosity.

It looked like a goth club—black velvet drapes covering the
walls of a long hallway, plush, velvet carpet underfoot. Jimmy led
Angie to a door that bore an intricate painting of a beautiful, dark-
haired man standing proudly atop a cliff. He was nude, save a
leather contraption that covered his groin—a sight that made
Angie blush furiously. She was glad for the dim lighting and

averted her eyes. What the hell kind of place was this, anyway?

On the other side of the door, Jimmy was greeted by an extraordinarily tall woman whose pale hips and breasts were covered in the tiniest scraps of leather, a long, sheer dress covering her from shoulders to knees. It was impossible to judge her age. She had a strange, timeless beauty about her.

Jimmy took her outstretched hand and brushed a kiss along her knuckles.

"James, it's been a while since I've seen you here. I thought you'd forgotten about me." Her smoky, low voice was pleasant and warm. Jimmy laughed lightly, shaking his head ever so slightly, not breaking eye contact.

"How could I forget you, Madam Midnight? I've merely been busy." He paused, took a step aside, and folded his hand around Angie's, drawing her forward. "I want you to meet my dear friend, Angie. She has little to no experience in...the finer art of pleasure...so go easy on her. But I hear she's a quick study." He wiggled his eyebrows and winked at Angie, whose blush deepened. "And I think her lover would be most appreciative of your services."

The madam took Angie's other hand and gave an encouraging squeeze. "Of course, James. It gives me great pleasure to be the one to educate such a beautiful woman." She graced Angie with a lingering, suggestive smile and made her involuntarily shiver as the madam brushed her thumb across her knuckles. "Come with me, dear, and I'll introduce you to a great many things."

The trio made their way through a heavy oak door decorated in cast iron, one that looked like it belonged in a castle. The room they entered appeared to be built of stone, but Angie was sure the look was fake—it couldn't be real, they were in a warehouse after all. Lit torches illuminated the room, flickering light bouncing across shiny black leather and metal objects hanging from the walls.

"What do you hope to accomplish with your visit here?" the madam asked, her eyes lingering on Angie appraisingly.

Angie swallowed, her eyes trying to make sense of the various objects on the wall. She didn't have the faintest clue what half of them were, though she recognized a few items that looked like restraining tools, a few whips, and one table clearly displayed an assortment of handcuffs. She cleared her throat, suddenly entirely too uncomfortable, not knowing how to answer the question, the urge to bolt and curse at Jimmy nearly overwhelming.

The other woman laughed—a note of amusement mingled with understanding.

"Come here, take a seat," she instructed, indicating a black leather sofa against the left wall. Angie hesitated for a moment, then sat as instructed. Jimmy took a seat next to her, his lips twitching with the effort to conceal a smirk. Her mind raced for an excuse to leave in the following silence, then concentrated on figuring out a way to get him back. The silence stretched, and she realized she'd have to at least try to answer the question.

"Er...I don't know," she muttered uncomfortably. "I mean...Can you repeat the question?" It was a cop-out, she knew, but couldn't figure out a way to explain. She cleared her throat again and dropped her eyes to her lap.

Madam Midnight knelt and placed her hands on Angie's knees. "Tell me how you like it," she ordered in a tone that clearly wouldn't tolerate a refusal. Angie looked at Jimmy pointedly, not entirely comfortable with the idea of answering in front of him. He took the hint and quietly left the room. The door clicked shut, cutting through the silence. Angie looked into the woman's eyes and fought her inhibitions back.

"A little rough," she answered clearly, "but not too rough. I've never...tried anything like this before. I don't know what to ask for. I don't know how to tell Lauren that it's okay." The words were tumbling out unchecked. She took a deep breath. "She does get forceful sometimes, usually when we're both emotionally wound up."

"Do you want to be topped, or do you want to top her?"

Now Angie was not so naïve as to misunderstand the question, and the visions it drew forth were both a little frightening and yet darkly appealing. She shuddered, her pupils dilating in automatic response. She licked her upper lip unconsciously. Her breath hitched and an unbidden, low laugh escaped her lips. "Both," she whispered finally.

Madam Midnight nodded and took sauntering steps along the wall, her knee-high black leather boots clicking on the floor as she took down this piece and that, examining it, then put it back.

Every few minutes, she'd ask a question—"Do you enjoy deep penetration?" or "How secure is your lover in bed?"—before replacing an object on the wall. With each passing minute, Angie's reservations slipped away and she started describing Lauren's lovemaking with increasing animation. It was freeing for the woman who'd generally kept tight wraps on her love life, not even allowing herself to speak about it in detail with her best friend. At some point, she realized that she'd been longing to discuss the sex with someone more experienced, someone who'd been there and could appreciate her craving to learn more.

The madam answered questions with a lilt of amusement in her voice, gave Angie ideas she'd never dreamed of. And when the madam disappeared from the room for a few minutes to "retrieve a few things," Angie couldn't help but wait in eager anticipation. Her eyes grew wide at the assortment the woman brought back, her hands gliding over the smooth black leather and latex appreciatively. The handcrafted pieces were outrageously expensive, but by the time the prices were revealed, her head was full of visions that outweighed the cost. She handed over her credit card without hesitation, blushing pleasantly at the look of approval in the madam's eyes.

She let herself be led outside, where Jimmy was waiting patiently, smoking a cigarette, an excited sparkle in his eyes. He had his own black bag of goodies in his hand. They walked silently to the car and got in before each rifled through the other's bag giddily.

Angie's fingers trailed across silky smoothness and she pulled out a lilac scarf, the faint throbbing between her legs ending abruptly. She dropped it on the floorboard, her mouth open in silent shock.

A cool breeze drifted along Angie's skin and she sighed, relishing the pleasant feeling of the temporary reprieve from the otherwise humid Texas summer. A hand on her shoulder applied pressure in a soothing manner and her head dropped to her chest, a groan escaping her lips. She was sitting on a bench with Jimmy outside the police station in downtown Fort Worth, waiting for Detective Key to come back with a verdict.

It could be any old scarf. It could be completely unrelated. It could… She was guiltily praying for a connection so the police might have a decent lead. But it would be such a bizarre coincidence that she tried to quell the rising hope that had filled her chest during the drive from Dallas to Fort Worth.

Jimmy had tried to dissuade her theory with his typical jokes and sincere concern. He also didn't want to get his acquaintance in any trouble. After Midnight, he'd tried to explain, wasn't just a store where one might buy sex toys and exotic costumes. He'd admitted that after midnight, the place was more like an orgy center, and trusted customers could buy other types of services that he didn't exactly elaborate on but that Angie's imagination readily supplied.

In the end, though, he reluctantly agreed that it was worth checking out. He'd called Madam Midnight on his cell phone, giving her fair warning just in case. She'd been most displeased and had harshly revoked his privilege to visit. He'd informed Angie with more than a touch of bitterness, hoping the madam would forgive him soon.

The click of a lighter announced the detective's presence and Angie reluctantly dragged her eyes to meet his. "So?" she asked with a touch of impatience. They'd been waiting for two hours.

"Our lab tech says it's the same material, exact shade of color, and shape." He took a long drag and released the smoke quickly. "There's also a tiny imprinted logo in one corner, which matches the ones we found on the other scarves. We'd originally thought 'A.M.' was the killer's initials, like he was taunting us." His voice was bright and clear, the deflated fatigue erased. "I called the owner of After Midnight. I had to threaten to inform Dallas police of what I suspect are shady activities going on in that place—not that'd I'd know any such thing, and I don't even want to know why the two of you were there—and she agreed to let me in." He took another drag and chuckled. "Gave me some ridiculous password and told me I'd better be 'selectively blind.' I'm about to head out there."

His eyes lingered on Angie and she thought she saw a question there but chose to ignore it. He shrugged at her silence and turned to leave. "Thanks for the tip, Angie," he tossed over his shoulder. "And don't worry about your friend, Jimmy. I'm sure my blindness will take hold long enough to not get her in any trouble."

He put his cigarette out on the pavement and strode down the street with quick, anticipatory steps, disappearing around a corner without so much as a glance back.

Jimmy grumbled about his scarf being admitted into evidence, and Angie's eyes narrowed. She grabbed his arm and rounded on him.

"Why would you buy such a thing at a time like this? It's completely distasteful considering what's been in the news."

He shrugged out of her grasp and shot her an angry look. "I've been using scarves for years. It's not my fault I happen to shop at the same place as that psychopath. And how dare you judge me."

She took a step back, her narrowed eyes softening with regret, though no immediate apology shot to her lips. The thought that the detective may have thoroughly questioned him about the same thing came suddenly to mind, an image of her friend's flustered face floating to the surface. Detective Key had asked her to wait at his desk for a few moments and had led Jimmy into a conference room. She'd thought the detective wanted to interview Jimmy about the madam and her establishment because he'd clearly have better information.

"Did he accuse you?" she whispered and read the answer on his face. "I'm sorry for being rude. I'm sure he doesn't really think you have anything to do with the murders. But he has to explore every possibility. Don't worry about it."

Her friend nodded, though it was clear he didn't quite believe her. The drive back to his apartment was wrought with tension. She was sorry to leave him but respected his desire to be alone. She felt like calling the detective and chewing him out. It didn't matter that he was just doing his job. It took all her willpower to resist the temptation.

It was late when she trudged up the stairs and unlocked her door, dumping her black bag and purse carelessly on the floor. She sighed into the silence and wandered into the kitchen, forcing herself to push aside thoughts of the investigation, the most recent murder, and the new link she'd inadvertently discovered. She wondered what the detective was learning at that very moment and had to cut the thought short.

She rifled through her pantry, frowning at the sorely understocked shelves. After several minutes of debating whether making noodles with ketchup constituted a real meal, she gave up and ordered takeout from her favorite Chinese restaurant, vowing to visit the grocery store after dinner. She and Lauren, it seemed, had eaten most everything in the house, and she had a bad craving for snack foods and ice cream.

Nearly an hour of watching CNN later, she answered the door with a scowl, wondering what the hell the holdup had been. Thrusting a twenty-dollar bill in the deliveryman's direction, she snatched the bag from his hands and quickly shut the door. Grumbling, she sat back in front of the television and satisfied her rumbling stomach with orange chicken and fried rice.

Between bites of an egg roll, she wondered how her lover was doing. She resisted the urge to call. Surely, Lauren was still studying. Her best friend, Leslie, was in a similarly unavailable state—patching together a dissertation for her art history doctorate. Angie hadn't seen her in weeks and wondered if her friend had gotten lost in the dusty aisles of the university's library.

She sighed and stuffed a piece of chicken in her mouth, eyes glazing slightly as she stared at the television without interest. It was times like these when she most missed running. A good, hard trek along Green Oaks Boulevard would do her some good. Her eyes fell on her new cast and she groaned in frustration. She'd be wearing the damned thing for another four or five weeks, only to be replaced by a smaller brace. And then…who knows if she'd be able to run again. Ever. Anger bubbled up, as it did so frequently these days, and she thought again about the meeting she'd be having the next week with her lawyer.

No amount of money would satisfy the dark monster within that wanted real revenge. But it would hurt Henry nonetheless, which is why she'd agreed to file a civil suit to begin with. Her lawyer had only wanted to wait this long so she might recover a little, get settled back in to her life before undergoing the long and likely emotionally draining process of suing the twisted man.

The thought that she'd have to testify soon in his criminal case shot through her head, and she lost her appetite. She carefully put the fork in the Styrofoam container she'd been eating from and leaned back into the couch, deep creases lining her forehead.

She'd signed sworn statements. She'd turned in photocopies of all her notes from the Carpenter/Henry reporting. But it wasn't enough. The detectives needed her to describe the cold-hearted way in which Henry had shot off Carpenter's head, how he'd tried to set her up for the murder, and how he'd physically abused her before she could escape. Angie felt the familiar cold clenching in her full stomach, and she momentarily felt sick.

Slowly, she opened her eyes and let the room come back into focus. She decided then and there that she couldn't let the two men run her life forever. She'd get the help she'd thus far refused. The nightmares had to stop. The icy feeling that spread in her gut every time she thought about it had to stop. She'd let the mess go on long enough. And there's no shame in needing help, right? Right.

She grunted at herself in acknowledgment and stood up. She couldn't very well go find a counselor right that minute. But she felt like she had to do something.

Her leg. She could force it to heal, damn it. She'd done the exercises. It could handle something a little tougher.

Balancing carefully on her good leg, she tentatively put some weight on the other leg and hissed as pain shot up to her hip. Gritting her teeth, she leaned a little heavier on the encased limb and grunted at the lightning heat that made her upper thigh quiver. She let up the weight, took a deep breath, and repeated the exercise, sweat beading on her forehead.

She was going to recover, damn it, and to hell with what anyone else said to the contrary. She had to.

Half an hour later, she gave up the effort and raked a hand through hair damp from the exertion. The last few times, she'd put a decent amount of weight on the leg and it didn't hurt as much as the first time, though she suspected the limb may have simply gone numb. She grabbed her cane and delivered the food to her refrigerator. A glance at the clock told her it was ten o'clock. Definitely not too late to make a trip to the grocery store. She popped a couple of over-the-counter painkillers and took deliberate care to take slow, easy steps after pushing herself so hard, but made it safely down the stairs and into her car.

When she turned the ignition, an old favorite song came on the radio and she pumped up the volume, singing the lyrics in carefree abandon.

It took seven grueling trips to get the damned groceries up to Angie's apartment since she could really only carry two bags or so at once, her other hand occupied by maneuvering the cane. And by the time she'd locked the front door, breathing heavily, she didn't really give a crap whether the milk went sour in its bag on the floor. She tried to argue that the twenty dollars she'd spent on items that definitely needed refrigerating and the additional thirty dollars on items that must be stashed in the freezer wasn't really worth the effort of straining herself further. But after a few minutes of leaning against the wall, glaring at the pile of food, she reluctantly decided that she'd best put it all away. She muttered things like, "need a damned personal shopper," and, "bribe Jimmy to carry my shit."

Grateful that the task was finally completed, Angie was about to flop down on the couch when a flickering light down the dark hallway caught her attention. A shiver of fear ripped through her chest and she dropped the phone she was carrying, with which she'd intended to call Lauren despite her earlier decision not to.

Angie held her breath, her heart pounding, and sneaked down the hallway. She tried to, anyway, but it's difficult in a cast. Her back flat against the wall, she reached a trembling hand around the corner and flipped the switch, bathing the room in bright light.

A low chuckle nearly buckled her knees, but only a second later, she realized she recognized that particular laugh and abandoned the safe spot against the wall.

She was ready to deliver a heated, "You nearly scared the shit out of me!" But her mouth went dry instead when her eyes fell on the bed.

Lauren was sprawled across the sheets on her stomach, her face propped up on interlaced fingers with a smoldering look in her eyes, a feral grin curling red-painted lips. A thin, cream satin sheet covered her from the hips down, but her strong back was bare. She'd taken the care of lighting a dozen candles, interspersing them across the room.

"Turn off the light," she ordered, her voice husky and low.

Angie flicked the switch without looking, unable to tear her eyes away from the beautiful woman waiting in her bed. It suddenly occurred to her that she'd dumped the groceries in the exact spot where she'd disposed of the black bag earlier. She swallowed a lump in her throat, heat rising to her cheeks. She opened her mouth to say something, realized the words were lodged firmly in her throat, and closed it, rubbing a hand along the back of her neck instead.

She felt like she couldn't move, keeping eye contact with Lauren. Lauren's smile widened and she stretched out a hand, beckoning. Angie willed her legs to work and took the offered hand that drew her closer to the edge of the bed.

"It seems, my dear, that you have some interesting plans," Lauren drawled, rubbing her thumb over her knuckles. She drew the hand closer to her red mouth and a moan rose from deep in Angie's throat when she felt those soft lips wrap around her index finger, teeth lightly grazing its surface. "The black bag proved too much temptation for my curiosity. I hope you don't mind," Lauren said when she released the finger.

Angie shook her head slowly and licked her dry lips, wondering what her lover had done with the things she'd bought. Her blush deepened, creeping down her neck and along her chest. She was simultaneously grateful Lauren had apparently decided to take the lead and mildly annoyed that was the case, confusing her.

Lauren pushed herself up with one swift move so that the sheet fell away and she was kneeling in front of Angie, firm, full breasts at eye level. Angie ached to lean forward and wrap her lips around a tempting dark nipple, but her eyes fell lower and she took in a sharp breath, heat warming her instantly. There it was—that leather-strapped, rubber-tipped contraption that had cost her a fortune. She reached out and touched the length of the strap-on with trembling fingers, her eyes meeting those dark orbs she loved so much, a touch of fear running along her spine.

Lauren wrapped strong arms around her shoulders and pulled her in for a tender embrace. Angie felt the length hard against her stomach and sagged into her lover's arms. Hands ran along her back in soothing, sensual movements, lips nuzzling her neck softly.

"Shh, it's okay," Lauren whispered, hot breath tickling her ear. She shivered and ran her hands along the length of the taller woman's back until they reached the leather strap. She traced it slowly, a tiny whimper escaping her lips.

Lauren's hands retreated and wedged between them, infinitely more patient with the blouse's buttons than she had been the last time. Angie leaned back, allowing her better access, watching the long-tapered fingers with utter fascination as they peeled away the blouse, dropping it to the floor, before wandering lower to work open her denim skirt. Her breath hitched at the sound of a zipper opening. Her skirt fell to the floor and she carefully stepped out of it, eager for her lover to continue. Goose bumps were marching along her arms and legs in anticipation, her steadiness faltering under the fluttering fingers removing her panties and bra.

Lauren slid off the bed and picked Angie up, placing her carefully on the bed before crawling on top of her, letting her weight down slowly. She grabbed Angie's wrists and held them over her head with one hand, her other hand dipping along the curves and shallows of Angie's body with practiced ease, kneading the creamy breasts, rolling a nipple between index finger and thumb. Her tongue swirled in Angie's ear. Her teeth biting her earlobe gently, teasingly, until she drew out a frustrated groan.

Her eyes twinkled with mischief, and Angie tried to focus on them, tried to keep contact even when the roving hand slid down the length of their intertwined bodies and found her slick opening. She cried out when the fingers lingered there, refusing to enter, and Lauren's husky laugh filled the room, ringing in her ears.

Those red lips lowered to Angie's, barely touching, agonizingly soft, lingering for long seconds before crushing their faces together while fingers slid inside her in a singularly exquisite moment of relief. Angie groaned into her lover's mouth, thrusting her hips upward, struggling for more and unable to voice her demands.

Lauren's lips retreated and she bit Angie's neck almost savagely, not nearly enough to draw blood, but certainly harder than she'd ever dared before. Angie's hips momentarily ceased their rocking and she whimpered under the assault, struggling against the strong grip on the hand confining her wrists. The sharp pain mingled with dark pleasure and her half-lidded eyes slid shut.

Suddenly, Lauren was gone and Angie cried out in protest when she felt the fingers inside her retreat and disappear. She opened her eyes and sat bolt-upright, clutching at Lauren, who laughed dangerously just out of reach. The taller woman leapt forward and pushed Angie's shoulders back roughly until her back hit the mattress.

"Turn over," she growled and Angie's eyes went wide at the tone, but she swallowed hard and obeyed, settling on her stomach. Her lover's hands gripped her upper thighs tightly and spread her legs apart before a long tongue slid between the lips of her swollen center. Angie inhaled sharply, the breath coming out with a hiss, her hands clenching and unclenching fistfuls of sheets.

The tongue snaked through her folds, up along her crack, and followed the path of her spine before centering on the back of her neck where teeth sunk in unexpectedly. She felt the length of her lover's body settle over her and she moaned, desperately needing that hard object pressing against her to slip inside.

"You have to ask for it, Angie," Lauren growled, nibbling along her neck until she found an earlobe to wrap her lips around.

Angie shuddered and struggled, her mouth moving without sound. "Please," she finally managed in a hoarse whisper, but the other woman only blew hot breath in her ear.

"Please what?"

She groaned in frustration and her hands balled into fists. She cleared her throat and licked her lips, "Please, inside, now."

"You want this?" Lauren whispered, taking hold of the strap-on with one hand and running it teasingly along Angie's center.

She moaned and nodded, a strangled, "Yes, yes, damn it," rising to the surface in high-pitched desperation.

Finally, she felt the tip pushing into her, wedging its way deep inside her, filling up the empty space with aggravating slowness until it would go no farther and she let out a muffled cry, half-silenced by her mouth pressed against the mattress. Her lover wriggled her hips to adjust her position, forcing a shudder from Angie's oversensitized body. Lauren slid in and out of her in a few tentative thrusts, and receiving muffled shouts of encouragement, began to pick up speed.

Angie felt it bump her cervix repeatedly and she moaned at the sharp pain that brought torturous pleasure. Her lover's hands dug into her shoulders rhythmically, matching the rapid in-out rhythm that set her body ablaze. Her clit rubbed against the satiny sheets with each thrust and she could hardly catch a breath deep enough before it was expelled. Spots danced before her eyes even as she alternately cried a savage version of her lover's name and desperate pleas to go faster and harder.

She felt Lauren's sweat trickle down her sides and along her thighs—the movements like a blur of speed. Angie's inner muscles quivered, tightening, and she let out a strangled groan, her fingers and toes curling for the precious infinite seconds she hung in suspense before the orgasm crashed through her. She went completely limp.

A low chuckle next to her ear brought her back to the bedroom that smelled of Lauren's musky lavender and sex. Hands ran soothingly along her back and legs in tender caresses, and Lauren wiggled her hips experimentally, apparently delighting in the shiver it caused. Angie mumbled, "Mmm, no, stop it."

Minutes passed slowly as they waited for their breathing to slow before Lauren finally withdrew and removed the leather straps. Red marks crisscrossed along her hips and lower abs. Angie rolled over and traced the lines lazily, a lopsided grin plastered across her face. With her hands, Angie started to wander into sensitive territory and Angie's eyes filled with determination. She stretched her hand out until her fingers touched leather and she pulled it close.

"Help me put this on," she demanded, amused by the wide eyes that met her own.

The lovers sat side by side on Angie's balcony, enjoying the crisp breeze that ruffled their hair. Raindrops prattled along the railing while they watched the lightning flash across the sky. A deep rumbling filled the air, and Angie sighed contentedly. It was three o'clock in the morning and they should have been in bed, but they'd spent the last several hours playing with her new toys. She made a mental note to thank Madam Midnight in person soon and to beg for her forgiveness for the earlier transgression of her trust.

Angie's hands were wrapped around a warm cup of jasmine tea, and she took a soothing sip, enjoying the warmth that trickled down her throat. She didn't care about the way she'd feel the next day—unfocused and tired. Being able to sit next to her lover in companionable silence, watching the beautiful thunderstorm, was worth it.

"Jimmy told me about the scarf," Lauren said, and Angie's head turned to regard her. She was pleased to find the woman utterly relaxed. Lauren turned to meet her eyes and a smirk shot across her lips. "That's how I knew what you'd been up to." She paused and turned her eyes back to the horizon. "I was done studying anyway. I just wanted to see you, maybe tease you a little, but...the bag was so tempting I couldn't stop myself." Her rich laughter reverberated along Angie's flushed skin. "What a wonderful surprise it was."

"Yeah," Angie murmured, fighting a matching smirk, the corners of her mouth twitching. "I'm glad you...um...approve." She giggled in spite of herself and dropped her eyes to her tea, deciding to take a sip to kill the giggles.

"I definitely approve." Lauren flashed her a grin and nipped at her ear, causing Angie to splutter and dribble tea down her chin. They laughed softly.

"Look," Lauren broke through silence that followed. "I've been thinking." She paused, raking a hand through her disheveled hair, snorting when she ran into several tangles. "I don't want to be the overbearing girlfriend. It's just not me, you know? I just want you to know that I'm going to chill out about the investigation." She turned and cupped Angie's face. "I care about you so much and, well, I don't want to push you away."

She took a deep breath and let it out slowly. Angie searched those dark eyes that looked black by moonlight. "The concerns you've expressed—you have a point and believe me, I'm taking it seriously. It's just something I've got to do. Even if there are risks."

"Okay," Lauren said and graced her with a tender smile. "Talk to me if you need to, though. I'm not as stupid as I look, you know. I might have some insight to offer. After all, I am 'old.' Doesn't wisdom come with that?"

Angie snorted and giggled at the same time, forcing a cough from her throat. She shook her head and laughed until the other woman joined in. And just like that, it was as if the last two days' confusion and troubles had been erased. They sealed the refound easiness of their relationship with a slow, exploratory kiss that made Angie's heart swell with joy.

Chapter Twelve

Angie was barely able to keep up with the following week's insanity. First, there'd been the Saunders funeral to attend and write about. The mayor had additionally given her several exclusive interviews on the FBI's involvement and a police task force that had been assigned to aid them in finding the "bastard who killed my son."

She'd written a story about the Fort Worth gay community's efforts to help warn people who didn't keep up with the news— their telltale fliers plastered on every bar wall and venue gay men might visit. It was a small article, but Angie was glad to get it in the paper. North Texans may not be as conservative as the rest of the state—Dallas County in particular was more blue than red— but gay articles were still difficult to get past upper management who worried about infuriating the good ol' boy reader base in Fort Worth and the rest of Tarrant County. Murders are different. You can't really get around covering them. The side stories were the problem.

On top of that, there was of course the issue of the mayor having a gay son to begin with. It was a family secret that could have become a scandal under any other circumstances, but the right-wing groups were surprisingly quiet for the first couple of days after William Saunders' death, likely out of respect for the grieving father they knew as a good Christian man and upstanding citizen. The day after the funeral, however, brought a couple of dozen protesters to city hall who claimed the mayor's "moral standing" was now in question since he'd obviously failed to impart "good family values" in his own son.

It was disgusting, to say the least. But as a reporter, Angie couldn't very well ignore the matter. She'd prayed that her boss would sic the city reporter on that story, which is what happened, but the mayor refused to grant any interviews. In an act of desperation, Tom had demanded she give the man a call and ask for a few quotes about the protest.

"You know I don't want to talk about this," the mayor had fumed. "Especially after the media ran their damned footage of my grief for days and days." He had paused, sighed, and added, "But you've always been fair. So here's my statement: A good Christian man will love his child no matter what because Christianity is about love, family, and faith. And I consider myself a good Christian and a good father.

"You can't choose who you love, and no amount of therapy and ridicule will change that. William taught me that. As for the protesters, I say, 'Judge not lest thou be judged.' Loving my son has never affected the way I run this city. If anything, I've learned to be a better man. So drop it."

The city reporter, her former colleague Larry Jones when she shared his beat, had jumped on the quotes and run to the mayor's pastor for comments, who had given a lengthy interview that boiled down to his steadfast resolve to stand behind the mayor and his family. Much to everyone's surprise, the pastor denounced the protesting as an act of tastelessness and indecency, which pretty much killed the protesters' motivation. After three days of picketing, only three people showed up and the trio had gone home after an hour.

And nothing makes news fade faster than fresh blood. That very day, when the protesting ended, there was another signal twelve. Another body. Another mess. And this time, it was the FBI that was controlling the crime scene, crawling all over an apartment complex in north Fort Worth in their black suits and crisp white shirts—not two miles from where William Saunders had found his untimely demise.

Detective Key was involved as the city's lead investigator, but he had become more of a footnote. He'd been specifically ordered not to speak to the press, though he called Angie off the record to give her a rundown on the crime scene so she could ask very specific questions of FBI investigators. She'd been grateful for his consideration, understanding of his frustration, but to say interviewing the FBI was like pulling teeth was a grandiose understatement. She'd be lucky to get any details beyond the actual death.

Matters were further complicated for the media by the fact that the killer's fourth victim was a Latino man from Tijuana, Mexico. He wasn't an illegal immigrant—he had a green card and had been living in Texas for seventeen years—but was supposedly a loner-type with no family or friends to interview. The *Tribune* was under intense pressure by the Hispanic community to provide equal quality reporting and coverage lest it appear it was producing smaller articles because of the victim's race.

The FBI wouldn't tell the press where the man worked and couldn't immediately release his identity because agents were having difficulties locating his next of kin in Mexico. The word was that reporters wouldn't get a name for at least a couple of days.

And that was right about the time when Angie thought she would go crazy from too many stories, too many interviews, and too much frustration. She'd nearly torn her hair out at the demands her boss was making—"Find somebody, anybody to tell us what this guy was like, damn it."

"Yeah, I'll just pull a buddy out of my ass," she muttered as she smoked a cigarette in the Los Torres Apartments parking lot. She was getting desperate. None of the neighbors appeared to know anything about the victim except that he lived in apartment 2A.

Her phone buzzed, indicating she'd received a text message. She flipped it open and stared at her phone for a full minute. "CR8-92P. Red." She didn't recognize the incoming number and dialed it, waiting to see who'd pick up. After six rings, a Spanish-speaking man informed her she'd called a cell phone that a man had accidentally left behind at the convenience store only two blocks from the crime scene.

Angie looked around the parking lot and back at her message. "CR8-92P. Red."

Her eyes fell on the many news vans and parked cars. Then it clicked. The caller wanted her to look for a red vehicle with the listed license plate number. She strolled through the parking lot, trying to appear nonchalant, scanning every red car and truck in sight. She finally found a beat-up Nissan pickup in the far east corner of the lot—far from other prying media eyes.

She didn't know what she was looking for, but as soon as her eyes grazed the back windshield, she found it. In popular Latino fashion, the owner had paid for his last name to be painted across the length of the window in gothic block lettering—Ramirez.

Well, she snorted, that narrowed it down to about one hundred thousand people living in the Metroplex. After a quick glance over her shoulder, she walked around the truck and peered into the front seat. She caught sight of a royal blue polo work shirt with a nametag attached that read, "La Isla, Guillermo."

Angie's mouth opened and closed for a second as she took stock of the situation. She'd recognized the work shirt immediately—La Isla was her and Lauren's favorite restaurant, after all. So she had a first and last name and knew where the man worked. The only problem was whether this was actually the victim's truck. And the more she thought about the text message, the more unnerved she became.

More specifically, exactly how accidental was it that a man had left the cell phone behind? Making a decision, she jotted a couple of quick notes in her notepad and trekked over to the corner convenience store in question.

"Por favor, describe el hombre..." she began when the clerk asked if she needed anything and got a rough description from him. When he started talking about red hair and a strong build, Angie nearly dropped her notepad. She couldn't help looking over her shoulder and scanning the nearly empty parking lot outside. As far as she was concerned, there was little chance the phone had been left by anyone but the killer. It was equally unlikely that he was still anywhere near the crime scene. Angie thanked the man and dialed Detective Key's cell number the second she stepped out into the unforgiving Texas heat.

Detective Key marched up to Angie with quick, efficient strides. The first words out of his mouth were not "hello" or "thanks for calling" or at least a "tell me what you know," but more of an aggravated, "Give me your phone."

She stared at him, her eyes narrowing, but thrust the thing into his outstretched hand. He punched a few buttons and pulled up the text message. Then he swore for several seconds, balling his fist around the phone. For a second, Angie was torn between concern that he'd crush the thing and surprise at his outburst. Before she could express either thought, he handed it back and dug in his pocket for his cigarettes. He lighted one and drew in the smoke harshly, expelling it just as furiously.

"Before you ask, I'm not supposed to tell you this, but it is the correct vehicle," he finally said, pinning her with his eyes. "And I'm on a coffee break, not out speaking with a reporter or checking on a lead." He took a long drag of his cigarette so that the cherry burned halfway down the length of it. He released the smoke in twin streams from his nose and dropped the butt on the ground. "Let's go inside and get coffee."

Getting coffee turned into Key flashing his badge and speaking rapid-fire Spanish with the clerk for several minutes while Angie tried to keep up. Her knowledge of that language was a bit rusty, but she caught small pieces about security cameras and monitoring systems. He pulled out his tiny notepad and began taking notes while Angie shook her head, looking around the store. She seriously doubted the rundown place in a dubious neighborhood had a working security camera, even though she could clearly see a small device mounted two feet above the clerk's head. Places like these typically installed fakes to scare would-be criminals. It was just cheaper.

"Angie," the detective caught her attention, and she turned to face him. "This way," he said and pointed at another man she hadn't noticed. He must have come out of a back room. "The manager is going to let us look at the security tape."

At her look of surprise, the manager laughed. "We get it new today. Just installed. Too many criminals taking money from register. Maybe it works already, eh?"

She nodded and mutely followed the two men into a cramped back office, where indeed a monitor was recording the store's interior. The manager stopped the tape and rewound it to the approximate time the detective wanted.

And clear as day, there he was—flaming red hair, giant sunglasses, a beard covering his lower face. He was wearing a sweatshirt, which was extremely odd this time of year. The clerk appeared to be nervous, kept glancing at the backdoor, apparently under the impression that he was about to be robbed.

The redhead wandered along the rows of junk food and pulled a phone out of his pocket, spent twenty seconds punching in numbers, then turned his phone off, grabbed five bags of chips, and proceeded to harass the clerk to hurry it up with the check-out. When he rushed out of the store, his phone lay on the counter. The clerk looked at it quizzically, made to run after the man and hand the phone back, but appeared seconds later, speaking into the phone. Angie knew that's when she'd placed her call.

The detective stopped the tape, a strange look on his face.

"Señor, I need a copy of this for the police department," he demanded in an authoritative voice. "And I'm going to have to ask you not to speak of this to anyone because it's part of an ongoing investigation. Comprende?"

"Sí, I will tell nobody. I make copy now." And the manager did just that.

Once outside the store, Detective Key held the tape in his hands, gripped so tightly his knuckles were almost white. A frown creased his face and he stared in the direction of the Los Torres Apartments. He was silent and unmoving so long Angie began to fidget and was on the verge of interrupting the man's pensive staring when he suddenly said, "You're not writing about this. Not a single word. And what I told that manager—that goes for you, too."

"You're not going to hand that over to the media?" she nearly shouted, incredulous. "Don't you want a picture of the killer displayed? Don't you think you'll get a lot of tips? What the hell's going on with you?"

She realized she'd stepped way the hell over the line a split second before he rounded on her. The look on his face almost made her take a step back.

"I know what I'm doing, damn it," he growled. "Yeah, this tape is pretty fucking important, but I don't want our killer to know his freaking picture was taken. The camera was installed today, Angie—today—not yesterday or the week before. I'm willing to bet the killer thought the camera was a fake, just like every other convenience store in this area. So for now, it's a fucking secret. Got it?"

She gritted her teeth and slowly nodded, wanting to scream in frustration. She still didn't know what the hell to do about her story. And how the hell had the killer gotten her cell phone number? She decided to voice the last question out loud, needing to know.

"Oh, it's not that hard," the detective said offhandedly. "Do you shred your bills? Does the *Tribune* staff have explicit instructions not to hand it out? There are a number of ways to get your hands on that kind of information."

"Damn it," she grumbled, a mental picture of her paper recycling bin popping to the foreground of her thoughts—a stack of old, unshredded bills and junk mail sitting in plain view. The killer had already proven he knew where she lived. He could have followed her two days before, when she'd taken the load to the nearest recycling Dumpster.

Detective Key suddenly stood up straighter, peering down the street, and let out a stream of muffled curses. Angie craned her neck, trying to figure out what he was looking at, and spotted a youngish-looking man in a white T-shirt and khaki shorts with flip-flops. The man was talking on his cell phone, looking like any of the other crime scene bystanders calling their friends and family to talk about the homicide.

"What?" she asked.

"Your tail is currently informing his supervisor that we're standing in this parking lot. And I bet he's seen the tape I'm holding. Damn it."

"Okay," she drew the word out, not understanding. When the detective didn't immediately answer her unasked question, she said, "Why does it matter if he saw the tape? You were going to hand it over anyway, right?"

Detective Key turned to look at her, a series of emotions racing across his face before he could slip the mask back in place. A grin broke out across his face and he said, "Yeah, of course. I just don't want to be sidelined by the FBI. It's a pissing contest, you understand, and this piece of evidence would give me a much-needed boost in this bureaucratic game we're playing. I was..." he trailed off, looking down the street, spotting two suits heading their way. He sighed overly dramatic in an "Aw, shucks" kind of way. "Well, here come the feds. They'll claim this as their own work. So much for the promotion this year." He grinned good-naturedly at Angie, a forced relaxation taking hold of his shoulders and hands so that it looked like he was just hanging out by the time the suits met them in the parking lot.

Angie's eyes narrowed at him as she watched the sudden change in his demeanor, not entirely convinced.

"Jay, Miss Mitchell," one of the agents acknowledged. The pair looked so identical they could have been brothers. Maybe it was a trick of the stark light or maybe it was just FBI. Angie held out her hand and they took it in turn.

"Security tape?" the other asked, peering at Detective Key's hands.

"Sure is," the detective drawled. "It takes a good cop to do the legwork. This, my friends, may help us break the case." He placed heavy emphasis on the word cop, and Angie recognized the not-so-friendly banter for what it was, what he'd said earlier—a pissing contest.

"We'll take that, Key," an agent smoothly replied, apparently deliberately dropping Jay's title. He held out his hand for the tape, but the detective didn't cooperate.

"No can do, Hicks. How do I know you won't go tell the boss you drummed this up yourself? No, I'll hand it over myself, but thanks for the offer."

Agent Hicks narrowed his eyes in a most unfriendly manner for several seconds, then abruptly laughed and dropped his outstretched hand. "Okay, Key. If you need to show the boss so desperately that you can do your job after all, then you can take the tape to him like a good little cop."

The other agent snickered, but the detective's falsely pleasant smile didn't falter.

"Miss Mitchell," Hicks addressed her, shifting gears. "How did you know where to find the victim's car? Our man says you got a message on your phone, then immediately started looking at cars."

"Looks like you answered your own question," Detective Key interjected, a note of amusement in his voice. "Perhaps you should ask who called her."

"Jay, I think you should report back to the boss," Hicks shot back. "He's looking for you, wondering why the hell it takes you half an hour to walk two blocks and 'get some coffee.'"

The detective grinned at the agent and held up the tape before turning to walk toward Los Torres Apartments. Before he left, though, he touched Angie's shoulder and said, "By the way, you don't have to answer a single question if you don't want to. Make 'em haul you downtown." And chuckling, he wandered off.

Both agents frowned after him, then pinned Angie with their dark lens-covered eyes. "Tell us about the phone call," Hicks demanded.

"What phone call?" Angie asked, her eyes a bit wider and eyebrows raised for added innocence effect. "I think I'd better talk to your boss if I'm going to give any information."

The agents groaned in unison and tried several more times. But Angie was damned if she was going to spend the whole day answering questions for several different people—talking to the top dog should solve the problem. And maybe then she could try the quid-pro-quo approach and get some decent information for her story. So there.

She ended up being marched toward the crime scene between the two men who acted as though she might bolt. Yeah, right—run with her cast and all. Angie liked the feds about as much as the detective did, albeit for different reasons, the primary of which was their tendency not to give good interviews. So she made a show of limping and forced the men to match her slow gait.

"Ever wonder if the FBI has a file on you?" a voice asked from behind, and Angie spun around to face the stranger. He disturbingly resembled Clint Eastwood if said actor had gone bald and grew a bushy mustache. The man held out his hand, tacking on a gruff, "We do. Agent Moreno Silas, pleased to meet you, Miss Mitchell."

Angie shook his hand and tried to get the mental picture of him riding a horse into the sunset out of her head. He led her over to a nondescript black van, and they climbed inside where it was comfortably cool. She'd been waiting for an hour and was getting anxious. Any minute now, she expected a call from her boss about the homicide story for which she had very little information.

"I'll make this quick." Agent Silas broke through her worries and pulled out a notepad. "Tell me about the phone call."

Angie cleared her throat and debated the best words to choose to get what she wanted without ending up in an interrogation room at the North Texas FBI headquarters in Dallas. She discarded several options and finally settled on, "We both need to do our jobs and there's no reason we should make things difficult for each other. So how about this: I'll tell you all about the call and you give me some decent information about the homicide. Fair?"

The agent dragged his eyes from his notepad to her face slowly, an exasperated but amused expression on his face. He remained silent for several seconds, letting the question linger, and Angie was tempted to fill the conversational gap and was just barely able to resist doing so. His agent eyes seemed to pick her apart piece by piece in that silence, but she bore the scrutiny, fidgeting as little as she could manage.

"I'd dare to venture that my job is a bit more important than yours, so let's continue, shall we?" he finally said and smiled at her patronizingly.

"Fine," she said. "I'll need to call my lawyer."

His smile crumbled and his eyes widened. He shook his head and jotted down a few notes before looking up at her again. "Why make this difficult?"

"Because you are," she answered honestly. She sure as hell didn't want her lawyer involved, and she certainly didn't want to get on this man's bad side so quickly. Detective Key had spoiled her with his willingness to share information so freely. But the agent's patronizing tone had struck a nerve and she wasn't going to back down now.

He regarded her for another minute and finally the smile returned.

"You'd have us drag you in for questioning just because you need a few quotes?"

"Yeah, I would. And it's not just a 'few quotes' I need, sir. It's more like a whole story I need. I never understood why you feds have to be so damned tight-lipped about everything. I mean, you won't even give us the basic facts. Come on, man. Just give me the who, what, when, where, and why. Then give me a how. And then I'll give you what you need. Quid pro quo or no go."

She'd sat up straighter, her shoulders strung tight, chin raised. This was the exact attitude that both annoyed and thrilled her boss. She was a stubborn, frustrating, aggravating... Well, she did her job. And looking into the bemused sparkle now shining from Agent Silas's eyes, she knew immediately that she'd get what she wanted.

"Damn," he said, trying hard not to laugh. He closed his eyes and wiped a hand across his sweaty brows. "Can't give you the who, you know that. I guess I don't have a choice about the rest."

"Guillermo Ramirez, works at La Isla in Arlington," Angie said evenly, watching his reaction carefully. She wasn't disappointed. She would have loved to play poker with the man, the way his mouth drew into a tight line, his brows furrowed, and his eyes hardened.

"Next of kin has not been notified yet," he said, the words clipped and harsh.

"It won't take a couple of days, either. We know he had a green card—been living here for ten years, your PR person told us so—and a man like that usually provides correct information in his paperwork. I bet you have a contact already from his work application where he listed an emergency contact name and number."

"Give me another hour or so," he relented, his frown deepening. "You're right, and an agent is on it."

Finally. Angie willed her lips not to form a grin. She had a starting point. She could go to La Isla the second the agent let her leave and start interviewing coworkers.

Agent Silas tolerated her questions for the following ten minutes, providing her with enough information for a decent story. The crime scene was nearly identical to the last one, though the door wasn't spray painted as she'd already discovered when she'd arrived early that day. The man had not reported to work the past three days. Investigators were pretty sure he was also gay, though he apparently had a wife and kids in Tijuana whom agents were trying to contact about his death. There were other details she pulled from the reluctant agent, but they were so similar she could have taken previous articles and changed the names, addresses, and ages and it would fit.

The only difference they'd discovered so far was the vic's race and the fact that he lived in a lower-income apartment complex than the others. He'd also just moved into the Los Torres Apartments two months prior, which explained why none of his neighbors seemed to know anything about him. And agents found some ecstasy tabs in a nightstand drawer. Much to Angie's surprise, Agent Silas added, "Just like in the other apartments. Always in the nightstand drawer. About a hundred bucks worth of ecstasy."

Angie swallowed her surprise and kept on writing notes as though it were typical. Inside she was fuming—Detective Key had been holding out on her. She wasn't sure how much the drugs had to do with anything, but it was suspicious that they were all found in similar locations and similar amounts.

But when the ten minutes were up, the agent shut her questions down and started in on his own. Quid pro quo. Angie gave her information, showed him her cell phone, and described the tape. Curiously enough, Agent Silas still hadn't received said tape and made a radio call for other agents to go fetch the detective with the tape. Twenty minutes passed. Finally, the detective slid the van's door open and popped his red head in.

"Here it is," he said and thrust the thing into Agent Silas's waiting hand. "Got the manager to agree not to speak about this," he quickly added.

"Good, good," the agent said. "Took you long enough to bring it to me, but good job in getting it in, Key. I'll be out in a few, then we'll talk about this."

The detective nodded and closed the door. Angie reanswered each and every question about five times until finally, flustered and anxious, she was released from the van. Her cell phone rang that very instant, and she launched into a lengthy explanation before her boss could lecture her on deadlines.

As soon as she finished, rather breathless, he demanded she read back her notes and typed up the story with pounding keystrokes. She didn't even get a lecture on deadlines or the incident with her cell phone. He just asked to see it when she got back to the office and told her to hurry over to the restaurant. Angie suspected his lack of outburst was because he thought they had an exclusive and was excited. At that point, she didn't really give a crap why he wasn't yelling at her as had happened too damned often lately.

She rushed over to her car and took off, glad that the other media crews seemed completely clueless about her interview with the lead investigator and that she'd have the victim's name online in a couple of hours.

"Angie!" a breathless voice gasped loudly just over Angie's shoulder, scaring the crap out of her. Her fingers slipped on the keyboard she'd been pounding as she jumped in her chair. After a deep breath, she slowly turned around in her seat, wondering what the hell was going on.

Gavin panted as though he'd just run twenty blocks and wasn't used to it. His bright face was flushed, but his eyes sparkled with intensity. Angie had been more than annoyed with her team. Both he and the intern had been missing in action all day. And while she'd dealt with the FBI and later with a hysterical restaurant staff, Tom had been unable to locate her backups— despite about twenty or so phone calls to their respective homes.

But staring at the fellow, seeing his fiercely anxious eyes so focused, Angie's annoyance drained away, the bitter lecture she'd wanted to deliver replaced by a burning curiosity. She couldn't help but ask, "What is it?"

"Well," he took a deep breath, trying to steady himself. "I got a tip-off. There's a connection between all the victims we didn't know about. And it's so freaking bizarre, you'd think it came straight from a movie plot." He took another deep breath and rushed on with, "They all went to high school together. Martin High in Fort Worth. Classes of '90 and '91. But that's not the best part." He paused for effect. "They were all in this clique— Calamus, they called themselves, whatever the hell that is—did poetry shit late at night, like some gay Dead Poets Society or something." He stopped abruptly, apparently realizing that he was babbling. Silently, he thrust a bound book toward Angie, who reached out and took what looked like a stack of paper copies strip-bound.

The card stock, purple cover was worn and looked thoroughly abused. A strange-looking plant was on the cover and she wondered why the word "calamus" was printed in bold block letters on the front, tickling a memory that wouldn't quite surface. She frowned at the thing and flipped it open. As soon as she did, she understood why Gavin was so excited.

There they were: Ben Whittaker, Chance Lockett, William

Saunders, and Guillermo Ramirez—no names, and though the copies of their school pictures were not of high quality, Angie recognized them immediately. Time had been good to them. Change their hairdos, take away two sets of braces, and they looked strikingly similar to the pictures that had run in the *Tribune* for weeks. There were two more pictures of men she didn't recognize, which made her frown deepen. If the killer was targeting this group specifically, then the two others...

"Do the feds have this?" she suddenly demanded.

"No, just brought it in myself," Gavin said evenly, having finally caught his breath. "Why? Do you think we should turn it over?"

Angie's eyes widened and she opened her mouth to deliver a sarcastic, "No, Gavin, let's just hang on to this piece of potentially helpful evidence and wait till the other two get killed," but forced back her biting two cents. Holding the book, she tried to seriously consider keeping it to themselves. The thought was ridiculous, and yet... No, they had to turn it over.

She flipped through another few pages, eyes scanning the angsty teen poetry. She couldn't very well sit there and read through the hundred or so pages while Gavin stood there, but she was reluctant to give it up quite yet. She flipped to the back and began flipping pages in reverse. On the third to last page, she discovered a poem called, "After Midnight."

Her eyes darted down the forty-eight lines of text, her heart racing. She snapped the thing shut, her mouth dry, her hands becoming clammy.

"Here's what we're going to do." The words came out nearly breathless. "We are going to copy this shit right now. Then I'm calling the feds." She paused, reconsidered, and amended, "The detective, not the feds. We'll request a messenger from the station come by to pick this up. Then we're going to leave—that's right, you and me, don't look at me like that." She snorted at the straightening of his shoulders and the frown that cut across his face. "I have a hunch and there's a place we need to visit. On the way, you will tell me exactly how you got this."

"Um." Gavin gulped, looking suddenly very nervous. "I don't want to get anybody in trouble, see, and..."

"If we're going to do anything about this," she waved the

book at him threateningly, "you'll have to tell me what the hell's going on. And where the hell is Mandy, anyway?"

"I'll tell you on the way, it'll take too long otherwise," he interjected, resigned.

"Fine. Let's get this show on the road."

Angie rushed down the long rows of cubicle desks until she hit the far-end wall where the copy machine was located. She ground her teeth—mostly excited but partly frustrated at how long it took to copy one hundred pages—and drummed her fingers on the machine cover. She'd assigned Gavin the task of telling her boss they'd need to make a trip to Dallas and would be out of commission for the next several hours, a job she was more than glad to delegate.

Angie punched a series of familiar numbers in her cell phone and growled anxiously for Detective Key to answer his phone. On the third ring, he picked up with a gruff, "No comment, Angie. You know I can't."

"I don't need a comment, damn it. I have something for you that you're going to love. Send a messenger over and you can have it. Tell whoever comes over here to ask for Tom Brunsfeld, you know, my boss. He'll have it."

"It what?" he asked, his voice dropping an octave authoritatively.

"You'll see. Gotta go, my phone's about to die," she answered quickly and hung up before he could object. The last thing she wanted was to be dragged down to the station—again—when she wasn't even the one to come up with a piece of evidence this time. Besides, she was on a mission that didn't need inconvenient interruptions. She turned her phone off to ensure that he wouldn't be able to reach her.

She limped back to her desk and grabbed her purse and a notepad, then snagged Gavin by the arm on her way out the door. Tom looked a little flustered, she couldn't help but notice as she walked by, but she was too excited to care.

What she and Gavin were about to do was more like true investigative journalism—none of that sit-back-and-cover-shit-that-hits-the-fan kind of stuff. This was real. And it didn't matter that she wasn't the one to get the tip-off. Actually, it was kind of a relief.

Preying On Generosity

Chapter Thirteen

"Pick up, pick up, pick up, pick up… Damn it!" Angie groaned at the voicemail message that greeted her and waited impatiently for the beep. "Jimmy! I need you to call me back ASAP. I need your help. It's important. I'm going to Dallas and need to get into that After Midnight place again." She was about to hang up, but quickly added, "By the way, does the word calamus mean anything to you?"

She tossed the phone back into her purse and shot a look at Gavin. His driving was proving to be a test of her nerves. Not that he wasn't going fast enough—no, the problem was he was speeding like hell. They'd just barely escaped three wrecks on I-30. Her right foot kept pressing into the floor in an unconscious effort to hit the brakes. He swerved left to avoid another collision. Angie ground her teeth and closed her eyes.

When she'd told him where they were headed, he'd become increasingly withdrawn and nervous. She didn't understand what the hell his problem was and chalked it up to his apparent prudishness.

"So we're not going to get in, right?" Gavin asked hopefully.

"Like hell," she snorted. "We're going to that damned place and we'll try to talk our way in. Detective Key is not a stupid cop. He'll put two and two together quicker than I did. I give him less than an hour before he shows up. We need to beat him there, Gavin, and get the interview before he shuts the madam up."

Gavin bit his lower lip and slowly nodded. Angie watched him for another minute in silence, wondering why this was such a big deal. So it was a…stranger kind of place. It wasn't like he was going on his own. She was tempted to dig at him until she understood his attitude, but there were more pressing matters.

"Tell me how you got that book," she demanded, her notebook out and ready. It's not as if he couldn't add his own narrative to a story, but she wanted the notes for her record. In case anybody asked. Especially in case anybody doubted.

He took a hand off his steering wheel and wiped sweat off his forehead, rubbing his hand nervously on his wrinkled khakis. Angie flinched at the look of utter internalized concentration that drew his attention away from the road. A horn blared and Gavin hit the brakes—another close miss.

"Um…" he stammered, cleared his throat, and tried again. "Well, Angie, I got it from a guy who went to my high school— coincidentally, Martin High School. I didn't know him. He was years ahead of me." He paused and glanced at Angie. "I had, um, been out all night with my brother drinking. It was really too late to go to bed and still make it to work. We, um, went to IHOP to sober up." He smiled sheepishly and cleared his throat. "Anyway, we'd been there for a couple of hours and the drinks were seriously wearing off. Right when we were about to leave, I overheard a rather heated debate coming from the booth behind ours…"

Angie could almost see the scene unfolding as Gavin told his tale—his reckless driving fading into the background.

Gavin had stopped his brother midsentence, his hand held up to still the conversation, his ears straining to hear what was going on behind them.

"Don't you see how serious this is? Three of them—gone! Murdered, for Christ's sake!" an unfamiliar voice had hissed. An acknowledging grunt from another person had followed, likely to get the agitated male speaker to lower his voice. People were starting to stare.

"All I'm saying is that I'm not making this shit up. Read the freaking news, man."

"I'm sorry if it's hard to take you seriously, Jeff. You've always been a conspiracy nut—there's no denying that."

An uneasy silence followed. Gavin's brother leaned forward, still drunk, and demanded to know what the hell was going on in a low whisper, his words slurred.

"Shut up," Gavin had ordered.

"Are you listening in on that dude's conversation?"

"Shut up." This time more urgent.

"He went to our high school, that guy. I recognize him. Hung out with those fags." A look of utter concentration had crossed his face. "Hey, I think he was a fag, too. Yeah, I remember he was one of those guys who hung out with the others. Doing theater plays and shit."

"Damn it, Sean, shut up."

But it was no use. Sean was too drunk to understand the concept of discreet eavesdropping. Worse yet, he'd slid out of the booth, taken four unsteady steps to the other booth, and very loudly said, "Hey, I know you! We went to high school together. Remember?"

As Gavin pinched his nose, trying to stifle an annoyed groan, his brother had continued to babble at the man for another couple of minutes. Someone excused themselves from the table and left the room. Exasperated, Gavin got on his feet and was about to drag his brother away when the man said, "Yeah, I remember you. You're that asshole who used to spray pink shit on my locker."

Shit, Gavin thought, and grabbed his brother's arm, ready to haul him away before a fight broke out. His brother didn't usually respond well to name-calling. But Sean surprised him with an easygoing, "Yeah, I was kind of an asshole in high school." He'd paused. "Why don't you let me join you, pick up your bill—for being such a dick back then and all? Unless your friend's coming back?"

Gavin looked at the man, curious to see how he'd respond, surprised by the relieved smile that replaced the earlier frown. He nodded, saying only, "No, my friend went home."

Maybe he hadn't wanted to be alone.

Sean plopped down in the booth. "Thanks, Jeff. Don't remember your last name. Sorry."

"Breaux. And yours?"

"Sean Austin. This is my brother Gavin."

The look that crossed Jeff's face piqued Gavin's curiosity—brows furrowed, lips parted in a half O—and he responded with a puzzled smile.

"You don't work in newspapers, do you?"

"Actually, yeah, I do. Good to meet you." The hand that shook his was limp and clammy-cold.

"I thought I recognized your name," Jeff mumbled and sat silent for several minutes while Sean babbled about his brother's fellowship at the *Tribune*—the typical proud, bragging relative. A confused waitress came by and cleared the other booth, listening apprehensively as Sean requested their bills be combined. A few minutes after she left, Jeff interrupted Sean's high school reminiscing monologue.

"Gavin, you're working on the gay murders, right?"

The fellow nodded, completely alert. He hadn't been mistaken about what he'd overheard. A lurch of excitement threatened to let loose a flood of questions he could just barely restrain.

"We need to talk. I have something you might be very interested in for your stories."

And that's when Gavin had been handed the poetry collection. He listened with rapt attention as the man described his theory that he and his friends were being picked off one by one, though he apparently didn't have any idea why this was happening. In the end, Sean had fallen asleep in the booth while Gavin and Jeff talked for three hours—much to the frustration of the IHOP staff.

Angie's eyes slowly refocused on the road. Gavin had stopped telling his story two or three minutes before and she hadn't realized it was over right away, her mind busy at work processing the facts.

"Where did he get the book?" she finally asked.

"He made it nearly fifteen years ago. He's one of the people pictured on that first page. And he's terrified he'll be the next victim. He came to town the second he heard what had happened to his friends."

Gavin added that Jeff had been out of town for the past month, trekking around Europe like he'd dreamed about doing for years. He'd apparently missed the first couple of stories on Ben Whittaker. But when he returned to Lubbock, he discovered a new story online that had made him sick.

"Oh…" Angie sighed and understood why Gavin hadn't wanted to elaborate. He probably didn't want to get that guy in any trouble, his lack of extensive journalism experience making him uneasy with the situation.

Her eyes drifted to the smiling faces and she tried to imagine learning that three dear friends had dropped out of her life during the time it took to read an online article. The thought made her shiver. She'd have been sick, too.

"How close were they?" she wondered aloud.

"Jeff had seen them all seven weeks ago at Whittaker's apartment," Gavin said evenly. "Jeff says they're all pretty busy but try to meet up once a month or so."

"Damn." She shook her head. That had to be tough. Her initial assumption had been that the six had drifted apart after high school, perhaps losing touch as some went to college and others didn't. This story—the Fort Worth gay homicides—had made national headlines. It was nearly unheard of for so many murders to happen in Fort Worth in such a quick time frame, especially considering the similarities pointing toward a single serial killer.

If Jeff had been in Texas the past month, he'd have known of it immediately.

She asked if Gavin had gotten the sixth man's name and he had—a Trey Greenly who lived in Vail, Colorado.

Her eyes remained fixated on the spot where she'd jotted down the last man's name. Something about Vail… There'd been a story about Vail on the wire a few weeks before.

She dug in her purse and flipped open her cell phone, rapidly punching in her boss's number. One, two, three rings. Then, "*Tribune* city desk, this is Tom."

"It's me," she said, urgency in her voice. "I need a favor. Can you look up a Trey Greenly in the archives?"

He grunted and she heard keystrokes rattling in the background.

"There's an AP brief that mentions Trey Greenly—found murdered in his summer condo on September 10 in Vail, Colorado." He paused. Angie could almost hear the wheels grinding in his brain. "You don't think…" he trailed off as though the question were absurd.

"He has everything to do with the homicides here," Angie whispered and cleared her throat. "That book Gavin told you about has a picture of him in it. There's no name, but another person who is also in the book confirmed it." She paused. "Tom, is Mandy back in yet?"

"Yeah, just got here. You won't believe what she's been up

to…"

"Tell her I think she needs to get the Vail cops on the phone and get some stuff from them. And she needs to do it now," Angie cut him off.

He was silent for a minute as though weighing options. "Okay, will do," he finally said and made to hang up but tacked on a quick, "You be careful, Angie."

His voice was gone before she could say, "I will."

She relayed Tom's end of the conversation to Gavin, who was shocked by the news. Jeff, he said, was going to be devastated. And it was all the more reason for the feds to get their hands on the purple book.

"If the killer went all the way to Vail…" he started and couldn't finish the sentence. He didn't need to. Angie knew exactly where his thoughts were headed. The same worry had crossed her mind the second she remembered there had been a major crime in the otherwise quiet resort community. That the two dots connected so easily was anything but a coincidence. It was another piece of the puzzle. Another story to write. But she couldn't focus on that right now; there were other matters at hand. They were about to hit I-35 and head north, racing closer to their destination.

And Jimmy still hadn't called. How the hell were they going to get in without a password? A headache started building behind her temples and she closed her eyes. She needed something else to focus on. Tom had started to tell her that Mandy had been up to something.

"Where's Mandy been?" she asked the driver, who for the first time shot her an excited grin, temporarily erasing the worry lines on his sweaty forehead.

"I called her from the restaurant while Jeff went to the bathroom," he said proudly. "She's been at Martin High School half the day to confirm their attendance there, drum up some yearbooks, and get comments from past teachers, that sort of thing. Then she ran employment and criminal record searches to see if there were any other commonalities. I haven't heard from her since she started working on that."

"And I guess after hanging out with your brother and Jeff all night, you went home and crashed for a while."

He shot her a sheepish grin. "Yeah, but I found out a lot of stuff that I haven't gotten to yet, and I took notes the whole time, filled a third of a notepad. I wasn't just sitting on my ass. Honest. That hourlong nap I was going to take just kind of...er...took more like five hours."

She pretended to give him a menacingly threatening scowl, as though to say, "Not good enough," but was unable to suppress the rising grin that gave her away. She snorted at his alibi for being absent all day and had to admit that he hadn't done half bad. In fact, he'd done a hell of a lot better than she'd ever thought he would. And despite her earlier frustration, she grudgingly acknowledged that he wasn't such a bad reporter.

Sure, the source had practically stumbled across his path. So what? He got the info, brought it to her, and now they could take the valuable puzzle piece and work it into a brilliant story. Not to mention, it just might save a man's life. Not bad. Not bad at all.

Angie could sense her boss salivating over the juicy soon-to-be article. And she had a feeling he would be a lot less angry with her over the next couple of weeks. Come what may.

Her heart was pounding. The story would be a blockbuster. But that was only part of the excitement. She had the distinct feeling that whatever they learned at After Midnight would provide the climax for this investigation. It had to. Her gut told her that the vague, rambling poem bearing the same name was not a coincidence. It was dark and troubling. Something had happened there that night. The last lines, "Horror-struck, we left the terror behind/ Never to speak of it again/ That experiment gone wrong/ Oh how naïve we have been," promised as much. It was dated May 31, 1990. The poem suggested something had happened the night before.

"Thanks, Gavin," she said into the long-stretching silence. He nodded in acknowledgment and exited I-35 onto Oak Lawn Avenue. They were almost there.

"Come on, Angie, let's go for a little walk," Gavin said as he grabbed her by the arm and gently led her away from the call box. She protested vehemently, pissed that they had been denied.

They'd pulled into the appropriate lot ten minutes earlier and she'd marched straight up to the door, rang the bell, and announced, "This is Angie Mitchell. I was here with Jimmy the other day. I need to speak with you."

A crackling silence had followed.

"You are not welcome here," the madam's voice had shouted back, then there was only silence. No amount of ringing the call box's bell had brought another word from the woman's lips.

Angie had called Jimmy but only reached his voicemail. Again. And then she cursed for five solid minutes while Gavin stood by with his hands in his khaki pockets, staring at the ground. When he'd had enough, he took her arm.

They walked along the industrial back roads for a couple of blocks while Angie furiously smoked a cigarette. Gavin stopped suddenly and she almost ran into him.

"We'll wait here five minutes and head back," he said, not meeting her puzzled eyes. "We'll get in. I have a password."

"What?" Angie nearly shouted. If he had a damned password, why had they just wasted their time?

He turned his back on her and mumbled, "I...um...come here from time to time," he slowly turned, his eyes finally meeting hers, and he quickly added, blushing, "but not often. Just when I'm on vacation. A friend introduced me a couple of years ago. She'll remember me. We just need her to think you left." He paused when he was met with silence and nervously folded his arms across his chest.

"And why exactly didn't you try that first, rather than let me make a fool of myself?"

His arms dropped and knotted his hands together, fidgeting.

"I didn't want anyone to know."

Angie snorted, then slowly began to laugh.

"Gavin, how did you think I knew about this place? Jeez. So you're basically telling me that you were completely freaked out that I'd learn 'dirty secrets' about your sex life. And by freaking out, you didn't stop to consider how strange it was for me to recognize an obscure reference in some guy's poem about this place if I'd never been here?" She laughed again. "Your secret is safe with me. And I'll tell you something in return that not many people know about at work." She hesitated only a second. "I'm dating a woman."

She watched him replay the words in his head. He stopped

knitting his fingers and a smile slowly slid across his lips. "Good point. And cool about the woman," he finally said, his blush deepening. Relief flooded his face and he visibly relaxed.

"Okay, let's go back." And he led the way. He punched the call box button and answered the nervous, "Who's there?" with, "Your Adonis, crowned in the forest." The door buzzed immediately to admit them. Angie resisted the urge to pump her fist in triumph and Gavin smirked.

Before they reached the door with the painting that had made Angie blush on her first visit, Gavin stopped and blocked her path. "Listen," he whispered. "Maybe you should wait behind the door and I'll see what I can get out of her before she realizes you're here. Give me the copies."

Angie hesitated a split second but reluctantly nodded and handed over the paper. She could easily listen behind the door if he left it cracked just an inch. And if he wasn't getting anywhere with his inquiries, she could always step in and take over. She handed the man the photocopies and watched as he slid through the door, leaving it open just enough not to look conspicuous.

"Gavin, dearest, it's been ages," Madam Midnight purred when he greeted her.

"Too long, too long," he agreed and gave a flirtatious laugh. Hiding behind the door, Angie felt free to let the smirk slide into place. The fellow's voice had dropped more than one octave. Yeah, he was laying it on thick.

"So what brings you to my abode after such a long absence? Are you requiring any…services?"

"Maybe another time, dearest," his baritone voice carried easily, and Angie suspected he'd raised it for her benefit. "I'm living in the area now. Maybe we can see a little more of each other in the coming months while I'm here."

"You got transferred?"

Transferred? Angie wondered exactly what profession he'd given in previous conversations. You don't get transferred in journalism unless you're a manager for a major chain. Which he wasn't. At his level, you work, you quit, you find another job. She suddenly seriously doubted whether his little plan had been such a good idea and had half a mind to cut him off—false representation and all that jazz. But she decided to wait. For now.

"Oh, I'm hurt, madam," he said melodramatically, the statement followed by a low chuckle. "Have you forgotten already that I'm a newspaper man?"

Now Angie really wanted to snort and laugh. She bit her knuckles to keep from doing exactly that. Gavin the dork by day, Gavin the tacky Casanova by night.

"That's right, how silly of me," she muttered, and Angie was barely able to make it out. Her tone of voice had abruptly changed. She was on to them.

"You're here with her, aren't you?" It was more of a statement than a question. The negative emphasis on the word "her" made Angie's smirking lips turn upside down.

Silence.

"Yes, I am, madam," he answered obediently. Just like a good little masochist. "I swear I would not have brought her if this weren't important. We need your help. A man's life is at stake."

Another long silence. Angie heard three muffled steps and the door flew open, nearly knocking her smack in the face. She'd just barely been able to dodge it when the woman burst through.

She lowered her face to less than an inch from Angie's nose.

"I can't get involved," she hissed. "What do you want from me? The detective's already been here. You're making trouble for me. You have to leave."

Angie couldn't see Gavin's reaction around the face looming so closely and she swallowed, a touch intimidated by the tall and enigmatic woman's forcefulness. But she did not inch away to get Madam Midnight out of her comfort zone.

"You're already involved, one way or another," Angie replied evenly, the words enunciated with clear precision. Her mind was racing. She could not let this woman throw them out. She needed words—the right words—to plead their case. It was hard to think with those scarlet-painted lips drawn threateningly into a snarl so close. The urge to back away was draining her creativity dry.

"Five men are dead," the reporter pressed while the taller woman continued to loom over her. "And it sure as hell has something to do with this place." She paused for effect. "We need to know what happened on May 30, 1990." Angie prayed that she'd read the poem correctly.

The woman's snarl melted away, replaced by a fleeting,

haunted look that dashed across her face and slid beneath the mask. A lazy smile replaced the expression and the woman purred, "I don't remember. Gavin, where were we? Discussing a possible business transaction, I believe." She turned her back on Angie and strode up to the fellow.

"Don't you walk away from me," Angie shouted and took two steps forward. "You lying bitch. Don't tell me you don't fucking remember what happened that day, but you can remember who knows how many bizarre-ass passwords and customer's names."

Desperate times call for desperate measures. Angie willed her body not to tremble when the woman spun on her heels, her face a map of emotions—outrage being the primary reaction. But there was another, clearly distinguishable look in those burning eyes, proving Angie's gamble was not in vain. Even as Gavin gasped and rushed forward to apologize on his colleague's behalf, the reporter read the flickering of excitement in the dilating pupils and crinkling skin around the middle-aged woman's eyes.

The tactic had come to her in the kind of stroke of genius that seldom comes without intense pressure and a short temper: Push any button you can find to trip your opponent up. And when the madam had turned her back, when Angie's temper rose, a string of crass barntalk came to mind. Jimmy had said it: "Butch on the streets, femme in the sheets. Everybody puts on an act. If you're tough and controlling, you just want to be thrown against the wall by someone who seems all sweet and sincere."

"What did you say?" the madam demanded and Angie laughed. It was perfect. The way she'd acted the last time she was at After Midnight—blushing, naïve—it was a shocking contrast to the words she'd chosen for maximum trip-up effect.

"You heard me," she hissed at the woman, and threw in a "Shut the fuck up, Gavin," over his mumbled, "She doesn't mean it."

Angie stared into the hazel eyes, let the last month's frustrated anger boil to the surface until her whole body was awash with a raw fury. She thought about the package, her fight with Lauren, the threat of being fired, her lost sense of security. She thought about her slow recovery, her hatred for Ted Henry. And when she saw a small spark of fear light up the other woman's eyes, when the head slowly shook to deny her demand, Angie gave up control

Angie was led through the painting-covered door, along another side hallway, and up to a bookcase at the far end of a cozy-looking room that hid what looked like a small cubby hole when Gavin shoved the case gruntingly aside. He pulled it back into place, and they waited in the dark of the closet-sized niche. It was pitch black, save for a faint outline of light coming from under the bookcase.

Moments passed in utter silence. Then, to both the reporters' surprise, they heard muffled voices headed their way. For a moment, Angie thought the madam was leading Detective Key straight to them. She stifled a curse, trying to hear past her pounding heart.

It wasn't as though they would be in any real trouble if the detective found them. But Angie preferred that he remain ignorant of her little visit until the story ran on page one. If he caught them, he was likely to order they not print any part of the interview Gavin had just taken down. The detective couldn't force them not to print it—not really—but ignoring him could end up killing any contacts she'd made on the police beat. Cops don't forget when you print something they don't like. They share their dislike and distrust with anyone who will listen. The only excuse is to plead ignorance afterward. And Angie was pretty sure she could pull off the dumb act, using her brief history of crime reporting as the perfect excuse.

Such are the games of police-media politics. It's always a fine line between reporting the facts and warning the public but doing so without compromising an ongoing investigation. Both sides almost always think the other is screwing up.

And besides that, Angie was more than a little interested in hearing a real live Detective Key questioning. So she tilted her head toward the sounds and strained to decipher the words.

The voices drew nearer. Gavin's fingers dug painfully into her shoulder in anticipation of being discovered. But just when they thought the bookshelf would be moved, an angry detective would yell at them, and they'd be thrown out, Angie made out the madam asking, "Please, take a seat."

Right—there'd been a couch next to the bookshelf. Relief flooded through both journalists' bodies, making Angie feel almost weak-kneed with the constant emotional back-and-forth of the day.

"I have something I'd like to show you," the detective was saying. Angie's interest piqued. She'd forgotten to show the pictures to the other woman.

Seconds ticked by so slowly Angie began to tremble. There was no response.

"Do you recognize any of them?"

"You know the answer to that, Jay," she said apprehensively.

What the hell did that mean? The fingers in Angie's shoulder dug in harder and she reached up to pry them away. She'd have rather stomped on Gavin's foot.

"I want to hear you say it," Detective Key's voice shot back angrily.

"You'll have to take me down to the station."

A string of furious cursing followed, ending in, "Damn it, woman, you know what's at stake here. I need to know. Is this man the one we've discussed or not?"

"Jay, I'll tell you again. I think you need to turn this investigation over to someone else. You're too close, and this will end very badly."

Silence.

"I'll be back with a warrant, you have my word," he shouted. "And I'm not the lead investigator anymore. The FBI's taken over my case."

"Good" was all the woman said before pounding footsteps announced the detective had shown himself out.

Moments later, the bookshelf was eased forward and they were beckoned to come out. Angie delivered a slew of questions about what she'd just heard, and even Gavin managed to shoot off a few of his own.

But they would not learn anything else at After Midnight that evening except a quick acknowledgment that the six men in the pictures were the six men she remembered beating her Apollo. After that, all Madam Midnight said was, "I've told you too much already," before she showed them out.

Angie was extremely bothered by the conversation she'd overheard. It nagged at her curiosity in a savage sort of way. Her reeling mind finally settled on two thoughts: It was no accident that the woman had led the detective to a spot where they could hear what he said. And there was no way in hell Angie wouldn't find out what the detective was hiding. No matter what it took.

"You're too close, this will end very badly."

A man terribly wronged. His hard eyes and emotional outbursts. She remembered the early impression, and it stuck with her all the way back to the office.

Chapter Fourteen

T he race back to the office came to an abrupt halt just past the Beltline exit in Grand Prairie on I-30. Traffic was a complete standstill—flashing blue lights half a mile ahead. It could mean only one thing: a major wreck. Cursing, Angie began reading over Gavin's notes, inserting a couple of comments here and there. After ten minutes and no movement, she looked up at the parked cars and let loose another sting of expletives. She pulled out her cell phone and dialed the *Tribune's* Arlington office.

"Hey, Joe, this is Angie. Can you tell me what's going on with I-30 near Beltline? Traffic's completely stopped. Is it shut down?" The cop reporter put her on hold and she waited impatiently for him to pick back up, muttering. "Six-car pileup, two fatalities, cops shut down the highway. Expect to see a couple of Careflight helicopters take off soon." He paused. "Gotta get out there. Thanks for the tip, Angie."

"Damn it, damn it, damn it," she shouted into the now-silent phone.

Just then, people started getting out of their cars and walking toward the flashing blue lights ahead, trying to get a better look. Angie glanced sideways at the drop-off to the access road. They couldn't even pull a Texan and make their own exit to escape the delay. Damn it, indeed.

Gavin shut off the engine and opened his door. "Come on, Angie, there's nothing we can do."

Grudgingly, she got out and lighted a cigarette. She puffed the smoke in the humid Texas heat—far too warm for an early October evening. She refused to follow Gavin as he walked toward the lights like the other spectators. To hell with it. She tugged at her crumpled blouse, trying to straighten it.

Her cell phone rang, pulling her thoughts away from mentally composing paragraphs with the knowledge she'd just obtained.

It was Jimmy. Finally.

"Too busy to call me back, are you?" she immediately teased.

"Nope, just waited what I thought was long enough for you to give up on gaining entrance to After Midnight. Did it work?" His voice was lighthearted, but she detected a note of concern that erased the teasing smile from her lips.

Her pause was apparently too long. "You got in, didn't you?"

"Yeah." She sighed. It had been a long day. Her head was hurting with stress and too much excitement. She didn't want Jimmy to be mad at her but swallowed the apology that was threatening to surface. She didn't need to say she was sorry for doing her job.

She could almost hear Jimmy formulating a response in the seconds that ticked by in silence—interrupted only by the stray blaring of horns farther down the back-up, where drivers couldn't see the flashing blue lights.

"Okay," he finally said, resignation heavy in that single word. "Guess I'll just find another place to buy my toys." He paused again—but this time much shorter. "What's this about calamus, anyway?"

Relieved, Angie gave him the nutshell version of what had happened that day.

Jimmy whistled low into the phone, then said, "So because gay men put that thing together, and I'm a gay man, you assume I'll know the answer."

"I guess...I mean...Damn it, that's exactly what I thought," Angie stammered, fighting a grin that wouldn't stay hidden. "Come on, tell me what it means."

"What do I get out of it?" he demanded, chuckling at her flustered response.

"What do you mean, 'what do I get out of it?' It's just a freaking question," Angie play-huffed, adding a tiny touch of whining for effect. "Please tell me."

"Oh, don't give me that girly crap." His chuckling turned to laughter. When he caught himself, he added, "Try a bribe, darling.

194

You owe me. You practically ensured that I'll never be admitted to After Midnight again."

Well, crap. Angie sighed, raking a hand through her blond hair. Jimmy was good at not-so-subtle guilt trips. The good news was that they didn't happen too often, and the bribes required were usually not very pricey. She went through a list in her head—buy him a massage, buy him dinner, take him out for drinks. No, no, no. She'd used all of those up. And this particular game required that she come up with something new each time.

She weighed her need for instant gratification against her willingness to wait until she made it back to the office and had access to the Internet and its search engines. But in the end, her insatiable curiosity won out.

"How about a trip to the movies?"

"Not good enough. Try again."

Damn it. "Er…how about…I cook you a meal?"

"Are you trying to kill me? Hell no. Try again."

Angie ground her teeth to keep from laughing, which would surely result in more teasing. She closed her eyes and thought long and hard, distracted by Jimmy's lack of interruptions—now that he seemed like he was in a better mood—or suggestions.

"How about a picture of your two dearest friends," meaning her and Lauren. Actually, she thought, that wasn't a bad idea. They could use a couple of good pictures, and Jimmy's photography hobby would come in handy. Of course, that meant he had to make his own bribe. Angie decided she liked the idea and smirked.

"Nude?" he shot back, apparently catching that fact.

Angie gulped and spluttered for a couple of seconds before Jimmy cracked up, his laughter high and clear. Despite the blush that crept up her neck for sheer embarrassment, she was surprised to realize how much she'd missed that sound.

"Gotcha," he said triumphantly when the last few guffaws died off. She could picture him doing a little victory dance. "It doesn't have to be nude, but you may want to consider it anyway. And yeah, I'll take that as my bribe."

"Fine. Now tell me about calamus."

"It's a poetry thing. A lesser known gay symbol. I mean, we have the triangle and rainbow, of course, but the intellectual types prefer the calamus. It's a type of plant. Walt Whitman—whose poetic homoeroticism was the only thing that kept me awake in freshman English, by the way—used it to symbolize masculinity in some of his racier pieces. And if you ever see a calamus plant, you'll understand why." He paused for effect. "I don't know shit about plant anatomy or what's called what, but it looks kind of like a long, thick grass, and it has pieces that jut out and look just like miniature penises. Minus the heads, of course, but very phallic. I wrote a paper on that my senior year in high school."

Angie's mouth formed a large O as she tried to imagine what that paper had been like, knowing her friend's saucy sense of humor. Her mouth finally closed and she began to snicker.

"How very juvenile of you, dear," Jimmy interrupted flatly. "Anyway, it makes sense that a group of gay high school teens interested in poetry would pick a gay symbol that comes from poetry." He waited for a response, then sighed in exasperation. "Woman, stop your silly snickering. You wanted to know and now you know," which, of course, only made her laugh harder.

Tell any giggling person not to do so and they'll get louder. Try as she might, she couldn't stop. It wasn't even that funny. But her day had been one of those extremely draining days after which you needed a good, hard laugh. For the exhausted reporter, this was it. And damned, it was good.

She could feel some of the strain drain away as her shoulders shook with mirth. Things had been entirely too damned difficult lately. If she wasn't running from murder scene to murder scene, collecting bits and pieces for that blockbuster she planned to build, she was stressing out over that crazy-ass serial killer so intent on "helping" her. Not to mention dealing with her boss's anger, her lover's worries, and her incompetent team—thank God they turned out to be all right. Life was becoming too serious. There were too many damned fires to put out and she was tired of playing the firefighter.

What she needed, now that she'd gotten her dose of laughter, was a good backrub. And maybe a couple of drinks. Throw in a cuddling session with Lauren, she thought, and maybe she could salvage the last remnants of the week. It was Friday, after all, and she had two days left.

The giggling finally died away and she managed, "Thanks,

Jimmy. You have no idea how much I needed that. What are you doing tonight? It would be fun to have a few drinks—you, me, and Lauren. What do you say?"

"I thought you'd never ask," he said, and Angie could picture a grin on his face. "Is nine o'clock okay? Think you can tear yourself away from your desk by then?"

"I'll have you know," she shot back, "that I'm not at my desk at all. I'm stuck on I-30 behind a mega-wreck." Just then the blades of two helicopters came to life, a roaring sound even from where she stood, half a mile away. Squinting into the setting sun, she was just able to make out Gavin coming back toward his car. "Hey, I gotta go," she shouted above the roaring choppers. "It looks like maybe they'll clear the highway in a few minutes. I'll see you at nine."

"Until then, darling." And the friendly voice was gone.

Indeed, fifteen minutes later, the first cars inched past the freshly swept accident site, where the bashed-up cars had been moved and dumped on both shoulders. Police officers were urging rubberneckers to move along, but Angie could hardly blame the slow-moving drivers. When she'd told Jimmy it was a mega-wreck, she hadn't realized how extensive the damage had been. The smashed-up vehicles made her shudder and shot a pang of guilt straight through her middle at having been so angry over the relatively small inconvenience of being delayed half an hour—especially since two people had died on the skid mark-blemished site.

"Angie," Tom called out from halfway across the newsroom when she and Gavin rounded the corner from the hallway. He didn't look nearly as excited as Angie thought he should. She'd supposed he would be practically bouncing. Even if the story they planned to write wouldn't run the next day. They simply needed more time than that. But shouldn't Tom be elated over the scoop that would bury their competition?

She marched toward him as quickly as the cast and cane would allow, Gavin close behind. The three met halfway, right at Tom's office door. "Just Angie," he said gruffly, dismissing the fellow with the wave of his hand. Gavin frowned and headed over to Mandy's desk.

Once inside her boss's office, Angie noticed a large, white envelope on Tom's desk with the words, "For Angie Mitchell," scrawled across the front in now-familiar handwriting. Her heart sank. Her eyes darted up to meet Tom's, and he quickly looked away.

"It's not that bad," he said, stopped himself, and snorted. "That is, the messages are not bad, at least the ones I can read— guy can't write for shit. What is bad, though, is that you got another freaking correspondence at all."

He pulled out the contents of the envelope—printouts of her earlier online stories, this time marked up with red ink instead of black. The killer had apparently been eager to make his remarks sooner rather than later, unable to wait until the next day's paper came out with a fuller account. The online stories looked like graded essays. In fact, one article sported an encircled B in the top right corner. What the hell was up with this guy?

"I can't be certain, but it looks like the first posting wasn't good enough." He pointed to the many markups. The page was so red it looked like it was bleeding. "The only thing I can make out for sure is, 'far below her standard.'" He paused, put the paper on his desk, and held up another. "This one obviously has less markings, isn't nearly as angry-looking." He put it down and selected the final printout. "This one, on the other hand, is interesting. Look here," he said, and motioned for Angie to come closer. "Check this out: 'And more sins are revealed,' right next to the paragraph about the drugs. It's hard to tell, but I think the next line below that is, 'with many more to come—the writer is getting closer to the root of the matter.'"

Tom watched her examining the printouts. He wasn't exactly angry—more concerned than anything. When she finished, she sighed heavily and sat in his chair. She definitely needed to just go home. But there was no way in hell she could expect such a wonderful thought to become reality anytime soon. There were paragraphs to construct, an intern and fellow to supervise, and investigation results to relate and explain.

"Jay will be on his way in a little while," he said. "Seems he was stuck in traffic and had to get back to the station to take care of something when I called. The package came more than an hour ago, dropped off anonymously at the front door. I made copies,

198

though."

"I'd like to make my own copies," she immediately said.

"Already done," Tom said.

Good. There was no way she'd sit around waiting for hours to find out what the hell that guy had written all over the printouts like last time. Not when she had a perfectly fine chicken scratch translator waiting at home. And just maybe, if she asked for Lauren's help this time instead of trying to hide the shit that hit the fan, it would make her lover feel more like she was behind the scenes, had some semblance of control with the shared knowledge they'd gain. At least they would both know what was going on this time. Besides, the idea of speaking with Detective Key after what she'd overheard earlier did not seem very appealing.

Not knowing how much time she had before the detective would show up, she gave Tom the nutshell version of what she and Gavin learned at After Midnight. Her editor leaned forward in his seat, listening raptly, interjecting an excited question here and there. When she finished, he leaned back in his seat and knitted his fingers, eyes focused inwardly.

"Listen, Angie, I've been thinking…" her boss finally started, stopped, and shook his head. A small smile shaped his lips before he continued. "When's the last time you were indicted on obstruction of justice charges?"

"What?" Her eyes widened and she mouthed several mute words before answering, "Never, Tom. You know that."

"You and me both." He chuckled at her puzzled expression. "Don't you think it's about time?"

"What the hell are you talking about? Hell no, it isn't 'about time.'"

"Angie, what we have here," he picked up the printouts and waved them in the air, "is one hell of a story. It's important stuff." He slid out of his chair and rounded the desk, paced several seconds behind Angie's chair so that she had to crane her neck around to watch him, and stopped. "Don't you want this to be in your story?"

She stared at him for a good thirty seconds, trying not to reject the idea outright. What would happen if they did? Was this supposed to be solely a private message, or did the killer want his handiwork plastered across the news? For that matter, did she really care what said killer wanted?

Angie was pretty damned sure that their killer was the man who'd gone by the name Apollo. And said man had already proved that he had a tendency for ultra-violence and for theatric flare in his modus operandi, if the crime scenes he left were any indication. Not to mention he seemed to be a touch narcissistic in his belief that he could "educate" Angie on the finer aspects of her work, delivering commentary on the most pertinent articles.

Which led her to believe that just maybe he wanted to see more of his efforts in print. What made her believe this the most was the pink spray paint he'd left on his third victim's door and the text message she'd received earlier that day. He'd actually helped her get the story.

And why not print his comments in the paper? Part of her job was to get all sides of the story. So far, she had a bunch of mourning relatives and investigators. Usually, readers don't get the third side—that of the accused killer—until he or she hires a lawyer after arrest and the defense attorney becomes the public relations liaison for the arrested party. That's just the way it usually is.

Still, the killer might just freak out. Maybe he'd enjoy being even more in the spotlight than before. The thought that it might put her safety more at risk than it already was seriously worried her. He did, after all, know where she lived. Besides, Detective Key had expressly ordered her not to print "one single word" the last time she'd received such an envelope. That had pissed her off. Of course, he hadn't ordered her yet not to do so with the second set of marked-up articles. Angie conveniently blocked out the voice inside that shouted, "He hasn't had a chance yet."

Very slowly, she nodded in response to her editor's question—grudgingly admitting that her desire to see what happened outweighed legal consequences. But it was one thing to be curious as to what the killer would do. It was a different matter altogether imagining the legal headaches such a brazen act might cause.

Tom gave her a long, appraising look before saying, "I won't force this into your story." He put his hand on her shoulder and squeezed, the first comforting and friendly gesture he'd given her in weeks. "But this is one of those 'once in a lifetime' type of deals. I want you to understand that. And besides," he chuckled and dropped his comforting hand, "I'd say probably ninety percent of all good investigative reporters have been indicted once in their careers. Or at least they were threatened with such."

Angie looked up into his expectant face. The more she thought about it, the more she thought she wanted to print the comments, too. And so with less hesitation, she gave him a go-ahead nod.

"I've cleared it already with the big boss," Tom said. "He says it's not like the cops can claim you leaked a big secret that wouldn't come out if we went over to the station right now and demanded a copy of the police report Jay made when the first package came, using those first comments instead of these." He went back to his chair and typed in a series of commands. "Come here and read this."

Angie forced her tired body to rise from the chair and limped around his desk to peer over her boss's shoulder. He'd composed a couple of simple paragraphs, which said:

"Shortly after seven p.m., a security officer working at the *Tribune* building night entrance was handed an envelope by what he described as a white man with medium build, red hair, wearing a blue ball cap and gray sweatshirt. The security officer contacted an editor in the newsroom, who retrieved the envelope and discovered several messages inside.

"Someone scrawled extensive commentary in red ink across printouts of several online articles that were posted Friday morning and afternoon recounting the latest murder in the string of homicides over the past five weeks."

Tom interrupted her reading to say that he and Mandy had already typed up information on the Vail homicide to be included in the story.

"Police have confirmed that they believe the envelope came from the killer and was written by the killer.

"Next to a paragraph relating that police had found drugs in all of the Fort Worth victim's apartments, the commentator scribbled, 'And more sins are revealed, with many more to come—the writer is getting closer to the root of the matter.'

"There are many more comments written in the margins of the printouts, but the *Tribune* staff was unable to read them. The *Tribune* has handed over the envelope and its contents to

201

investigators. A team of laboratory analysts will examine the documents carefully for further clues."

Angie read and reread the five paragraphs several times. She asked about the police confirmation, which hadn't happened yet, and Tom said it would surely come up in conversation when the detective came to his office. She read the paragraphs again before deciding that they would do.

"You were pretty sure I'd go along with this," she remarked off-handedly and snorted. "You think you know me that well, huh?"

"Of course I knew. Like I've said a thousand times, you're my most brazen, bull-headed, gutsy reporter. You're a damned handful, Mitchell, but it comes in handy sometimes."

And he laughed. She hadn't heard him laugh for weeks. It felt incredibly nice.

"Since I wrote all of that, I'm putting my name in the byline—not to take away your glory," he smirked, "but because I won't ask you to risk indictment without someone to share the burden."

Angie opened her mouth to object, closed it, and nodded. He was sharing the target, and it was a noble move. Stupid, but noble.

He checked his watch and told her to go on and "get the hell out of here." Angie was only too glad to leave—more because she didn't want to bump into the detective than anything else. She was worried that if pressured, she'd give away the story that would be in the next day's paper. Which would likely result in a visit to the police station. Which in turn would not only be extremely unpleasant, but would also considerably delay her from having drinks with Lauren and Jimmy.

The bigger story—the notes from After Midnight—would hold for a couple of days. It was the kind of article that needed a lot of fine-tuning, that simply couldn't and shouldn't be rushed to the presses. It was unlikely that the *Tribune* would be scooped on it anyway since the path that led them to After Midnight had begun by sheer coincidence. The feds had probably tracked down Jeff Breaux by now and tucked him safely away somewhere. At least, that's what Angie hoped.

She got all the way to the elevator before Madam Midnight's statement to Detective Key crossed her mind again.

"You're too close, and this will end very badly."

Angie had already punched the down button. But when the door chimed and opened, she stood there, gnawing her bottom lip, extremely bothered. She let the door slide shut and turned around, heading back down the hallway. She didn't take the left side entrance into the newsroom but continued instead to the news research office.

She scribbled a few notes on a piece of paper and tore it from her notepad, handing it to the night-shift researcher.

"I want anything and everything you can find on him, no matter how mundane. Something happened—something bad—and I want to know what it was. Please put whatever you find in my mail slot."

The brunette nodded, straightened her shoulders, and started pounding away on her keyboard, already immersed in the task by the time Angie said, "Thanks."

The decision to have info pulled on a law enforcement officer made her uneasy—she shouldn't have a reason not to trust him—but if for nothing other than her own peace of mind, she couldn't let that gnawing gut feeling go unanswered.

It was dark outside when Angie strode across the parking lot and unlocked her car with exhausted, trembling fingers. The next day, she knew, was going to be a bad day. She sat in her car for several seconds with half a mind to call her boss and say she'd changed her mind about those last five paragraphs. But she didn't.

Angie turned the ignition and reached for the volume dial on her radio, determined to drown out the last few hours with the sultry, beautiful voice she knew so well. She'd let her lover's music wash over her in blasting, hot waves. And maybe, if she focused on the lyrics, she'd be able to forget about the day's events long enough to relax her body and mind.

Preying On Generosity

Chapter Fifteen

L auren gnawed at the end of a pencil, her nose nearly touching a printout on the sticky bar table. Occasionally, she'd stop gnawing, jot down a note, and return the writing utensil back to her busy teeth. Watching, Angie wondered how long the pencil's end would hold out before breaking under the distracted biting and chewing. Jimmy snapped his fingers in front of Angie's face, giving her a pointed frown when she dragged her eyes ever-so-slowly away from the pencil to face him.

"Sorry," she muttered and took a sip of lukewarm beer.

He huffed, lighted two cigarettes, and handed her one. They took a long drag in unison—the smoke they expelled swirling above the dimly lit booth toward the ceiling.

As soon as Lauren finished transcribing the comments in her much more legible handwriting, the three could celebrate properly. Lauren's midterm papers had come back with excellent markups, and she was the most relaxed Angie had seen her in weeks, which was plenty reason to celebrate on its own.

Better yet, Jimmy had managed to secure another gig for Fearless—this time at a larger venue with better payment. The band would make three times what they had during their last performance at the Art Bar.

Angie nudged him in the ribs with her elbow. "What exactly did you have to do to get that gig, anyway? I heard there's a lot of under-the-table sort of stuff that goes on in the music industry. You didn't provide any…special services, did you?"

Jimmy coughed on smoke released a bit too quickly. He glared at her for a few seconds, but the twitching corners of his mouth gave away that he wasn't really offended.

"You'd like that, wouldn't you?" he snorted and took another drag. "That would suit your fetish with seedy underground business dealings just fine, wouldn't it?"

"I don't have a fetish for…"

"We found a bunch of trashy mystery novels under your bed that would indicate otherwise."

Now it was Angie's turn to cough and clear her throat.

"What did I tell you last time about going through my stuff?" She caught his satisfied smirk and snorted, her eyes drifting back to Lauren, who looked suspiciously as though she were over-concentrating on the task at hand. She slipped a hand below the table and drew a line from Lauren's knee to her upper thigh, finding a particularly sensitive spot where she dug her fingers in, making the other woman jump.

"What?" Lauren demanded, taking the pencil from her mouth and looking up from the printout. Angie looked from one to the other and sighed.

"I can't trust either of you, can I?"

Lauren stuck the pencil back in her mouth and smirked around it. "Duh," she said. Jimmy grinned outright, shaking his head.

Damn.

"Are you almost done yet, or what?" Angie shot at her lover.

"You want me to do this half-assed or the right way?"

Angie drained her glass and set it back down on the table with a clank. She wasn't really upset. And likely, this sort of reaction was the exact reason why Jimmy loved to break the rules. He was the troublemaker, after all; Lauren just went along with his antics. Sometimes, they were like a couple of misbehaved children. But at least they weren't boring.

She flagged down their waitress and ordered another beer for herself and Jimmy. Lauren had hardly touched hers. She'd been too busy examining the printouts for the past half hour.

When Angie had first come home, on time for once, she'd interrupted a game of poker—Jimmy seemed to be losing miserably—and immediately handed the photocopied printouts to Lauren, whose happy expression had faltered only for a second, worry lines flitting across her forehead, before she settled on a forcibly pleasant smile. And though Angie had caught the brief look of extreme worry, she kept her mouth shut.

They had gone on the Internet and printed out matching articles, minus the commentary, so Lauren could transcribe the messages in the exact same spots the killer had chosen. Then they'd headed out to the bar instead of working on them at the apartment because, as Jimmy said, "you look like you need a damned drink." Angie had been uncertain whether he had referred to her or Lauren. In either case, he was probably right.

Waiting for Lauren to complete the transcription was proving a test of Angie's patience for two reasons: She wanted to know what the hell all that red ink said, and she wanted to get it over with so they could relax.

Jimmy began to babble about the upcoming gig. He'd begun to set it up two weeks prior but waited until he got the official go-ahead before telling anyone. At least this time, Lauren would have a month to prepare. Which was a damned good thing. Angie didn't know if she had the energy to deal with another weeklong freak-out. Not that she could blame the woman—performing relatively cold on stage was not her idea of a good time, either.

That article in the *Dallas Alternative* had provided sufficient leverage to get the band in at the Gypsy Tea Room, and Jimmy hadn't had to "provide any special services." It had been a good write-up for a band that didn't take itself too seriously. Angie had clipped the article from the paper and hung it on her fridge.

With a pang of guilt, Angie realized she hadn't shown much interest in the band's dealings lately. She'd been so preoccupied with work that she hadn't bothered to ask when the next gig was or how the site that Jimmy had created was doing. Her eyes drifted back to Lauren and the guilt intensified. The woman was working hard on the last page of the Internet articles. She was almost done with a task Angie had practically demanded she do, yet Angie herself hadn't even bothered to ask for weeks how school was going or how the band was doing.

Angie drew a long breath and took a sip of beer. Her shoulders were tight with dread and stress. She stared into her glass and took another sip. She looked up and caught Jimmy watching her.

"So," she drew out the word, not knowing how to formulate the questions without showing how much she'd missed in the last couple of weeks. In the end, she decided to try off-handed. "How's

Fearless's site doing?"

Lauren looked up from the printout, a surprised look on her face.

"Better than expected, actually," Jimmy said before Lauren could say a word. "Thanks for asking. We thought you'd forgotten the band existed."

"Not forgotten," Lauren interjected, shooting him a look.

"Anyway," Jimmy plowed ahead, ignoring the interruption. "We've gotten a lot of donations through PayPal. I set it up so you can download any song for a dollar."

"Really?" Angie couldn't keep the surprise out of her voice. The one and only time she'd visited the site, there hadn't been such an option.

"Really?" Jimmy mocked her and snorted. "It's been like that for two weeks. Seriously, you need to get with the program."

Angie dropped her eyes to the table and began fiddling with a napkin. She felt a hand squeeze her knee under the table. Lauren leaned in and brushed lips along her cheek, settling on a quick kiss.

"I know you've been busy," Lauren whispered, her breath tickling Angie's ear. "I knew you'd ask eventually. Some of us have more patience than others." She snickered and nipped Angie's ear playfully. "But a little more interest would be nice."

Angie shivered and nodded. Yeah, she needed to be a little less self-absorbed, too.

Lauren slid back into her spot and set the printouts aside. "Later," she said when Angie looked up and reached for them. "Right now, we're at a bar, and we're going to enjoy our time here." She pointed at the stack of paper. "Those are not conducive to us enjoying ourselves."

There was a note of disgust in her voice, which practically tripled Angie's curiosity. But she ground her teeth and nodded in silent surrender. Her lover was right, after all, and it wasn't as if she could do much with the comments at that moment anyway.

Angie lighted another cigarette. "How much money have people donated?"

Lauren's soft smile grew into a big grin. "You tell her, Jimmy. It was your idea."

Jimmy rested his chin on interlaced fingers, leaning forward.

Very slowly, he said, "Three thousand dollars in two weeks."

Angie's eyes nearly popped out and she dropped her cigarette on the table.

"Three thousand dollars?" she asked, incredulous.

"Three thousand dollars," Lauren confirmed, her grin widening. "In two weeks."

"Holy crap."

"Yeah," Jimmy agreed. "I checked our PayPal account this morning and thought there was a mistake. Then I did a search online and discovered that the band is being talked about in all these blogs and forums. It seems the word is out."

"And the money?"

"Wired to a Peace Corps buddy of mine in Micronesia. They'll be able to buy a hell of a lot of books for the library we built last year."

Angie laughed. She couldn't help it. Not because buying books for a tiny island library was funny, of course, but because it was almost too good to be true. And because such a big deal had happened in the last couple of weeks and she didn't even know about it. Her laughter was the kind of guilt-ridden, laugh-or-cry response. Her lover should have been disappointed, maybe even furious. That she wasn't was extremely relieving.

"Since I've been such an ass," she finally said, "I'll tell you what. I'll do my best to sell your story to a reporter in the features department—get you some more hits and donations. And if that doesn't work, I'll help you any other way I can." She paused. "This is really good news, you two. Congratulations."

"Hey, you can't take my job," Jimmy said and grinned. "I'm the business manager. I get to talk to the press."

"You just miss seeing your name in print," Angie interrupted, smiling.

"Yeah, well, since you don't write about cool computer geek stuff anymore, how else am I supposed to get in the paper?"

"You could set something on fire…"

"Or kidnap somebody…" Lauren joined in.

"Or jack somebody's car…" Angie continued, louder now.

"Or you two could just shut up," Jimmy shouted, cutting the two women off with a wave of his hand, trying not to laugh and failing miserably.

Their conversation dissolved into a fit of ruckus laughter, which began to draw attention until they were finally told to calm down by the waitress. Not that it stopped them or that they cared. They were just three friends out having a good time. And, Angie thought, after all the drama, to hell with anyone who tried to stop them. She needed it.

It was the first crisp morning of the season. Texas weather typically does a bizarre flip-flop thing halfway through October— you get up and it's hot as hell; you go to bed, and the next day, it's really freaking cold outside. There is no autumn. Not really.

Angie and Lauren were sitting side by side on the balcony, wrapped in a rust-colored wool blanket, shivering as the winter air swept through their hair and tickled their rosy cheeks. Since it was the first cold day, they'd decided to enjoy it outside with a couple of steaming hot cups of cinnamon tea. They shivered together and said nothing, eyes drifting along the outlines of barren trees and gray skies—both lost in unpleasant thoughts. Angie scooted a little closer to Lauren, and the taller woman wrapped a comforting arm around her shoulders.

They'd made it back to the apartment far too late to deal with the printouts. Even Angie, who'd practically chewed her bottom lip raw in an effort not to snatch at the papers while they were still at the bar, had relinquished her quest to find out what the hell was written when they walked through the dark apartment—her eyes bleary with exhaustion. Lauren had set them on the coffee table and they'd simply gone to bed.

But when morning light first pooled in streaks onto their bed, draping lines across Angie's face so that she woke, she couldn't resist the temptation of slipping out and reading what her lover had transcribed. Shivering in her T-shirt and pajama pants in the living room, she'd scanned the comments line by line until she'd checked and double checked every word.

She'd dropped the papers back onto the coffee table and wandered into the kitchen to brew a pot of tea, muttering the comments back to herself.

Most of the written lines were more of the same-old, same-old—the writer needs to learn this or that; the writer needs to respect this aspect of the crime; the writer asked a good question here, left off an important one there. Only a few comments truly troubled her, made her stare into space in contemplation as the teapot sputtered and hissed.

"Four reported, one unmentioned, two more to come."

The "four reported," she knew referred to the local victims— Ben Whittaker, Chance Lockett, William Saunders, and Guillermo Ramirez. The "one unmentioned" must be Trey Greenly, the man murdered in Vail, Colorado, that until the day before she hadn't realized was connected. Paragraphs about that crime would be in the Saturday paper but wouldn't have been in her online stories. It made sense. What made Angie pause was the last bit—"two more to come."

There were only six faces pictured in the calamus poetry book. The last member was Jeff Breaux, who as far as she knew, was not yet a victim. And with the feds crawling all over Fort Worth and in possession of said poetry book, he should have been picked up and safely tucked away somewhere.

Who then was this seventh person? The one whom the killer suggested in his comments would join the other victims? "Two more to come," it said, not "one."

Angie realized with a start that the teapot was emitting a high-pitched screeching sound and she jumped, quickly removing it from the burner. She was extremely glad she'd closed the bedroom door. It was still early, about eight o'clock, and she hadn't wanted to spoil her lover's rare sleep-in opportunity.

She added a chamomile teabag to her cup before pouring the boiling water. She needed something to calm her racing heart. She wasn't so much worried for Jeff Breaux as she was for this unknown seventh person. For the life of her, she couldn't figure out why she was so troubled. All she knew was that a bad feeling had begun to spread through her gut and tighten around her heart, making it hammer hard in protest—a terribly unpleasant feeling that made her feel slightly weak-kneed at the same time.

Angie stepped into a pair of worn slippers and threw on a winter coat before stepping outside. She trudged through the piercing wind to her car where the photocopies of that poetry book lay scattered across the passenger seat.

Back inside her apartment, she cranked up the heat, her nose scrunching slightly against the musty smell blasting from the central air unit, which spoke of months without use. She sat on the couch and flipped through the pages, scanning the names below each poem, looking for a seventh name. She didn't find one. Frustrated, she tossed the stack onto the floor and sipped her tea, with worry lines etched across her forehead.

She felt as though she was missing something, as if the answers were all in plain view but she couldn't quite see them. The killer was dropping hints left and right, but she couldn't understand half of what he was trying to tell her.

Angie went to take another sip and realized the cup was empty. She'd been sitting on the couch for longer than she'd thought and sighed.

"You're up early," a warm voice said over her shoulder, the statement followed by sleep-warmed hands touching the back of her neck, digging in and massaging in slow, soothing circles. Angie closed her eyes and let her chin drop down to her chest in appreciation.

"You're wondering about the seventh person, aren't you?" Lauren's rich voice drew her attention back to the problem at hand. Angie nodded.

The pleasantries of the prior evening had ended with a brief discussion on the way home about the poetry book, how it was obtained, and its ramifications. It wasn't even Angie who'd brought it up; Jimmy had tossed it into the midst of tipsy conversation halfway back to Angie's apartment, wondering if anything new had come of it. Lauren had grown rather quiet and had made no comments on the matter.

"Yes," Angie said, rolling her head until her neck popped after her lover's kneading hands retreated. "I just don't understand it. There's not a seventh person anywhere in the clique's book."

"Maybe the seventh person doesn't have anything to do with the clique."

"But that wouldn't make any sense…" Angie began, stopped, and slowly opened her eyes, which had drifted shut during the pleasant ministrations. "Unless…" She paused, considered her words as if to make sure they were logical, and continued, "Unless the seventh person was a more recent addition to the group, say, after the book was made."

"Could be," her lover had acknowledged while sitting next to her.

Angie frowned and thought about it some more. As she reflected back on her conversation with the madam, it didn't seem to make sense since the woman had agreed that there'd only been six men. Why would the killer go after a seventh, if there had been only six?

"Lauren, if you worked at a place like After Midnight and got attacked by six crazy people while you were...um...working, would you be pissed off at your boss more or less than at your attackers?"

Lauren's eyebrows shot up at the unexpected question. She hesitated several seconds before saying, "It depends on what the boss did about it, I guess." She thought about it for another minute or so. "If the boss did nothing—didn't go to the police or take care of me or whatever—I think I'd be pretty pissed off, yeah."

Angie nodded and glanced at the photocopies of her articles on the table. Maybe the madam was in as much danger as Jeff Breaux. The thought bothered her, but she couldn't quite believe that this seventh person would be the owner of After Midnight. She couldn't have said why, but it just didn't seem right.

Of course, she wasn't a serial killer and couldn't begin to figure this one out. She wondered if the feds had hooked up a behavior analyst with their evidence yet. And if so, she'd sure like to get her hands on whatever notes the profiler had taken.

The only thing Angie felt sure of was that Apollo was out for revenge in a very sick and twisted way. And so far, he'd been quite successful.

Lauren had gotten up from the couch and made a fresh pot of tea, filled two cups with cinnamon teabags, and had tempted Angie outside with promises of cuddling and refreshing cold air. It wasn't as good as the idea of rain on her face, but Angie had taken the offer anyway.

The two women sat on the balcony and shivered—Angie's nose pressed into the crook of Lauren's neck, both troubled over the murderer's comments. The day was promising to be a solemn one.

Angie's cane and cast clicked down the *Tribune's* third-floor hallway in quick, efficient steps. She was here for one purpose and one purpose only. She told herself she'd stop by the research department—hopefully without anyone other than the research assistant seeing her—and she'd get the hell out of the office. She wasn't on the schedule that Saturday, and she preferred to keep from getting roped into some assignment or another. Not to mention that she absolutely had to make it to class that day. She'd already used up all of her absences, and it would be pretty damned stupid if she flunked the course for the sole reason of not being able to show up.

The sports department was empty. Good. The little side hallway leading to the newsroom was empty. Good. Three more doors and she'd make it as far as the research office without being noticed. With a sigh of relief, she put her hand on the door and slipped inside.

"Hi, Rose," Angie greeted the dayshift researcher and wandered over to the counter behind which a woman in her late forties was busy sorting through a mountain of papers.

The woman looked up and smiled. "I'm glad you came in today. Now I can get some of this crap off my desk."

Angie's eyes followed her pointing finger, which indicated a folder marked, "Angie Mitchell. Info requested 10/19/05." The folder was thicker than she'd expected. She raised her eyebrow in a silent question.

Rose chuckled and picked up the folder, holding it out for her to take.

"It looks like you got more than you bargained for, huh? Your note did say, 'everything and anything.'"

"Yeah, I guess I did request that. Thanks," she said and tucked the thick folder under her arm, wondering what the hell Detective Key had done to manage so many references. It's not as if the *Tribune* researchers would have access to his employment reviews or anything like that—more like mentions in other newspapers, on television, that sort of thing. Angie remembered the boxing photograph she'd spotted in his cubicle and resisted the urge to roll her eyes. Of course. She'd be willing to bet that a good chunk of the folder was comprised of old tournament results.

"Thanks again," she sighed and hurried out of the office and down the long hallway to the elevator. She actually made it to her car without bumping into any of her regular colleagues. She pulled out of the parking lot with a sigh of relief.

It was almost noon and she decided to read over the folder's contents in the university's library, conveniently located next to the building where she'd have her afternoon class. She plunked a couple of quarters into a coffee vending machine and eagerly retrieved the cup, snorting when the hot, bitter stuff touched her tongue.

"Tastes like shit," she muttered with half a mind to toss the cup in the trash as she marched over to the library's main elevator. She took another sip and her eyes watered in sympathy for her mouth. She shuddered and tossed the damned thing in a nearby trash can once she stepped out of the elevator onto the third floor.

The library was eerily quiet that Saturday afternoon. It wasn't close enough to finals yet for it to be bustling so "early" on a weekend. Angie found her old favorite spot—an ancient sofa in the far west corner behind the foreign newspaper collection—and plopped down with a sigh of relief that no one had taken "her" spot.

As she'd suspected, a bulk of the folder was printouts of tournament results that had been copied onto microfiche some time before. Apparently, the detective had been quite good at boxing, but Angie didn't care too much about that part of his life. Her eyes quickly scanned the top of each page, found the boxing association heading, and discarded the information quickly. The stack of photocopies in the folder was quickly dwindling, and she worried that she might have wasted the researcher's time.

But halfway through the pile, just when she began to think that she couldn't trust her gut anymore, her fingers touched the top of a page that didn't contain tournament results. The page was stapled to several others. As she read the following ten pages, her eyes widened and her mouth opened in surprise.

The stapled pages were a basic report—the kind any person can get for fifty bucks off the Internet—a cross-listing of a person's Social Security number associated with various aliases a person has used and possible first-degree relatives said person might have. Most people have aliases, even if it's unintentional. Edward is sometimes "Ed" or "Ted." But in Detective Key's case, it wasn't "Johnny" and "John" and "Jay."

It was Nathaniel Howard Gillyworth.

He'd changed his name, as affirmed by an attached report.

"Nathaniel Howard Gillyworth?" she muttered, scanning further aliases of "Nathan" and "Nate" and "N.H."

Her mouth felt dry and she wished she hadn't thrown away the paper cup of nasty, cheap coffee. She licked her lips in an effort to wet her mouth. Her eyes kept darting back to the unfamiliar alias for Detective Key.

She set the report in her lap and reached for the next page in the folder. It was a copy of the afternoon edition of the now-defunct *Dallas Star*—a paper that had gone under a decade before. It was dated July 6, 1987. Angie read the first few lines and swallowed hard.

"DALLAS — Police released today that the bodies of Charles and Alissa Gillyworth, two affluent Dallas socialites, were discovered in a mansion that went up in flames shortly after midnight on Friday.

"The bodies were found in two separate bathtubs. Their deaths do not appear to be accidental, said Dallas Detective William Sooner. He declined to elaborate.

"The couple's two children were not harmed. Matthew Gillyworth, fifteen, had spent the night at a friend's house and has been taken into child custody for the time being. Nathaniel Gillyworth, twenty-four, does not live with his parents..."

Angie expelled a breath of air she hadn't realized she'd been holding. She flipped through numerous additional *Dallas Star* articles that further detailed the double homicide. Apparently, no one was ever arrested for the crimes. Both sons had been thoroughly questioned and had been ruled out as suspects. There'd been speculation that they stood to gain a hefty inheritance. A later article revealed that their parents had lost most of their money in poor stock market choices.

But by the number of articles written about the fire and murders, Angie knew there had been quite a media frenzy on the subject.

Angie reviewed the report on Detective Key. It said he'd been born to an Alissa and Robert Key. His birth record read Nathaniel Howard Key. A hand-scribbled note from Rose said that Robert and Alissa divorced in 1971, when Nathaniel was eight years old. Alissa had then married Charles Gillyworth less than a year later.

Matthew was born in 1972. Robert Key had died in a car crash in 1976.

The would-be detective had been twenty-four years old when the fire happened. His mother and stepfather had been murdered and no arrest was ever made in their case. And with the media circus, just maybe, Angie thought, he'd changed his name to get away from it all. He'd taken back his father's surname to ditch the recognizable "Gillyworth." But why change the first name? It's not as if a background check at any job wouldn't turn up the same result that was included in Angie's folder. It didn't seem to make any sense.

What did make sense, though, was that the double homicide at least partly explained the sense she always got from the detective that he was a man terribly wronged. He had been wronged. He'd lost his parents, and their murderer was never found. Perhaps the events had led him to become a cop, although Angie couldn't be sure. There was no indication that he'd ever wanted to be something else—no colleges he'd attended, no trade schools he'd enrolled in—only a long list of crappy, dead-end jobs he hadn't been able to keep for more than a few months at a time. Burger joints. A couple of bars. A car wash. A gas station.

And then the sudden turnaround in 1988, when he'd enrolled at the North Texas police academy and had changed his first name from Nathaniel to Johnny. It all seemed to fit with her hypothesis that his parents' murder had inspired him to follow a path in law enforcement and ultimately in solving homicides.

She wondered about his half-brother, the fifteen-year-old who had ended up in a foster home in the Dallas suburb of Grand Prairie. Angie leafed through the stack of papers and again looked at a photocopy of the July 6, 1987, article. A blurry black-and-white picture showed a young teenager sitting on the sidewalk outside the fire-gutted home. She thought he looked like he was staring into space, completely numb. His face was expressionless—at least that's what Angie thought. It was hard to tell, looking at the copy of a copy of a poor-quality newspaper photograph. The caption read, "Matthew Gillyworth, fifteen, sits on the sidewalk in front his parents' charred home. Authorities said his parents, Charles and Alissa Gillyworth, were found murdered inside."

Angie searched the remaining stack of paper and didn't find much else of interest, save a tiny brief that mentioned Matthew having been mugged and robbed in Oak Cliff in May 1990 and a short article reporting that Key and another Dallas police officer had been put on administrative leave after having been involved in a shootout where a teenage gang member had been fatally struck in the chest. That Detective Key—then Officer Key—had been put on administrative leave was standard policy. Officers who shoot people are generally sent to shrinks while an internal investigation is conducted to make sure the officer hadn't screwed up. That his career hadn't ended meant the outcome of the investigation had been in his favor.

The only other research results were a ton of articles in which Key had been quoted as a police officer, then a detective on various Dallas crimes over the previous decade. And of course, Angie's most recent articles on the Fort Worth murders.

The detective didn't have a wife or any children. His home wasn't worth much. He owned a boat that he kept at Lake Arlington. Nothing exciting about any of that.

Angie rested her head against the high back of the sofa and closed the folder and her eyes. She wasn't sure if she felt relieved to know why the detective behaved the way he did or whether she was upset because of it. But the two emotions swirled around in her head until she felt a familiar throbbing behind her eye sockets.

He'd lost his family. He was allowed to be bitter.

But curse the damned madam at After Midnight—her words kept coming back like a taunting earworm: "You're too close, this will end very badly."

The report had been thorough. Angie knew a hell of a lot more about Detective Key than she had before. But that "too close" business didn't make a damned bit more sense than it had before she'd spent the last two hours poring over the research department's findings. Unless this person who killed the five gay men was the same person who killed his parents—highly unlikely; not even remotely similar MOs or targets—there was no connection whatsoever that she could see.

Angie pinched the bridge of her nose and groaned in annoyance.

Chapter Sixteen

The sun sat squarely on the horizon—just a quick little rest—before it would dip out of view and let the chilly October night take its course. Angie was damned if she was going to let the day slip away so easily without at least trying to complete a full circle of her usual running route—cast or no cast. She squinted at the setting sun, checked a mile-marker in the park, and cursed between gasps for air for a full minute as she hobbled straight ahead, leaning heavily on her cane.

The park would close before she could get back to her car. That didn't mean she couldn't get out, just that she was likely to be questioned by a park security officer. And it meant that she definitely couldn't walk four miles in less than ninety minutes. At one time—it seemed like so long ago but was really only three months past—she'd been down to seven-minute miles.

Her leg muscles screamed in protest, but she paid them no attention. To hell with them. She'd been denied her frustration-venting outlet for too long. A breaking point had been reached. And she told herself her doctor didn't know what the hell he was talking about.

It was the Monday after an extraordinarily long weekend. She'd visited her doctor that morning for the twenty-second of what seemed like a bazillion follow-ups, and he'd given her the bad news: "I'm afraid, Miss Mitchell, that you aren't making sufficient progress to justify removing your cast quite yet. Either you aren't doing enough exercises, or your physical therapist isn't challenging you enough. Regardless, I'm scheduling you for another visit in two weeks, then we'll see where we go from there."

One foot in front of the other. Deep breath. Ignore the pain. Repeat.

Angie was a runner. And for a runner not to run... Well, her temper was suffering hellishly. After leaving her doctor's office, she canceled a physical therapy session and called her lawyer.

"When the hell is that meeting we were supposed to have?" she demanded when his receptionist finally put her through. It's not like yelling at her lawyer was going to solve any problems. But she couldn't very well go running to blow off steam. She called because she was mad at the situation. She was ready for revenge. And going after Ted Henry's pocketbook was the next best thing to ripping his head off, which she couldn't do because he was sitting in the Tarrant County jail.

Her lawyer used the sort of voice one would use on a crazy person to calm her down. He told Angie in that overly soothing voice that they'd have their meeting soon enough and not to worry. Angie had hung up on the man halfway through his goodbyes.

She had then called her boss to tell him she wasn't coming in to work that day; she was too upset and too pissed off. He had listened to her and replied in the same tone her lawyer had used. "Everything will be all right, Angie. Take the day off and relax. I'll see you tomorrow."

She'd replied rather sarcastically and snapped her cell phone shut. She'd called Jimmy, who for once was unable to console her. She'd called Lauren, who didn't answer her phone because she was likely in class. She'd called her mother and complained for a solid hour while the older woman added cautiously, "Oh, that's terrible," every time Angie slowed her ranting long enough to take a breath.

By noon, she was at a chocolate shop consoling herself with truffles and brownies. That kept her mood elevated to "acceptable" for about an hour, by which time she felt sick for all the desserts she had consumed. The sick feeling caused her mood to drop several notches until it was back at the "really freaking pissed off" level.

She tried to make some special treats in the kitchen, succeeding only in creating a new look for the place, namely, a disaster-torn, science-experiment-gone-bad sort of look. She didn't bother to deal with the mess. She was in a full-blown temper tantrum.

Angie was supposed to be wearing a brand-new brace, something she could take off when she slipped into a tub full of steaming hot water with bath salts. In anticipation of her first cast-free day in so long it seemed like forever, she and Lauren had gone to the mall and shopped for expensive bath oils, salts, and other fun body products. They'd spent half a fortune. It was supposed to be worth it.

And then that damned doctor had made his statement and shattered her happy anticipation. Somewhere, in the logical part of her brain, she knew it wasn't his fault that her bones were refusing to mend at a reasonable rate. It wasn't his fault that she was constantly missing her therapy sessions or that she frequently ignored his orders to stay off her feet. No, her leg wasn't royally screwed up. Yes, it would continue to heal and the cast would eventually come off. Yes, it was better she keep the damned cast on for another couple of weeks so that she healed properly and didn't rebreak the bone right away, making things far worse than they already were.

"But damn it, I can't stand this," she muttered over and over again, hell-bent on proving something by completing the four-mile circuit in River Legacy Park. What that was, she wasn't sure. It didn't matter anyway.

A stiff breeze blasted through the barren oak trees along the path and froze her cheeks. She stopped, momentarily surprised. She touched a finger to her face and realized it was wet. She didn't even know she'd been crying. Angrily, she rubbed her sweater sleeve across her face.

Her legs were heavy. The cast weighed a thousand pounds. She could not put one foot in front of the other, take a deep breath, ignore the pain, and repeat. Now that she'd stopped, it felt as if she'd never get going again.

Angie sat on the sidewalk. She pulled a crumpled pack of Marlboro Lights from her pocket and lighted a cigarette. She took a drag and watched the tiny gray cloud be whisked away. She took another drag, slower this time, and released the smoke with a long sigh.

She didn't have her purse, which meant she didn't have her

phone. Both were tucked safely under the driver seat in her Mitsubishi Eclipse, which was parked approximately nine-tenths of a mile away.

Already it was growing darker. She sat for ten, maybe fifteen more minutes. The sky was a brilliant shade of crimson with dark violet splotches where a few tiny clouds had gotten lost on the mostly cloudless October sky. The temperature was also dropping.

Angie pushed up with her arms and tried to stand on her good leg. It wasn't used to so much effort—the type she'd forced it to endure for the past hour—and protested with a spasm that made her knee buckle. She was just able to catch herself without landing on the more vulnerable limb. Her butt plopped down heavily on a sharp rock. Angie yelped.

She cursed, tried again, and gave up.

"Now what?" she muttered and suffered another internal temper tantrum that threatened to launch a headache. She was so absorbed that she didn't hear the footsteps approaching. When a hand touched her shoulder, she screamed.

"Whoa!" a familiar voice shouted through the noise. "I didn't mean to scare you, but your message kind of freaked me out."

And damned if it wasn't Lauren, come to the park to see if that wasn't where she was hiding. Lauren took three quick steps around her and squatted down.

"You scared the crap out of me," Angie announced, a determined grin splitting across her face despite her horrid mood and worse day.

"I gathered that much." Lauren grinned back at her and sat down. She looked at Angie appraisingly for a long while before saying, "So I get out of class and get this crazy message about a 'lunatic, shit-for-brains doctor,' something about 'screw work' and something-something-something 'chocolate.' I didn't understand much else, too many four-letter words spoken too quickly. Any idea who that might have come from?"

Angie snickered and dropped her eyes, blushing furiously. Good thing it was rapidly growing darker outside. She could feel the weight of her lover's eyes continuing to scan her body, calculating how bad her mood really was. But Lauren's presence alone was enough to dissipate some of Angie's anger.

"So anyway," Lauren continued, "I rush over to your place to see if there's anything I can do and find the kitchen totally wrecked. It looks as if someone," she hooked a finger under Angie's chin and forced the grass-green eyes to meet her own, "tried to conduct some sort of science experiment in there and didn't clean up after themselves." She paused. "For the life of me, I couldn't figure out what you were trying to make."

"Italian cream puffs," Angie muttered. A mental picture of her lover's shocked face at finding the kitchen the way she'd left it forced further snickering past her protesting, emotionally roughened throat. She coughed, cleared her throat, and continued to snicker.

"You. Are. Impossible," Lauren said with a half-laugh, before ruffling Angie's hair and wrapping long arms around her shoulders. "I don't know what you think you're doing out here, but whatever it is probably isn't too good for you. So let's get out of here, okay?"

Angie knew by the way Lauren's arms squeezed a touch harder and remained a second longer than usual that the woman had been seriously worried but was trying not to show it. After all, Angie hadn't said anything about going to the park, had only called to vent, had left a long and angry message—apparently fairly incomprehensible at that—and had then disappeared for several hours.

And it was a damned good thing Lauren knew her well enough to know where to look for her. It might have been a long time before anyone else came by to help her out. Her legs were in no shape to continue, even if it was for less than a mile.

She peered up at Lauren, who had gotten back on her feet.

"Um," she hesitated, feeling stupid, "I'm going to need some help."

"I figured," Lauren smirked. "It's what—another mile back to where I found your car?" She offered both hands and Angie took them, allowing herself to be pulled up. Almost immediately, Lauren had to catch her around the waist because her knees shook too hard. The taller and much stronger woman cradled Angie in her arms and started walking down the path.

"We'll be taking a few breaks," she huffed after a couple of minutes and Angie wasn't able to repress a little snicker. "Ha-ha. When I break a leg and make you carry me, let's see how long you last."

Angie snorted in response. It was hardly a fair comparison. Lauren was much heavier with all that lean muscle.

Forty steps later, Lauren sighed heavily, stopped, and gently set Angie down on the path. She stretched her arms out and rolled her shoulders, then sat next to the other woman. She tucked an errant blond strand of hair behind Angie's ear and rubbed the backs of her knuckles along the rosy cheek.

"Thank you for finding me," Angie mumbled sheepishly.

"I was kind of hoping I wouldn't actually find you here." Lauren sighed, then chuckled. "I figured you were at the coffee shop, but you weren't. I checked a couple of places." She paused. "Then I sat down and wondered where your stubborn ass would end up if you were pissed off enough with something to prove. And voilà, here you are."

"Couldn't I have come here just because I like this place?"

Lauren gave Angie a look that plainly said, "No way."

"Puh-leaze. I caught you red-handed."

Angie snorted and dropped her eyes. Then she looked across the path and found a familiar underbrush behind which stood a gigantic Texas oak tree.

"Maybe I just wanted to reminisce," she teased and pointed. Lauren followed her line of sight. A giggle escaped her lips and color crept up her neck and cheeks.

They'd sought refuge under that same tree during a raging summer thunderstorm. They'd kissed there for the first time. That kiss was out of control before their lips even touched.

"Er..." Lauren said and gave a half-laugh.

Angie watched her lover, curious. The tiny laugh lines around the woman's eyes crinkled and her lips twitched with the effort not to giggle.

Angie opened her mouth to ask a question, but the sound of quickly nearing footsteps interrupted her train of thought. Distracted, she peered along the direction from which they'd just come and spotted a jogger heading their way. She and Lauren watched as the man came at them in easy, confident strides, muttered, "Evening," at them as he passed, and disappeared around the bend.

A piece of paper fluttered in the air where he'd just jogged past and Lauren called after him, "You dropped something." The thudding footsteps didn't slow but instead gained momentum. Puzzled, Angie pointed at the piece of paper and Lauren obediently retrieved it for her.

Angie unfolded the paper with Lauren peering over her shoulder.

It was a page ripped from any old regular composition notebook, college ruled. A paragraph of sloppy writing was scrawled in the first three lines. Angie couldn't make out anything but the very first word, which said, "Angie."

She closed her eyes and crumpled the page, dropping it to the forest floor.

She mentally rewound the last three minutes, back to where the jogger was approaching. She saw a blue ball cap, a bright yellow windbreaker, and white tennis shoes. She tried to focus on the man's face or his hair or anything other than the bright-yellow jacket. But try as she might, Angie couldn't remember a single distinguishable feature. Damn it.

When Angie opened her eyes and let her surroundings come back into focus, Lauren was on her cell phone, speaking with a police dispatcher. She was shouting.

"No, you listen to me. You need to get an officer out to River Legacy Park right now. This man is a serial killer and..." Lauren shut up momentarily, her jaw muscles clenching and unclenching as she ground her teeth. "No, I'm not reporting a mugging. No, we're not freaking hurt. You know what? You probably just gave a psychopath killer another chance to slip through the police's fingers because while we're arguing, he's jogging right on out of the park. Congratulations."

Lauren snapped her phone shut, seething with anger. She muttered something about "worthless dispatchers" for several more seconds. Angie blankly stared at the woman's clenched fist, which held the crumpled paper.

"What does it say?" she asked the furious woman, who momentarily stopped her muttering, focused on her, and snapped, "You don't want to know."

Angie took a deep breath. "Yes, I do."

"No, you don't." Lauren's voice rose a notch and she looked away.

"Lauren." Angie reached out and touched the woman's shoulder. "Please."

Lauren's dark eyes, black by dusk, found and locked on Angie's for several silent seconds. She opened her mouth, closed it, and opened it again. She cleared her throat, glancing down at the paper. "It says: 'A thank you note for the wonderful article in Saturday's paper. I feel like you truly understand the importance of what I'm doing, Miss Mitchell. It gives me great comfort. And don't fret too much more about the visit to your doctor; there is much work to be done, many more stories to write. Sincerely, A.'"

Angie heard the words but didn't. Her mind simply rejected them as too ridiculous—at least at first—and she had to make Lauren repeat herself. The woman did, but it didn't make the paragraph, or the situation, seem any more real.

The notebook page was too close, too personal. It was one thing to have received a couple of envelopes. But reading between the lines, this one said clear as day that the man had followed her. Not to mention he'd found her in the park. Or maybe he gave the note to someone to drop off. But Angie doubted that.

Lauren's cell phone rang. She hesitated, her eyes locked on Angie's, but finally flipped the thing open and discovered she had an incensed Fort Worth police dispatcher on the line.

"Officers are on their way, Miss Lucelli," Angie could hear the man practically shouting into the phone. "Please don't go anywhere. Please don't hang up."

"Oh, so now you take me seriously?" Lauren snapped back.

"The Arlington dispatcher didn't know about..." was all Angie could make out. But by the way her lover's aggressive voice calmed, she knew an apology had just been made. Not that it would make much of a difference. Precious minutes had passed. The jogger—surely the killer himself—was more likely than not safely out of the park by now. And all a police officer would accomplish at this point was a lengthy delay.

Lauren hung up the phone. "I'm sorry, but it looks as though we're going to be stuck here for a while."

"Yeah," Angie sighed. "It's okay." She thought about the note and the jogger. "I'm damned glad you came to find me." The last was said with feeling.

Lauren put an arm around her shoulders, and they sat in

226

silence for several seconds. Far in the distance, they could hear police sirens. They sighed dramatically in unison, looked at each other, surprised, and burst out laughing. Not because the incident had been funny or because they had a wonderful evening to look forward to, but because it was a laugh-or-cry kind of deal and they chose the more pleasant of the two routes.

Their laughter was abruptly interrupted. They heard shouting, two male voices, coming from the parking lot area. Lauren jumped to her feet. Angie tried, stumbled, and was caught in strong arms just before she would have fallen.

"What the hell's going on?" Angie demanded of no one in particular.

The screeching sirens were getting louder.

Lauren picked Angie up and walked them around the bend. There were too many trees. They still couldn't see. The taller woman's pace quickened into a light jog. Her breath puffed out in regular, steamy intervals. The shouting continued, growing more urgent. Lauren's arms began to quiver and Angie was worried she'd get dropped on her butt. Just when she was about to start shouting herself, primarily an order to be put down, Lauren's legs carried them around the last bend, out of the trees, and into a circus of flashing red and blue lights.

A yellow windbreaker lay on the ground not three feet from Angie's car.

"Security see something?" Lauren asked, confused, as she set Angie carefully down on the sidewalk, trying desperately to catch her breath.

Angie watched the cops pour out of the vehicles and start running across the park.

"No," she said, realization dawning. "The feds are after him. My tail—the guy who's following me—probably overheard you yelling at the dispatcher. I'd be willing to bet he's the one who lit a fire under the cops' asses."

Lauren snorted and sat next to Angie. They watched the scrambling chaos for several minutes. Angie scanned the parking lot full of cruisers, wondering when someone would come over to take their statements. A chopper's blades sliced through the night and the shouting. A floodlight blasted through the dense shadows from trees.

Then an unmarked car pulled in behind the flashing lights and a redheaded man got out. Detective Key looked decidedly winded. Or agitated. Possibly both.

"Angie," he gasped at her as he marched toward them, digging in his pocked for his notepad. "He was...here...got the call and came fast...the note...tell me."

Angie pinned him with her eyes, scrutinizing the flushed face and rapidly rising and falling chest, watched the puffs of steam escape his lips. His shoulders were shaking as he shivered against the cold air. He'd apparently left his jacket somewhere.

"Been running?" she asked slowly.

"To my car...yes." He paused and took a deep breath. "Give me the note."

His changed demeanor toward Angie was immediately noticeable. He didn't even bother to try with the niceties, even though Lauren was sitting nearby. He was likely excited, of course, because of the evening's events. But she suspected he was none too pleased about Saturday's article.

She handed him the crumpled note without a word, then waited.

The outburst that followed was as predictable as it was unprofessional. A uniformed officer came over to make sure everything was okay. The detective shoved his badge under the fresh-faced cop's nose and ordered him to "fuck off."

Lauren was back on her feet. She never could sit still when something was going on that she perceived as being wrong in any way. She opened her mouth to say something, but Angie grabbed her ankle and squeezed a silent warning.

Lauren shot her a look but clamped her mouth shut. Angie nodded approvingly and let her eyes return to the detective's face.

He was pissed as hell. He wasn't even shivering anymore.

"It's him, all right," he finally said when he'd caught his breath. He ran a hand through his hair and ground his teeth. Then he pulled out a pack of cigarettes, lighted one, and sighed into the flashing lights.

"He'll get away," he deadpanned when no response from either woman was forthcoming. He focused his attention on Angie, took a drag, and released the smoke in an angry expulsion of breath. "You didn't even try to stop him, did you?"

Angie's eyes widened and her jaw dropped.

"Excuse me," Lauren interjected angrily. "But how the hell is she supposed to 'try to stop him?'" She gestured toward the cast and raised a challenging eyebrow. "And anyway, aren't you cops supposed to tell people to let cops do their jobs and not try any vigilante shit? That's what I was always told."

Angie closed her eyes and swallowed hard. She couldn't, she shouldn't.

"What the hell is your problem, Jay?"

Damn. So much for being a good, polite citizen.

He spluttered for several seconds, then cleared his throat. He pinched the bridge of his nose, eyebrows furrowed. And then he laughed.

"What's my problem, indeed?" He opened his eyes. "I got a little carried away. Pressure from the upper brass. I'm frustrated. We're getting nowhere. We have tons and tons of evidence and still no real suspects, nobody we can haul downtown and charge with murder."

"Not my problem," Angie said flatly.

"You're certainly not helping with the pressure part of my job. Let me tell you, that piece you put in Saturday's paper..." He stopped himself and shrugged. Then he switched gears so abruptly it made the two women blink. "Please describe the jogger."

Angie let it go. She wasn't so sure Lauren would. But the other woman unclenched her fists, took a deep breath, and began to talk about the jogger. The detective took her statement, then took Angie's. In the meantime, more FBI showed up to join the cops crawling all over the park. A second chopper joined the police helicopter. Channel Five was shooting footage for the nine o'clock news.

Suddenly, not ten seconds after the detective had asked his last question, a commotion drew their attention to the west end of the park where the trees grew thickest. They heard distinct shouts of "Over there!" and "Come out with your hands in the air!"

"Stay here," Detective Key ordered, drew his gun, and jogged across the park.

Angie itched to follow. She wanted desperately to see what was going on. She tried to stand and grumbled in frustration when a warm hand pushed her shoulder back down. "Angie, no."

A news van peeled around the corner and parked behind Detective Key's unmarked cruiser. Two cameramen jumped out and ran toward them. Angie shook her head and pointed toward the commotion. They jogged toward the crowd of uniforms.

And then Angie saw him, highlighted under the floodlight—big, beefy officer hands clamped over his struggling arms. His head shook wildly, desperately back and forth. He was screaming.

"What the hell's going on? I didn't do anything! I didn't do anything! Get off of me! Let me go!"

He wrenched an arm free and took a swing at the nearest officer. His body suddenly convulsed, and he fell to the ground. Angie knew he'd been shot with a Taser gun. The electronic prongs probably hurt like hell, judging from his surprised scream and subsequent silence. Then there were too many officers in a tight knot around the man to see what was going on. Angie dropped her eyes to the sidewalk and knitted her fingers.

"They got him," Lauren said and slowly sat beside Angie.

"They got somebody," Angie muttered.

"You don't think it's him?"

"That would be too good to be true. And you know how that always works out."

Angie and Lauren barely made it home in time for the ten o'clock news. Once the man had been detained, officers had insisted the two women take a good, long look at him to make sure it was the right guy. Lauren had been certain it was. Angie wasn't so sure. In the end, the cops had lugged him downtown for questioning. And not until after that were they released from the scene.

Of course, Angie knew they could have just walked off. The police couldn't force them to stay. But she felt leaving without the go-ahead would cause far more damage than it was worth. So they'd stayed.

When they pulled into the apartment complex's parking lot, Jimmy was sitting on the stairs leading up to Angie's apartment. He jumped up when he saw them and jogged between their two cars.

"I saw the news," he announced, nearly breathless, his face pale. "I got in my car and headed over there, but the park's entrance was blocked off." He paused, took a deep breath, and took two steps back so Angie could close her car door. "I'm glad to see you two are okay."

Angie's eyes narrowed. What the hell... "What did they say on the news?"

He hesitated, knitting his hands. "Er... They said the killer had sought you out in the park. They said he delivered a message to you personally. They gave your name on the news."

The color drained from Angie's face. A string of nearly breathless profanities slipped from her lips. Lauren seemed equally unimpressed, the muscles along her jaw clenching rhythmically. She was grinding her teeth again.

"Did you really meet the guy?" Jimmy couldn't help himself. He didn't look eager or excited. He wasn't bouncing on his heels. His shoulders were strung tight and he couldn't stop twisting his fingers. The words appeared to have just popped out.

"I don't know," Angie snarled and strode past him. She wasn't mad that he'd come over or angered by his question. Actually, the heads-up was probably nicer to get from him than to see it on television without warning. But she was too damned tired.

And she felt stupid. It was bound to happen. She shouldn't have been surprised. The cameramen recognized her. The cops would have had to explain how they got the emergency call, why they arrested that man. Angie's name was bound to come up.

She hated being in the news. It caused more problems than she could usually deal with. And just when the Ted Henry fiasco had started to drop off the radar, this shit popped up. She'd be in the news again the next day. And they'd bring up the summer incident. There was no doubt about it.

She hobbled up the steps, leaning heavily on her cane. She unlocked the door most unenthusiastically, while Lauren and Jimmy stood over her shoulder, eager to get inside and turn on the television. She knew that's what they wanted but didn't feel like complying. Angie thought about hiding in the bedroom while they watched the news, pretending she wasn't on television again.

But in the end, she knew she had to deal with it.

She sat down on the couch slowly and grabbed the remote. At exactly ten o'clock, she hit the "on" button and the black box flared to life. Lauren sat to her right; Jimmy sat to her left.

"First on news at ten, we have breaking news in Arlington. Clive Johnson reports."

The anchorman vanished, replaced by a live shot from the station's news chopper, where the flashing red and blue lights still lit up River Legacy Park.

"Police arrested a man in his mid-thirties earlier this evening who they believe may be connected to the recent rash of Fort Worth gay murders." The chopper scene switched abruptly to footage shot during the arrest. The man in question was screaming his confusion. The image was jostling, likely because the cameramen kept having to shift positions. It looked like a scene straight out of "C.O.P.S."

"Police received a call from two women on a pathway in the park shortly after eight o'clock. The women claimed a jogger had passed them a note that could only have come from the serial killer who has already killed five men—four in Fort Worth and one in Vail, Colorado. One of the women is *Fort Worth Tribune* reporter Angie Mitchell. According to police, she has received numerous messages from the killer. Investigators have declined to tell us what the most recent note said, only that it was specifically addressed to Miss Mitchell."

Angie cursed at the screen and received smacks on both shoulders to shut up.

The scene switched and Detective Key was saying, "Miss Mitchell recognized the handwriting from earlier correspondence she received from a person we believe is the killer. She was in the park with a friend. They did the right thing and called police."

The scene switched to include Angie and Lauren sitting on the sidewalk. They were speaking with a police officer. The scene changed to crime scene tape around the yellow windbreaker.

Clive Johnson stepped in front of the camera and continued, "Right now, police are trying to determine whether the man they arrested is the same man who committed the horrendous crimes. A police officer told me that the man in custody claims he was paid twenty dollars to deliver the note by another man. We will bring you further updates throughout the hour. Reporting live in Arlington, Clive Johnson, Channel Five."

Angie put the television on mute, disgusted. The next day, she knew, was going to be hell at work. And frankly, she was surprised Tom hadn't yet called to chew her a new one. Maybe he'd finally wised up and realized that none of this was her damned fault. Or maybe he felt responsible after pushing to include the comments from the online articles in Saturday's paper.

Jimmy got up and wandered into the kitchen, where he let out a surprised, "What the hell?" Receiving no response from either woman, he shrugged and opened the fridge door, retrieved three bottles of beer, and headed back into the living room.

"So I decided to fire myself today," he said awkwardly, clearly trying his best to distract from the current situation. Neither woman said a word. Angie looked up briefly, then went back to her internal grumbling.

"Hello? Is anybody home? No? Guess I can strip down to my boxers and do the Macarena then." He got so far as to undo his belt buckle before Lauren jumped up and stopped him, the scowl on her face not quite convincing because little chuckles kept popping out.

Angie dragged her eyes from the carpet and focused on the two. She watched the silly struggle—Jimmy trying to pull down his pants, Lauren trying to stop him—and finally processed what he'd said.

"Wait," she cut through their giggling. "Did you say you fired yourself?"

The giggling stopped, and he reluctantly redid his buckle, pouting just a little. "Yeah, I did say that." He looked as if he regretted the announcement, as though he'd used it only as kind of a trump card, a bomb dropped to obliterate any current foul moods.

"Why?" Angie asked, curious in spite of other goings-on.

Jimmy began to fidget with his hands again, just like he had been twisting them in the parking lot less than half an hour earlier.

"Come on, why?" Lauren echoed the question, jabbing him in the rib with her index finger.

"Er... Quit poking me, damn it." He paused, sighed at the expectant expressions, and caved. "I don't want to be a computer geek forever. I want to do other things."

"Like what?" Angie and Lauren demanded in unison, looked at each other, and snorted.

"Like what I did for Fearless. That was pretty cool. I want to do more stuff like that," he finally answered, twisted his fingers some more, and laughed nervously. "You might think it's stupid, but I just...felt like I needed some change in my life."

There was an awkward silence. He threatened to unbuckle his pants again.

"So, ah...I guess you'll have a lot of time then, huh?"

"I'm not going to stop working, Angie. I just want—well, you and Lauren are doing important stuff. I'm fixing computer shit. I'm sick of it anyway. I'll figure something out. And for now, I'm set. Some guy bought my company for a nice chunk of cash." He paused and held up his finger to silence the question that shot to Angie's lips. "And it's none of your damned business how much money I got."

Lauren smirked and was about to add her own two cents when her eyes caught something on the muted television. She scrambled for the remote and turned up the volume.

"...Officials are now saying that the man they arrested is not the man they are seeking in the Fort Worth gay murders. The man they arrested—Max Stephens of Arlington—was paid twenty dollars to deliver the handwritten note that police believe came from the killer and was intended for *Fort Worth Tribune* reporter Angie Mitchell. Mr. Stephens described the man who paid him as having red hair, being of medium build, and standing about five feet eight inches tall. His description matches those police have released from witnesses connected to the murder investigation.

"Mr. Stephens has dark brown hair and is over six feet tall. Police still have him in custody for further questions but will likely release him soon."

Angie took the remote from Lauren and muted the television. She twisted the cap off the bottle of beer Jimmy handed her, set the cap on the coffee table, and took a long drink.

"So that's it then," Jimmy said, sounding thoroughly disappointed. "He's still out there, preying on our community."

"Picking off specific targets," Angie interjected.

"Right," Jimmy said as though he didn't quite believe it. Angie couldn't tell if his tone was sarcastic or not. But it was laced with something other than humor and wit, no matter how he tried to disguise it with that high-pitched laugh of his.

Even Lauren gave him a funny look.

Jimmy shrugged, took a sip of beer, and proceeded to tell them how he'd managed to auction off his business on eBay.

Preying On Generosity

Chapter Seventeen

There's something we need to talk about, and it's important. But not tonight. Give me a call in a couple of days. I'll be busy until then—settling up things with my business."

While Angie buckled her seatbelt and backed out of her parking space, she couldn't help but think about what Jimmy had said right before he left. Lauren had been in the bathroom and he'd clearly waited until they were alone.

She'd tried to press him for specifics, but he'd refused to elaborate.

Angie put her car in drive and pulled out of the parking lot. It was really starting to bug her. She wondered if she couldn't just call him later. But he'd said he would be busy. She turned up the volume, tried to drown out her curiosity with light rock, but she kept drifting back to the look in his brown eyes—so uncharacteristically serious. Why couldn't he have just told her? More importantly, what could he possibly have to tell her that he couldn't say in front of Lauren? Unless, of course, it was another surprise. But it hadn't sounded like something along those lines. And Angie was pretty damned sure there was very little about Jimmy that her lover didn't already know if it wasn't a surprise. And that's what was bugging the hell out of her.

With a start, she realized she was almost at the office downtown. She took a sip of Coke—gotta get that caffeine in the system—and shook her head.

"Never a good thing when you can't remember a single stoplight being red," she muttered, trying to wake up just a little more and get Jimmy out of her head.

Her allotted parking spot was occupied. Damn it. She'd almost struck the bright yellow car as she swung hers around the bend with practiced ease. She came to a screeching halt barely an inch from its bumper. She put her car in reverse to pull around. The whole lot was full—highly unusual so early in the morning.

She was forced to pick a spot in the paid lot on the other side of the *Tribune* building. Fuming, she hobbled across Taylor Street and marched toward the entrance with half a mind to ask security to tow the offending yellow car.

Angie strode through the sliding glass door and flashed her ID badge at the guard. She got so far as to punch the up button for the elevator before she realized she was being spoken to.

"Excuse me?" she asked, turning to face the security guy.

"I was wondering if you were okay, Miss Mitchell."

She stared blankly at him for a few seconds, wondering what he meant. If he spoke to her it all, it was usually things like, "Good morning, Miss Mitchell," or, "Have a good one," or the occasional, "Enjoy the nice weather," when she was marching out of the office for a midafternoon pick-me-up at Starbucks.

A chime announced that the elevator doors would spring open momentarily.

"Sure," she muttered, still puzzled.

"Must have given you a fright, though. I can't imagine."

"Oh," she muttered, realization dawning. "A little bit, yeah."

She didn't want to talk about the night before at River Legacy Park. Nine o'clock was too early to be so damned serious. The elevator door opened and she slipped inside, hurriedly hitting the button to close the door and go up three levels. The man peered after her, a worried look on his weathered face. Angie ignored him.

She walked down the long hallway to the newsroom, her one heel clacking along the white marble floors, her cast making a soft thump-thump noise in between clacks, her cane completing the rhythm. Before she could even make the bend, she ran into three other people—separately—each of them greeting her with statements like, "Glad you're okay, Angie," and, "I can't believe what happened to you," and, "Damned scary thing last night, Mitchell."

She quickened her pace and didn't stop. She walked past her

coworkers without a word or glance back, choosing not to respond. She didn't care how rude it was. She could tell that Tuesday was going to be a day like her first day back after the Henry fiasco—everybody dropping by, interrupting her work, wearing the same worried frowns, offering the same advice and comfort.

Her mood dropped a notch when she turned a corner, walked down another hallway, and made it into the newsroom. A dozen reporters were milling about the first row of desks, chatting. When they saw her, the buzzing conversation suddenly stopped. She groaned internally.

It took nearly half an hour to get to her desk. Every last reporter, it seemed, had come in early—curious about what they'd seen on the news. And reporters don't keep their curiosity in check for the sake of politeness. She was thoroughly questioned—"What did the note say?" And harassed—"Maybe you shouldn't have put that bit in the paper Saturday."

Realizing that she couldn't ignore them all like she'd ignored the security guy and the three people in the hallway, Angie slipped into the mask she'd built over the previous three months, the one that hid her annoyance and chagrin. But after half an hour, the mask began to crack and she didn't know how much longer she'd be able to field the incessant questions without snapping at somebody.

Tom finally came to her rescue. He stepped into the newsroom and told everyone to "get back to work." He'd gently took Angie by the arm and led her past her coworkers, depositing her at her desk with a whispered, "I'm sorry."

The tone of his voice indicated that he wasn't talking about the five gazillion questions. He was referring to the Saturday article. She was almost certain that he knew exactly what the note said, had probably made good on his promise to demand copies of all correspondence from the killer. Her suspicions were confirmed when he stood by her desk for several seconds, shifting from one foot to the other, and quietly said, "Most bizarre thank you note I've ever seen."

She nodded. There was nothing to say about it. He'd called the note for what it was.

He remained where he was while she booted up her computer.

A minute later, when he still hadn't left, she looked up at him. "Yes?"

"About the follow-up," he started, stopped, and cleared his throat. "Do you really think it's a good idea?"

Ah. Her boss was getting cold feet.

"Did the police give you crap for the Saturday piece?"

He smirked and nodded. "Got a call from that federal agent—Silas—who went on about compromising the investigation. He threatened to charge me with obstruction of justice, and I told him to go ahead and try. Your name didn't come up."

Angie's lips formed an O, and she took a breath to say something, but Tom cut her off before she could get a word out.

"I talked to our lawyer. I'm told there's not much he can do. We didn't do anything illegal to obtain the information we printed. I'm just..." He paused and scratched the back of his head. "I'm just, well, if the last article got the response it did, then what kind of response will the investigative piece get?"

"I don't know, Tom. But we've got to write it."

"Remind me why."

"Because people are scared. We haven't reported that this killer isn't just picking off random gay men. They think this psychopath is preying on generosity. And maybe that's how he's luring his targets, but he's not after the general gay population. The public thinks he is."

"Mmm," he mumbled and nodded. "Okay. You're right. Let's do this."

"That a boy," she said and touched his shoulder. "I'm assuming we still have the go-ahead with this?"

Tom nodded. Not only did the executive editor give them the green light, he told her, but the story would go on the wires for other papers across the country to pick up and print. It was still national news.

He began to walk off but turned and added, "Hey, I'm going to send an e-mail to the staff with the answers they're looking for about last night. And to tell them to lay off."

"Thanks," she said with more than a little relief and smiled. He nodded and headed for his office.

Angie went through her flooded e-mail inbox—more than a hundred messages from her coworkers and people who'd seen the news—and deleted half of them without reading past the first two lines. A headache was starting to build. Damned television and its insistence in putting her in the news.

Her voicemail was similarly full of messages and took her nearly half an hour to make it through until she'd deleted everything and the flashing red light went out. Sighing, she leaned back in her chair and cracked her knuckles.

She looked around the office and caught several sets of curious eyes that darted back to computer screens guiltily. She let out an aggravated sigh and rubbed her temples.

An hour passed without interruption. Angie was so wrapped up in writing the big story—she'd completed a thousand words already— that she didn't hear the footsteps approaching her desk. When Gavin touched her shoulder by way of greeting, she jumped. Smiling, he set a venti caramel café latté on her desk with a couple of croissants. A grateful grin split across her face, much to his obvious amusement as reflected in his grin.

"Tom said these are your favorites, thought you'd need them today."

Her grin crumbled and Gavin quickly pulled up a computer chair and sat down.

"Oh, don't be like that. I got the e-mail. We're not going to talk about last night, okay?" He paused, took a sip of his own coffee, and continued with, "No, I'm here because I want input in this story you're so diligently typing up."

A fraction of her grin returned while she picked up her coffee and took a long sip, her eyes returning to the many paragraphs of text on her screen. Of course, she thought, they're a team. He had every right to make the demand he'd just made.

She returned her eyes to his and nodded, then scooted her chair aside.

"Read what I've got, add whatever you think you need to. I already put in a lot of your notes, but this isn't anywhere near done yet." She paused while he pulled his chair closer to her desk. "Hey, where's Mandy? Shouldn't she be here for this, too?"

"She'll be here. The cop reporter called in sick this morning and Tom made Mandy cover for him. She's at some wreck on I-20."

Angie watched him intently while he read. It was fascinating to watch his facial expressions—his nose scrunched up in concentration. She munched on the croissants and sipped her coffee while watching him. Occasionally, he'd stop, type a few words, and continue with a self-satisfied smile. She smirked because she knew he couldn't see her.

Angie didn't know what he was adding but was sure it would be appropriate. After he'd come through with the most recent lead—getting his hands on the poetry book and their trip to After Midnight—her initial skepticism had all but died away. She knew he was a good writer. And she trusted him.

Thinking about After Midnight, she couldn't help but think about Jeff Breaux. So much of the story they were working on had come from him. She wondered where he was, if he was indeed tucked away safely like she'd assumed.

She set down her coffee and dug through her purse. After rummaging for several minutes, she pulled out a battered business card and glanced at the scrawled cell phone number on the back. She picked up the phone and punched in the ten digits.

"Agent Silas?" she asked when a gruff voice answered.

"Speaking."

"This is Angie Mitchell and I was just wondering…"

"I don't really care what you're wondering, Mitchell. My only comment from now on is no comment. Period. Got it?"

"Yes, sir. I understand. But I'm not trying to get a comment…"

"Then what the hell do you want?" he barked.

"If you'd please let me continue…" Angie paused, sure she'd get cut off again. But all she heard was the crackling of his cell phone signal. She cleared her throat. "I was wondering what you guys had done with Jeff Breaux."

Silence. Then, "Who?"

Angie's heart almost stopped. She took a shaky breath. "Um, didn't you get a copy of the poetry book we got ahold of? We gave it to Detective Key. It has pictures of all the victims in it, and Jeff Breaux seems to be the only one still alive." Her voice was quivering and her heart sank when he didn't give any sound of recognition. The words started to come out faster. "Calamus, that's the name of their clique. They all went to high school together. Martin High. Another reporter spoke with Jeff Breaux, who told

242

us..."

"Hold on," Agent Silas said. She heard rustling paper and muted voices. A strange click followed. "Say all of that again, Miss Mitchell."

"Am I being recorded?"

Another seconds-long silence. "Yes."

She thought about asking why but chose not to. It didn't matter. This was too damned important. She repeated everything she'd said, slower this time, and included an account of what she and Gavin had overheard at After Midnight.

She glanced at Gavin while she spoke. His face had gone completely pale. He was breathing hard, as if he'd been running.

"Put Gavin on the phone," Agent Silas ordered and she did so without complaint.

Gavin nervously gave his own account, spoke at length about the conversation he'd had with Mr. Breaux at IHOP. The conversation ended with a heated, "You didn't know anything about this?" His tone was desperate. "I mean, Jeff is still at the Motor Inn, unprotected?"

Angie couldn't make out the other end of the conversation, but it was rapid-fire sentences and Gavin was nodding vigorously. "On Lancaster Avenue," he said at one point, and shortly after that, "No, the last time I spoke to him was that day at IHOP. He said he'd be staying there for a little while. I just assumed..."

The line went dead. Angie stared at Gavin. Gavin stared at her, phone still in hand.

"Maybe he went home..." he said weakly, but clearly didn't believe it.

She opened her mouth to say something when her cell phone rang. Before she could answer it, Gavin's phone rang.

Detective Key was calling for Angie. Mandy was calling for Gavin.

What the calls had in common was a message that there was another signal twelve on Lancaster Avenue.

Angie was off the phone first and began to pack her things in her purse, readying herself to head out. She could hear Mandy's excited voice shouting into Gavin's phone. She had the scanner with her and had heard the call for the homicide unit. When he hung up, his face was an ugly shade of green. He gagged once, twice, and threw up in the trash can under her desk.

She put a trembling hand on his back while he heaved. She didn't hold it against him that he threw up. Even she felt sick. A voice in her head was pointing out that she could have—obviously should have—checked up on Mr. Breaux's whereabouts sooner. It would have been, she realized, an important piece of her story. The whole let-readers-know-he's-safe paragraph.

She squashed the voice with grim determination. They'd given the evidence to Detective Key. It had been his job to ensure the man's safety. Neither she nor Gavin were at fault. If anyone was to blame, it was that damned unprofessional, weird investigator with the bad temper. And like hell she wouldn't find out why he hadn't turned the book over when a man's life had been at stake.

"Come on," she told Gavin when he put the trash can down. "Let's get you to the restroom so you can clean up. Then we have a murder to report. It's the least we can do." She paused, patted his back, and when he looked at her, added, "It's the only thing we can do."

To Angie, the most notable thing about the crime scene was the absence of a certain redheaded detective. But considering her earlier conversation with Agent Silas, she had no doubt he'd been yanked off the investigation for his blunder. That is, she began to wonder, if it actually was a blunder.

She knew a pissing contest was in progress. He'd told her as much. And even if he hadn't, no police precinct appreciates it when the feds show up. It's not just an invasion. Most detectives consider it an insult. Because when the feds are called in, it means the locals are in over their heads. And that was definitely true for the Fort Worth PD. But Detective Key had made it clear to her that he neither appreciated their involvement nor thought it necessary. Could he then, she wondered, have kept the book private to wrest back a piece of the investigation—to conduct his own behind the feds' backs so he could find the killer himself? Or was there another reason? She couldn't think of a single reason why he'd done what he'd done that made any damned sense. Even if he thought he could solve the murders on his own, he had to have realized he was gambling with a man's life.

The Motor Inn was in a seedier part of Fort Worth, that section of Lancaster Avenue notorious as a hangout for junkies and prostitutes. Angie couldn't imagine staying in that hotel. It was beyond rundown. It looked like it needed to be condemned. But maybe that's why Mr. Breaux had chosen it. She just didn't know.

She and Gavin met Mandy in the parking lot. She looked particularly flustered, and when Angie asked why, wondering if she was upset as Gavin had been, Mandy pointed at Agent Silas across the lot. "He shut me down. He said he won't answer questions for *Tribune* reporters."

Angie's eyes widened, and the surprised look was almost immediately followed by a deep scowl and furrowed brows. "We'll see about that," she hissed and stomped off toward the yellow crime scene tape. They didn't have time for a damned arm wrestling match. They had to hurry. She had to do something before the media circus showed up. She didn't know what that was, but she just had to.

She was almost there when Agent Silas turned, gave her an expressionless once-over, and turned his back on her, continuing to issue orders to uniformed police officers behind the tape. Angie ignored the gesture and got as close to him as she could, stretching the crime scene tape as far as it would go without tearing.

She called his name several times and he didn't respond. Baffled, not used to even getting a "No comment, damn it," or maybe even a tell-off, she stood silently for a full minute, twisting her fingers. In her head, she could hear the seconds ticking by like thunderbolts. Or maybe it was her anxiously racing heartbeat.

Then the solution came to her. She called Gavin and Mandy over and whispered feverishly, "You made your own copy of that book, right?"

Gavin nodded. "It's in my car."

"Get it. Bring it here. I still have mine, so we don't need yours."

He jogged to his car without a word. He apparently understood that they needed to hurry. He came back less than a minute later with a tattered copy in hand, giving it to Angie.

"Hey, Silas," she shouted, "I've got something you might want."

Finally, he turned to face her and she waved the copy at him. He stared at her hard for a few seconds, then took quick steps toward her. He reached out to take the copy and she handed it off to Mandy, who took three steps back.

Agent Silas scowled at them.

"All we need are a couple of quotes. Five minutes, tops. Then I'll give it to you," Angie dared and waited.

"That's blackmail," he barked and held out his hand, but Angie shook her head.

"You'd never have known about this if I hadn't called." Well, that was half a lie, considering the article that was going to run in the next day's paper, but she decided to conveniently neglect to mention that. "Come on, Silas. It's a fair trade. You can't ignore the press. In five minutes, this place will be swarming with reporters and you know it. Lance Tucker will show up and give us the basics. But I need something special from you."

Tucker, Fort Worth PD's spokesman, was good about press conferences. But every reporter from every agency would have the same quotes. No, Angie wanted a little extra—as much for her readers as for herself.

She locked eyes with the agent, who appeared as though he was trying not to look at Mandy. He sighed.

"Two minutes," he snapped "Starting now."

"Take notes, guys," she shot over her shoulder, hoping they had notepads and pens at the ready. Then she fired off the first three questions. "Why isn't Detective Key here? Is he off the case? If so, why?"

"He's off the case because I ordered it. He's not here because I called the police chief and told him what happened and now Key is on administrative leave."

"What happened with what?"

"You know what."

"I need you to say it for the record."

His eyes narrowed and Angie thought he wouldn't do it as several precious seconds ticked by. But he did. "Detective Key failed to turn in a vital piece of evidence that may have prevented the death of this most recent victim."

"This homicide is definitely related to the others? The victim is Jeff Breaux?"

"Yes and yes."

Angie gnawed her lower lip. She was running out of time and

it was making her nervous. She watched the agent check his watch and give her a knowing smile. Her temper flared.

"How is the investigation going? Any promising leads yet?"

The smile slid off his face. "Not good. Some leads. This killer knows what he's doing," he growled.

"What about Key's competence? Was that a factor in his being taken off the case?"

"Detective Key has had a lot of success in the past in solving crimes. But his failure to turn evidence over to the FBI was a big mistake. And that's all I'll say about that." He checked his watch again. "Now, Miss Mitchell, your time's up. Hand it over."

Mandy stepped up and handed the copy to Agent Silas. He snatched it from her fingers as though he was worried she'd change her mind. Then he looked Angie in the eyes and said, "I thought I was doing you a favor when I kept your name out of the conversation I had with your boss the other day. I thought you'd appreciate not getting charged." He paused significantly. "But if you pull one more stunt like this, I'll have you brought to my office. And you won't like it. I admire a woman with guts, Miss Mitchell. But I have very little admiration for you right now. I hope there isn't any other evidence you have that we don't."

Angie nodded and stepped back. "I've told you everything I know."

"Good. No more quid-pro-quo games." He turned his back on them and marched off toward uniformed officers. Another agent approached him and he handed the woman the copy he'd been given. Then he went around a corner and disappeared.

Angie sighed in deep relief and sat down on the blacktop parking lot.

"I can't believe you just did that," Gavin whispered.

"Neither can I," she said quietly. "You get all of that?"

"Every word."

"Good job, you two." She said it with feeling. "Mandy, call the info in to Tom. I'll call Detective Key, see what I can pry out of him—if anything. Gavin, go find the hotel management. Let's get on it."

One ring, two rings, three rings, then, "I guess you know."

"Yeah, Jay. What the hell were you thinking? We trusted

you."

"I took a gamble and it didn't work."

Silence.

"Was it worth losing your badge?"

"Yes, it was."

"What…" Angie started, but the line went dead.

She tried calling him back but he'd turned off his phone.

"Damn it," she said to no one in particular. "Damn it, damn it, damn it!"

Screw it. She'd quote him on that shit.

While Mandy and Gavin tried to keep up with the media circus, Angie sat in the car. She was worried sick. With Detective Key off the case, she didn't know if she was supposed to continue on as she had been—as per his plan—or hide like her gut was telling her to. Agent Silas wasn't speaking to her. She didn't know if she still had the promised protection. She kept glancing around the parking lot, trying to figure out if anyone in the crowd were an undercover agent watching over her. But nobody seemed to be doing so. Of course, said agent's job was to blend in and not seem conspicuous. So really, there was no way for her to know. Which was exactly why she was so worried.

She was muttering to herself, pissed off at Key, feeling guilty over Breaux's death, trying to figure out what to do next.

She thought about calling Tom but called Lauren instead and told her what had happened. Every detail. Angie expected an outburst from her protective lover, but no such thing came shouting her way. Instead, she soaked up the words of comfort Lauren gave, that soothing, rich voice she loved so much doing a considerable amount to calm her frayed nerves.

After the call ended, she leaned her head against the cool window and closed her eyes. Yes, Angie thought, she'd go back to the office in an hour, finish the big story, and drop her investigation after that. She would have no part in any more stories involving the serial killer. Not even a freaking brief. At this point, it was simply the right thing to do. Mandy and Gavin could handle it. Mark could take her place. Tom would understand.

But somehow, she suspected, her decision wouldn't make any difference.

After all, she had a knack for finding trouble. Or maybe it was that trouble had a knack for finding her. Whichever way the equation worked, it didn't matter. Something bad was going to happen soon—to her, not to some poor victim like Breaux and the others. She could feel it in her gut like a tiny monster gnawing at her insides.

Angie closed her eyes against the sick feeling and tried to think of something—anything—else.

She failed miserably.

Preying On Generosity

Chapter Eighteen

O n the hurried drive back to the office, all Angie could do was compose paragraphs in her head. She tried to block it out, but the only other thoughts that would pop up when she tried to distract herself was that statement Jimmy had made—the one about needing to talk about something important. Sighing, she pulled out her cell phone and called his number. She got his voicemail. She couldn't figure out why, but it pissed her off.

She wrote the emotion off as being stressed out of her mind. And then she went back to composing paragraphs in her head, giving up on the attempt to distract herself, and began jotting down a line here and there in her notepad while Gavin navigated through the dense, rush-hour traffic.

Back at the office, Angie, Gavin, and Mandy had a quick meeting with Tom to discuss their options. Instead of having a gigantic mega-story, which is what they'd have to do if they just included the day's events in the working story, they decided to break it up into three pieces: the breaking news of Breaux's murder, Detective Key's dismissal, and everything else. They'd have to hold some national news to fit it all in. But, as Tom pointed out, "local hard news always wins."

Angie typed while Mandy and Gavin watched the news reports on television and came back with various updates, after which they'd scramble to get the cops on the phone to verify the newest information. Mark was out in the field, too, sticking around in case investigators released any new info. To say it was a mess—the writing and rewriting, scrambling, and cursing—was a bit on the nice side of the descriptor spectrum.

Three hours later, Angie read over the big story one more time with her team. She read it out loud, and more than a few reporters were lingering, trying to hear what she'd written. When she was finished, Mandy and Gavin nodded eagerly and gave her a thumbs-up. Their eavesdropping coworkers began talking excitedly about the story. Angie nodded to herself and dropped the file in the work flow to join the other two stories they'd completed.

Her head hurt. Her fingers were sore from typing so much. Wednesday's front section would have two pages dedicated to the crimes. It was time to go home.

She drummed her fingers on her desk, waiting to get the go-ahead from Tom. He was editing the stories and had already called her extension four times with questions or clarifications. On a story as long as her investigative piece, it would take him at least forty-five minutes.

"Definitely need to go home and get a backrub," she grumbled and pulled up her Internet browser. Her computer beeped at her, indicating she had a new e-mail message. Not all that surprising, considering they'd posted the breaking story online, and people were likely responding. But since she didn't have anything better to do, she pulled it up. And it wasn't just some reader. It was from Jimmy.

"Sorry I missed your call. Your phone's dead, by the way. Can't call you back because I'm about to head out. We'll talk soon."

Angie stared at the postscript for a few seconds before giggling. "Busy indeed," she finally muttered and giggled because it said, "P.S. The cute bartender at 1970 said he'd trade me dinner and a movie if I fixed his computer. So don't call tonight."

She shook her head, still smiling—God, smiling felt good— and got out of her chair. She stretched her back for a few seconds and decided she needed some food as dinner had been forgotten in the rush to get the stories in. She hobbled down the hallway to the break room, plunked some quarters in the vending machine, and withdrew a pack of Twinkies with a sheepish smile. She got herself a Coke and sat at a table with a sigh. For several minutes, she contented herself with sipping Coke and eating Twinkies. When the snack was gone, her thoughts went back to Jimmy.

Damn, she wished he could get past his relationship hang-ups and find someone decent. She didn't think the bartender was it. He'd have some fun and that would be that, more likely than not. As usual. And he deserved some fun, sure. But, she thought, he deserved so much more. Needed it, in fact.

Still, she couldn't help snickering about the trade—dinner and a movie for some computer help. Dinner and a movie was probably a hell of a lot cheaper than what Jimmy usually charged clients for his expertise. But then again, he'd sold his business and technically wasn't charging for fixing things anymore. Still, unless sex was involved, she thought and nearly laughed out loud, the bartender was getting the better end of the bargain.

"Jimmy is a sucker," she muttered and snorted. She took another sip of her drink and stifled a yawn. "Gotta get more caffeine in my system," she mumbled around another sip and closed her eyes after checking her watch and discovering that she'd only been in the break room for ten minutes.

Back to Jimmy and his generosity. She thought about the treats he brought over—usually chocolate- or alcohol-related goodies—and all the things he'd done for Fearless. And all the times he'd come through for her. All those necessary conversations and pep talks. The trip to After Midnight that had resulted in such bizarre but incredible sex with Lauren.

Yes, he was a good, generous guy. A little devious and terribly sarcastic, but giving and fun. Maybe it was her turn to give something back. She tried to think about little treats he might enjoy. She could consult Lauren. Yeah, that's what she'd do.

Her eyes drifted shut and she began to softly snore.

Half an hour later, she was startled out of her nap with a loud, "There you are!"

Her head snapped up, and she muttered, "I was paying attention, professor, I swear," before the drowsiness completely left. She rubbed her eyes and face, discovering to her slight horror that she'd drooled down her chin. She tried to discreetly wipe it away but made it only more obvious by doing so.

Tom's laughter filled the room and she groaned.

"Go home, Angie. Your story's solid. I made a few minor adjustments, but I think it's pretty air tight. I can't wait to see what Silas has to say when he calls me up tomorrow. And it felt damned good to have the designer put the *Tribune* exclusive logo next to your byline." He put his hands in his pockets and rocked on his heels, the earlier doubts clearly erased.

"And since you worked so late and are obviously damned tired, take tomorrow off, okay? You look like you could use it."

Angie nodded and got up, walking back to her desk with him. She didn't have the heart to tell him she wanted out this late in the game. She didn't want to destroy his good mood, which had been so rare lately. She reluctantly resolved to deal with the issue on Thursday. Early. As soon as she saw him.

It was nearly nine o'clock when she was halfway home on I-30. Her eyes felt sticky and dry. She wanted to crawl into bed with Lauren as soon as possible. She hit the gas hard, ignoring the pesky responsible voice that started going on and on about speeding tickets and earning negative points on her license for driving all crazy-like.

Warm arms wrapped around her shoulders when she stepped into her apartment and she sagged against Lauren's body with heartfelt gratitude. She nuzzled her lover's neck and inhaled the rich, comforting, lavender scent. Damn, it felt good to be home. This, she thought, was all she needed out of life. No crazy news stories. No psychopath killer mailing her weird shit. No angry federal agents or dishonest detectives. Just Lauren.

She loved her job. And she hated it.

She wanted the big stories—minus the danger.

She wanted to make a difference, to help people with her reporting. But she didn't need the trouble and headaches that were becoming all-too-common. She was twenty-five years old, hadn't even reached the five-year mark in her career, and was already starting to burn out. That wasn't supposed to happen. Not in quiet Fort Worth. In New York maybe, but not here.

Lauren was rubbing her back in soothing circles, humming a soft, comforting tune. Angie hadn't realized that she'd started to cry. It was such a surprise that she abruptly pulled back and angrily wiped the wetness from her face, not meeting her lover's eyes. She tried to argue the tears away as exhaustion, frustration, disappointment, disillusionment. In the end, she knew it was all of those. But primarily, it was her pride and drive being shattered.

She was giving up. And it hurt like hell to admit it to herself.

A finger hooked under her chin and forced her eyes to meet Lauren's. A question was in those dark eyes. And Angie knew she had to answer it.

"I didn't realize I was crying," she muttered, feeling completely drained and a touch guilty. "I'm going to drop the story. I want out. And I feel like a fool. And, well..." She ran a hand though her hair nervously. "And you were right."

She got a raised eyebrow in response. A soft smile curled Lauren's lips, but it wasn't one of relief, as Angie thought it would be. "What?" she asked.

"So there's a limit to your stubbornness after all," Lauren said softly and ran her knuckles along Angie's damp cheek. "I never thought I'd see it."

Angie harrumphed and turned away. Lauren caught her around the waist before she could take a single step and whispered in her ear, "I'm sorry about what happened with Detective Key. And I wish things could have gone differently. But you did what you were supposed to do. Is that why you're dropping the story?"

"Partly," Angie whispered back. She didn't know why they were whispering, but her throat felt raw and the word came out hoarsely. She sighed. "I'm tired of all this bullshit. I'm not helping anybody. They're all dead and the cops are completely lost."

"There's one person left, right? A seventh person?"

"Well, yeah..." Angie paused. "But it doesn't make any sense."

"Maybe not yet, honey."

"Weren't you the one who was rooting for me to give this mess up?"

The responding chuckle tickled Angie's ear and she squirmed.

"Yes," Lauren said, the whispering gone. "But I don't like to see you beating yourself up. Don't get me wrong—I hate thinking you're in danger, which you are... But you've worked so hard. Your work is so important to you. It's a quality I find quite admirable, at least most of the time. I'd hate for you to give this story up and regret it, let it ruin your passion for your job."

"It won't." Angie was proud of how steady her voice was. "I'll think about it. Tom gave me the day off tomorrow. I won't do anything crazy."

Lauren snorted and laughed. "Won't do anything crazy," she

repeated after Angie and laughed again. "Come on, let's get you some tea. Then I'll give you a backrub and you can go to bed. How does that sound?"

"God, I love you." Angie sagged back against Lauren's body and sighed. "Very, very much."

Lauren laughed harder and shook her head, took Angie's hand, and led her to the couch. She continued laughing as she made her way to the kitchen, while she brewed a pot of tea and still hadn't shaken off the last few chuckles by the time she returned to the living room with a steaming cup that smelled of mint and chamomile.

Angie dreamt that she was in an alley. The images were fleeting, distorted, and disjointed, but she knew it was an alley and it was dimly lit. She felt as if she were being watched, but every time she turned around, nobody was there. Just the long, grimy alley with a Dumpster at one end and a pile of trash at the other.

She began to shiver. She didn't feel cold, but somehow it was right that she should shiver. It was cool in October, after all.

There was a flash of white light and she closed her eyes against it. She felt like she was floating—it was dizzying and highly disconcerting. She opened her eyes and there was only the alley with its Dumpster and pile of trash. Angie started walking.

It was like she was moving through water. Her legs wouldn't move properly, as though she were in a movie and it was set on slow-motion. She tried to run. She couldn't.

She stopped and sat down. She had something in her hand. It was a police photo spread. Six angry faces looking up at her. They were moving, their lips forming words she couldn't make out.

A deep voice said, "I'm right here."

Angie looked over her shoulder, puzzled, but again there was nobody there. The photo spread was gone, replaced by a lilac silk scarf in her hand. There were no stains on it like there'd been on the one that came in the envelope. It felt cool and smooth. It looked beautiful and she felt herself smile as she wrapped it around her neck.

"Ecstasy—it's a wonderful thing," the deep voice echoed in her head.

She felt the scarf tighten around her neck. It wasn't painful—

just as she wasn't really cold but shivered anyway—and she began to struggle. Light in the alley was growing dimmer and she tried to scream, but no sound came from her lips.

"Terrible things happen after midnight," the voice said.

Her world fell into darkness.

"Angie, Angie!" Lauren was shaking her shoulders and she sat bolt upright. Cold sweat ran down her back and hair was plastered to her forehead.

Angie licked her dry lips and struggled to wake up. The nightmare had been different. There was no stale cigar smoke smell, no cognac, or 9 mm revolver. But she couldn't hang on to the details. They were too slippery and slid out of her mind before she could grasp anything concrete.

"Alley," she mumbled. "Silk scarf and a picture."

And then it was completely gone.

She squinted against the light in her bedroom. When her eyes adjusted, she looked up at Lauren, who was fully dressed. And if Lauren was dressed, that meant it had to be…

"What time is it?" she asked, her voice rough from sleep.

"Ten o'clock. You didn't even budge when the alarm went off at nine. I would have let you sleep longer, but you were making these noises," Lauren shuddered, "and it sounded as if you were having a terrible nightmare."

"Yeah," Angie said uncertainly. "I think you're right."

"You said something about a silk scarf and a picture."

It was Angie's turn to shudder. She could only imagine what she could have been dreaming about. Then something else Lauren said registered.

"Ten o'clock? Damn. It's late. I guess you're off to class, huh?"

"Yeah," Lauren sighed. "Wish I could stay here, but I have to go. I'll call you later."

Angie reached forward and snagged her lover's arm, pulling her in for a quick kiss before she released her. When she heard the door click shut, she rolled over and lay in bed for a while, trying to remember her dream.

Not that she wanted to relive the nightmare, but she had the feeling she'd let go of something important. The gnawing feeling that she'd missed something followed her into the bathroom while she brushed her teeth and into the kitchen where she made coffee and poured herself a bowl of cereal. It wouldn't let up, even while she tried to zone out in front of the television. Exasperated, Angie hobbled out onto the balcony—still in her pajamas—and leaned against the railing, staring up at the sky.

The steel-gray sky would distract her. The chilly breeze would numb her. The occasional gust of wind would blast along her body and grind away that nagging feeling that was starting to make her stomach cramp unpleasantly. Fresh air. It was healing—like summer rain. Come on, wind, she thought, take me away.

The wind didn't come in time. An idea dropped from her head into her stomach like a cement block. Puzzle pieces she'd been collecting started to fit and she didn't like the picture it was forming.

Apollo. After Midnight. The assault the madam had described. Revenge. Calamus. Six smiling faces, all dead. The photo spread on Detective Key's desk—bottom left corner, wide mouth, arching brows, goofy haircut. Matt, the bartender at Club 1970. The redhead Jimmy liked.

Jimmy was supposed to have had dinner and a movie with him. Matt had offered a trade. Jimmy was supposed to help. The killer was asking his victims for help. He was preying on generosity. Jimmy gave a generous offer.

The comments in the margins. The seventh person. Jimmy.

"Fucking hell," Angie shouted and spun around, wrenched open the balcony door, and stumbled inside. She grabbed her home phone and called both Jimmy's numbers but got his voicemail both times. She tried again and again, but he didn't answer.

She searched frantically for that tattered business card. She punched in the number.

Four rings. "Damn it!" Five rings. "Please pick up!"

Finally, "Agent Silas speaking."

"I know who the killer is!" Angie shouted into the phone, panic taking over.

Agent Silas hung up on her.

Angie screamed into the empty living room and hit redial.

"Look, I don't know what you think you're doing, Mitchell,

but..."

"Shut up and listen to me, damn it! A friend of mine is in some seriously deep shit. Now I know who the killer is and..."

The line went dead again. The bastard hung up on her. Again. He didn't believe her. And Jimmy... Angie groaned in frustration, her racing heart drowning out the sound and anything else. Her temples were throbbing painfully. She felt lightheaded. Her head began to spin and she slumped down along the wall until she was sitting with her head between her knees.

She had to do something. If she was right—she was praying furiously that she wasn't—there was still time. If the killer was true to his M.O., she might have as long as a day to find Jimmy. But where the hell was she supposed to start looking? Jimmy's apartment.

The phone clenched tightly in her trembling, white-knuckled left hand, she punched in 911. An operator picked up and she started babbling. She was told in the sort of voice one might use on a crazy person that a report was being filed. She was asked to call back when twenty-four hours had passed since her last contact with Jimmy to file a missing person report.

Angie argued with the operator and got a lecture on police procedure. When the call was over, she threw the phone against the wall where it shattered a glass picture frame with a loud crash. She dropped her head between her knees and took long, deep breaths.

Jimmy had said he had something important to tell her.

Still shaking, Angie stumbled across her apartment, into her bedroom, and started ripping open drawers, tossing clothes across the room—completely panicked and desperate—until she found a skirt she could wear and a T-shirt to pull on. She ripped off her pajamas and changed as quickly as she could.

She was having trouble seeing. The tears wouldn't stop.

"Please," she kept muttering. "Please, please, please..."

She was begging to be wrong. She didn't know who she was directing her pleas to, but it didn't matter. She wished she was crazy, just like the operator had apparently believed. Jimmy would be fine if she was just crazy.

Angie stumbled through the living room to the entrance, wrenched open the lock, and swung the door open, nearly hitting herself in the face, and grabbed her purse and keys. She jarred her leg twice on the stairs she was trying to take two at a time and didn't care.

She couldn't get to Jimmy's apartment fast enough. She was gunning the engine along Beach Street, half hoping a cop would spot her and come racing after her Mitsubishi Eclipse with lights flaring and sirens blaring. At least that way, the cops would show up at Jimmy's doorstep. Because there was no way in hell she would pull over for a damned ticket.

The thought that she might run into the killer at his apartment never crossed her mind. She was too freaked out. Too hysterical. Maybe she was crazy.

She came to a screeching halt in a parking spot near Jimmy's front door. She struggled up the front steps, her leg beginning to throb in protest, but she pulled herself along the railing until she made the top landing. She began pounding on his door in utter desperation.

There was no answer. For a minute, she stood there in disbelief and almost felt relieved. But the panic would not subside that easily, nor could she dismiss the sick, icy feeling in her stomach. She pulled out her cell phone and dialed his number. Still no answer. She began pounding again. Then she started shouting.

The door next to his opened and an elderly man stepped out.

"What the hell is going on?" the man demanded, and she turned bleary eyes on him. He took a step forward, his annoyance immediately replaced by concern. "Miss, what's going on?" he asked, putting a hand on her elbow to steady her. Angie had started to sway.

She sat down and tried to catch her breath.

"Hey," the man said suddenly. "I recognize you. You're that reporter who was on the news the other night…"

"Yes, yes," she nodded vigorously. "Angie Mitchell. From the *Tribune*. Been reporting about the murders in Fort Worth. Jimmy's my friend. I think," she fought another attack of hysterical tears, "he's in trouble. I have to get inside."

The man's eyes widened and he lowered his voice, "You don't think he's…"

She nodded. The color drained from his face.

"Wait here," he said earnestly. "James gave me a spare key the last time he went to Mexico. I still got it somewhere."

And he disappeared through the door he'd come from.

Angie closed her eyes and prayed like she'd never prayed before. The time it took the man to return seemed like forever. Any minute, she'd scream. Any minute, she'd get sick and pass out. She couldn't think straight. The puzzle pieces were swirling around her head.

Jimmy's neighbor touched her shoulder and she gasped, her eyes snapping open and focusing on him. He reached out his hand and helped her up.

"Let's go inside," he murmured and put the key in the lock with trembling fingers while Angie waited at his back.

There was a click. The door swung open.

Preying On Generosity

Chapter Nineteen

Angie couldn't see around the heavy-set neighbor as he stood in the entryway. He didn't say a word. He also wouldn't get the hell out of the way, and she could barely fight the urge to push him. Finally, at the end of her patience, she said, "Excuse me, I need to go in there."

"But there's nothing wrong," he said slowly with a note of astonishment and turned to face her. "Are you sure he's in trouble? I'd hate to let in just anybody."

"What do you mean, there's nothing wrong?" The question was clipped and strong, but her knees didn't feel quite as weak anymore. Maybe someone had listened to her furious praying. "Everything's okay?"

The man nodded, turned, and gave her a skeptical look.

"Look, sir, I hate to be rude, and I understand your concern," Angie started with a forced calm. "But I have to make sure. Trust me. I'm his friend." When he still showed no sign of budging from the entryway, she sighed exaggeratedly and huffed, "You can follow me through the apartment, okay?"

"If he's in trouble," the man drawled, "why aren't the police here?"

Angie pinched the bridge of her nose and groaned. Did everybody think she was nuts? Why was nobody listening? But even as the questions echoed in her head, she couldn't help but feel a tiny shred of giddy relief. The man had said everything appeared to be in order. Surely, he'd have noticed crazy shit spray-painted on the walls or if there were upturned furniture.

"I called them, and they told me I had to wait twenty-four hours to file a missing person report. I tried explaining what I

263

know, and they didn't believe me." She paused and dropped her hand. "Jimmy e-mailed me last night and said he had a date with the man I suspect is the killer, and I didn't figure it out until this morning." She paused significantly. "I called the lead investigator—an FBI agent—and we're not on speaking terms because of the articles I've written, so he hung up on me. Twice."

The man's eyes widened at that—not the FBI bit, but the dating part. For a second, Angie thought he hadn't known Jimmy was gay and she had inadvertently outed him. She was about to say something about it when the man started spluttering.

"Yes, right," he said, knitting his fingers. "The man they're looking for—a redhead, right? I always watch the news—need to know what's going on in the world." He took a deep breath. "I saw James let in a redhead last night—'round about midnight. I was out smoking a cigar and I told them to keep the noise down…" He stopped, took a step aside, and ushered her in with a hurried, "Go on. Go find out what you can."

About damned time.

Jimmy was a clean freak. She knew that. Every time she had visited his apartment—even on little or no notice—it had been spotless. Lauren had once said something about him getting bored late at night when he couldn't sleep and scrubbing it top to bottom. She'd said it happened at least once a week or so. And as per typical fashion, everything seemed to be sparkling clean and in its place. Except for a computer case and various computer components strewn across the dining room table. A couple of tools lay nearby and the equipment looked like it was in some state of repair.

Jimmy had promised to fix the guy's computer. Maybe Matt had brought it over. She wandered into the bathroom—spotless—and into the study, then the bedroom. Even his bed was made. His four plants by the window were as green as ever. Jimmy took care of his shit.

But when she walked around the bed, Angie found a pair of pants and a shirt on the floor. She couldn't imagine him leaving clothes on the floor, but perhaps he'd been in a hurry. Maybe he'd planned to pick them up later.

She paced around his apartment like a caged, limping animal for several minutes. Kitchen, living room, dining room, study, bathroom, bedroom, back to the kitchen. She was muttering to herself. "Why the clothes on the floor?" and "What's up with the computer pieces?" while Jimmy's neighbor stood silently in the living room.

"His rug's missing," he said quietly, which stopped Angie in her tracks. She looked at the spot where he stood, and indeed, there should have been a burgundy rug on the cream-colored carpet. She couldn't believe she'd missed that. He'd bought it a couple of months before and had called her over for her opinion— "Does it go, Angie? I mean, really, does it work?"

She stared at the spot and rubbed her throbbing temple. He'd decided he liked the rug. There was no reason to get rid of it. Not really. Unless he ruined it.

She began pacing again.

She sat at his desk in the study. She needed to think. Which was extremely hard at that moment. She set her cane against the desk and spotted a pile of mail, ready to be dropped off. She flipped through it halfheartedly because she could, and well, she didn't really know what else to do at that moment.

The last envelope was addressed to her. It was in Jimmy's sloppy handwriting. She looked at it for several seconds. It was probably another one of his silly pranks—find some dirty picture on the Internet, PhotoShop the president's or some other celebrity's faces on the bodies, print it out, and send it to her. Ha-ha. He'd started doing it when she went back to work because she'd yelled at him for sending such photo illustrations by e-mail. She'd opened up one of those at work and closed it as quickly as she could, praying none of her coworkers had seen the damned thing. It had only happened once. She'd made sure of that.

Glancing over her shoulder, she folded the envelope and stuffed it in her jeans skirt pocket. She didn't know what it was, but it was hers. It had her name on it and everything. But there was no reason to freak out the neighbor, make him think she was stealing Jimmy's mail. She got out of the chair, glanced around the room helplessly, and decided there was nothing she could do in his apartment.

"I'm very sorry," she said to the neighbor. "Other than a few little unusual things, I can't find anything to suggest that what I feared was true. Not here, anyway."

The man nodded mutely, scratching the back of his head, still staring at his sandaled feet, which were planted on the cream-colored carpet. He sighed then, and muttered, "Hope he's okay." He looked up at Angie. "Please come let me know if you find anything out. And forgive my manners—the name's Chuck, though James calls me Charlie."

Angie nodded and stepped out through the open front door.

Her body ached. She felt in sore need of a nap, but the adrenaline was still pumping through her veins without any sign of letting up soon. She said goodbye and took the stairs carefully to the parking lot. She got in her car, shivered once, twice, and sagged into the seat. She watched Chuck lock up Jimmy's apartment and go inside his own. When his door was shut, she reached into her back pocket and pulled out the envelope.

She slid her pinky under the flap and tore it open. There were no dirty pictures inside. But there was a typed, one-page letter, signed by Jimmy.

Her eyes scanned the first paragraph and widened. With each subsequent paragraph, her breathing quickened. The panic that had gripped her earlier slammed back with full force. She read the letter again and again, trying to will the words to be different. But it was always the same.

Angie fumbled for her cell phone and sent a text message to Lauren. All it said was "911. Call me. Now."

"No wonder he wanted to talk," she was muttering, weaving in and out of traffic on I-30, racing back to her apartment. "It's important," she groaned. "No shit, Sherlock!"

She slammed on her brakes to avoid hitting a semi and swerved into the left lane, horns blaring after her. She didn't give a crap. She hit the accelerator and continued ranting—"I can't believe you didn't tell me!"

She cut across three lanes to make her exit and came to a screeching halt at the stoplight before she could turn right. She tried to will herself to calm down, but it was no use. Her fist struck the steering wheel and she revved her engine. When the light turned green, she peeled out, tires screaming.

Lauren hadn't called yet. Angie knew she was in class, but damn it, hadn't she indicated it was a freaking emergency? "Get your ass on the phone," she hissed, taking a sharp left turn, then another. Amazingly, she made it back to her place safely.

She took the stairs two at a time, her leg a hot, throbbing mess. It took three tries to get the key in the lock and open the door. She dumped her purse on the floor and stumbled across the apartment into her bedroom. There, she flopped down in her desk chair and took a moment to take deep, four-second breaths.

An idea popped into her head and her closed eyes snapped open.

"Key," she growled and dug her cell phone out of her pocket.

She punched in his number and waited, her fingers drumming on her desk. After six rings, she got his voicemail. He was avoiding her. Probably because she'd quoted him on the taking a gamble bit. Damn. She left a message—near-breathless and hasty—then hung up and groaned in frustration.

Her phone rang. It was Lauren.

"What's going on? What's wrong? Are you okay?"

"No, I'm not okay. Listen, you have to come home right now…" And Angie told her everything. She finished by reading the letter over the phone to shocked silence on the other end of the line.

"Tell me you called police."

"I called. They think I'm crazy—told me to wait till eight p.m. and file a missing person report."

"Sonofa…" Angie had never heard Lauren swear like that before, but she shared the woman's sentiment. "I'll be there in fifteen minutes. Don't go anywhere. Promise."

"I'll be here."

The line went dead. Angie set the phone on the desk with trembling fingers. Lauren was upset. So she wasn't the only one who thought this was pretty freaking bad. She'd half-hoped her lover would see something she didn't, point out a problem with her logic.

She tried calling Detective Key again. He didn't answer, but her call rang through to his voicemail. He was most certainly avoiding her. She closed her eyes. There had to be something else she could do. She checked her watch. It was almost one o'clock. Seven hours before she could even file a missing person report. Seven hours till the cops would get involved.

She got up and went out onto the balcony, lighted a cigarette, and let the smoke out slowly. "Think, Angie, think," she mumbled. "When you can't call the cops and you can't call the FBI, what the hell do you do?" She took another drag. "Damn it!" Another drag, sigh. "Damn it!" A curled fist, knuckles white. "Damn it!"

She raced through everything she'd learned during her reporting on the murders. Nothing helped. But there was still that sticking point—the one where Detective Key screwed up and let them down.

A man terribly wronged. A man who fucked up royally.

"You're too close, and this will end very badly."

Angie's thoughts focused on the statement made by Madam Midnight and shuddered. It wouldn't get out of her head. It was suffocating her thought process. Detective Key was too close. It would end badly. He'd taken a gamble with a man's life. And why the hell would he do that? He was too close. How could he be too close?

"You're only too close if the investigation is personal, if you're emotionally involved somehow, if..." she trailed off. Could he be? No way. He did have the red hair, though. But it didn't fit. Not in any way, shape, or form. She crossed the possibility off her list. But he had screwed up.

"You're only too close," she started over, trying again, "if you're emotionally involved, if you're investigating a crime that's personal, or if any of the suspects or victims are friends or family, or..." She stopped abruptly and dropped her cigarette.

"Matt," she whispered.

She swung around and ripped the door open, rushed into her apartment, and was just about to reach for the phone book and look up a number when the front door swung open. Lauren ran in—pale, breathless, and sweaty-faced—and crushed her in a hug. "Sit down," she ordered and led Angie to the couch. "Show me the letter."

Angie dug the crumpled page from her pocket and handed it over. Lauren scanned it, her jaw clenching and unclenching. "It's his signature, I'm sure of it," she whispered and dropped it on the floor.

"Listen," Angie began but was cut off.

"We have to do something."

"I know, but…"

"We have to find him."

"I agree, but…"

"Damn it, Angie, what the hell are we going to do?"

Angie gaped at her helplessly and shook her head. She could read the fear on Lauren's face and knew it was reflected on her own. She scrambled for something, anything, to say. Lauren was a woman of action. She needed something to do. Searching for a task helped calmed her own nerves, but only by a tiny bit. Enough to think a little clearer.

"Silas doesn't want to talk to me. Fuck him. You call Tom and tell him what's going on. Demand that he give you all the FBI contacts that we have. There's a main number. We'll call and get somebody who cares. We'll try to speak with anyone who isn't Silas. It's better than nothing." She paused. "I'm going to check on something else."

Lauren nodded and scribbled down the number Angie gave her, then disappeared in the bedroom and closed the door.

Angie grabbed a phone book off the shelf and started looking for the number to Club 1970. She found it, checked her watch—it was early for the bar to open, but maybe a manager was in—and dialed the number. Seven rings. Then eight. She was about to give up when a male voice said, "Club 1970. Jason speaking. What can I do ya for?"

She took a deep breath. "Hi. I have a strange question for you."

"I like the strange and weird. Shoot."

"Do you know Matt, the bartender?"

"Matt, Matt," the man paused. "Redhead?"

"Yeah, that's him. Is he there?"

"Nah, he quit about a month ago. Said he was too busy."

"Do you know his last name?" The man didn't.

"Could you possibly give me any contact information?" At that, the man's friendly voice changed and she got a lecture on privacy issues.

"Please, this is important. Is his last name," she struggled to remember. She should have consulted her notes first. "Is it something like Giller or Gillworth."

"Gillyworth," he said. "That's the one. Weird name. Can't believe I forgot it." He paused. "Why do you need to know?"

Angie didn't answer. Hell, she could hardly breathe. She hit the end button on her cell phone and slumped along the wall until she was sitting, her head sagging forward.

Matt Gillyworth. Or Matthew Gillyworth. Related to a Nathaniel Gillyworth—a.k.a. Detective Johnny "Jay" Key after his name change.

"You're too close, this will end very badly."

Madam Midnight had known. She'd lied to Angie and Gavin. She had known her Apollo's name. How could she have been blindsided so badly? No wonder the investigation was getting nowhere. The killer had a protector on the inside—his half-brother—who was getting rid of evidence.

Angie was willing to bet a year's salary that the photo spread she'd seen had somehow "disappeared." She couldn't explain any other reason why Detective Key hadn't been yanked off the case sooner. His name was different, but if she knew, others had to know. Name changes leave a trail. You can't just change your name and start over.

Then Angie thought about the note she'd been handed at the park. It was signed "A." A for Apollo. Apollo was the guy who'd been beaten half to death by the Calamus clique. Her mind pulled up the brief she'd read in the background folder on Detective Key. The brief had said Matthew Gillyworth had been mugged and robbed in May 1990 in Oak Cliff. "Mugged. Right. They falsified the police report," she whispered hoarsely.

She hugged a knee to her chest and closed her eyes. She could hear a one-sided, muffled conversation going on in the bedroom. She heard a door open and footsteps approaching. She opened her eyes and looked up at Lauren.

"I have an FBI agent on the phone and she's listening. She wants to speak with you. She keeps saying something about the M.O. not being true to form if nobody was in Jimmy's apartment," she said and held the phone out to her. "It's on mute."

Angie unmuted the phone. "This is Angie Mitchell."

"Miss Mitchell, this is Agent Brock." The female voice was not entirely unpleasant—courteous and professional, one hell of a nice change from dealing with Agent Silas. "I understand you believe your friend is in danger."

"Yes," Angie said and nodded at the same time, relief flooding through her body. "I'm so glad you're listening. I have so much to tell you."

"Tell me," Agent Brock said, and Angie heard a click she knew was the start of a recording device.

Angie paced around the apartment while she spoke with the agent. At one point, she stopped, picked up a notepad, and scribbled a couple of notes. She ripped off the page and handed it to her hovering lover. Lauren read the note, gave her a questioning look, and at Angie's shooing motions, headed back to the bedroom.

"Read it again," Agent Brock instructed. "Slowly, clearly."

Angie took a deep breath and let it out through her nose. She took a drag of her Marlboro Lights cigarette and exhaled with a sigh. It was almost three o'clock. She'd been on the phone for over an hour. Lauren had made her tea. She was sitting next to her out on the balcony, where the temperature was rapidly dropping. When the weatherman said a cold front was moving through, he hadn't been kidding.

Angie unfolded the note and cleared her throat. She put out the cigarette and sighed.

"It says: Angie, I have something to tell you and it's important. I know I said we could talk, but I'm too nervous and too ashamed. Writing it down is hard but easier than telling you in person. I hope you'll understand.

"I should have told you that first night when you called me about that Calamus group and told me what you'd learned at After Midnight. I was there that night in May 1990. I know better than you do what went on.

"I was barely eighteen. I was naïve and stupid. I went with a friend who had a password. We hired a top. We went into a room and let him do whatever he wanted. When our session ended, we left the room and walked down the hall. I heard screaming— terrible, horrible screaming. I barged into the room where it was coming from. Six men my age were beating up another top who went by the name Apollo.

"I ran for the madam. Together, we put a stop to the beating.

We couldn't stop the six men from running. I wanted to run, too, but the madam made me help her carry Apollo to her car. She drove him to the hospital and told them he'd been mugged.

"I didn't go to After Midnight for several months. When I finally dared going back, Apollo was there. He wasn't working anymore, just visiting. He wanted me to come forward with what I had seen. I refused. I was scared of getting in trouble and stayed away from that place for three years.

"I never saw his face, Angie. He always wore a black leather mask. I should have told you anyway. I should have gone to the police a long time ago. I feel partly responsible for what's been happening in Fort Worth. That's one of the reasons I didn't tell you sooner. But I'm telling you now in hopes that you'll forgive me.

"Your friend, Jimmy."

Angie crumpled the note in her fist and stared up at the sky. Please, she thought, don't make me read it again. She was sure she'd used up her well of courage.

"Thank you," Agent Brock said. There was a long pause and the sounds of rustling papers. "I'm going to contact Agent Silas with this information, and we will try to find your friend." Angie started to object, and the agent cut her off. "If Silas refuses to cooperate, I'll figure something out." Another long pause. "Miss Mitchell, I want you and Miss Lucelli to stay where you are. And hang on to that letter."

Convinced that something was finally being done, Angie promised they would do just that and hung up.

Lauren wrapped an arm around her shoulder and pulled her close, kissing her cheek and temple, rubbing circles along the base of her neck.

"I did what you asked me to," she said softly. "I ran that report."

"And?"

"He has a couple of priors for attempted assault and drug possession." She paused. "Tom is worried as hell, by the way."

"I bet. I should probably call him."

"There's something else," Lauren whispered.

"What?"

"Most recent address was reported six weeks ago—6227

Calloway Drive."

Angie's eyes widened. Six-two-two-seven Calloway Drive. The return address on the first envelope she'd gotten was 7226 Calloway Court, if she remembered right. The killer was playing with fire. Detective Key had said there was no such address. But Key was... he'd probably picked up on the similarities right then and there. "Damn it," Angie hissed.

She looked at Lauren. Lauren looked at her. They stared for several silent minutes, searching each other's eyes.

"Let's go," Angie said and pushed her tired body out of the plastic chair.

"Yeah," Lauren nodded and helped her up.

They were still grabbing purses, keys, and cell phones when there was a knock at the door. Angie cursed and grumbled, "Probably some cop wanting us to stick around. Guess they don't trust us, huh?"

"And with good reason," Lauren said, deflated, and headed for the front door.

A brown-suited, UPS deliveryman was standing on the doorstep, holding out a clipboard. Angie had an unpleasant sense of déjà vu. She knew what the white envelope under his arm would contain—had a fairly good idea, at any rate—and told Lauren to go ahead and sign for it.

Like hell she wasn't going to accept the package now. She hadn't wanted anything more to do with the whole affair, but now Jimmy's life was at stake.

Lauren closed the door and locked it. She sat heavily on the couch and dumped her keys on the coffee table. Angie took the envelope from her and ripped it open.

Another silk scarf, this time minus the blood stains. More newspaper articles. All of them fresh from that morning. How could she have not expected this to happen? The *Tribune* had run the big investigative piece. She unfolded the clippings with eager fingers.

There were only a few comments, and one lengthy paragraph in the right margin. Angie squinted at the writing, shrugged, and handed the clipped article to Lauren, who studied it silently for several minutes.

"It says here," she began, her voice wavering, "that 'It's time

273

for the grand finale. The one who would not be just will pay the price for his cowardice.'" It was next to a paragraph that alluded to the killer's comments in other articles' margins, the one where it said "two more," which had baffled Angie because it would indicate a seventh victim.

If there was any doubt in her mind—even the tiniest, quietest voice that always said anything is possible—that Jimmy hadn't actually been abducted, that he was just being a shit and not answering his phone, hiding in some coffee shop, it was obliterated.

Lauren closed her eyes, rubbed her forehead, and took a wavering breath before continuing.

"What he wrote here," she pointed at the scribbled paragraph on the right, "says, 'The writer is more clever than I thought she was. She has indeed learned. And she has listened. And I suspect she knows more than is written in this article. Congratulations to her also for ousting that incompetent detective. His attempts to stop me from achieving justice were both inadequate and foolish. These articles have exposed many crimes. And these men's legacies will be forever tainted with their sins revealed.'"

Lauren stopped. There was one more scribbled comment. Angie squeezed her forearm encouragingly. "What's the last one?" she whispered.

"An avenger stays true to form. But I am the exception."

Silence.

Angie muttered the two sentences. Once. Twice. Then her eyes widened.

"An avenger—serial killer—stays true to form," she started and swallowed hard. "Stays true to form—has the same M.O., maybe a similar or accelerated version." She paused. "But I am that exception. He's going to break his M.O. He's going to... Oh, God."

Lauren's eyes locked on hers. "He beats them for days. What if he decides to make that one day—as in, singular," she said, gripping Angie's hand hard.

"He could make it more days—as in, a week—or change the way he kills or the fact that he's not doing it in the victim's apartment."

That's right, Angie's mind interjected, say victim instead of

Jimmy. That'll keep her head on straight.

Lauren jumped up. "Let's go!" she shouted, clearly not comforted by Angie's suggestions. "We have to do something. We have to stop this. We can't just sit here."

She was practically screaming. Angie gawked at her, wide-eyed, for several seconds. This was the woman who'd begged her to stay out of trouble. The woman who worried like hell. But she was also the über-protective Lauren Lucelli, who would be damned if she would sit on her butt while something bad happened to someone she loved.

Angie grabbed her keys, nodded, and got off the couch.

"Six-two-two-seven Calloway Drive it is," she said and headed for the door.

Preying On Generosity

Chapter Twenty

T he wind had picked up. It was beating along the length of Lauren's car, forcing it to swerve with each gust of blasting cold air. She cursed, her knuckles white around the steering wheel with the effort to maintain control.

Angie sat in the passenger seat and looked up from her tattered Mapsco.

"Take a left at the next light," she said. "And...watch out!"

Lauren slammed on the brake and barely avoided ramming a light blue pickup.

Angie bit back the order to stay calm. Deep breath, let it go. At this point, there were no words that would have any effect on Lauren.

Angie's fingers curled around the edge of the Mapsco and bent its pages. Her jaw was clenching and unclenching. They'd been in the car for ten minutes already. It had been enough time to make her seriously question what they were doing. But they couldn't call the police. A call to Agent Brock had gone unanswered—likely because she was either speaking with Agent Silas or because she'd left the office. And in her emotional turmoil, Angie had failed to get a backup number.

She thought about calling Detective Key again. But he hadn't answered her message. And he'd probably avoid another call. She pinched her nose in aggravation.

The killer knew who she was and what she looked like. He'd followed her. She couldn't just show up on his doorstep and expect him not to recognize her. Or Lauren, for that matter. Surely he'd seen them together at some point.

"Turn left here?" Lauren interrupted her thoughts, and Angie nodded.

"You'll take a right on Varsity Lane, but it's a ways up, past Westway Boulevard."

Lauren grunted in response and hit the accelerator when the light turned green.

Angie had a sudden idea. She dug through Lauren's purse and pulled out her lover's cell phone. Detective Key wouldn't recognize that number.

Four rings, five—she thought he wouldn't pick up, but she was wrong.

"Johnny Key speaking," he grumbled in a low voice, as though he were afraid of being overheard. Or maybe he was distracted.

Angie hesitated a second or two, not knowing what to say, then decided to take a gamble and steeled herself. "I'm on my way to your brother's house."

Silence. She thought he'd hung up on her, but she could hear soft music in the background. He coughed and cleared his throat. "What?"

"You heard me," she growled. "I'm going over there. Right now. I don't know what kind of crap you decided to pull. I have a pretty good idea, though, and I think I know why you did it. But none of that matters right now. He has my friend—you met Jimmy—and I'm going to go get him back."

"What the hell do you think you're doing?" Lauren shouted and hit the horn, flipping off the driver of the blue pickup in front of them, the one they'd nearly struck only minutes earlier. It had swerved hard to the left and back in its lane, striking the curb but then correcting itself.

Angie shot Lauren a look and indicated the cell phone. She was still waiting for a response from the detective. He was cursing furiously, something about "some crazy bitch driver in her piece-o'-shit Dodge Neon." She couldn't make out the rest.

"Talk to me," Angie demanded, not giving a damn what his problem was.

"I'm here," he said. "You nearly made me have a wreck, Mitchell." There was a long pause. "Now I don't know what the hell you're talking about, but..." he trailed off suddenly. Lauren gasped. Angie looked at her sharply, realized she was looking out

278

the passenger-side window, and followed her lover's eyes.

She came face to face with Detective Key, the driver of the blue pickup. He was in the lane next to them. It seemed Angie and Lauren weren't the only ones on their way to pay Matthew Gillyworth a visit.

"I-I wanted," Lauren stammered, "to get around that crazy driver."

Detective Key was staring at Angie, who was staring back, forming words soundlessly. His eyes darted from her to the road ahead.

"You weren't kidding," his voice came over the cell phone and scared the crap out of her. She jumped and dropped the phone, scrambled for it on the floorboard, and brought it back up to her mouth to say something. The line was dead.

"Shit," Lauren muttered and hit the gas.

The blue pickup—and Detective Key—was rapidly pulling ahead. Angie gripped the armrest hard, her heart hammering almost painfully. Her eyes were wide. Her palms sweaty. She didn't want to know what would happen if they caught up with him.

He ran a red light and barely avoided smashing into a motorcycle. Lauren slammed on the brakes, her car coming to a screeching halt three feet past the white marker.

"He's going to warn him," Angie whispered, knowing in her gut that they'd just screwed up big-time. Lauren revved the engine again, screaming at the red light to turn green. The pickup truck was a dot down the road. It took a bend. And then it was gone.

The light turned green and Lauren peeled out. Angie's eyes were frantically scanning street signs. "Up there," she shouted, "Two signs down, take a right."

Lauren crowded out a postal vehicle just in time to take the turn. She ignored the honking and whipped her black Dodge Neon around the corner.

"After the stop sign, take a..." Angie was about to say "right," but her eyes caught sight of the blue pickup truck parked straight ahead. "Park behind Key's truck," she said instead.

They scrambled out of the car. There was no sign of the detective, his truck empty.

"Why did he park here?" Angie muttered, peering into the

pickup.

"Who the hell cares?" Lauren snapped and grabbed her arm. "Let's go."

"We need to be careful," Angie snapped back and yanked her arm away. "We can't just go barging in there. Key beat us. He's going to warn his brother."

But Lauren was already marching down the street. Well, hell. Grumbling, Angie hobbled after her. "Wait," she gasped, unable to keep up. "I'm coming."

Lauren stopped, her shoulders rigid and fists clenched. She was pointing at a house.

"There," she said when Angie came up alongside her, "6227 Calloway Court."

Angie looked at the house and realized why her lover had stopped abruptly. She hadn't done so for her to catch up. She'd stopped—shocked—and was simply rooted to the spot.

The front door was open. The two women stared at it for several seconds.

"I have a bad feeling about..." Angie began but never got to finish. A hand clamped over her mouth and pulled her back against a tall, masculine body. Another arm wrapped around her waist and hefted her off the ground. She could do little more than whimper.

Lauren turned to say something. Her eyes widened. She opened her mouth—likely to shout—and shut it abruptly, nodding. Angie was carried backward several dozen feet, into a front yard, around the back of a house, until she could no longer see the street. Lauren followed, her face grim and hands curled so tightly they looked white.

"Now," a voice whispered, tickling her ear. "I'm going to put you down and let you go. But you will not scream and you will not move. Got it?"

Angie tried her best to nod. She gripped her cane harder, readying herself.

The man let her go. She swung around to strike him, but he caught her cane easily.

"Stop it, Mitchell," he barked. She knew that voice. It was Detective Key. She knew they should have looked around a little more earlier. Damn it.

280

Angie froze for only a second or two. Then she turned and looked up into his face. His eyes darted nervously to Lauren, then back to Angie.

"Keep it down," he whispered, though he was the only one who'd been loud.

"What the hell are you doing?" she whispered back furiously.

"You were about to make a big mistake," he shot back, voice still low. "You have no idea what he's capable of. You can't just march in there."

"I have a pretty damned good idea..."

"No, you don't," he cut her off viciously.

"How could you?" She couldn't help herself. She had to know. She gave him accusing eyes, tugging at her cane halfheartedly. He let go and she set it on the ground, leaning on it heavily. He dropped his eyes to the ground guiltily.

"I thought..." He stopped, ran a hand through his hair. "Never mind." He looked like he was about to say more, but a fist suddenly smashed him hard in the face. He stumbled sideways and fell to his knees.

Lauren kicked him in the side and he was on his back. She dropped to her knees and punched him solidly in the face. She pulled back and did it again. And again.

Angie was so shocked that she couldn't move. Seconds ticked by before her mouth would obey her. "No!" she shouted and stepped forward quickly, grabbing her lover's arm.

Lauren gave her a bewildered look, wild eyes darting from Angie to the fallen man. She flexed her hand, wincing, as though it hurt like hell—gave it a long, disbelieving look—and straightened, her jaw set, her lips a thin, narrow line.

Angie expelled a breath she hadn't realized she'd been holding and bent over Detective Key, touching his face with the tips of her fingers. He didn't respond. A line of blood was trickling from his lower lip.

"What the hell..."

"We have to go get Jimmy. We don't have time for his bullshit. And who's to say he won't get us in more trouble than we're already in? He's that psychopath's brother, for God's sake!" she shouted exasperatedly.

"But..."

"No, Angie." Lauren lowered her voice and took a deep breath. "He already proved we can't trust him." She took Angie's hand and held it up to her quivering lips for several seconds, placed a kiss on each knuckle, and released it. "The door's open. Let's go."

If only Agent Brock would call back. Angie had left a message. Damn that woman and her slow response. If only the dispatcher had believed her. Precious hours had passed. She tried not to think about what could have happened inside the house across the street in those hours. She shook her head but couldn't get the sickening images to stop.

Her mind was also giving her five gazillion reasons in rapid-fire succession as to why they should stay exactly where they were. But her heart was singing a different song. It was telling her to burst through that open door and find their friend.

Too many thoughts. Too little time. Desperation was sucking the logic from her brain. The cold spot in her stomach leapt upward and sapped the air from her lungs. She felt as if she couldn't breathe.

And then that God-awful internal noise crept up on her—that screeching, wailing sound of Lauren's grief-stricken scream—and she could taste copper in her mouth. She started hyperventilating. Cold sweat broke out on her forehead and trickled down her back. She shook her head violently and dropped her cane, pressing the palms of her hands into her face. She felt lightheaded and groaned. It was too much. She couldn't do it. She was going to fail Jimmy. And herself. And Lauren.

Strong arms caught her around the waist before she could hit the ground. A soothing voice was in her ear, but she couldn't make out the words. The sound of screaming drowned them out. She started to tremble. She couldn't suck the air in fast enough. It was too much.

She felt a sudden, sharp pain explode on her wrist. Her eyes snapped open. She could smell lavender and hear the words her lover was muttering.

"Snap out of it. Slow breaths," she was saying, counting, "one, two, three, release." Angie listened for several seconds and tried to do as instructed. Her wrist hurt like hell. Lauren was tracing a circle over a bright red spot with the tips of her fingers. She'd pinched her hard. It was going to leave a bruise.

She realized they were sitting on the cold, crisp grass.

"What happened?" Lauren whispered minutes later, fear in her voice.

"Flashback," Angie muttered and hated herself for the admission, for the weakness she hadn't dared confide. She'd thought it had gone away. It hadn't happened in weeks. But she was wrong. And it pissed her off.

Lauren nodded and didn't say anything else. Seconds ticked by in silence—only the sounds of rustling trees and an occasional car driving by. The rest of the world came back slowly. And with it the knowledge that Jimmy might be in the house across the street being tortured. While she just sat there.

Angie cleared her throat and rubbed her face, brushing away blond strands of hair that were stuck to her forehead and hung in her eyes. She sighed and took a deep breath. "Help me up."

Lauren moved slowly, as though she was unsure if that was such a good idea. But she did it and reluctantly handed Angie her cane.

Detective Key still lay unmoving on his back, a thin trail of blood trickling down his chin. The two women spared him a glance, then turned away.

They rushed through the front door, squinting at the dim light within. It was open—a blatant invitation. There was no point in bothering to sneak around. Angie sincerely doubted Mr. Gillyworth was just airing out the place.

She was furiously praying that she was right in thinking the killer had taken Jimmy there. Because if he hadn't, who knows where their friend would be.

The inside of the house was like a cave—dark curtains shutting out the light. Lauren was in front, Angie behind. They didn't say anything, moving as quietly as they could into the darkness. They followed a long hallway, running fingers along the wall, until it opened up into a larger room. Angie was sure her eyes had adjusted to the dark, but she still couldn't make out any features in the room.

"Miss Mitchell," a baritone voice shattered the silence and stopped them in their tracks. Light flooded the room and made them blink. Squinting, Angie's eyes frantically searched the now-illuminated room, searching for the speaker, and she gasped.

It should have been the living room. Maybe it had served as a living room for someone else at some point. But it certainly wasn't a living room for Matthew Gillyworth.

The walls were painted solid black. The floor was black. Black-lacquered tables lined the far wall where bookshelves or a couch and a television should have been. And the tables were littered with dozens of objects similar to those she'd seen on the walls at After Midnight—restraining gear, whips, clamps, gags. Dozens of candles filled every available surface space.

And there was a big something in the middle of the room, draped in heavy black velvet. A man stepped out from behind that mountain of material.

He was like liquid grace. His body moved slowly, deliberately, like a lazy cat, as though he were at ease with himself and his belongings. This was his kingdom. And they were at his mercy. They knew it, and he knew it.

His chest was bare and beautiful—though a few thin, short scars marred the flesh on his lower abdomen. His legs were clad in black leather, ending in black boots. A matching mask wrapped over his head, exposing only his eyes, square chin, and lips, which curled into a self-satisfied smile. She could well imagine why people had paid to be with him.

Angie tried to remember what he'd looked like at the bar without the mask and black leather pants, but she couldn't do it. Only the police spread came to mind, and mug shots seldom do people justice.

"So nice of you to drop by," he said in a tone a host would use to greet the guest of honor. "I thought that was you outside. I was under the impression that it would take you longer to find my home." He paused long enough to sweep his arms around the living room and bow, then straighten, before continuing, "but this may work out better than I'd planned. It's so wonderful to finally meet you in person."

Angie willed her body not to tremble and took a step forward. She calculated the odds of rushing the man cast, cane, and all. Then she calculated the odds of Lauren rushing the man the way she'd handled Detective Key. She tried to figure the odds of them rushing him together. None of the odds looked good. Not because he was a muscular man, but because she knew what he'd done to his victims.

Standing there, she felt very weak and small—vulnerable.

She risked a glance sideways and saw twitching muscles around Lauren's mouth and eyes. She was sure her lover was going through the same scenarios she'd just imagined. Or at least similar.

Angie willed her nerves to calm. She had to do something. Anything. Before Lauren did something rash. She also had a feeling that if she hesitated too long with a response, on which the masked man was clearly waiting, something bad would happen.

"Mr. Gi— I mean, Apollo, I would like to see my friend," she said, proud of how steady and strong her voice sounded. "I know you have him."

He laughed and waggled a finger at her. "Ah, ah, ah," he chided, smirking, and walked around the draped object in the center of the room. "You're being rude."

Her eyes widened and her mouth went dry. What the hell? She stared at his mask, her mind racing. Of course she was being rude, damn it. He was a psychopath. He was also a top… Of course. A sadist. He expected respect. And obedience.

"Forgive me," she said, bowed her head, and paused. She looked up and caught Lauren's look of disbelief out of the corner of her eye and ignored it. "It's nice to meet you, too, Apollo."

He studied the fingernails of his right hand and rubbed them against his chest nonchalantly, like he had all day to consider whether he should forgive her. She stared at that hand. The middle two fingers were missing and there was something decidedly…wrong with the thumb. The angle, she thought, it didn't bend right.

"That's better," he finally said and graced her with a smile. "I love it when I'm right. I knew you were a fast learner, and you prove me right again and again."

She guessed that a sign of gratitude for his praise was then appropriate. She could barely choke it out. "Thank you," she half whispered, struggling not to shudder. She made eye contact, catching what she thought was a sparkle of mischief in those icy blue eyes. He was halfway across the room now. "Sometimes it's good to be right."

"Only sometimes?" He laughed, hands on his hips, shoulders shaking delightedly.

"Sometimes it's better if you're wrong."

"Such as?" He took a step closer and stopped. His eyes had pinned her but slid sideways to regard Lauren. Before Angie could answer, he said, "How rude of me." His head tilted slightly to the left. "You're the friend. I'm afraid I don't know your name."

Lauren made a low growling noise in her throat. It was her only response.

"One of those, hmm? Well, Miss Mitchell, would you care to introduce your friend? She seems to be more lacking in manners than either of us." And he chuckled, a low, throaty sound that raised the hair on the back of her neck.

"Apollo, this is Lauren." Her throat was dry and she had to clear it again. She swallowed hard. "Lauren, this is Apollo." She didn't dare look sideways.

"I know who the hell…" Lauren spat but quickly clamped her mouth shut.

Apollo's sensuous smile had morphed into a horrifying grimace. He hissed at her and reached behind his back. He's got a gun, Angie automatically thought.

Seconds ticked by. Slowly, his expression returned to the lazy, Cheshire-cat grin, and he relaxed his posture. "Think before you speak," he said pointedly to Lauren. "You may not like what will happen to you if you don't." He paused. "Unless you enjoy deep, penetrating, long-lasting pain."

And then he took a deep breath, rolled his neck, and stretched his arms, laced his fingers together—though a few were missing on both hands, Angie realized—and cracked his knuckles. He shook out his arms. Angie watched him in fascination. He didn't get that he was busted. Surely, he wouldn't think that she hadn't notified the authorities. Surely, he didn't think he could get away with his crimes. And yet he acted like an entertainer putting on a show. Of course, it was his "grand finale," as he'd informed her in the envelope she'd received earlier. She couldn't help but wonder if he'd already completed his work.

"You don't choose your friends very wisely, Miss Mitchell," he said. "I wasn't sure if James was a friend of yours until I went into his apartment. I'd seen you talking to him once or twice, and I was hopeful that he was just an acquaintance." He gave her a regretful smile. "I'm afraid this last lesson I will teach you will be the hardest one." He paused importantly and raised his chin. "You will learn to understand why some people simply must die. Some people are just not meant to live among decent human beings."

The icy feeling in her gut threatened to creep inside her head and force out a scream. By sheer will, she was able to keep her mouth clamped shut.

"No thoughts to share?" he asked, watching her with curious eyes. He folded his arms across his chest. "Surely you, of all people, would have a question or two. Come on, don't be shy. Ask me anything."

Angie was getting damned tired of this game. But so long as they were talking, he wasn't torturing or killing Jimmy. Of course, while they were chatting, Jimmy was probably hurt somewhere. And Lauren's patience wasn't going to hold out much longer.

"Do you want to get caught?" she caved, unable to help herself.

"What I want is to leave a legacy," he said. "Getting caught doing the right thing would merely be an unpleasant, but expected, consequence. You see," he uncrossed his arms and walked over to a table, picked up a long, coiled whip, and wrapped it around his stomach, turning back to her, "I didn't have a purpose after they broke my body." He walked the length of the room in slow, pensive strides, his eyes focused inward. "And no one would believe what happened. I almost died in the hospital. And then again when I plunged a knife into my own stomach."

Angie's eyes fell on the scars. It looked like he had tried more than once.

"But after many months passed, I had a dream. And I was born again."

He stopped and faced her. His mouth was half-open, his eyes heavy-lidded. He took a deep breath and let it out explosively. "I was forgiven for my past transgressions for I had undergone a purification by severe pain. And my new task was to purify those who had committed crimes against me. It was my reward for turning to the light!"

Angie gawked at him. He was a mad, raving lunatic. She had

thought it was about revenge—still believed it—but he had apparently twisted it around in his head somehow. She was about to say as much, but Lauren beat her to it.

"Let's untwist your logic. You're killing them because they hurt you," she growled, apparently unwilling to remain silent any longer. Angie groaned internally.

He laughed at her, a shockingly loud, barking laugh. "No," he cut the laughter off abruptly. "They broke me because I was living a life in sin. They were not acting of their own accord. Those innocents would never have touched me. But they were being punished for their sins, as I was being punished for mine." He gave a significant pause and crossed his arms. "They chose to ignore the message. So I was sent to purify them."

"They had a bad batch of drugs." Angie couldn't help herself.

"There are no coincidences in life, Miss Mitchell," he said patronizingly and shook his head as though he were deeply disappointed. "It's the first thing one should learn. He has a plan for us all. And He does not play games. He is infallible."

Great. They were stuck in a theological logic circle.

"So you gave up your life of sin," Angie drawled, crossing her own arms. "You became an avenger, a savior, by your statements." She paused, raising an eyebrow. "You write to tell me you're demanding justice, but here you stand before me and say you're just saving these poor, poor sinners. I see a contradiction there. You can't be saving them, avenging your injustice, and be the hand of God that purifies all at the same time."

His smile turned into that vicious grimace again and he hissed at her, uncrossing his arms. It did not scare her as it had before. She expected it this time. She unconsciously took a step closer to Lauren, unsure what he'd do next.

"I thought you appreciated my work," he spat, his easy confidence crumbling. "I thought you came to watch and learn."

"We came," Lauren growled, "to get our friend."

"Fine," he shouted and stepped into the center of the room. "It's time to see your precious friend."

He grabbed two handfuls of black velvet and yanked the cloth up in the air.

Lauren took a stumbling step back. Angie screamed.

Chapter Twenty-One

L auren recovered first and took two quick steps forward. But Apollo was faster, reaching behind his back and withdrawing a ten-inch, serrated blade—whipping it around in an arch until it rested against Jimmy's throat.

Lauren froze.

It was hard to recognize Jimmy. He was strapped to a metal chair, his wrists, legs, and neck tied to it with lilac silk scarves. He was stripped to his boxers, revealing a rainbow of bruises scattered across his chest, arms, and legs. His eyes were swollen shut. He seemed to be mercifully unconscious. Angie couldn't help but whimper looking at him, tears welling up in her eyes.

The ice in her gut started to melt. Her vision began to blur. Blood raced through her body, and she felt as if she could rip the arms from the masked man's body with her bare hands. She was breathing hard.

"Exhilarating, isn't it?" Apollo demanded in a low voice. "It is the greatest reward I have ever received. My past life had been a series of failures and disappointments. But my new life is rich and full."

That wicked blade was too damned close, Angie thought, wishing she had a gun.

"And now, Miss Mitchell, you shall see how it is done right."

He inched the blade away by a fraction and slapped Jimmy upside the head with his free hand. "Wake up, you coward," he shouted and repeated the motion.

Neither woman dared move. They were terrified, rooted to the spot.

Jimmy whimpered through the gag around his mouth. The

sound broke Angie's heart into a million shards of glass that slit up her insides. Sweat beaded on her forehead.

"No," she whispered. Then stronger, "No!"

Apollo looked at her, a feral grin on his face. "Why? I have told you what I must do. There is no way around it."

"Please," she begged shamelessly and realized tears were running down her cheek.

He frowned then, hesitating. "You beg so eloquently," he said, sighing, and licked his lips. His icy blue eyes stared into hers for several seconds in complete silence that was shattered when Jimmy whimpered again.

Apollo suddenly shook his head and started mumbling, "No, no, no…" He pulled away the knife and pressed the butt of it into his temple, rocking back and forth. "I know, I will," he muttered, nodding furiously, his eyes tightly shut. He groaned and scratched an index finger along his cheek until he drew blood. "A tiny moment of weakness," he said, his voice growing stronger. "I am only human. Forgive me."

His eyes snapped open and he hissed at Angie, all recognition gone from his face. "Stay back, demon temptress, you will not sway me!"

There was a crash behind Angie and she jumped.

"Freeze!" a familiar voice shouted. "Hands in the air!"

The room filled with Apollo's laughter.

"Or what—you'll shoot me?" he drawled, the easy confidence back. The change was so sudden it made Angie blink.

"Key," Lauren whispered.

Angie already knew. And she wasn't entirely sure he'd follow through with his threat. She turned to face him, to read his expression, and saw only pain. And regret. Maybe he would follow through. But the trembling of his arms as he held the gun—trained at his half-brother—made her nervous. She stepped a little to the left and noticed Lauren stepping farther to the right.

Her eyes darted back to Apollo, who shrugged and said, "Pathetic."

"Matt, put down the knife. I mean it," Detective Key said, but his voice quavered. He cleared his throat and licked his lips, wincing. "Please, brother."

"I have no brother," Apollo said, spitting the sentence out like it was a curse. "No brother of mine would be as foolish as you have been. No brother of mine would dare raise a hand to stop my noble cause." He paused, a nasty smile curling his lips. "I have not had a brother for years."

The color drained from Detective Key's face. "I believed you," he whispered.

"And how stupid of you," the masked man drawled. "I would never abandon my duty. I would never stop short so close to the climax. I have spent years building up to this moment. That you believed I would turn myself in shows how weak you are."

And then Angie knew what the gamble was that Detective Key had taken. He'd gone to the killer directly, thinking he could convince his brother to give himself up. If the killer walked in of his own volition, the act would surely be rewarded with a lesser sentence. Although, he had killed several people already. And when the next batch of bodies came in, the detective should have told somebody what went wrong and why. How stupid, indeed. And how heartbreaking.

"You were supposed to stay here, but you disappeared. I couldn't find you," Detective Key said and stopped. "You killed all those people, Matt. They have families. What they did was terrible, but..."

"We are not having this discussion again," Apollo growled, the words harsh and enunciated with vicious determination. "Now put down the gun before you shoot someone by accident."

Detective Key's eyes dropped to his arms, as though he hadn't realized they'd been trembling. He did not lower his gun. But he steadied his stance, took a deep breath, and let it out through his mouth.

There was a long, chilling silence as the brothers stared into each other's eyes.

Where the hell was Brock? Panic was starting to take over again. Apollo didn't care if he got shot—at least that's what Angie thought—and he could cut Jimmy's throat before his brother would shoot him. Her heart pounded. She looked into her friend's puffy face. She looked across at Lauren and they locked eyes. There was desperation there, too. Angie shuddered. The moment seemed like an eternity but was probably only a couple of seconds.

Sirens echoed in the distance, shattering the silence. There seemed to be dozens of them, and they were getting louder. Two seconds ticked by. Then three.

Apollo moved an inch. Detective Key shouted for him to stop. Lauren took a step forward. Angie reached out to grab her but realized she'd be in the line of fire. There was nothing she could do. She stood helplessly and watched the scene unfold.

Detective Key's finger tightened around the trigger. He shouted, "I always loved you, brother. I'm sorry."

Apollo's eyes widened and he screamed with rage, as his knife-wielding hand began to move.

A gunshot blasted through the room so close to Angie and Lauren that they clapped their hands over their ears and screamed.

Apollo's left shoulder whipped back—blood dripping down his chest—and he stumbled, screaming, "I hate you!"

He flung his body around, flipped the knife until he was holding it by its tip, swung his arm back, and sent the blade flying forward with unbelievable strength and speed.

Another gunshot blast struck him square between the eyes and for a single second, there was a surprised look on his face, before he fell backward and lay still.

Jimmy whimpered and Angie raced forward to untie him, but Lauren stuck out a trembling hand, grabbing her gently by the elbow. "I'll get him," she said. "See what you can do about Key."

The sirens were close now. They'd be at the house any second. Angie didn't want to turn around and see what she could "do about Key."

But she turned slowly and found him lying on the floor—the wicked blade lodged in his throat just below his Adam's apple. Gurgling noises were coming from his lips, and he had his hands wrapped around the hilt. Angie dropped her cane and sat on the floor beside him, folding her hands over his.

"Don't move it, Jay, let go," she said, her eyes widening.

For a few seconds, he stopped struggling, his eyes searching for and finding hers. He tried to say something, but only a raspy, wet sound came from his mouth and bloody spittle clung to his lips. Angie watched his lips and it looked like he was trying to say, "I'm sorry."

Angie shook her head—she didn't know how to respond to that or if she was even right about what he was trying to say—and she tried to stop the flow of blood with her hands. She didn't know what to do.

The sound of approaching sirens was a constant stream now, accompanied by squealing tires. Any minute now, police would come bursting through the door. And when they did, they'd see the detective and call in the paramedics.

It seemed like an eternity before Angie heard the first rushing footsteps. She called out to the police—"We're in here, we need help!"—and turned back to face Detective Key.

His eyes widened and darted back and forth for a second, then he reached one bloody hand up to Angie, grabbed her shirt, and yanked her down closer.

"Shut down After Midnight," he rasped, choking, struggling for air. He looked like he was going to say more, but footsteps were in the house now.

He mouthed the words "I'm sorry" again, gripped the hilt of the knife with both hands, and yanked the blade out of his neck.

"Shit!" Angie cursed and tried to put some pressure on the wound. She was screaming for help and officers came bursting in the room. "Officer down, officer down!" she screamed at them and they scrambled to get the paramedics in.

She was pulled away from the detective's body as the medical team started working on him. But she'd seen the life fading in his eyes. She knew he wasn't going to make it. Which upset her somehow. Not because he was such a great guy or because it was just the sentiment of tragically lost human life, but because he had tried. He had screwed up, but he had tried. In his way. And then—in his way—he made up for it. Jimmy was alive, after all, thanks to him. And his psychotic brother was dead.

Angie shivered against the body that held her, and she realized it was Lauren who had pulled her away. She sagged into those protective arms and sighed, forcing her wound-up body to relax if only for a minute.

"They're taking Jimmy," Lauren whispered in her ear and began to move. She helped Angie to her feet and collected her cane.

Jimmy was on a stretcher, wrapped in a blanket, strapped down. He was not whimpering. In all likelihood, he was unconscious again. The two women silently followed the paramedics carrying him.

They got as far as the hallway when a uniformed officer stepped in front of them and said, "Excuse me, ladies, but I'm going to have to ask you to stick around."

"Fine," Angie snapped at him. "Arrest us. Because unless you do, we're going to the hospital with our friend."

She was not going to stick around this time. As far as she was concerned, nobody could boss her around so long as she wasn't cuffed and in the back of a police cruiser.

"Then I guess we're going to do this the hard way…" he started, his eyes cold, but was cut off.

"You will do no such thing, officer," a woman's voice said, coming down the hallway. She stepped around the corner and shoved a badge in his face. "Agent Melissa Brock. I'm here with Agent Moreno Silas, who is the lead investigator of this case." She paused significantly, folding her arms and raising an eyebrow at his lack of response.

"Got a problem?" she drawled.

The officer stammered and shook his head. "They were going to leave the crime scene of a signal twelve and possible second."

"They are the reason all of us are here to begin with, officer," Agent Brock said slowly. "Let them go."

Grumbling, the officer marched outside without a look back.

"Agent Brock, pleased to meet you both, glad you're okay," the woman said and turned to Angie, holding out her hand. Angie took it, glad to meet the investigator who would listen.

"Thank you for coming," Lauren said.

"I'd say no problem, but it is a problem. A law enforcement officer died in here today, and it might be because you two decided to play heroines. If you'd done what I told you to, he might not have died."

Angie's eyes widened. "I don't think you understand what …"

"I understand a great many things." Agent Brock paused. "Look, we're going to do an inquiry. Both of you will have to provide a statement. But not now. Go to the hospital—John Peter Smith—and be with your friend."

She turned to dismiss them, but added, "I'll be seeing you in a couple of days."

They nodded and dragged heavy feet down the dark hallway

until they stepped out into the clear, cloudless, October dusk.

"Jimmy's going to be disappointed," Lauren said softly, twisting her fingers. "He's going to miss the big Halloween bash in Cedar Springs."

Angie nodded. He'd been talking about it for months. "Come on," she said and grabbed her lover's hands, prying her fingers apart. "Let's get to the hospital."

Lauren sighed, looked up at the sky, and shivered. Then she glanced at their hands and let out a rattling breath, "At least he's safe now."

"Yeah, he's safe now."

They walked silently down the street hand in hand, ignoring the flashing blue lights, the fire engines, and the media vans. They were in a bubble of wonderful relief and nothing could burst it, not the cameras in their faces, not the questions shouted their way. They got in Lauren's car and left Calloway Drive.

Hours went by slowly. The day grew dark. The moon was full and bright when Angie stepped out into the cold to smoke a cigarette. She stood shivering with other people, whose faces wore similar grim expressions of concern and exhaustion.

It was right that they should stand there—total strangers—and share why they were at the hospital. But Angie kept her mouth shut. She knew her story wouldn't go over well.

The emergency room was crowded. A little girl walked up to Angie and asked if she was there because she was sick. Angie shook her head and started to cry.

Lauren paced the length of the emergency room. Every once in a while, she'd get on her cell phone—talking to Jimmy's parents—and hang up even more agitated than she was before. She'd stomp over to the reception desk, demand to know how Jimmy was doing, and turn away dejectedly—denied information again.

Angie and Lauren weren't family, after all.

Tom called Angie's cell. She'd been sitting in the hospital for four hours. It was after midnight. He called to say he was coming by and to stay where she was.

She watched him stroll into the emergency room with an air of authority. His eyes scanned the room meticulously until they met hers. It was like he zeroed in on her, then marched over.

He sat heavily and folded his arms.

"This is one hell of a mess," he said and sighed.

Angie nodded. There was nothing else to say about it. He was right.

"I'm glad you're okay, and I'm sorry about James."

"Thank you," she whispered, knitting her fingers.

"I have to take you off the crime beat," he said in a low voice. She looked up at him, surprised. She'd been expecting to be fired. Things had blown up in his face again, after all.

"You're getting two weeks forced vacation," he said. "You'll need it, anyway, to deal with this, all of it." He paused. "Then we'll talk."

They sat in silence for several minutes.

"I love crime," Angie said finally, surprising herself. After all she'd gone through, after all the heartaches and headaches, she still wanted the beat.

"I know, Angie, but you can't have it anymore. Not for a while, anyway."

There was another long pause. Finally, Tom got out of his chair and handed her an envelope. "For James," he said and turned away.

Angie held the envelope and tried not to cry. She got up and went to find Lauren.

Lauren was sitting on a bench in the courtyard. She was staring up at the sky, muttering. Angie approached slowly, unsure if she was interrupting anything important.

She reached out and touched her lover's shoulder. A hand wrapped over her own and squeezed gently. "It's a beautiful night."

Angie nodded. Lauren was right. It was crisp and cloudless, exposing the full moon and sparkling stars. It smelled fresh and clean. She sighed and watched the puff of steam be whisked away.

"It feels as if I've spent hours sitting on this bench," Lauren said. Her voice was calm and soothing. It was not the ragged, weary voice that was making demands at the receptionist's desk. But there was something in that voice—a question maybe or a thought.

"I'm so glad we found him," Lauren said and dropped her head, taking a deep breath. "I don't know what I'd do..." She stopped and raked a hand through her tangled, raven hair. She bit her lower lip and met Angie's eyes. She looked nervous as hell.

"I think, maybe, after this, we should all go see a shrink."

Angie snorted and grinned. "Yeah, it's about damned time."

The *Tribune* delivery truck pulled up to the hospital at four o'clock, before the sun had risen, and a couple of guys started unloading stacks of freshly printed, bound papers. Angie watched them from the entrance. The newspaper stand nearby was completely empty. People get tired of reading old copies of Newsweek and People Magazine if they're stuck in the hospital for more than a few hours. Eventually, they'll grab a newspaper.

She waited, shivering in her sweatshirt. She wanted to see the paper.

The deliveryman smiled at her before he set a stack of papers on the ground and unlocked the newsstand. Angie's eyes fell on the cover and saw a picture she really didn't like—the paramedics carrying Jimmy out on a stretcher under flashing blue and red lights. She sighed and changed her mind about the paper. She could get one later. It's not as if she wouldn't be hearing about what was on the front page for a long, long time.

What she needed was a strong cup of coffee, a nice, long hug, and for that silly, sarcastic smartass to crack a joke. Even if it was a lame one.

Jimmy was sleeping on a crisp, white hospital bed. Tubes were hooked to various parts of his body. He was still in the ICU, but Angie hadn't really expected him to be moved out of emergency care after only twenty-four hours.

She sat next to his bed and held his hand. She wondered if he'd done that while she had been in the very same hospital, the very same emergency care facility. Somehow, she knew he had and it made her smile.

"It's time to go," a strangely familiar voice said over her shoulder and she turned.

And damn if it wasn't the same nurse who had taken care of

her—Grace with her crinkly gray curls and round, elegantly wrinkled face. Angie couldn't help but smile, wondering if the woman would even recognize her.

"Miss Angie?" she said, putting her hands on her hips. "I thought I told you to stay out of the ICU."

"I'm here for a friend," Angie said, her smile dissipating, her eyes falling back on Jimmy. "He looks pretty bad."

Grace pulled another chair up and sat down.

"Where did you find him? The paramedics bringing him in were talking about it in the hall." Angie told her and she looked extremely disturbed.

"Is he going to be okay?" Angie asked. She couldn't help it. The doctors wouldn't tell her or Lauren what was going on because they weren't family. Which is another reason Lauren had called Jimmy's parents so many times to get their butts to Texas.

Grace studied her face for several long seconds, gnawing her lower lip. It was making Angie terribly nervous.

"Now you know I'm not supposed to say anything about that," Grace finally said and lowered her voice. "But if I were you, I'd want to know. So I'll tell you this—the doctors were surprised as hell. There's not a broken bone on his body—save one tiny fracture on his left cheek and a cracked lower rib. All the damage is minor, relatively speaking." She paused, glancing over her shoulder guiltily as though she'd said far too much, which she had, and ended with a quiet, "No permanent damage whatsoever. So he'll be fine. Physically anyway. Eventually."

Angie squeezed the nurse's forearm gently. "Thank you," she whispered. "I needed to hear that. He just looks so… Well, I'm glad to hear it'll go away."

Grace nodded and stood up. She checked the stats on several machines, nodded to herself, and made a couple of notes in Jimmy's chart. "I'm going to let you stay a while longer. You know that boy hung around here last time, trying to take care of your girl. He'd kick her out, try to make her get some food and sleep. Sometimes they'd argue for twenty minutes until I had to come in and tell them to shut up." She chuckled to herself, remembering. "I'll take real good care of him."

"I know you will, Grace."

Just then, Lauren walked into the room, carrying a Taco Bell bag and a couple of drinks. She grinned at the nurse as she strode out the door with a quick, "Those had better not be for James," said over her shoulder.

Lauren flopped down in the chair next to Angie and handed her a couple of burritos.

"Jimmy's parents will be here in half an hour," she said between bites. "They called from the airport." She gave Angie a significant look and rolled her eyes.

Lauren did not like Jimmy's parents. Most recently, because they kept insinuating that the attack on their son had happened because of his lifestyle. They liked Lauren only because she'd had a hand in getting him to drop the drugs. Otherwise, she'd told Angie, she was likely to be treated disrespectfully.

"It's not that they're just assholes," she said, sighing. "They're sheltered. They come from some tiny hicksville town in Wisconsin. They moved here—the big city freaked them out—and they moved back to hicksville a decade later. They're not bad, just small-minded." She paused, sipped her soft drink, and bit into a taco. She swallowed and added, "Try to hold your tongue, okay?"

"I can behave myself, you know," Angie said and harrumphed. She finished her burrito and put the wrapper in the empty bag.

"Right." Lauren snorted.

"I can, damn it."

"Sure..." Lauren stopped. "Did you hear that?"

"Hear what?"

Lauren stood and walked around the bed and leaned over Jimmy's body. She placed her ear over his mouth and hovered, unmoving, for several seconds.

And then Angie, too, could see the lips moving ever so slightly. She watched Lauren's face, scrunched up in concentration. "You're in the hospital," she said softly and took his hand. "Your parents will be here soon."

His chapped lips moved again.

Suddenly she whipped her head up and looked at him sharply. "Okay, smartass."

Angie stared at them for several seconds, waiting for an explanation. Then she couldn't stand it anymore. "What did he say?"

"He said, 'Where's my hot nurse?'"

Silence. "Oh," Angie said, snorted, and started giggling. She took his other hand, the one Lauren wasn't holding, and squeezed before saying, "Your nurse is a fifty-year-old, heavy-set woman. But she's very, very nice."

Jimmy sighed and coughed. Lauren walked out of the room to go get said nurse to tell her he was awake.

Angie watched him closely. If he made even a single joke, he was going to be just fine. And he had. So she was content to finally let herself relax. Just for a little while.

The last bit of worry in her gut disappeared. She let her eyes close and her head lean against the back of the chair. "Glad you're starting to feel better," she mumbled and drifted off to sleep.

Chapter Twenty-Two

D etective Key got the twenty-one-gun salute as befit an officer fallen in the line of duty. His casket was driven along I-30 with a police cruiser procession that lasted more than half an hour. The bugler played taps while officers folded an American flag into a triangle. It was a fitting tribute. It didn't matter that he'd screwed up. He had still managed to save a man's life. He was still one of Fort Worth's finest. And neither Angie, Lauren, nor Jimmy begrudged anyone for treating him as such.

The families of the victims attended the memorial. They spoke of how he'd given them peace with his actions—that he'd been faced with an excruciatingly hard decision in having to take down his own brother and that he'd paid the ultimate sacrifice. Those who disagreed kept their mouths shut. Family members of Jeff Breaux stood silently and refused interviews after the service was concluded.

The FBI subpoenaed Angie's notes. Every shred of information and evidence she'd collected starting on the date of that first homicide. She hadn't argued. There weren't any sources she needed to protect. She didn't have anything that was off the record. She gathered her notepads, copied every page for her own files, and turned them over in a box. There were dozens of them. She couldn't believe that she'd taken so many notes. But then again, she could hardly believe how the story had played out. It was still too fresh and far too surreal.

Agents Brock and Silas were conducting an internal investigation to see if she and Lauren could be blamed for Key's death. As far as she knew, they were inclined to assign them no blame. She sincerely hoped they didn't change their minds.

The two agents had also gone after the proprietor of After Midnight. The madam was to face myriad charges from promotion of prostitution to employing minors and covering up a crime. The hand-painted sign at the establishment's entrance had disappeared. Every time Angie checked, there were no cars in the parking lot.

Tom was not mad at her. He was tired of her crap, but he wasn't ticked off. He'd been pressured by his boss to reassign Angie to a beat they felt would keep her out of trouble. That so much crazy crap had happened wasn't exactly what you'd call normal, but they didn't want to take any more chances. It had hurt—the forced vacation and reprimand—but she'd agreed early in the game that she would accept the consequences of her actions if things "blew up" in her boss's face again.

Angie let it go. She knew she could do well in education. She would find important stories there, too. And they would be stories that could be completed without having to deal with psychopaths, screwy detectives, and mourning relatives. She'd give it a try. If she absolutely hated it, maybe some other newspaper or agency would take her. She tried not to think about it too much. She'd decided to burn that bridge when she got there.

In the meantime, she spent her days visiting Jimmy in the hospital, entertaining his parents, and taking long naps with Lauren after she got out of class. It was a time of reconnection and healing. And if it hadn't been for Jimmy being hurt, she'd have enjoyed it immensely. Because there wasn't a madman sending her envelopes with crazy shit inside anymore.

It was a Wednesday morning and Angie was lying in bed, thinking about the previous week. Jimmy was leaving the hospital that afternoon. She sighed, stretched lazily, and snuggled closer to her softly snoring lover.

Lauren mumbled a halfhearted protest and muttered something about "go back to sleep" and "damned morning people." Angie snickered and nipped at her bare shoulder playfully. Her hands sneaked along Lauren's side and targeted a tickle spot she knew would wake the woman up in two seconds flat. Angie tensed, readying herself for the attack.

"Don't you dare," Lauren growled and rolled over so quickly

Angie was momentarily shocked. Then she was pinned to the mattress by the long, lean, evilly grinning woman with mischief in her eyes.

Their lips met, and they forgot that Lauren had class that morning. They forgot that Angie was supposed to visit her doctor. They forgot that anything else existed outside each other's arms.

It hadn't rained in weeks. The grass and trees of north Texas were brittle and dry, like a gigantic tinderbox. Every day, there were grassfires. It was unusually warm for late November, and Angie wished the cold front they'd been promised would blast through already. It just didn't feel like winter.

She imagined closing her eyes and tilting her head up to the sky. She could almost feel the cool raindrops pattering on her face, sliding down her chin and neck, making her shiver. But the rain never came. Not when she wanted it to. Not when she needed it.

Her eyes were not open. She was listening to the wind rattle through the tree, staring off into space. She was waiting in the park. He'd be there any minute.

She heard his car come screeching around the bend. He was so reckless these days. He whipped his car around hard and slammed on the brake, coming to a rocking stop two inches from the curb. He slipped out of the door and slammed it shut, peeling off his sunglasses.

His easy smile curled his lips. If it weren't for the last remainders of a few deeper bruises—barely brown now along the edges of his eyes and his left cheek—no one would ever have known what he'd been through.

"Hey," Jimmy shouted and strolled across the parking lot.

Angie and Lauren had tried to talk about the abduction. They'd tried to talk about his letter or about Matthew Gillyworth and Detective Key. They'd bring it up from time to time, and he'd talk straight through their questions—ignoring them entirely—or walk out of the room. It had been hard lately for the three of them to spend time together.

Angie sighed. She had not yet reached the limit of her patience, but she was beginning to get desperate. Their suggestions that he see someone about what happened got them nowhere. He didn't see anyone. The only people he'd talk to about what had happened were Agents Brock and Silas.

Jimmy stood in front of her and lighted two cigarettes. He handed one to Angie and took a drag. She accepted the offer. He was being generous that day with his smiles and his cigarettes. He had not been very generous since he'd left the hospital.

"How's it going?" she ventured, offering him a seat on the bench.

He gave her a fake smile, waggled his hand in a "so-so" manner, and sat down.

"So I guess you decided to go back to work." He took a long drag. "Tom gave you your job back."

"I wasn't ever fired," she huffed. "I was on suspension. Two weeks. I made it three when I found out they'd put me on the education beat." She snorted. "You know, that's exactly what I wanted them to do a month ago, and so they do it, and I decide that's not what I want anymore." She paused and ran a hand through her hair. "Guess you can't have it all. I'll have to see how this works out."

He nodded and put his cigarette out on the bottom of his shoe. "Want to go have a drink? To celebrate you rejoining the American work force?"

A beer sounded nice, but she knew she shouldn't. Not when drinking had become so much more common in their lives lately. She gave him a long, searching look. She tried to pin him with her eyes, but his darted away and he slipped his sunglasses back on.

"Guess not," he grumbled and lighted another cigarette. He offered her one and she declined. She didn't want to sit there and chain-smoke. She wanted to talk.

"You can't keep this up forever," she said quietly, hoping he wouldn't run again. "You can try, but it won't do you any good." She paused, encouraged when he didn't stand up. "I don't know what you're hiding from. It's not like we don't have a pretty damned good idea what happened to you. You need help."

He turned his face slowly toward her and pulled the sunglasses from his eyes. The look there was one of disappointment and anger. He was furious. His brows furrowed and his lips tightened. He took a deep breath and let it out through his nose.

"You're one to talk," he said in a low, forcibly calm voice. "I heard about what happened that Wednesday. About your flashback. Can we say PTSD?"

"I do not…"

"Angie, don't give me that crap," he snapped and turned away. "I'm not ready, okay? I'll go get checked out in a few weeks. It hasn't even been a month yet. But you—you've had months. And you never told anyone about this crap until it just kind of popped out." He raised a hand to silence the objection that shot to her lips. "Yeah, Lauren told me about your freak-out."

"Don't flip this around on me," Angie finally shot back and folded her arms. "We were talking about you. You flipped it around because you can't deal with it. Come on, Jimmy, talk to me. Tell me what happened."

He shook his head and stood. Then he started off at a brisk pace across the park. She watched him go for a few seconds before getting up and jogging after him.

She wasn't supposed to run—not quite yet—but what was a little jogging when it was important, right? Right. The impact of her weight hurt, but it wasn't the trembling, hot pins and needles it had been. She'd worn a brace for the previous two weeks and had taken it off that morning, as per her doctor's orders.

She was catching up when he turned to see if she'd followed. For a second, his jaw dropped, and he gave her the first wide, warm, real smile she'd seen in what seemed like forever. He started clapping, and when she reached him, he wrapped her in a hug and twirled her in the air.

She was grinning, too, she couldn't help it.

"I'd almost forgotten what you looked like without your cane. I didn't realize you could do that," he started and stopped himself. "You can do that, right? You're not ignoring any doctor's orders?"

"Oh, and like you should talk." She smirked back at him and he put her down. She leaned on her weaker leg and it felt a little unsteady but held. The jogging had not hurt it any. She'd only jogged a few hundred yards anyway. It wasn't bad, though, for a start.

"I'll take that as a yes," he said and tsked at her. She raised her eyebrow at his chiding and put her hands on her hips.

"What was it a few weeks ago?" she dropped her voice to mock his. "Oh, by the way, I had three cocktails and took a couple of Vicodins. Oh, well."

He snorted. "I took the painkillers before I drank the cocktails. You know how goofy you can get on that stuff. I didn't know what I was doing."

She gave him a skeptical look.

"Okay, fine. I was ignoring doctor's orders not to drink any alcohol." He paused. "But I needed a damned drink, okay?"

She did not ease up on her skeptical look but added a raised eyebrow.

"What, I don't get to need a drink after I get out of the damned hospital?" His smile was gone. "What's wrong with that? I needed to freaking relax. Especially after my parents were there with their constant blah-blah-blah bullshit about my 'unfortunate lifestyle' and wouldn't get out of my room. After that mess I saw on the news. After..." he stopped, horrified, and clapped a hand over his mouth. He snapped his eyes shut and turned his back on Angie.

She stepped around him quickly, reached out both hands, and grabbed his shoulders. She began to shake him—not hard but strong enough to get his attention. "Don't shut me out," she said over and over again. "Finish the damned sentence."

He shook his head. "Let me go."

"No," Angie whispered. "Just drop the act. This doesn't have to be some sappy talk. Just quit pretending everything's okay. Because it's not, damn it, and I'm tired of playing along."

"Let me go," he demanded again and pushed back at her. But he wasn't really trying. He took a rattling breath and gave up. He opened his mouth and closed it, forming a few helpless, soundless words. "Let me... I can't, Angie, it's too hard. You don't understand."

"But I do understand. That whole thing with Ted Henry and Carpenter ..."

"Bullshit!" he shouted.

Angie's eyes widened. "What the hell, of course I..."

"Bullshit," he growled this time, gripping her forearms and shoving her hands off his shoulders. "You may understand what it was like to get kidnapped—I'll give you that—and beaten. But, Angie, you are in no position to tell me how to deal with this. Not after you refused to get help and didn't tell us a damned thing that was going on in that head of yours."

They stared at each other for a few seconds in the middle of the open park while children played with kites and gave them curious looks. Angie's breath was coming out in short bursts. She hated it when she was painted into a corner.

He was right. She knew in her heart that he was absolutely right and she hated it.

"Jimmy," she started, stopped, and sighed. "Let's make a deal. We'll talk—about my stuff and your stuff— then we'll figure out what to do from there. Because this," she indicated their stance with her hand, "can't continue."

He breathed in through his mouth and let the air out through his nose. He closed his eyes and nodded. "Deal," he whispered.

He wrapped an arm around her waist and they walked across the length of the field, found a path, and followed it into the trees. They spoke in hushed voices in between long silences. It was the most they'd shared in months.

It would be hours before they would stop in front of their cars—eyes red and puffy—and decide to go find Lauren. She'd surely be waiting for them, wondering what had kept them so long. They'd have to tell her what they'd told each other. Without the sugar-coating and rose-colored filters. It scared Angie a little, but it had to be done. She told herself so. She believed it. And Lauren, after all that had happened, deserved it.

THE END

Preying On Generosity

About the author

Kimberly LaFontaine is a photographer living in the great city of Fort Worth, Texas. When she's not out chasing brides and grooms with her camera, she can typically be found at IHOP hashing out the plot for her next book. Writing is her passion, her therapy, her hobby, and her favorite activity.

She was born in Mobile, Ala., in 1979. She spent her childhood in Germany, where she discovered her love for writing fiction. She has grown to love Texas and the Dallas-Fort Worth Metroplex, though she makes frequent trips back to Europe.

OTHER TITLES FROM INTAGLIO

A Nice Clean Murder
by Kate Sweeney; ISBN: 978-1-933113-78-4

Accidental Love
by B. L. Miller; ISBN: 1-933113-11-1

Assignment Sunrise
by I Christie; ISBN: 978-1-933113-40-1

Bloodlust
By Fran Heckrotte, ISBN: 978-1-933113-50-0

Code Blue
by KatLyn; ISBN: 1-933113-09-X

Compensation
by S. Anne Gardner; ISBN: 978-1-933113-57-9

Crystal's Heart
by B. L. Miller & Verda Foster; ISBN: 1-933113-24-3

Define Destiny
by J. M. Dragon; ISBN: 1-933113-56-1

Gloria's Inn
by Robin Alexander; ISBN: 1-933113-01-4

Graceful Waters
by B. L. Miller & Verda Foster; ISBN: 1-933113-08-1

Halls Of Temptation
by Katie P. Moore; ISBN: 978-1-933113-42-5

Incommunicado
by N. M. Hill & J. P. Mercer; ISBN: 1-933113-10-3

Journey's Of Discoveries
by Ellis Paris Ramsay; ISBN: 978-1-933113-43-2

Josie & Rebecca: The Western Chronicles
by Vada Foster & BL Miller; ISBN: 1-933113-38-3

Misplaced People
by C. G. Devize; ISBN: 1-933113-30-8

Murky Waters
by Robin Alexander; ISBN: 1-933113-33-2

None So Blind
by LJ Maas; ISBN: 978-1-933113-44-9

Picking Up The Pace
by Kimberly LaFontaine; ISBN: 1-933113-41-3

Private Dancer
by T. J. Vertigo; ISBN: 978-1-933113-58-6

She Waits
By Kate Sweeney; ISBN: 978-1-933113-40-1

Southern Hearts
by Katie P Moore; ISBN: 1-933113-28-6

Storm Surge
by KatLyn; ISBN: 1-933113-06-5

These Dreams
by Verda Foster; ISBN: 1-933113-12-X

The Chosen
by Verda H Foster; ISBN: 978-1-933113-25-8

The Cost Of Commitment
by Lynn Ames; ISBN: 1-933113-02-2

The Flip Side of Desire
By Lynn Ames; ISBN: 978-1-933113-60-9

The Gift
by Verda Foster; ISBN: 1-933113-03-0

The Illusionist
by Fran Heckrotte; ISBN: 978-1-933113-31-9

The Last Train Home
by Blayne Cooper; ISBN: 1-933113-26-X

The Price of Fame
by Lynn Ames; ISBN: 1-933113-04-9

The Taking of Eden
by Robin Alexander; ISBN: 978-1-933113-53-1

The Value of Valor
by Lynn Ames; ISBN: 1-933113-04-9

The War Between The Hearts
by Nann Dunne; ISBN: 1-933113-27-8

Traffic Stop
by Tara Wentz; ISBN: 978-1-933113-73-9

With Every Breath
by Alex Alexander; ISBN: 1-933113-39-1

Forthcoming Releases

She's The One
Verda Foster & BL Miller
June 2007

Revelations
Erin O'Reilly
July 2007

Away From The Dawn
MK Sweeney
August 2007

The Gift of Time
Robin Alexander
September 2007

Heartsong
Lynn Ames
October 2007

… And Many More

You can purchase other Intaglio Publications
books online at www.bellabooks.com,
www.scp-inc.biz or at your local bookstore.

Published by
Intaglio Publications
P O Box 794
Walker, LA 70785

Visit us on the web:
WWW.INTAGLIOPUB.COM